Sometimes
It Feels Like
Far

GARY SPETZ

Printed in the United States of America

v3j
First Printing, March 5th, 2021

ISBN-10: 0977092267
ISBN-13: 978-0-9770922-6-0

Sky Pond Press
PO Box 374
Lakeside, MT 59922

For my wind,

Marlene

Author's Note

While I have walked in some of the protagonist's footsteps, I am not Haakon. This story is fiction, inspired by a time and a place and people that I once knew.

ALL THINGS BELONGING...

to the earth will never change—
the leaf, the blade, the flower,
the wind that cries and sleeps and wakes again,
the trees whose stiff arms clash and tremble in the dark,
and the dust of lovers long since buried in the earth—
all things proceeding from the earth to seasons,
all things that lapse and change and come again upon the earth—
these things will always be the same,
for they come up from the earth that never changes,
they go back into the earth that lasts forever.
Only the earth endures,
but it endures forever.

Thomas Wolfe

1
SNOW GLOBE

The quiet was profound. Having just left the all-pervading clamor of a bustling city, Haakon was taken aback. Yet, it was not silence. So acute were his unruffled senses, he could detect—hear *and* feel, actually—the faint, collective rumble of thousands, perhaps millions of weightless snowflake impacts against the powder-covered landscape.

He stood in a white universe surrounded by infinity. The falling flakes were so large and their dense, combined breadth, so vast. Each snowflake appeared to defy gravity. They reminded him of tiny, toy parachutes. Their unhurried descents tempted the adolescent in him to catch one on his tongue. But he was too old for such silliness, so he reluctantly allowed them to fall on his head, unchallenged.

Misty was not as reserved. When a flake floated between her eyes, she instinctively snapped it into her jowls and then patiently awaited the next. The Labrador in her mixed breeding obligated such a response.

Looking down at Misty, he smiled. Haakon was happy to be back in Montana—giddy, really.

It was springtime and the falling snow surprised him, though it should not have. He reminded himself that he was in the mountains. The seasonal rules were different here. They told him it *had* been green and everything was growing. Yet, what greens had been, now lay buried. The landscape before Haakon was a blank palette of white. Only the river below refused to be erased. Its fast moving-water, swollen by the recent runoff, devoured the descending snowflakes and carried their essence to a faraway ocean.

It had been a long time since he stood on this spot. The view was as he remembered, even with the snow. Etched in his brain was the panoramic scene of a narrow, shallow, rock-lined river, running left to right for as far as he could see in both directions. A thick forest of pine and fir walled its distant shore. Through the thin, clear water, he could see red and green and tan rocks—scoured from an ancient earth, then carried and rounded by unrelenting glaciers—lining its visible bottom.

But behind him, there *were* changes. A stout log cabin now stood where the little camper trailer once resided. And many trees had been felled, presumably to open up its view of the river. It was a handsome structure set in a perfect wooded backdrop. Haakon thought it could have easily adorned the cover of *Log Home Living* magazine.

This had been his uncle's retirement home for the better part of seventeen years. But after he passed, having no direct descendants, he bequeathed it to Haakon, his favorite nephew—well, his only nephew and the person he knew would treasure it the most. Other than from photographs, Haakon had never seen the home, but he knew the five-acre lot well. He knew it from long before.

Haakon had promised, back then, to return to Montana before summer. He never did—not until now, forty-six years later. He had promised to be back after his spring quarter ended. But he did not return that summer, or the summer after that, nor when he finally completed college all together.

As Haakon observed the river through the veil of white, he thought about her. Even though their youth and vows and shared dreams had long since faded, he still wondered where she was. He had often wondered. And now, back in Montana, standing in falling snow, he remembered his last sight of her as he drove off—*her* standing forlorn in a snow globe of memory. Gazing down at the familiar landscape, he recalled the many times they had studied the river together, often sitting tightly, side-by-side in an embrace. He questioned how the inevitability of them did not come to pass.

After their parting and, eventually, after Haakon's return to college, he met and fell in love with another, just as she had feared. He did not fall *out* of love with her. He did not believe that would have been possible. Rather, Haakon fell in love again. And his life, in rapid succession, went off on a new trajectory with his new love. Haakon never told her this. He had been a coward. He allowed their frequent and tender letters to become less frequent—and less tender from his end. Presumably, she read the not-too-subtle signs. Then, in time, she must have mustered her dignity and moved on, exiting Haakon's life as he had so ungracefully designed. He never told her he would not be returning to Montana, but she surely came to know this.

Had he not been launched into a fast lane upon returning to Minnesota, things might have turned out differently. Haakon would never know. Life seemed to hang from a fine thread and the lightest breeze twisted it in one direction or the other. Fate? Maybe. Back then, so much of life was steered by where he was and when. In many ways, life's treadmill became a distraction. Everything after college arrived in a tidal wave of monumental events: graduation, marriage, children, and career. The simplicity of life abruptly ended. Goals, deadlines, commitments, and schedules became the overlords of the day.

It would disappoint her that Haakon did not follow his true passion and become an artist. Instead, he punted and pursued a profession as an architect, thinking it a more practical means to provide food and shelter and all the nonessential material stuff that one can convince oneself is needed. Nevertheless, being an architect proved itself a rewarding career in which he flourished. He even grew to like it in time.

Despite the regimen of duties, Haakon relished his life—at least until he did not. It had been a seamless existence, mostly. He envied no one. But, over the years, his wife, for her own incomprehensible reasons, grew to love it less. And concurrently, she grew to love Haakon less. He supposed there was negligence on his part to, as these things were rarely unilateral. And he supposed they both had changed and their aspirations had altered over the years. Regardless, by the time their younger of two daughters drove off to college, their marital flame died out. Soon after that, or perhaps before, Haakon's wife found someone else. So they ended and went off to live separate lives. She quickly remarried. Haakon did not.

He resented the betrayal and they spoke very little after their divorce. But, eventually, Haakon picked *his* ego up off the floor and resumed life. He dated and spent time with women whom he genuinely enjoyed, but none with whom he trusted with love. He had jilted and he had *been* jilted. As Haakon found both sides of this coin to be painful, he resolved to remain the noncommittal "bachelor playing the field." And, while this approach to relationships had some advantages, it was all in all a lonely row to hoe.

After *their* college days, his daughters married, had children, and then moved with their respective new families to the opposing coasts. By then they were accustomed to their father living alone, though not "in the backwoods." After his retirement, he told them he needed to return to Montana. It had been his plan for so long that it was unimaginable not to do it.

"You're going to live alone in the wilderness?" the first exclaimed. "If something happens, who's going to help you?"

Haakon tried to explain to her that northwest Montana was not the northern reach of the Yukon. It had towns and roads and people. And he was healthy. At sixty-five years of age, if he avoided looking into the mirror, he could persuade himself that he was much younger. He felt younger. But this discussion was futile. It was like trying to convince a teenage daughter he was a "cool" parent. It was all unimaginable to her—inconceivable. From his daughter's perspective, sixty-five was one slip and fall away from the nursing home.

The second said, "But we'll never see you!"

"I won't see you any less than I see you now," Haakon replied. "Both you and your sister are a plane ride away from me now and you will still be a plane ride, well maybe two, away from the cabin."

"What about the grandkids?"

"I can't think of a better place for the grandkids to come visit. It will change their lives. It changed mine."

They knew all of this was true. Growing up, they had heard their father's countless Montana tales. But their hearts did not *want* it to be true. They did not want him to move. He suspected it had more to do with selling their childhood home. By leaving it, they would say a last goodbye to the family they once were. Haakon understood this all too well. It was a big part of why he *had* to go.

"You'll get bored in Montana. What are you going to do with all of your time?"

"A little boredom is not necessarily a bad thing," he answered. "Sometimes it can help you collect your thoughts and get your head screwed back on."

"It's a little late for that, isn't it?"

Haakon glanced at his girls with an exaggerated scowl.

"Don't worry, I'll have plenty to do. There's hiking, fishing, and finally a perfect opportunity for me to become the painter that I always wanted to be. Don't you want to have a famous artist dad? Picasso, van Gogh, Monet, Dali, Pollock, and then me, Haakon."

"You had better purchase all your paints here before you go, Vincent van Haakon, because I doubt if they'll sell art supplies in their trading posts."

"Sure they do. If you have enough fur pelts, you can trade for just about anything in Montana. But what I probably should do is buy me a rifle and some traps."

"Very funny. Please don't become one of those unbathed, long-bearded recluses."

"I won't. I promise to shave and take a bath once a week… whether I need it or not. And I'll write. I think they even have email and phone service there."

Haakon's daughters traveled back to Minnesota to help him pack up the family home and to take possession of various lifetime mementos they valued. Before he drove off in his loaded SUV with its U-Haul trailer in tow, both daughters gave their father the worried look one might expect if embarking on a solo sailing circumnavigation of the globe. As he sat behind the steering wheel with Misty by his side, his younger daughter motioned to open the window. When Haakon did, she repeated a line from his favorite movie, *Jeremiah Johnson*—a movie he had subjected both girls to more times than they could count.

"Watch your topknot!"

Haakon's eyes watered as he replied.

"Yep, watch your'n."

Two deer emerged from the snow-clad trees on the river's far side. Misty watched them with silent curiosity. They ambled to the water's edge. The falling snow eased up and a narrow ray of sunlight found its way through the clouds and fell upon them for nearly a minute, illuminating their sleek reddish spring coats. As one drank, the other cautiously gazed up in their direction. She sensed the man and dog's presence, yet was not compelled to flee. Then they both drank.

Haakon stood watching with his heart flooded in sentiment and memories.

2
MONTANA BOUND

Hitchhiking is a crapshoot. You never know how long you are going to wait for a ride and, once you get one, how far it will take you. It is a pursuit of place where planning is pointless. You are a sailboat on an asphalt river in want of wind. And you stare off anxiously at approaching chrome grills the same way a becalmed sailor looks to the horizon for a hopeful distortion of flat sea. When it comes, and it eventually does, the wind carries you along the course that you have set with rudder and trimmed sails. But it can, and ultimately will, randomly drop you. So you travel along your route in fits and starts. You may well have an intended destination, but hitchhiking like sailing is not about expediency, it is about economy—and with economy comes compromise. And compromise invites the inadvertent. So the journey, by its very nature, is capricious—its foundation based upon adventure.

By his nineteenth year, Haakon had hitchhiked the nearly 1,400 miles from his Minnesota home to northwest Montana, twice. And twice the wind dropped him, inexplicably, in Whitehall, Montana. Probability-wise, it is not easy to land in Whitehall, Montana. The tiny, freeway-side town is close to nothing and it is the crossroads to nowhere. Yet, twice his ride ended there and twice after sunset.

When your ride ends after dark, your hitchhiking day is over. Nightfall makes hitchhikers look shifty and, when illuminated by the harsh glare of headlights, downright terrifying. You might as well stand on the shoulder of the road, dirt-covered, with disheveled hair and tattered clothing, holding out a thumb in one hand and a bloodied axe in the other. A ride is unlikely. And if there are two of you hitchhiking, forget it—it will not happen. So, rather than take part in a hopeless roadside creep show that was sure to yield zero miles, Haakon chose to sleep under a noisy freeway bridge in Whitehall, Montana—twice.

"Damn! What are the odds?" Haakon asked himself, both dismayed and amazed.

He wondered if it was a divine sign of some sort. But of what? He tried to convey his astonishment to his traveling companion, but Brady replied with silence and his all-too-familiar "I don't give a shit" glare. Brady was a man of few words who, like a mime, mastered artful non-verbal communication. He did not appear to be in a good mood, though he rarely exhibited happiness even when he was. Brady liked to hold his emotion cards close. But he knew well that they had a problem. Haakon knew they had a problem too, but preferred not to think about it. What was the point, he thought? It would have made no difference. They were out of options and without sleeping bags, and the early spring temperature was dropping rapidly. There was no twenty-four-hour truck stop in which to seek warm refuge. The town of Whitehall before them, what there was of it, was rolled up and closed. This assured them of a long, cold, miserable night.

The two of them began there trip with sleeping bags, of course, as they had planned on camping their way across the West, both for monetary reasons and to demonstrate to themselves how rugged they were.

"Who needs a stink'n soft bed and a warm motel room," Haakon would say, in an attempt to imitate a Hollywood tough guy, jabbing his index finger into the air to emphasize "stink'n" and "warm."

The truth was—using a term from Haakon's Great Depression surviving grandfather—they barely had "two nickels to rub together," so thrift of travel was paramount. Indeed, it was compulsory. But being young, they imagined themselves tougher than they probably were. So, each acquired a worn brownish-green Army surplus, down, mummy bag that, while not as lightweight and pretty as those brightly colored nylon-shelled counterparts sold in the sporting goods stores, was guaranteed to keep them "snug as bugs" in anything that springtime nights might deliver—or so they thought. Their reasoning was, if it was good enough for Army grunts, it would be good enough for them. And, part of that belief may have hatched from a subconscious guilt for coming of age at the heels of the Vietnam era, after the draft had ended and no one they knew was enlisting. But ultimately, the price was right. Cheap. They tightly stuffed the bags into their respective backpacks, which contained other pertinent traveling items, like toothbrushes, extra clothing, candy bars, and tobacco products—Marlboro cigarettes for Haakon and disgusting chewing tobacco for Brady. Their packs' contents were carefully planned. What was *not* planned was the mishap in Spearfish, South Dakota, that separated them from their packs.

"Brilliant idea, King Haakon!" Brady blurted, as they climbed the berm underneath the freeway bridge.

He usually called Haakon by his nickname, Hawk, but when trying to annoy, Brady would use Haakon's formal name. And when he really wanted to get under Haakon's skin, he would preface it with his name's Norwegian source—a bit of trivia Haakon forever regretted telling him. Haakon knew he was not referring to spending the night up on the ledge at the top of the berm. Rather, Brady was referring to the Spearfish incident. He had been bitching about it ever since, hundreds of times throughout the long preceding day, like a skipping record.

"Yeah, it was my fault," Haakon replied, sarcastically.

It did not matter to Brady that Spearfish was not Haakon's idea. He knew this, but he did not *want* to know this. Brady was not about self-accountability. It was easier to blame others. However, Haakon was familiar with his bullshit, so he took it in stride as part of the daily discourse. Haakon knew the Spearfish incident was one of those unforeseen, unfortunate occurrences that unraveled before them, like a fumble on a football field that turns a sure touchdown into its ugly inverse—a 14-point reversal of fortune. It turned out that Haakon and Brady's luck in Spearfish changed just as quickly.

The previous day, they thought they had struck "hitchhiker pay dirt." A car that was going beyond their destination of northwest Montana picked them up in eastern South Dakota. Hitchhikers dream of such lifts. This would be a 1,000-plus-mile ride! And all that was required for admission was to be well-mannered, polite, and, if appropriate, jovial. This was nearly always the fare for hitchhiking.

Even before they climbed into the car, Haakon had a good feeling. As he ran towards the powder blue Plymouth Duster, which had abruptly stopped 50 yards beyond them—its brake lights implying a ride offer—wondering how anyone could purposely choose such a hideous color for a car, he noticed that it had a Wisconsin license plate. It was centered between a Green Bay Packer and a Blatz Beer bumper sticker.

"He is one of us," Haakon thought.

Being from neighboring Minnesota, Haakon was not a Packer fan—actually, he had been taught to loathe the Packers—but during his first year of college in Wisconsin, he had become a fan of Blatz Beer. At three bucks per case it was hands down a campus favorite and, by good fortune, it tasted pretty good too. Yet, despite its Wisconsin notoriety, Haakon had never seen Blatz Beer branding beyond the state's border. So right away he would have something to talk about with the driver. And this was important, because while hitchhiking it was incumbent upon the hitchhiker, if you were a hitchhiker of any merit, to always have a topic of conversation. This helped cut through what could otherwise be the awkward silence of riding through an often-featureless landscape with a stranger. Drivers usually picked up riders because they were lonely. In Haakon's admittedly short hitchhiking career, he had already observed a correlation between driver loneliness and an inability to easily strike up a conversation. So, while Haakon was not a born extrovert, for a free ride he figured that he should make an effort.

But this driver *was* a conversationalist.

"Where you guys headed?" the driver asked cheerfully as the car rolled back onto the near-empty freeway with the two hitchhikers now aboard.

"A small town in northwest Montana called Renfro," Haakon answered, being the designated speaker for the two of them.

Brady, being a selective introvert, instinctively climbed into the back seat, always yielding the front seat to Haakon when it was available. With the front seat went the duty of being the spokesperson.

"Well, you're in luck, because I'm going through to Seattle," the driver answered. "I'm not sure how far I'll go today, but I'll at least get you a lot closer."

"Wow. That would be great," Haakon replied. "Thank you for the ride."

"Where ya guys from?"

"We're from a small town northeast of the Twin Cities called Spirit Lake, not far from the Wisconsin border."

Haakon thought mentioning their close Wisconsin proximity would win them favor. He did not reveal that he usually disparagingly referred to this same border as "The Cheddar Curtain"—a term derogatorily embracing the dairy state's notoriety of cheese production. Minnesota and Wisconsin, as with most bordering states, had a long rivalry that aroused belittling comments about each other. It did not escape Haakon's attention that this car's rear window ledge had not only a Green Bay Packer bobble-head, but thrown into its corner was also a Green Bay Packer cap and jersey. This guy had a strong state allegiance. Haakon would have to choose his words carefully.

"I'm Carl," the driver said while taking his right hand off of the steering wheel to shake. "I'm from Sheboygan, home of the bratwurst."

Haakon tried quickly to think of something Spirit Lake was known for, but came up empty. This made him feel like an inadequate representative of his hometown. Surely, it was recognized for something—the proud hometown of a movie star, a famous athlete, a revered politician? Something. But nothing came to mind, so he simply stated their names.

"I'm Haakon and that's Brady."

Brady on cue said, "Hi."

"Haakon? Like the bird?" Carl asked.

"No. Like the Norwegian king," Haakon answered. "I guess my primarily Swedish parents were into the names of Norwegian royalty for some unknown reason. Go figure."

"Well, it's a cool name. Different. That's a good thing," Carl said.

"Maybe. I guess. But it nearly always requires explanation. Sometimes I wished that my parents would have just named me Bob or

Pete… or even Sue," Haakon said while thinking that talking about a name was as good as anything to discuss.

Carl looked to be about their age. He had rounded features and long curly brown hair—not fat, yet far from thin. He looked to be someone who could consume a respectable quantity of bratwursts, cheese, and beer—someone who, Haakon thought, may be destined to have a date with a cardiologist in his later years. He was as affable as he looked, so they had no difficulty conversing about all topics imaginable—all the things that have ample time to come to mind while crossing the Great Plains. As they talked, Haakon watched out his window for anything unique that might appear, like a deer, or a tractor, or even a tree. He wondered how, back in the covered wagon days, travelers could have possibly filled their time with conversation. It seemed unimaginable that there would be enough words for a slow roll across South Dakota.

"Thank God for freeways and combustible engines," Haakon thought to himself as he stared out the window into its vast emptiness.

Carl asked why they were traveling to Montana and Haakon explained to him that being unsuccessful at finding summer jobs in construction and having no steady girlfriends back home, they felt compelled to try their fortunes out West—following the famous frontier-day-words of journalist Horace Greeley: "Go West, young man!"

It was 1976, the year of the nation's bicentennial. It also was the year of a severe building recession. Construction jobs were few and far between. In previous summers, the relatively good pay of construction jobs had spoiled Haakon and Brady. The minimum wages of fast food, gas station, and grocery store jobs no longer sufficed them, as it did for most of their friends. Haakon and Brady were willing to work physically harder to make more money.

They were both young, large, and strong, and they were "union brothers." When the laborer union business agent's car drove towards their job site two summers before, their foreman let out a call: "All laborers get off the job, NOW! BA's coming!"

With that order, all seven dropped what they were doing and ran in the opposite direction of the approaching car, scurrying away like rats off a ship's deck. Then, just before they were out of view, the foreman yelled out again, "Brady, Haakon! You two back here!"

The two of them stopped dead in their tracks and looked at each other. Brady had a "this can't be good" expression written on his face and Haakon shrugged his shoulders in reply. Then they both gaited back towards the foreman, looking remorseful, as though they had been caught doing something wrong. A heavyset, tie-wearing man in a white shirt with rolled-up sleeves approached the foreman from the now parked car, carrying a clipboard. But Haakon and Brady arrived at the foreman's side first.

"How old are you guys? I need the truth," the foreman whispered to them.

"Seventeen," they each responded.

"Well, Happy Birthday, you're eighteen today."

He then strode off to greet the approaching union business agent halfway.

"These two need to be signed up," he said.

"Didn't I see more than just them?" the BA inquired.

"Nah, just punks hanging out on the job site. Hooligans really. I told 'em to scram."

The BA smirked at hearing the familiar lie, but he accepted Haakon and Brady as a consolation. So, lying about their ages, both were enlisted as "brothers" in the Minneapolis Laborers Union, Local 563. In doing so, they immediately gained its benefits and increased wages, as well as the penance of weekly union dues. Both felt fortunate.

After the BA drove off from the job site and all of Haakon and Brady's cohorts returned from their hiding spots, they were sent home permanently. The foreman knew they were now on the union's radar and that the BA would be back. He did not want to provoke the ire of "organized labor" and force a job shutdown.

Haakon and Brady were well aware it was not luck that kept them on the job. The two of them worked circles around the other guys and, even during those minutes when there was nothing to do, they had enough sense to *find* something to do. Few things irk a construction boss more than seeing a worker lean on a shovel or stand idly with hands in pockets. A boss sees neither the worker nor the shovel nor the pockets. He just sees dollar bills blowing off in the wind. To a boss, an idle worker is akin to watching the meter run in a parked taxicab.

Haakon and Brady were not geniuses, but they knew to abide by
Construction Rule #1: Always look busy—always.

Yet good work ethics is where their similarities ended. Unlike
Haakon, Brady was a skilled athlete, a born natural who stormed
through his high school years breaking numerous sports records. He
was "varsity everything" from his very first day as a freshman, leaving
many resentful upper-classmen sitting on the bench in his wake. He
depicted the stereotypical jock star and often walked between high
school classes with an entourage of letterman-jacket-wearing admirers.
Haakon was not one of them, nor was he "a jock." Rather, he was a
cigarette-smoking, fringed-jacket-wearing, "long hair" who worked at a
gas station after school. Sports was not Haakon's forte, nor his concern.

Despite Brady's high school notoriety, he was not popular with
all of his classmates. Given an audience, he could be an outspoken
ass—crude, rude, and loud. In these moments he was an unrelenting
ridiculer of underdogs, maliciously gaining hoots and snickers at their
expense. His surrounding band of laughing lemmings only fed into
this ugliness. If you were not in his horde, it was easy to recognize
this behavior as the product of hollow self-esteem. Haakon saw it,
yet it still did not make Brady a sympathetic figure to him. Not then.
Back in high school, Haakon and Brady were not friends, rather just
acquaintances through a mutual friend.

But, Haakon respected Brady's prowess as an athlete and was
impressed that he had won the favor of one particularly sweet, attractive
female classmate. Melanie was literally Brady's antithesis. Haakon did
not view Brady as good-looking or smooth-talking. Brady had the
same stocky build of Babe Ruth, which seemed unnatural for both,
considering their superior athletic propensities. And until Haakon
knew him better, he could not imagine that Brady could muster any
measurable level of verbal charm. But he could. Brady was a "diamond
in the rough." His girlfriend must have zeroed in on this quality and
then made a conscious decision to discount his many unfavorable
traits. Haakon could think of no other explanation. Brady and Melanie
married right after graduation. Soon after that, Haakon found himself
working with Brady on a summer construction job.

High school athletics and his romance with Melanie were Brady's
life's high-water mark. But sadly both were short-lived. When Haakon

phoned Brady nearly a year later to check on the following summer's job prospects, Brady seemed to be struggling with life. His high school celebrity status and his pretty wife had both left him. He lived alone in a mobile home with two dog-sized cats. After Haakon had gone off to college, Brady stayed at the construction job where they had worked together. He seemed content. By the time Haakon stopped by to see him the following spring, Brady was a broken man. Besides losing his wife and star-status, Brady had lost his job, his two cats, and even his new Ford pickup truck. Melanie had quickly outgrown him. The other losses could be attributed to time, the recession, an unfixed door latch, and burdensome loan payments, respectively.

Brady was down on his luck, but he still had a trace of humor.

"If I didn't have bad luck," he told Haakon, "I wouldn't have any luck at all."

With no job and no prospects, Haakon suggested that Brady travel with him out West. Haakon had a construction job lined up in Montana through his uncle. He was sure he could get Brady on too. Despite the deep national building recession of that summer, the northwest Montana building trades were benefiting from an influx of migrating Californians fleeing their once "Golden State." The pay was not as good as their former union jobs, but as Haakon's uncle used to say, "It's better than a stick in the eye." Haakon and Brady had nothing going in Minnesota, nothing to cling to—no wife, no girlfriends, and no jobs. A summer in Montana would be a welcome adventure for both.

Haakon explained to Brady that living there would be cheap but primitive. Haakon's uncle owned a wooded lot on a river with a tiny travel trailer parked on it. It had no electricity or running water. His uncle used it as his annual hunting camp and said that Haakon was welcome to stay there. But, Haakon made it clear to Brady that they would not be "bunking together" in the trailer. It was too small for two big guys and, even if it had been roomy enough, Haakon would still not roommate with Brady. Brady simply was not roommate material. In fact, Haakon considered Brady a slob and he suspected that this trait might have played a significant role in Brady's failed marriage. And Haakon's assessment of him had not factored in Brady's foul tobacco chewing habit. Brady would have to "tent it"—whether or not it rained or hailed or even snowed. Yet this was all right with Brady. He relished the opportunity to change his depressing surroundings.

"A wet tent in the woods," Brady said, "would be far preferable to a lonely mobile home in the city."

Eventually, the contour of the Black Hills broke above the seemingly endless two-dimensional plains. They stood prominently, silhouetted against the dimming backlight of a setting sun. As the Plymouth labored up the long, gradual grade, the previously pleasant May weather quickly turned cold and windy. Heavy rain, almost snow-looking, smacked against the windshield. Carl leaned over to turn up the heat and to divert air to the defroster. Haakon smiled to himself, still reeling from their good fortune of being in a warm car, continuously rolling towards their destination. Brady snored in comfort.

But less than an hour later, Carl struggled with driving. The blowing heat was making him sleepy and the constant rain made visibility difficult.

"I think I'm through for the day. I gotta get off the road," he suddenly announced.

The alarming words jolted Haakon and woke Brady up instantly. Carl might as well have thrown cold water in their faces.

"Tell ya what," Carl continued, "I'm gonna get a motel room up ahead in Spearfish. If ya want, I can pick you guys up in the morning where I drop you off, if you're gonna camp for the night."

Haakon gulped, still trying to find mental footing from the unexpected turn of events. In minutes, Carl would eject them from their heated bliss, out into the cold, wet, windy night.

"Or, we can split up a room together, three ways."

Haakon and Brady had not planned on spending any money on lodging.

"I'll check in as a single, then you guys can sneak in after I get the room. You can "bag it" on the floor. Split three ways, it won't cost us hardly noth'n."

Thus the seed of a criminal act was planted.

Carl pulled off of the freeway into the sleepy pre-tourist-season Black Hills town of Spearfish, then turned into a small U-shaped "Ma & Pa" motel with a brightly lit neon "Vacancy" sign. As he drove by the office, Haakon and Brady laid low in their seats. When Haakon peeked up, he recognized the office to be strategically positioned at the gateway of the "U." It stuck out in a glass-walled spur that oversaw the street, parking lot, and the entrance to each motel unit. If equipped with machine guns and bulletproof glass, Haakon thought it would have made an excellent military blockhouse.

After Carl registered, he drove his car right up to the motel room's door. In darkness, Haakon and Brady slipped inside.

After they awoke early the next morning, Carl loaded all of their bags back into his car. When he returned to the room, he looked nervous.

"They're watching me from the office. I think they're on to us," he said, confirming the expression Haakon saw on this face. "We're the only car here."

Carefully, Haakon peeked through the closed drapes and confirmed both the empty parking lot and the two figures staring through the large office window in their direction.

"What should we do," Haakon asked.

"You're never going to get out the front door. I think you'll have to sneak out the bathroom window and meet me in town," Carl said.

"You're joking, right?" Brady interjected. "Have you seen how small that window is?"

Brady's concern was justified. The bathroom had a window that opened into a back alley, away from the view of the office. But it was tiny and Haakon and Brady were not. To make matters worse, it was high on the wall. Both would need Carl's help climbing into it backward and then, if they could squeeze through, they would have to jump five feet or so to the alley below.

"It's the only way," Carl responded.

So, in desperation, they executed the plan. Since Brady was larger in girth, he went first. Both Carl and Haakon clumsily helped maneuver him backward into the small opening. Once his legs were through, his center of balance enabled him to move without assistance. He let out a groan, then wiggled out and fell down onto the dirt below. Haakon heard a thud, then a curse, prompting him to stick his head through the window to chastise Brady.

"Quiet, you idiot!"

Brady looked up at Haakon after brushing the dirt off his pant legs.

"*I'm* the idiot? Look at us… sneaking through a bathroom window into a dirty alleyway in Podunk, South Dakota! I don't think I'm the only idiot here."

Haakon thought it hard to argue with Brady's point, but they were already committed to their plan, as ludicrous as it may have been. With help from each side of the window, and having a narrower circumference than Brady, Haakon shimmied through the opening with relative ease. Brady uncharacteristically assisted the landing, so Haakon did not have to fall onto all fours.

"Okay guys," Carl's visible head whispered from the window above, "I'll check-out at the office, then meet you downtown."

Both Haakon and Brady nodded in agreement. This seemed reasonable to Haakon, as he recalled the "downtown" consisting of only a few blocks of small businesses and shops. At this early hour, they would likely be the only pedestrians and thus easy subjects for Carl to locate. So Haakon and Brady nonchalantly strolled out onto the main street—their large figures as inconspicuous as two zebras in the Sahara desert. The sidewalks were empty and the main drag had virtually no traffic. It was just Haakon and Brady futilely trying to blend into their environment, wishing to cloak themselves in some sort of "small town" camouflage. As they walked, both turned frequently towards the motel hoping to see Carl's car appear.

They came upon the lights of an open cafe. Inside its large street-facing windows was a littering of old men wearing plaid shirts and baseball caps. Some were conversing and some sat engrossed behind open newspapers as they sipped from white porcelain coffee cups. Haakon noticed a few of the cafe patrons looking up as he and Brady passed by. He correctly surmised that their youth and unexpected presence became the cafe topic of the moment.

A few doors down, a corner grocery store's lights were on as well. It also had large windows facing the street, so Haakon and Brady ducked inside thinking they could enjoy its warmth while watching for the car, without an audience of coffee-sippers. But as they stood there, it occurred to both simultaneously that the store was not yet open for business. An old man was stocking a shelf at the end of a long aisle. He glanced up at them but said nothing. Still, Haakon could feel his suspicion. He imagined that the old man thought of them as two escaped prisoners on the run.

Both stepped back outside into the cold, continuing their nervous scan for the powder blue Plymouth.

Eventually, it appeared in the distance, cresting a hill, and both vagabonds sighed with relief. It approached slowly and Haakon waved subtly to get Carl's attention. But once Haakon saw Carl's face, he knew something was wrong. He felt it even before he noticed Carl frantically pointing behind, as he passed by. His unexpected signal prompted Haakon and Brady to fall back into the shadows of a receding hardware store entrance. Within moments, another car appeared on the crest. The sedan sped up as it passed their hardware store refuge. The car contained an old couple, which both assumed to be the motel's "Ma and Pa."

"This isn't good," Brady said, expressing the obvious.

It was not good. Haakon and Brady waited and watched for several minutes before they saw Carl's car appear again, this time approaching from the opposite direction. It was still tailed by the old couple, but now a police car had joined the caravan.

"Oh, shit!" Brady said. "What do we do?"

"I don't know. Just stand here, I guess."

Haakon assumed that the caravan would stop in front of them and they would be arrested. He tried to imagine how he would come up with bail money and how he would explain being in a South Dakota jail to his uncle. But, the caravan did not stop. Carl, then Ma and Pa, then the police car each, again, drove by the hardware store. As they passed, Ma and then the policeman glanced over in Haakon's and Brady's direction, but neither car slowed. Two blocks beyond, at the town's only visible stoplights, the caravan turned towards the freeway entrance.

Haakon and Brady waited in vain for nearly an hour. Then, daringly and out of desperation, they walked past the police station, hoping to find the impounded pale-blue Duster. But it and Carl were nowhere to be seen. Haakon and Brady realized then that Carl had likely been ushered out of town and that their backpacks were traveling west without them.

"What are we going to do now?" Brady asked, knowing that Haakon knew no more than he did.

"I don't have a clue. This really sucks!" Haakon answered, looking as distressed as he felt. "I guess we just get back out on the freeway and hope that we see him stopped along the way."

"What are the odds of that?"

"Slim, I would think. But what choice do we have?"

Brady shook his head as they both stared at the ground, trying to think of something brilliant.

"Thank God we have our jackets," Haakon said, trying to give their dire predicament a positive spin.

"Yeah, but we don't have our sleeping bags. That's gonna be a problem."

"True. That had occurred to me too."

"And I don't have my chewing tobacco," Brady added.

"That's not a problem for me. Now, at least, I won't have to see your disgusting drool."

"Don't worry. I still have my wallet. I'll buy some more," he said, grinning for the first time that day.

"Well, don't piss away too much of your money on that brown slobber. With our stuff gone, we're gonna need the little money we have left."

Once back on the freeway, Haakon and Brady extended their thumbs and plied their luck again.

It is always a good idea to appear somewhat miserable when you are hitchhiking. Sympathy is your ally. So it is helpful to act a bit—but only a bit, since this can be overplayed. Like with most arts, it is a balancing act.

First, to make it work, never wear sunglasses. Drivers need to see your soul through your eyes. Sunglasses, particularly wraparound sunglasses, make you look shifty.

Second, do not appear too gleeful, like "man, this is the life standing here for hours with my thumb out waiting for a free ride." This would make you appear deranged and unstable. However, you should not seem cheerless either. Drivers do not want to be dispirited, nor do they want to deal with someone's hard-luck story. You just want to look a little uncomfortable, like "my life would sure be great if only you would make a small effort and give me a ride in your nice warm car, being you're already headed in my direction and all."

Haakon called it the hitchhiker's "Goldilocks Look": not too hot, not too cold—you have got to look "just right."

Sometimes wind, rain, snow, and cold could help you accomplish a pitiful demeanor without having to act at all. Few things look more pathetic than a hitchhiker being pelted sideways with wind and sleet, while the driver sits in a warm, soft bucket seat, cruising down the road, shielded from the harsh elements, thinking "God, I'm glad that isn't me!"

For Haakon and Brady, one benefit of losing their backpacks was that it gave them that "Goldilocks Look" without even acting. After retreating from Spearfish, they felt miserable, yet both tried hard not to look too miserable—both tried to shake it off.

In short order, they had a ride.

To their delight, their next driver was an attractive young woman in a scanty dress. When Haakon opened the passenger door, he nearly gasped when he saw her sweet face and, at the same time, the revealing side profile of her nearly exposed breast. It took considerable willpower for him to focus on her eyes.

"Thank you," Haakon muttered as he tilted the passenger seat forward so that Brady could climb into the backseat.

"You guys look as though you could use a lift," she said.

"Yeah, it's not pleasant out there," Haakon responded, still consciously forcing his eyes up.

With the seatback restored, Haakon quickly sat down and closed the door.

"That was nice of you to pick us up."

Out of the corner of his eye, he could see Brady's eyes, saucer-shaped. From the backseat, Brady had a favorable viewing angle of her dress. Haakon hoped that she would not notice his gaze through her rearview mirror.

She looked a bit tousled. Her short brunette hair was messy and her mascara slightly smeared. Haakon had the impression her clothing had been worn on the previous night, which this morning was, apparently, an extension of.

"Where ya headed?" she said, turning to Haakon briefly as she veered back onto the freeway.

Her eyes were big and round—disproportionate to her small stature, though favorably. They gave her the adorable look of innocence that her apparel seemed to defy. Had her dress not distracted Haakon, he would have initially recognized their bright green loveliness.

"Northwest Montana," Haakon answered.

"Close to Coeur d'Alene?"

He loved the sound of the name, particularly the way she said it.

"Pretty close," he answered. "We are turning north just before. Headed up to a little town near Colterville. Do you speak French?"

"I *do* a little."

She turned towards Haakon briefly, showing a face of appreciation. He relished being able to gaze into those eyes again, albeit for only a second.

"You pronounced the name so beautifully."

"Well, thank you," she said. "But it actually doesn't have such a beautiful meaning. It translates to 'heart of the awl' or 'pointy heart.' It was a derogatory term that French fur traders gave to their skilled and shrewd Indian trading partners."

She was smart, Haakon thought—likely college-educated. He scorned himself for having a different first impression of her—not a bad impression, just a less venerable one. "Don't judge a book by its cover," he noted in his mind. Then he recalled his first view of her dress and excused himself. "I'm only human," Haakon reasoned.

"I kind of wish I didn't know that," Haakon said, chuckling.

"Yeah, I know what you mean. The French language can make almost everything sound beautiful."

Haakon nodded.

"I'm going as far as Gillette, but that should help you some, yes?"

"Gillette would help us a lot," Haakon answered automatically, not calculating the miles in his head, but knowing that every westward mile ultimately helped their cause. "Thank you. We really appreciate it. I'm Haakon. That's Brady."

Haakon did not offer his hand, as he did not want to distract from her driving.

"Haakon. Like a hawk, like the bird?" she asked.

"No. Like the Norwegian king, I guess. My parents just wanted to burden me with a lifetime of introductory explanations."

"You're funny," she said, turning to smile at Haakon. "I'm Susie."

He smiled back.

"What's in Colterville?" she asked.

"Jobs."

Haakon went into a lengthier explanation of their story—with all the what, why, and where's—that concluded with their Spearfish motel incident. Brady sat quietly in the backseat as he usually did unless addressed directly. He watched lazily out his window, no doubt realizing that staring at her open dress risked abruptly ending their warm ride. But he listened. Not much got by Brady, despite his often-lackadaisical appearance. He took it all in. Haakon knew this because often a random conversation that he would have with a driver, in his attempt to be an appreciative and amiable guest, would come up later, mockingly. Brady was more than happy to let Haakon "put himself out there" so he could sit back and collect comedic material. Haakon had come to accept this as routine. So, he knew that even though Brady could masterfully disguise himself as being aloof, he was actually a human tape recorder with astutely keen ears.

"Wow, that sucks about the backpacks, guys. Wish I could take you all the way, but I'm on my way to work too. And I'm waaaay late. And you can see that I'm not dressed for it."

Haakon took that opportunity to study her dress again.

Then she laughed.

"Well, I guess you guys don't know what I do for a living so you don't know if I'm dressed for work or not."

This comment made both Haakon and Brady chuckle nervously.

"Would you believe I'm a nurse?"

Haakon wanted to tell her he would believe anything that she told him and that if she were *his* nurse, she would make being sick or injured a fair trade.

But instead, Haakon asked, "In Gillette?"

"Yeah, in Gillette. I'm a small-town girl, though not such a wise girl as I took up with some jerk in the Black Hills. You'd think I'd be smart enough to find a local guy, and a good guy."

For a moment, Haakon considered what it might be like living in Gillette and volunteering to be "her local good guy."

"Hey, can you hand me a smoke from the glove box?"

Haakon handed it to her, allowing his eyes to fall to her breast, hoping it was exposed again. But it was not and he felt bad for wishing it. Susie placed the cigarette in her mouth, seeming not to notice his wayward gaze. After it was lit, she explained her situation.

It was something about some guy she had just met and somehow ended up spending the night with, at his parent's Black Hills cabin. She drank too much. She smoked some pot. He turned out to be a jerk. He possibly slipped a drug into her drink. She slept in too late and now she would probably lose her job in Gillette, where she lived with a girlfriend and a cat.

Haakon did not get the impression the story was atypical for Susie. She seemed a scatterbrain, albeit a sweet and intelligent one. This was not a contradiction. He had known many people whose common sense did not rise to their IQ level.

Reliving the previous evening made her emotional, so her story did not come out as coherently as she might have thought. But from what Haakon comprehended, her sweetness made her a doormat. And this made him sad. He genuinely hoped she would find a "good guy," though he thought it improbable. For whatever deep-seated reason, Haakon did not think she was really looking for that good guy.

This revelation made Haakon rethink his brief alternative plan of moving to Gillette.

Haakon and Brady heard a lot of driver's stories while hitchhiking. They would usually debrief each other of the previous ride as they stood waiting for the next. Many drivers liked to have someone to listen to them. This became clear early on. Sometimes it was a confessional of sorts. It seemed to be one of a driver's greatest motivators to pick up a hitchhiker. The need to talk and be listened to often overrode a driver's innate concern for his or her own security.

When the car arrived at her Gillette freeway exit, both Haakon and Brady thanked Susie and bid her farewell and good luck. Her sad face mustered a smile as Haakon closed the passenger door. Then she sped off, back into her unnecessarily difficult life.

Standing on cold concrete again, the two hitchhikers turned their attention to the sparse oncoming traffic. Zoom. Zoom. Zoom. Car after car passed them without even a glance, for nearly an hour.

"God, she was beautiful!" Brady stated out of the blue.

"This just occurred to you?"

"Maybe she got fired and she's gonna come back out here and give us a ride the rest of the way."

"Yeah, that's gonna happen," Haakon said, shaking his head.

"I could sure use a chew right now."

Haakon turned to give Brady a puzzled look.

"Jeez, your mind sure jumps around. You go from something so beautiful to something so foul in the same thought?"

"I'm a complicated man," Brady replied.

"You're confusing complication with mental deviancy."

He glanced back at Haakon with an exaggerated smile.

"Besides," Haakon continued. "You'd put that foul garbage in your mouth while trying to catch a ride? What, do ya wanna guarantee that we stand here in the cold all day?"

"Look who's talk'n, Mister Smoke Sticks! At least my lungs don't look like stovepipes," Brady said.

"Even if I had my cigarettes, you wouldn't catch me smoke'n while trying to get a ride. That's taboo," Haakon responded. "Besides, I'm quitting."

"Right," Brady said in disbelief.

"No, I am. No better time than right now. I'm without cigarettes. I'm in an unfamiliar environment with a new schedule. Best time to break a habit, they say."

"I'll believe it when I see it. You're an addict," Brady said. "I expect to see you start shaking any minute now."

Haakon smiled.

"Maybe you're right. All the more reason to quit," Haakon said. "But you should think about it too. The girls aren't big on tobacco drool and spit cans, you know. Something to think about."

"What would you know about what girls like?" Brady asked, annoyed.

"I know plenty."

"You just know what *your* mom told ya."

"Actually, it was your mom," Haakon retorted, proud of himself for fielding Brady's unintentional setup.

Brady responded by giving Haakon the finger, but Haakon's eyes caught a sight beyond Brady's raised hand, far in the distance. Brady turned to see what had caught Haakon's attention, as though spurred by some mutual premonition. The broad chrome grill of a Cadillac was approaching at high speed and both hitchhikers instinctively sensed trouble. On a few occasions, cars purposely veered towards them—presumably to satisfy some perverse sense of humor. These were always speeding cars. So, without discussion, both Haakon and Brady braced for a leap into the adjacent ditch.

The Cadillac raced by, never feigning a threatening swerve. But immediately after passing, it slammed on its brakes, causing the tires to screech and smoke. Then the backup lights flashed on and the car raced towards Haakon and Brady in reverse—right in the middle of what was now an empty freeway. Both again braced for action. This time it halted alongside them, mere seconds before they would have jumped to safety. The big black car with dark-tinted windows sat motionless for an uncomfortably long time, during which Haakon and Brady tried to assess the level of impending danger. Its rumbling mufflers were like the low growl of a lion and its reverberating exhaust made the ground below their feet vibrate. Suddenly, the long passenger door swung open, revealing the driver sitting, slouched, on the far end of its wide bench seat. A cowboy hat sat beside the figure. The man behind the steering wheel appeared to be small, but Haakon was uncertain if his perceived size was skewed because of the large wide car and his distance. He glanced at the hitchhikers, then nervously up into his rearview mirror, then back at them.

"You boys need a ride or what?"

"Ya, sure," both answered somewhat reluctantly, without moving.

"Well, get on in. This ain't a parking lot," he quipped.

Haakon and Brady approached his vehicle cautiously, still evaluating the situation. Haakon tilted the front seat forward and Brady climbed in, once he determined that there was no one crouched down on the floor of the backseat, waiting to lunge at him with a knife to slit his throat. Then Haakon pushed back the folding seat and climbed in himself. Just as he sat—at the precise moment his posterior contacted the leather of the seat—the driver pressed down on the accelerator with his weathered cowboy boot. The large Cadillac's powerful V8 engine accelerated down the freeway concourse, as though trying to achieve lift. The resulting G-forces sank both Haakon and Brady into their seats and it slammed Haakon's door shut before he even had the chance to reach over and close it.

"Sorry if I startled ya boys. I'm an abrupt man. Where ya head'n?"

He had a bit of a drawl, like an accent Haakon would know from an old cowboy movie. He looked over towards Haakon impatiently for an answer, with his eyes off of the road for too long of a time. His lips moved slowly even after he had asked his question. Haakon realized he was chewing tobacco.

"Northwest Montana," Haakon answered, still looking forward, concerned.

The car continued to speed up. Haakon glanced over and could see the speedometer reading 80, 90, then nearly 100 miles per hour. If it were not for the outskirts of Gillette racing by in his peripheral view, he may have doubted what the gauge was showing. Even at high speed, the heavy car hugged the road. Yet Haakon was growing anxious. And, though he did not look behind, he knew that Brady was as well.

"I'm not goin' that far, but I can take ya to Buffalo."

This would normally be an hour-long drive, but at this speed it was anyone's guess. Haakon and Brady never filtered rides according to the distance that the drivers were traveling. If the driver was going in their direction, they got in—figuring that every ride was a step closer to their final destination.

"Damn!" the cowboy suddenly exclaimed loudly.

This raised Haakon's alarm level even higher. He glanced towards the driver for an explanation but, initially, was offered none.

"What's your name?" the cowboy asked frantically, as though it was suddenly important.

"Bob," Haakon answered, purposely lying.

"Well Bob, I don't know if you boys noticed, but I just passed a poleece-man. I was going a little over the speed limit," he said matter-of-factly while gazing intently into his rearview mirror.

The patrol car apparently had receded down a slight hill out of his view.

"I do suspect that he'll be come'n back for me," he said.

Then the cowboy-driver followed this statement with a question that raised the hair on the back of Haakon's neck.

"You boys wanna go for a little ride?"

Haakon knew his answer without even having to weigh it in his head. He was pretty certain he knew Brady's too.

"I'm gonna get off at this exit com'n up here," the driver said, gesturing towards a freeway ramp that had just come into view, "and try and lose'm. Shouldn't take long."

Haakon's mind was jumping all over the place, but each of his envisioned scenarios included a high-speed race down some back roads that would end at the local Dewdrop Saloon, where the cowboy and all of his cowboy friends spent their idle hours trying to think of ways to lure hapless hitchhikers into their sinister web.

"Ah… how about if we get out quickly at the stop sign at the bottom of the ramp?" Haakon offered. "We'll get out fast."

"Well, all right… if ya do it quick," the driver said, sounding disappointed.

Haakon had never seen Brady move so fast—even in high school when Brady had a football tucked in his arm and was racing his opponents to the end zone. Once the Cadillac squealed to a stop, Brady was throwing the front passenger seat forward before Haakon was fully out of it, nearly slamming his forehead into the car's doorframe. Both were out and on the shoulder of the freeway ramp in a flash. Haakon quickly thanked the cowboy, gave him a wave, and wished him "good luck."

"I'll watch for you boys when I get back on the road," he shouted as he sped away, once again with an open passenger door.

The smoking rear tires eventually gained a firm grip on the asphalt and the Cadillac shot off. The open door slammed shut in reaction to the acceleration. A minute later, the big dark car was a speck on the broad Wyoming horizon, save its large trailing plume of dust.

"*That* was interesting," Brady said, relieved to be back on solid ground.

Haakon smirked and nodded in agreement. The ride had only taken them a few miles, but they concurred that they were miles in the right direction, so both shook it off and walked up the freeway ramp to resume their imploring hitchhiking poses.

If Haakon and Brady were fishermen, they would have called it a good day. Within ten minutes their thumb hooks had a bite—a large, tall, noisy white pickup truck slowed and rolled onto the shoulder. As it stopped, Haakon hoped that the cab had room for all three of them, as it would be too cold to ride in its open back. Nevertheless, gambling,

Haakon feigned a pulled muscle and hesitated running to meet the truck, giving Brady a wide lead. By the time Haakon had caught up, Brady was opening the passenger door and when he saw Haakon hesitate again, he realized he had been duped into boarding first. This meant Brady had to sit in the center of the bench seat, between the driver and Haakon.

As he climbed in, Haakon heard him mutter, "You son of a…"

But it was too late. Brady knew that to contest the seating arrangement at this crucial moment would be a serious breach of hitchhiking etiquette. It could result in the driver angrily speeding off, leaving two fools standing on the roadside. So, he placed his foot on the running board and pushed up into the cab, having enough sense to say "thank you" to the driver as he did.

This was a tall pickup, even for 4-wheel drive. With some effort, Haakon pulled himself up alongside Brady, while thanking the yet-to-be-seen driver. Once plopped comfortably onto the bench seat, Haakon turned, as he always did, to say, "Hi, I'm Haakan and this is…"

Brady's ashen face distracted Haakon's speech.

"Bra… Braaaaty."

Sitting next to Brady, behind the steering wheel, was the largest Native American Haakon had ever seen. Aside from his hulky size, he did not look particularly friendly. His face was dark and rocklike—chiseled, with abrupt angles. It did not appear pliable or capable of projecting expression. He wore conventional cowboy-wear, with the exception of his hat. The creamy-white Stetson had a colorful and intricately beaded hatband. The base of a single large feather was tucked behind it.

Haakon had nothing against Native Americans, though he had known only one from college. But this man was intimidating, through no fault of his own. To Haakon and Brady, his appearance seemed alien and his size imposing.

"I'm going as far as Billings," the driver said in a deep, raspy voice.

"Great," Haakon responded, knowing it was a 230-mile ride. "Thank you."

The big man said nothing more. He stared straight ahead and sped back onto the freeway. Haakon and Brady stared straight ahead too and remained silent. Haakon presumed from the driver's body language, and the not-so-subtle fact that he ignored Haakon's introduction, that this driver preferred quiet. And, of course, this was his prerogative, but Haakon knew it would make for a long awkward ride.

Nothing was said for the next hour. Haakon sat and looked off across the expanse of rolling hills, while Brady and the driver gazed ahead onto the mesmerizing never-ending road. Each time the pickup truck passed an exit or rest area, Haakon scanned for the powder blue Plymouth that contained their backpacks.

A short time after crossing into Montana, as the sun fell low in its big sky, the pickup truck passed the exit for Garryowen. Haakon's idle mind pondered this odd name. This is when, after nearly two hours of silence, the big Indian spoke again. He turned to his two passengers, averting his attention from the road for a longer time than he should have, then pointed with one of his enormous hands off to the east.

"Over there… that's where Custer got his ass kicked."

Those were his only words. He said them matter-of-factly and then turned back to face the road.

Haakon realized that he was referring to General George Armstrong Custer and the Battle of Little Bighorn. He suspected Brady understood this too. But why would the big Indian break his silence to announce that?

Haakon was keenly aware they were located well within the Crow Indian Reservation and the day was ominously growing late. Was this a signal? Was the big Indian now going to deliver them to other big Indians who might want reprisal for the centuries of the white man's injustice? Had two hitchhikers narrowly escaped a group of malicious drunken cowboys only to fall into the hands of a band of vindictive Indians?

Haakon nervously waited for more cues of their fate, but none came. The cab returned to its former quiet state as the pickup truck rolled on. But the further they got from the Little Bighorn River, the better Haakon felt. Still, he was not convinced that he and Brady would live to see another sunrise until he could make out the tall oil refinery flare stacks of Billings, on the horizon. The massive torches were like welcoming lighthouses, assuring they were soon to reach land.

When the big man arrived at his Billings exit, he stopped to let us climb out.

"Here," he said, leaning towards the open door.

He held out a small paper wrapping. Haakon reached back up into the cab to receive it.

"Buffalo jerky… better than white man jerky."

That was all he said. Haakon looked up into his face, surprised. Then the up-until-then stoic man grinned as he reached over to close the passenger door. Both Haakon and Brady waved as he drove off, but were uncertain if he saw them.

With darkness soon upon them, Haakon and Brady were grateful to quickly snag another westbound ride. Though, after the exhilarating cowboy and Indian experiences, a part of Haakon was disappointed to be riding with a nonthreatening accountant from Chicago. However, the rational part of Haakon enjoyed the driver's familiarity. Without anxiety, they rolled comfortably through the darkening Montana landscape. So relaxing was the ride, Haakon struggled to stay awake. He considered it impolite to snooze while their host had to remain fully alert. Brady was not encumbered by this concern. He slumbered away in the backseat, breathing loudly, with his head tilted back unnaturally—a sore neck in the making, Haakon thought.

It might have been preferable on this evening to have ridden across the heart of Montana in the cold exposed back bed of a rickety old farm truck. Something less than a plush, warm Buick Riviera would have better prepared the two hitchhikers for the harsh transition to the frigid freeway underpass. For some forgotten reason, their host was headed for Silver Star and that meant turning off the freeway in, literally, the middle of nowhere, and in the middle of the night.

The exit sign read: Whitehall, Montana.

"What ta.. time is it?" Brady asked in the clattering voice of someone freezing.

A semi-truck passed overhead, creating a thundering roar. The sound and shaking no longer made them lurch in fear, as they had grown accustomed to it, like people who live under an airline runway approach. Haakon paused momentarily to answer him.

"It's a little pa… past fa… four. They'll be sa… sa… some light in just over an hour," he said, trying to buoy Brady's spirits.

They sat half asleep underneath the bridge at the top of the berm, in fetal positions, trying to retain heat. From Haakon's perch, he could see some lights in Whitehall. He kept hoping that its gas station would open so he could go buy a candy bar and take a long time eating it. Then maybe he would buy another. But it was wishful thinking. The gas station never opened during their bridge-stay. And not a single car or pickup truck passed by it.

"Next time you have an idea like hi... hitch... hiking out West, keep it to... to yourself, would ya?" Brady blurted. "You really fi... fixed us."

"You're ge... ge... get'n soft," Haakon replied, trying in vain to disguise his nearly violent shivering. "We're Mi... min... nesotans. This isn't even co... cooold."

"Yeah, ma... maybe. But there's something to be said about wear'n winter co... co... clothes in winter weather," Brady said. "I feel like I'm a little under... er... dressed."

"Jeez! Do you want my ja... ja... jacket? Will that get you to sta... stop whining?"

Their stuttered bickering went on for the next hour. It helped keep their thoughts off of their discomfort. Eventually, a faint glow distinguished the mountains from the sky. When assured this was the returning sun, they crawled out from under the bridge and walked to the upper end of the westbound ramp, resuming their attempts to garner a ride with extended thumbs. But it was still too dark and they still looked too shifty in the low light. At least they could dance around a bit to generate a little heat.

Haakon was amazed how slowly the sun climbs from beneath the horizon when its warm rays are desperately needed. He was wondering if the earth had been knocked off its axis, forcing the sun to move sideways instead of upward, dooming them to perpetual twilight. The backside of the distant Rocky Mountains seemed to softly glow pinkish-orange forever. But eventually, the giant fireball broke over the landscape's silhouette. It cast its intensity down upon the valley floor, illuminating and warming their concrete pathway. In the distance, reflected heat made the road appear distorted, like a dancing desert mirage.

The morning radiance renewed their confidence. When his core's comfort caught up, Haakon stared down the freeway and marveled at how gently it rode up and down the contours of the land, as though skimming over ocean waves. He felt like a sailor again.

Still, there was little traffic at this early hour. At times, there was no sound of cars *or* trucks, just the subtle awakening noises of the surrounding landscape—the slight rustle of a breeze passing over an unobstructed plane of grass, chirping birds beginning their day's work, the distant bay of a calf calling for its mother, and an even more distant bark of a dog.

As the earth warmed, Haakon smelled the strip of asphalt below his feet. It occurred to him that people racing upon its surface, detached by cold steel and spinning rubber, could not know this intimacy. The essence of the road could only be realized by those who stood on it for countless hours. Even the laborers that painstakingly created the road, pouring and pressing it inch by inch, could not have felt it like the hitchhiker. There is a familiarity that comforts the soul when standing on the edge of such a simple yet vast entity. The road goes on forever, or seems to, and in this enormity it represents to the hitchhiker possibility, renewal, and opportunity.

The whirl of car tires emerged against the other background sounds. It grew closer and more distinct. When a chrome grill popped up into view, it was met with the sun's low rays, making it glare brilliantly like a star, forcing both Haakon and Brady to shield their eyes.

Haakon knew they had a ride. Sometimes he could just feel it.

3
CAMP ONE

In what would turn out to be the final year of the "war between the States," Silas and Sarah left allegiance-divided Kentucky to seek peace and prosperity in the West. It was a long, slow journey that included many stops where Silas would take on various jobs as Sarah bore children. By the time they arrived in Montana Territory, Sarah had given birth to nine offspring.

Tired of moving and determined to settle down, Silas took on work as a millwright in the bustling postwar lumber town of Colterville. As his job title implied, he was tasked with keeping the mill operational. Sarah took in laundry while tending to their children and giving birth to two more. For a time, the family lived a modest and comfortable life along the quiet Saleesh River. But then Silas, twenty years Sarah's senior, dropped dead in the mill, leaving her a young widow with a large family.

With little means of support for herself and her brood, Sarah was compelled to gamble. She audaciously moved herself and her children 30 miles up a Saleesh tributary river to seek what she perceived as an opportunity. The upper waters and their surrounding woodlands were now clambering with lumbermen busy to fill the needs of a burgeoning nation. Sarah purchased cheap land along the Cedar River. Then she and her oldest boys built a small log hotel. It was near the landing where the sawyers dropped their logs into the river—the liquid highway used to usher their fallen trees downstream to the mill. The structure was modest and crude, but sorely needed. A bustling post-war, lumber-hungry economy was drawing more and more men into the virgin forests of the Northwest. With them came commerce.

Sarah foresaw wages descending from the mountains, so it was not long before she and her sons built a mercantile in which to sell the lumbermen various supplies. And soon after that, she established a saloon to quench their thirsts. Eventually, the thriving entrepreneur realized that she could sell portions of land around her businesses as lots for homes. This brought women, then families. A post office opened in the front of the mercantile. Sarah gave it her family's name. The town of Renfro was born.

Before the Great Fire of 1910, Renfro was a lively place where a steady stream of men would emerge from the woods ready to part ways with hard-earned cash. That was the boom. What followed the fire was the bust. The big timber not burned away was eventually logged out and depleted. So, the mass of workers that had moved in so quickly *during* the boom, moved out even more quickly *after* the boom. Renfro reverted to a quiet place on the river. Only a handful of inhabitants remained to scratch out a living.

Haakon and Brady arrived sixty-six years after the Great Fire. By then, a nationwide building recession had nearly finished off an industry that was already hobbling. Lumber had seen brief intermittent remissions since the fire, but they were short-lived and always a pittance of the glory days. The Renfro that they met stood quiet and hollow. Its ancient wooden walls hosted ghosts. Those that lived with the ghosts in 1976 were an odd mix of California retirees and the children of the children of the great lumber days. One group sought cheap land and solace from urban madness. The other just sought to eke out a living in the only place they had known or cared to know.

The hitchhikers' final ride fortuitously dropped them off at the Cemetery Road turnoff, a mile beyond Renfro. This gravel spur led to Haakon's uncle's lot. It approached the Cedar River, perpendicularly, then turned towards the town, following the river closely. After a half-mile, the road ended on a low hill that overlooked both the river and the town. A dilapidated cemetery occupied the top of the hill. Haakon's uncle told him that Sarah and her offspring were buried there, as well as dozens of others—men, women, and children who once, for a brief time, breathed, slept, loved, ached, laughed, cried, worked, and dreamed on this remote parcel of Montana wilderness.

Haakon thought of these ancient souls as he strolled towards the river. He wondered if he would feel their presence.

"So this is it, huh? This is what we hitchhiked halfway across the country for?" Brady asked as he followed behind like a puppy, purposely feigning indifference.

But Haakon knew him better. Brady liked what he saw and so did Haakon.

"Yep. This is it. Just a bunch of mountains and trees," Haakon answered. "Were you hope'n for somethin else?"

"No, this will do, I suppose," Brady relented. "But those mountains sure do block the view."

Haakon smiled at the audacity of the comment and walked on.

Strands of fog interweaved the treetops under an overcast sky. They were in a deep, narrow, wooded valley filled with the sweet spring scent of pine and fir. A breeze carried a tinge of moisture in subtle passing waves—the essence of the surrounding mist—making the air feel colder than it was.

The highway they left was the spine of the valley. It continued south as a dark asphalt ribbon rolling in and out of view before dropping into a distant band of thick fog. A railroad track tried to follow the course of the river, but its broad curves and steady grade forced it to meander the valley floor. Yet, all three conveyors of transportation—asphalt, steel, water—converged where the valley tapered into a cliff-lined canyon.

Where Cemetery Road curved to the north, they came upon a sagging wooden driveway gate. An overhead log archway, precariously close to collapsing, supported a weathered plaque. In faint letters it read "Camp One." This was the name Haakon's uncle gave his sacred hunting camp—the place he enjoyed for two weeks each year and dreamed about all the other weeks.

Together, Haakon and Brady raised and swung the heavy gate open. Then they proceeded down two tire ruts that cut through a plane of tall grass. It led straight towards the river, dropping gradually at first. Once the moving water came into view, the ruts pivoted to the right and descended more steeply. A third of the way down the hill, Haakon could see the drive abruptly end next to a camping trailer and an old faded vehicle.

He should have watched his feet because he nearly tumbled when his toe caught a protruding rock. But the sight of the river demanded his attention. It spanned the entire panorama that unfolded before them. Thousands of muted soft crashes—not loud in volume but broad in audible breadth—filled the air. Though not wide or deep, its presence dominated the property. In a contained, quiet, still, wooded setting, it was a relentless force of motion.

The bank on the far side of the river was steep and wooded. Their side was more gradual, its shoreline relatively clear of trees. Fifteen feet off of the near shore, a towhead with tall shrubs broke a small rivulet of water away from the main body. Haakon's uncle told him he had built a rudimentary rock dam on the small fork of water to form a shallow pool. It provided a place to bathe, he said, though not comfortably. Other than the river itself, his property had no running water. The two campers would have to be resourceful.

There was a flat granite outcropping just below the end of the driveway. It looked as though nature had designed it to be a patio for sitting and enjoying the view. Haakon and Brady instinctively walked straight to this overlook to assess their surroundings.

"This is pretty nice," Brady said, which was significant for one not prone to positive expression.

"Yeah," Haakon responded, nodding in agreement. "This will be all right."

The hovering fog above the treetops lifted to expose mountains far beyond the river. Their highest peaks still harbored patches of snow, but the lower ridges gleamed with the bright green of spring. Haakon could make out a staggered thread of white water descending from one of the snow masses into the tree line below, in a display of winter merging into summer. He wondered if it was the source of the river running before them.

The floating fog closed the mountain view window as quickly as it had opened. Haakon awoke from his momentary daydream.

"Let's see what we have to work with here," Haakon suggested to Brady.

There was a small tool shed a short distance up the hill from where they stood. Haakon found its key where his uncle told him it was hidden. Inside were some rudimentary landscape tools—shovels, a Pulaski, a chainsaw, a come-along, chains—along with items like gloves, chaps, hardhats, and oil and gas cans. There was a workbench with drawers that contained basic tools like wrenches, screwdrivers, and pliers. On top of it sat the battery and keys for the old 4-wheel drive International Scout. His uncle said it was his to use. Since it represented mobility, and thus freedom, getting it started was first on their work agenda.

The Scout was not a pretty vehicle. Beside being worn and rusty, its designers borrowed the visual aspects of both an automobile and a pickup truck in a purely utilitarian manner. Clearly, style and turning heads were not on their minds. The vehicle was an elongated, faded, pastel green box with cracked, graying tires. It was adorned with a once-white topper that enclosed its cargo bed and cab. This made it more practical for inclement weather and helped tone down its peculiar hue.

Haakon's uncle had made him aware that International Scouts had a reputation like their namesake farm tractors. Both were renowned as tough, reliable workhorses—built to labor, not to garner "oohs and aahs." And with its 4-wheel drive chassis, this vehicle was as off-road functional as an Army Jeep.

With tools, keys, and battery in hand, Haakon and Brady moved as swiftly as a racetrack pit crew. Within minutes they had the Scout's hood up and its battery secured in place. Haakon jumped up onto the worn vinyl bench seat, shifted it into neutral, and then held up two crossed fingers. Brady stood in front facing the Scout's grill as though an airplane mechanic awaiting a signal to swing its propeller. As instructed by his uncle, Haakon pumped the gas pedal three times then reached down to turn the key, holding his breath as the starter-motor churned. It spun away lifelessly for several seconds. But then one cylinder sparked briefly. This gave them hope. Haakon stopped, turning the key off to rest the starter. After a long minute, he glanced nervously at Brady again and then turned the starter back on. This time another cylinder sparked to life and the two clamored together, roughly. A dark cloud of smoke that smelled of unburned gasoline came out of the exhaust. Haakon grew worried. Then, suddenly, the two firing cylinders coaxed the other two along. Just as the battery began showing fatigue, all four cylinders fired into a harmonious rhythm. The Scout roared to life.

"Yes!" Brady exclaimed, raising his fists to the sky in celebration.

Haakon gave him the thumbs-up sign but stayed seated for a time, wanting to assure himself that the cold engine would not die. He lacked confidence there was enough battery juice remaining to turn it over again. When convinced the engine was warm and fully operational, he stepped out and let it idle unattended.

"Freedom!" Haakon shouted over the noisy engine. "No more begging for rides."

They were both ecstatic.

Following the Scout's revival, they each tended to their new living quarters. Brady found a flat spot some twenty yards from the fire ring to set up a tent. Haakon's uncle said he was welcome to use the old hunting tent stored in the tool shed.

"You know there's plenty of room for the two of us in that trailer," Brady said.

"That's not gonna happen," Haakon instinctively reacted, wanting to make his position known in no uncertain terms. "I told you that from the onset. I don't care how big the trailer is, we are not going to be roommates."

He knew it would be challenging enough to share 5-acres of land with Brady.

Though compact, the trailer was surprisingly complete. Across its back end, it had a bunk bed. Haakon designated the bottom bunk for his sleep and the top bunk for storage. The little trailer also had a propane refrigerator and stove. And next to both was a sink, though there was no running water to feed it. It even had a propane furnace if needed. There was a tiny room with a door with just enough space for a porta-potty, but it served as a closet instead. Haakon's uncle had built a much roomier outhouse next to his tool shed. It would be a rudimentary existence for both, but they each regarded it as an adventure.

Haakon quickly got the trailer in order, then went outside to check on Brady. He could hear him cursing from where a mass of dull-green canvas was dancing around. From a distance, it looked like someone had thrown a blanket over an unsuspecting cat. The movement within appeared frantic and confused.

"How's it goin'?" Haakon asked once he got up close to the activity.

The tussle stopped.

"Your uncle really fixed me!" a voice from within the canvas exclaimed.

Through the years, Haakon came to understand that someone was always "fixing" Brady.

"How's that?"

"The poles don't fit."

"Did you look at the instructions?"

Haakon could see a printed diagram lying in the tent bag out of Brady's view.

"Screw that! I don't need directions on how to put together a tent."

"Yeah, I can see that. But if you change your mind, there're some instructions here in the bag. Do ya want me to hand them to ya?"

After a brief struggle, Brady's head popped out of the canvas mass. His face was beet red.

"Sure, why not," he said, disdainfully.

Haakon reached over with the directions and Brady snapped them out of his hand, giving him a glare at the same time.

"Doesn't it make you feel just a little guilty making me live in this thing?"

"No. Not really. Not at all," Haakon replied, casually. "Listen, while you're wrestling with this tent, I'm gonna walk around and check out the property."

"Yes, do go and enjoy yourself while I'm fighting this thing."

"I fired up the propane fridge. Do you wanna drive into Colterville to get some groceries and stuff after you set up your little playhouse?"

"Yeah, that sounds good," he answered. "Maybe I'll just give up on this thing and sleep under the stars."

"Not a good plan. Eventually, it will rain and I don't want ya knock'n on my door in the middle of the night, whining that you're all wet and cold. I think I'd stay at this tent project if I were you."

"As soon as I make some money, I'm gonna buy a pickup with a camper top to sleep in."

"You could use one of the mattresses from the camper and it would probably be pretty comfortable," Haakon said. "Better than the bridge last night, anyway."

He left Brady to his canvas battle and walked off, retreating up the driveway. When the gate came into view, Haakon noticed a man attempting to pull it closed from the outside. He was tall and thin, clad in denim, and he appeared to be in his 30s. When Haakon got closer, he could see that the man had short, curly, red hair and a matching neatly trimmed beard. His face was redder than his hair. Haakon was uncertain, until he spoke, whether this was because of excess sun or anger. A small boy stood near him.

"Hi," Haakon shouted as he approached, to signify his presence even though he was sure they had seen him coming.

"You gotta keep this gate closed!" the man said brusquely, answering Haakon's question about the redness of his face.

"Okay," Haakon said with the tenor of a question.

"We've got cattle that can get out. You ever try round'n up cattle that get loose?"

"No."

"Well, I don't want to be doing it, so you gotta keep it closed."

"Sure. Sorry. My uncle didn't tell me… or if he did, I forgot."

"Well, it's gotta be closed," he stated again as if he had not adequately made his point or was disappointed Haakon did not react with his own anger.

"Sure. Sorry. Won't happen again. I'm Haakon," Haakon said, reaching out his hand.

Even at his young age, Haakon knew the best way to disarm a disgruntled stranger was to first try kindness. Often this made the agitator feel like an ass.

"Oh. Yeah," the man said, surprised. "I'm Sig."

After a slight hesitation, he met Haakon's hand.

"Haakon. Like the hawk… with wings?"

"No. But my friends do call me Hawk."

He gestured to the freckled, redheaded boy standing next to him, who looked up at Haakon, bashfully.

"This is my son, Sig."

"Sig and Sig," Haakon responded, smiling. "This will be easy to remember."

Haakon reached out for the boy's hand. He looked to be a miniature version of the larger Sig.

"Nice to meet you too, Sig. How old are you?"

"I'm seven," he answered shyly.

"Good age," Haakon said. "I would've guessed twelve."

The boy grinned as Haakon turned back to the larger Sig.

"I'm Bill's nephew. I'm here with my friend Brady for the summer."

"I'm from the farm over there."

He pointed to an older white house surrounded by outbuildings in the distance.

"I'm Sig and Anne's nephew. I came up from Georgia with my son," he explained. "I just got divorced. Brought my boy up here with me."

"Sig, Sig, and Sig?" Haakon asked, wanting confirmation.

"Yeah," he answered with a slight smile. "My uncle pretty much raised me. I had been named after him. I think the world of him, so I ended up naming my son after him too."

His lengthy answer convinced Haakon that he no longer felt threatened.

"Sounds like it can get confusing."

"Well, my uncle usually goes by Sigmund. I go by Sig. And my boy goes by Little Sig. Makes things a little less confusing."

Haakon smiled back down at Little Sig and the boy smiled back.

"Well anyway, I just wanted you to understand about the gate," he said, but now with the tone of a diplomat.

"Message received. I'll tell Brady. We'll keep it closed. You can count on it."

"Hey, I'm sorry to have barked at ya. Nice to meet you, Haakon," Sig said, hand extended again.

"Likewise," Haakon answered while shaking his hand a second

time.

With that, Sig and Little Sig strode back down the gravel road, then turned to make their way along the railroad tracks towards the farm.

Haakon walked the periphery of his uncle's parcel. It felt good to be moving around, after so many stationary hitchhiking hours. By the time he had circled back to the campsite, Brady was standing proudly next to his upright tent.

"You did well, pilgrim," Haakon said mockingly.

"Yeah, this is gonna be great… if the bears don't get me."

"Well, if they give you any trouble at night, just yell out. I'll pound some pans together to try to scare them. That should at least give ya a head-start."

Then Haakon thought the better of discounting his concern.

"But, seriously, I wouldn't put any food in there."

"No, I wouldn't want to do anything to spoil their appetite when they come for me," he answered.

"But I wouldn't worry *too* much. They'd have to be pretty damn hungry and desperate to want to eat you," Haakon said. "Just keep chew'n that vile tobacco. That ought'a keep'm away."

Brady gave Haakon a brief, forced smile.

"By the way, I just met a guy from the farm."

Haakon pointed in the farm's direction.

"He was kind of pissed that you left the gate open."

"What do ya mean, me?"

"You were the last one through it," Haakon said.

"You were right next to me! You never told me to close it!"

"Do I gotta tell you everything! Well, anyway, I promised you'd keep it closed."

"Why?"

"I guess they have cows that can escape. They don't like chasing down their cows, so we gotta keep the gate closed."

"Hmm… steak! I could go for a steak," Brady said with his eyebrows raised. "Maybe we let one through every now and then."

"Maybe. Or maybe, better yet, we go back to Colterville and get some cow already pre-packaged," Haakon said. "Listen, I'm gonna first go down to the river and clean up. I found soap and some towels in the camper. I don't want Montanans to get the wrong impression of us."

"Heck with'em!" Brady replied.

"More specifically, I don't want Montana girls to get the wrong impression of *me*. But suit yourself."

Brady waved off Haakon's concern with his hand.

"Yeah, like you're an authority on the topic. Just keep think'n that you smell like a rose. I'm sure it'll work out fine for ya," Haakon said sarcastically. "I'll be ready to roll in fifteen minutes."

With a bar of soap in one hand and a towel in the other, Haakon made his way down to the river. There he stripped down with confidence that he was in no one's view, and then searched for a place where he could fully submerge. Finding no water deeper than four inches, he settled for sitting on a boulder and taking a cat bath. The water was freezing, yet he proceeded anyway, realizing cold baths would be his daily penance for enjoying the semi-wilderness experience.

He made short work of the task and was aboard the Scout within the promised fifteen minutes. Brady climbed into the passenger side and plopped himself onto the bench seat beside Haakon.

"What is that stench?" he asked.

"Soap, Brady. It's called soap."

"You smell like a whore."

"And you know that smell, how?"

"I know things," he replied.

"Yeah, that's what scares me about you. You know things that might be left best unknown. But, I'd rather smell like a whore, as you say, than someone who sleeps under bridges."

Without turning towards him, Brady waved Haakon's concern off with his hand again.

"By the way, this is just one of the reasons you and I will never be roommates. This and that brown slobber you chew on."

Brady turned towards Haakon and grinned, then reached into his back pocket for his container of tobacco.

"Look what I found," he blurted gleefully.

"You're hopeless."

"That's not what your mom says," Brady replied as he placed a pinch in his mouth.

The sniping continued as Haakon drove the Scout up the dusty driveway, then down the one-mile of highway back towards Renfro. Passing through the tiny town, Haakon noticed the tavern.

"Why don't we have a beer first to celebrate our arrival," Haakon suggested.

The two were young enough to still think it a novelty to legally drink.

"Sounds good to me," Brady replied.

Stepping into the old tavern was stepping back through time. At first it was near-total darkness. The newcomers' eyes strained to adjust from the outdoor light. Haakon could hear and smell the inside of the bar before he could see it. A jukebox played a popular country song— something they had heard countless times on the car radio on their trip across the Great Plains. A pool ball made a sharp cracking noise as it slammed into another. A soft thud indicated the ball dropped into a pocket—followed by the hard phenolic resin reverberating against acoustic wood as it rolled into a collection trap. A light audible click signaled that it had met its other fallen cohorts.

The ancient building's musty odor mixed with the scent of beer and cigarettes created an unexpectedly comforting aroma, much like an old hickory chest. As Haakon's eyes adjusted, he could recognize two teenagers encircling the pool table like sharks, each seeming to take the game seriously. They glanced over in Haakon and Brady's direction briefly, but seeing unfamiliar faces, they returned their attention to the game. A leathery-skinned, gray-haired man wearing work garb with suspenders sat on a tall barstool near where Haakon and Brady walked in. His relaxed posture made Haakon wonder if he was a permanent fixture of the establishment. An arm propped his head off of the bar top like a kickstand. His other free hand held a smoldering cigarette. Its ash was exceedingly long, seeming to flout gravity. He, unlike the pool players, was *very* interested in the two of them. Haakon sensed his eyes were locked onto their every step. Yet, he said nothing.

Behind the bar was a young Native American woman of untapped beauty. She had the core features of attractiveness—large dark eyes, high cheekbones, long, straight, jet-black hair, and Haakon suspected, a petite, shapely figure—but she downplayed her assets by avoiding makeup and wearing the loose clothing of working men.

"What can I get you guys?" she asked as Haakon and Brady each climbed up onto a stool, midway along the bar.

"Do you have Lucky on tap?" Haakon asked.

"I do."

"I'll have that."

"I'll have a Heineken import," said Brady.

"Aren't you special," Haakon quipped sarcastically.

"Hey, if I'm going to spend my hard-earned money on beer, it's not going to be swill, like you drink. I have standards."

Haakon smiled, as did the bartender. He noticed that the old-timer on the far end of the bar continued staring at them. His cigarette, still hanging unattended from his hand, had lost its ash. Forgetting his roadside pledge, Haakon got off of the stool and walked over to the cigarette vending machine behind him, inserted some coins, then pulled the lever that dropped a pack of Marlboros onto the tray below. As he walked back to his stool, peeling the pack open, he could see, out of the corner of his eye, the old man was still surveying his footsteps. He was beginning to give Haakon "the creeps."

"One bottle of special and one glass of swill," the bartender said as she delivered their beers.

They exchanged smiles again. A door swung open near the other end of the bar, briefly exposing a kitchen. A good-looking young woman walked out, glancing over at us as she approached the bartender. She had long, lustrous brown hair and a sensuous full-figure. Haakon smiled at her and she shyly returned the gesture. As the two women talked, the brunette seemed aware that Haakon was watching them. Brady was engrossed in the pool table, now having spun his barstool clear around to watch the players.

"Can you tell me a good place to buy some camping gear?" Haakon asked loud enough to get the attention of the two girls.

The brunette turned and smiled at Haakon again.

"Sure. You want to go to Kuno's Supply in Colterville. They have a huge camping section," she said, as she approached Haakon. "Going in the backcountry?"

From a close perspective, her broad smile and gorgeous brown eyes captivated him. She wore perfume reminiscent of the Gillette nurse-driver.

"No, we're just trying to set up our camp right outside of town.

We came here from Minnesota for jobs. We're staying on my uncle's property."

Haakon held out his hand.

"I'm Haakon."

"Like the bird?"

"No, like the Norwegian king. But my friends do call me Hawk."

She accepted Haakon's hand then said, "I'm Rachel. My friends call me Rachel."

Both chuckled and held each other's hand for a longer-than-normal handshake.

"You know, your name's fitting. You kind of look like a Norseman. You've got that Viking thing goin'—tall, muscular, long blonde-ish hair, blue eyes," she said.

"Don't tell him that. He's already insufferable," Brady chimed in without turning towards them.

"Oh, this is Brady," Haakon said, gesturing towards him.

Brady turned away from the pool game briefly to face her.

"Hi," is all he said before turning back.

"He's special. He drinks imported bottled beer," Haakon said.

"I see that," Rachel said. "And you're *not* special?"

"My mom thinks I'm special. My uncle thinks I'm special. I once had a dog that thought I was special… but come to think of it, I might have been misreading the dog since I was his meal ticket and all."

"I'm sure your dog thought you were special too," she said, playing along.

"He didn't," Brady piped in, still turned away while facing the pool table.

"I don't even know you and I already think you're special," she said.

"He's not," Brady again interjected.

"This is your friend?" she asked, nodding towards Brady.

"Did I refer to him as a friend? Let's just say I know him."

Suddenly, a raspy voice thundered out from the far end of the bar.

"Damn long hair hippie!"

Haakon turned towards the outburst's source. The old-timer was glaring in his direction.

"Oscar! Behave yourself!" Rachel barked.

"That's okay," Haakon said to her before turning back to the old man. "I'm not a hippie."

"Well, ya got long hair!"

"Yeah, but that doesn't make me a hippie. You don't see any beads hanging around my neck, do ya? I'm not wearing sandals... or wearing a bandanna."

Haakon did not recognize him as a serious threat.

"I don't even smoke dope, so how can I be a hippie?"

"Damn long hair!"

Haakon found these words coming from the old man to be funny and he burst out laughing, as did Brady. Rachel was less humored.

"Oscar, watch your mouth," she scolded, "or you'll have to leave."

"Well, I don't like hippies," he retorted.

"Why don't you like hippies?" Haakon asked.

"Just don't."

Haakon took a swig of his beer, then lit a cigarette. Oscar had finally extinguished his, so Haakon held his pack out towards him. It was like holding an apple out to a horse. The old man got off his perch and moved down the bar towards Haakon, grabbing one of his cigarettes as he sat on one of the nearby empty barstools. Haakon held out his lighter and the old man leaned his cigarette into the flame.

"I'm Haakon," he said, offering his hand.

Oscar took it in his, but then did not let go.

"Hawken. Hawken? Like the rifle?" Oscar asked, seeming bewildered by his name.

"No... yeah... yeah, I'm named after the rifle," Haakon said, leading him on with a lie in hopes of getting his hand back without having to provocatively jerk it away.

This was the first time Haakon had heard anyone associate his name with the old mountain-man-era rifle.

"Brady here, he might be a hippie," Haakon said to the old-timer, hoping the diversion might free his hand.

"You're shittin me," the old man said.

He released Haakon's hand.

"He don't have no long hair."

"True, but I've always been suspicious of him."

"Bite me!" Brady replied, still transfixed on the pool table.

"You give me a chainsaw and I'll take care of any damn hippie," the old man started in again.

"That's nasty, Oscar. Really? A chainsaw?" Haakon asked.

"Damn straight!"

"Oscar!" Rachel exclaimed.

She had moved back behind the bar, relieving the other girl.

Oscar grimaced, then turned his head down while muttering something to himself. The outside door swung open, momentarily flooding the dim room with stark daylight. As it closed and the light receded, Haakon could make out the approach of a tall, slender man. He looked to be a few years older than Haakon and Brady. His long, thin, straw-colored hair extended unnaturally away from his head as though charged with static electricity. Wire-rim glasses with thick lenses added to an overall odd, though friendly appearance. He stopped at the bar, directly alongside Oscar.

"How ya do'n, Oscar?" he said.

"Not bad. How you do'n Landon?" Oscar asked in return.

"I'm okay," he said.

Then he turned his attention to Rachel.

"Is Swan around?"

"Yeah, she's in back. She'll be right back."

"Hey, Landon," Oscar suddenly blurted out. "This guy next to me is all right. He's a long hair, but he's not a hippie."

Landon looked over at Haakon and smiled.

"Well, that's a relief, Oscar."

"You got your chainsaw with you, Landon?"

"Nope. Left her home. But do ya think I would bring it in here for you if I had it?"

"Probably not," Oscar answered, dejected.

"Oscar, your friend here has long hair," Haakon said, gesturing to Landon. "How come he isn't a hippie?"

"Cause he's Landon! He's no hippie," Oscar answered, flabbergasted, as though this should have been obvious.

"Oooookay," Haakon responded. "That makes sense."

Haakon grinned at Landon and he grinned back, assuring his realization the discussion was in jest.

"I'm Haakon."

He reached out his hand to Landon.

"This here is Brady."

"Haakon. Like the bird of prey?" Landon asked.

"No. Like the rifle. Long story."

"Landon," he replied, while shaking Haakon's hand. "Nice to meet you. You guys new around here?"

"Sort of… for the summer anyway," Haakon said. "We are going to work for a contractor in Colterville."

"Really? Who?" Landon asked.

"Kingsley Construction."

"No kidding. That's who *I* work for," Landon said. "I heard about you guys. You're our reinforcements from Minnesota."

"We are," Haakon answered.

"Well, welcome aboard. You'll like working for Kingsley. He's a good guy. A little uptight at times, but a good guy," Landon said. "We have a good bunch of guys."

"Did you say Minnesota," the old man inquired, wanting to get back into the conversation. "That's alright, I guess."

The old man seemed to contemplate this for a few seconds, before continuing.

"My father came from Minnesota. At least you're not from California. I hate those California hippies!"

Haakon, Brady, and Landon each broke out in laughter. The original bartender appeared from the backroom.

"Excuse me, I need to talk to her for a second," Landon said.

He did, then returned a few minutes later.

"Is she your girl?" Haakon inquired.

"Yeah," Landon answered.

"She's a good-looking girl, if you don't mind me saying."

"I don't mind. But don't get any ideas," he answered, feigning a serious face.

They both laughed again.

"Can I buy ya a beer?" Haakon asked.

"If you insist."

Haakon signaled to Rachel, who was drying beer glasses on the other side of the bar, by pointed to his beer and then over to Landon. She nodded in acknowledgment.

"What about Rachel? Does she have a boyfriend?" Haakon asked.

Landon glanced to see that she was still out of earshot.

"No. Well, sort of. There's a guy who's been pursuing her, but I don't think she is that interested. Sometimes they date."

Landon lit a cigarette.

"She's got a few kids," he continued. "Been married."

"I'm surprised. She seems our age," Haakon said.

"She's only twenty-one. Started pretty early," Landon explained. "Do you want to ask her out? I can make it happen. She's a good friend of Swan."

"Well maybe. Thanks," Haakon answered as Rachel arrived with Landon's beer.

It surprised Haakon to see it arrive in a plastic cup.

Landon promptly placed his cigarette in his mouth, then grabbed the beer with one hand and extended the other to Haakon. The cigarette dangled from his lips as he tried to articulate.

"Well, I gotta go. Nice to meet ya. Thanks for the beer. I guess I'll see you guys in the morning."

"Yes, you will," Haakon said, smiling.

"And let me know about Rachel," he said. "I think you would like her. She's a sweet girl."

"I will. Thank you."

Both Haakon and Brady watched, amazed, as Landon walked out the door with the beer in his hand.

"Is he gonna drive with that?" Haakon asked Brady.

"I guess it's legal here," he answered. "You can drink and drive."

"No shit!" Haakon exclaimed. "They must have written *that* law when people drove horses."

"We're in the Wild West now, Hawk."

"I guess. Do you think we should get those groceries?"

"Yeah. Sounds good."

Brady took one last gulp from his bottle, then both stood up. Haakon turned to Oscar and held out his hand.

"It's been nice talk'n with ya."

"Yeah," he said. "Ya got another one of those cigarettes?"

"Sure."

Haakon tapped the top of his cigarette pack against his hand to make several of them extend out. Oscar grabbed all three.

"Much obliged," he said.

Haakon looked down at the pack, grinned, and then turned back to Oscar.

"On second thought, Oscar, take the whole pack. I quit."

Oscar looked up at Haakon, perplexed.

"You've been an inspiration to me," Haakon said to him as he turned to leave.

"Thank you, Rachel," Haakon said loudly as he and Brady walked towards the door. "It was nice to have met you. And thank you for protecting me from Oscar here. I don't believe that I would like to meet his chainsaw."

She laughed while drying a glass. Oscar held his hand up to his mouth and took a long draw from the cigarette as he studied Haakon and Brady, then cracked a slight smile and raised a few fingers on the same hand to indicate his goodbye.

"Hey, tomorrow night's Spaghetti Night. See ya then, right?" she said.

"I do not know about Spaghetti Night, but I think I should."

"It's our big weekly event. Three dollars. All the spaghetti you can eat, plus Texas toast."

"If there's Texas toast, I'm in. I'll see you tomorrow night."

Haakon smiled at Rachel again, then followed Brady out into the daylight.

"Scary place you have brought me to Hawk. People want to saw us up with chainsaws. Now I've got that to worry about at night besides the bears."

Haakon chuckled.

"It's like *Deliverance* meets *Call Of The Wild* around here," Brady surmised, citing two motion pictures that depicted wilderness life—one disparaging, one laudatory.

They drove the windy highway the sixteen miles to Colterville. Much of the route followed the graceful Cedar River. No longer did the waterway serve as a conveyor belt for felled logs. More efficient semi-trucks and trailers had replaced it. Now, its once quiet dignity was supplemented by the unremitting blare of jake brakes. Yet, portions of the river escaped the highway and ventured off into the surrounding woods where it would disappear for miles, as though wanting a temporary reprieve from the imprint of man.

Haakon and Brady purchased groceries, some general supplies, and much-needed articles of clothing. Most had been budgeted from the onset of their trip, but the unplanned clothing strained both of their reserves. Still, Haakon had just enough money to buy a pair of leather steel-tipped work boots.

"You know you're gonna look like a dandy wearing new boots on the first day," Brady said, looking down at Haakon's feet.

"I know, but my tennis shoes are shot. I don't think they would hold together through a full day of work."

"They will if you use enough duct tape."

Brady pointed to his feet. His right tennis shoe had a two-inch swath of gray duct tape wrapped perpendicularly around the bottom and over the lower portion of the laces.

"You're a slave to fashion, Brady. But if we both had duct-taped tennis shoes… well, I wouldn't want to take away from the statement that you're trying to make."

"Trying? I don't try. I *am* a fashion statement," he replied, indignantly.

"On that we can agree."

They grabbed burgers for the drive back to Camp One—still enjoying the freedom of having their own wheels and doing things on their own schedule. When they arrived back, daylight was ebbing. Brady made a fire and, after they stowed away the groceries and supplies, they both sat to enjoy its warmth and musky pine smell. The sky grew bright pink. As it tapered to dark wine, their world shrunk to what was within the audible range of the fire. Darkness impaired Haakon's vision and primal instincts began to separate the hissing, popping, and crackling noises of the burning logs and the low rumble of the river, from the sounds of the blackness beyond the campfire.

Brady looked up at Haakon from across the blaze, his face demon-like from the accentuated shadows and dancing orange hues.

"This is alright, Hawk."

"Yeah, this is good. We're regular mountain men now. This is gonna be a good summer."

An animal cried out from the surrounding darkness. It caught

Haakon's attention for a moment, but soon his thoughts returned to the mesmerizing flame and the imaginings of the summer before them.

4
KINGSLEY'S CREW

Colterville, Montana, was a quiet place at 6:45 in the morning. A few old men merged into the downtown cafe for their ritual of coffee and conversation. The town dog trotted along the Main Street sidewalk in pursuit of an intriguing scent. A handful of pickup trucks drove past the dog, but none of their drivers looked in its direction. Most of the town's early risers were already at work in the mill or were at home preparing for the eight o'clock shift change.

Haakon and Brady arrived at the Kingsley Construction shop with fifteen minutes to spare. Brady could not understand why they had to leave Camp One early, "needlessly giving up valuable sleeping time." Haakon could not conceive of arriving late, particularly on the first day. A fifteen-minute cushion was the absolute minimum he could tolerate. Nevertheless, no time was wasted. Kingsley, their new boss, was already standing in the parking lot sipping from a chrome thermos cup when they arrived.

"You must be my guys from Minnesota," he said jovially, grinning with his hand outreached towards the Scout's open window.

"Hi, I'm Haakon."

Haakon smiled back as Kingsley took his hand.

"And this is Brady."

"Well Haakon, your uncle says you're quite the worker. You come highly recommended, so I have high expectations."

Kingsley was a short, portly, balding man who wore wire-rim glasses and a pastel blue working jumpsuit. He had a fidgety air of nervousness about him that he tried to disguise with exaggerated smiles.

"And you two have worked together, I'm told," he said, looking at Brady. "Your uncle told me if Haakon recommends someone, I can take that to the bank."

"Thank you for the jobs. We'll do our best for you, Mr. Williams," Haakon said. "A lot of this will be new to us, but we're fast learners."

"Call me Kingsley."

He glanced down at his watch. Haakon could almost hear gears shifting in Kingsley's head.

"Well, I'm gonna get you guys goin' right away. Time is money in this business and times'a waste'n. Why don't you follow me in this... what the hell is this, an old International Scout?"

"Yeah, it's my uncle's."

"Oh yeah, I remember. Man, it's a relic. Looks like an old Forest Service rig."

"I'm not sure," Haakon replied.

"Who else would come up with such a God-awful color of puke-green for a rig than the Forest Service," he said. "No offense intended."

Haakon chuckled.

"None taken. I'm just grateful to have some wheels to use. I can live with the color."

"Just so no one shoots at ya, think'n you're Forest Service."

"People here don't *like* the Forest Service?" Haakon asked.

"Not particularly. They're just a bunch of college-educated, government idiots sent out here to interfere with our lives and burn up our forests in their so-called controlled burns."

Haakon sensed his question had touched a nerve.

"They don't think trees can grow without them tinkering. God knows how the forests ever got by without'em. Anyway, I could spend all day talk'n on that one, but they're already cost'n me too much money—speaking of which, let's get to work. Just follow my pickup."

Kingsley smiled, patted the Scout's hood, and then walked to his vehicle.

He had several jobs going at once, which was a rarity during the building recession of the mid-1970s. By trade, he was an electrician. But, to generate enough work, he needed to be a general contractor as well. This resulted in hiring two carpenters and a laborer besides his two electricians. Haakon and Brady would be a second and third laborer for the busy summer building season. However, despite any employee's particular job title, Haakon and Brady would learn that everyone did whatever was needed on any day. There was no union presence forbidding the crossover of trades. If necessary, an electrician would pick up a shovel, a carpenter would pull wire, and a laborer would hammer. Whatever needed to be done, *was* done by whoever could most expediently do it. In this rural part of the world, you did what you had to do to make things work.

They followed Kingsley's pickup truck through downtown Colterville and up a hill at its far end. After a few turns we came upon a gravel driveway, lined with large Ford and Chevy pickup trucks and stacks of lumber. At its end was a garage being built onto an existing house. Several men were moving about on the attachment's second story. They glanced at the approaching vehicles, but continued working.

The quiet of morning was absent here, replaced with a barrage of whining circular saws and slamming hammers. Kingsley walked the Minnesotans over to a man leaning over a makeshift table covered with blueprints. Haakon recognized Landon from the Renfro Tavern. He had a look of concern on his face. Haakon got the impression Landon was not eager to see Kingsley.

"Hi Landon," Kingsley said, approaching. "Here's our guys from Minnesota. Haakon and Brady. Meet Landon."

"We've met," Landon said. "Hi guys."

"No kidding. Good," Kingsley said. "Do we have a problem, Landon? You didn't seem too happy just a minute ago."

"No. Well, kind of," he answered.

Landon appeared very uncomfortable.

"We built the stairs a little too close to the parking stall."

Kingsley looked up to view the open garage.

"Jeez! It looks like the stairs are right in the middle of the left stall.

How can that be?" Kingsley asked.

His face turned bright red.

"Hell, Landon. What's the point of having a garage stall if you can't park a car in it," he continued. "The homeowner must have had a shit-fit when he saw that."

"He wasn't too pleased," Landon said, looking down at his feet. "He pretty much ripped me a good one."

There was a long pause before Landon added, "I'll get it fixed, boss."

Kingsley said nothing in reply. He took a deep gulp of air and then turned to march back to his pickup.

As he passed Haakon and Brady, he said, "See if you can get these guys' heads out of their asses for me, would ya?"

Neither said anything in reply. Landon grimaced as he watched Kingsley's pickup truck speed away. Then he turned to Haakon and Brady.

"Did I tell you guys yesterday that he is a good guy?" he asked. "Sometimes he can be a real prick too."

Then Landon chuckled and added, "He'll get over it."

Haakon and Brady smiled, nervously.

"But, we gotta get that fixed. In the meantime, how bout you guys pack that plywood up onto the subfloor," Landon said, pointing towards a stack of plywood. "Then we'll nail it down."

Haakon and Brady, eager to show their worth, quickly grabbed the sheets and hoisted them up on their respective shoulders, then carried them to the edge of the garage. After they had the plywood stacked on the subfloor, Landon handed each a tool belt with a hammer. They loaded the pockets with nails and the three of them, on their knees, hammered away at the flooring. Another man, who had been cutting sheets of plywood atop two sawhorses on the floor's far corner, walked over to Haakon's side. Haakon noticed his shadow falling over him before he spoke.

"Let me give ya a tip."

Haakon stopped pounding and turned to look up. He had the leathered face and red-tinted eyes of someone accustomed to working in the sun. A prominent scar ran diagonally across his left cheek, and his hair was long and disheveled. His sleeveless shirt exposed muscular bundles of tanned and inked skin. He looked tough, but worn. Haakon suspected that he was younger than he appeared.

"It's not how fast you hammer," he stated, with a toothpick dangling from his chapped lips. "It's how fast you reload."

"Huh?"

"Let me show you. Gimme your hammer and some nails."

He kneeled down alongside of Haakon and grabbed his hammer, then took a handful of 8-penny sinkers.

"See here," he said, staring at Haakon. "Watch how I reposition the next nail in my holding hand while I am hammering with the other. By the time I drive the nail in…" Bang-bang-bang. "I've already got the next one teed up. That's the key."

"Wow. Makes sense," Haakon said.

"It's all about learning how to juggle the nails in your non-hammering hand while you're hammering."

The toothpick swiveled in his mouth for a moment.

"Just like in a gunfight or spending the night with a beautiful woman, it's all about how fast you reload."

"Okay. I'll try it. Thanks."

He handed back Haakon's hammer, then held out his open palm.

"I'm Judd."

Haakon shook his hand.

"I'm Haakon."

"Haakon. What kind of name is that?"

"My parents named me after a Norwegian king."

"Seriously? I work for a guy named Kingsley. Now I'm working with a Norwegian king."

He shook his head.

"Kind'a makes me feel inferior. I guess I'm just a commoner… though all the women around here *do* call me a prince."

Haakon chuckled and then went about trying his nail-reloading technique. Judd was correct. By lunchtime Haakon's nailing speed had improved significantly.

"You're like a hammer'n machine, now Haakon," Judd said to him as they all walked off of the job to gather under the shade of a large lodgepole pine.

"Thank you. I'm sure faster than when I started," Haakon replied.

"You hammer like a schoolgirl," Brady blurted out, catching up from behind.

"Maybe," Haakon said. "But at least I hit the joist. I think half of *your* nails were pounded into air."

"I never miss. Never."

"You're a delusional guy, Brady. You live in your own fantasy world," Haakon said.

After everyone was sitting on the ground, Haakon dug through a lunch bag he had assembled that morning. Brady looked over at him like a dog expecting table scraps.

"What are *you* looking at?"

Haakon reached into his bag, pulled out a wrapped sandwich and threw it over to him.

"Thanks!" Brady said, appearing surprised.

"I knew *you* wouldn't do it, so I made one for you while I made mine. Don't ever say I've never done anything for you."

"That looks good. Will you make *me* one tomorrow?" Landon asked.

Then Judd asked, "What, are you guys married or something?"

"Well, we're camp'n on the same property," Haakon answered.

"Camping? *I'm* camping… in a musty old tent. *He's* not camping," Brady blurted out. "He's living in a lavish trailer."

"Lavish?" Haakon responded, chuckling.

"So, ya make his lunches because ya feel bad for him liv'n in a tent while you're liv'n in luxury?" Judd asked.

"Hardly luxury," Haakon replied. "But no, I don't feel sorry for him. I just didn't want him beg'n for food. I hate it when he begs."

Everyone laughed.

They sat near enough to the parked vehicles to hear Landon's CB radio.

"Foghorn Leghorn, Foghorn Leghorn. Papa Bear. Copy?"

"Shit! Just when a guy gets comfortable," Landon exclaimed as he got to his feet.

Dusting off his pants, he walked over to the open window of his pickup truck and reached inside to the cab's ceiling and pulled out the microphone. With its curly cord fully extended, he stood outside to answer. He must have turned the volume down, because Haakon could not hear the conversation.

"Well, the boss-man wants Brady and Haakon out at the stud mill," Landon said as he returned to the group. "You best head now and eat your lunch on the way. I'll draw you a map."

So, with sandwiches in hand, Haakon and Brady drove back through Colterville, then proceeded up a road on the other side of town that followed along the gentle Saleesh River. The heavily forested route only sporadically offered views, but when it did, a serene, windy waterway appeared. Its slow moving surface mirrored its far bank, distorted only by waterfowl and an occasional angler. Yet, like the Cedar River, the Saleesh was not just a pretty face. It was the original conveyer belt of felled timber and the power source of the lumber mills.

Ten miles out of town they came upon the Saleesh River Stud Mill. While Haakon knew that there were various types of lumber mills for various types of wood, he had not known there were mills that only produced a particular length of a particular wood. It made sense once he thought about it. In the building trades, there could not have been a more common piece of lumber than the standard 2" x 4" stud. Its universal 92-5/8" vertical length was the backbone of nearly every new home built in America.

When they pulled into the gravel grounds, mountains of wood—raw timber on one side and endless neat stacks of bundled blonde studs on the other—surrounded them. A giant front-end loader with massive grapples reached into the mountain of logs and extracted food for the hungry mill. Opposite it, across the lot, a giant forklift carried finished product out of a huge metal building. A semi-truck with a trailer of long tree trunks, bundled in place by tall vertical steel spikes, was having its load lifted off by another front-end loader. The yard was a beehive of activity.

Proceeding slowly, they eventually came upon the panel van with the Kingsley Construction markings. Asking various mill workers about the electrician's whereabouts led them inside a cavernous building. It screamed with enormous gnawing saws. Men donning yellow hardhats and plastic earmuffs stood alongside a track that carried pieces of freshly cut wood. They pulled less desirable pieces off the track and pushed them onto another.

At the far end of a corridor of machinery, Haakon and Brady

approached a man wearing a loaded tool belt. He was wrestling a long strand of wire.

"Hi, are you Carlos," Haakon nearly screamed, trying to compensate for the blaring, high-pitched saws.

Carlos smiled, then shouted, "Hi. You must be Brady and Hogan."

Haakon just smiled and nodded his head.

"How about you guys grab these boxes of wire and we'll go outside to talk," Carlos shouted.

He cupped his hands around his mouth to project his words. Between his hand motions and the few words that they made out, Haakon and Brady understood enough. They each grabbed a stack of boxes and followed to his van, back into the sunshine and relative quiet.

"Gets a little loud in there. Hi, I'm Carlos."

"I'm Haakon. This is Brady," Haakon said, taking his hand to shake.

Carlos looked to be in his late thirties. He was short and stocky with dark, muscular arms that each sported a US Navy tattoo. He had thick, wavy, black hair and a square jaw that accommodated a built-in grin. The lighthearted tenor of his speech fit his affable appearance.

"I'm glad you're here. I've got a big job for you. It's an easy job… that's the good part. But it's potentially dangerous… that's the bad part," Carlos said. "Now most normal guys couldn't do it, but I can just tell by look'n at ya that you two are not normal guys."

Haakon and Brady glanced at each other, confused, but Carlos's broad smile suggested he was kidding. They followed him a short distance around the backside of a newly constructed pole building. There, next to a stub of large plastic pipe sticking out of the gravel, stood another tool belt wearing man. He was wrapping the end of a bundle of thick strands of multi-colored insulated wire with electric tape.

"Guys, this is Sig. Sig this is Haakon and Brady."

Sig looked up at them, surprised. "Haakon!"

"Hi, I didn't know *you* worked here."

"I didn't know you worked here," Sig replied.

"What, are you guys old friends?" Carlos asked.

"I just met Haakon yesterday. He's living near the farm," Sig answered, then turning to me. "I didn't know you were out here to work. I thought you guys were rich kids or somethin—just out here to vacation."

"Well, we're not rich kids, for sure. We came to work," Haakon said. "But we came partly for the adventure, if that counts as a vacation."

"Sure it does," Sig said. "I think I'm gonna like you, Haakon." Carlos chuckled.

"That's say'n a lot. Sig doesn't like too many people. I know he doesn't like me."

"I don't like you because of all the shitty grunt jobs you give me. But now that Haakon and his friend are here, I have a feeling that's all gonna change."

"Absolutely!" Haakon answered. "Grunt work is what we do. We're not fussy... or proud."

Sig and Carlos smiled.

"Sig, this is Brady," Haakon said. "He's the guy who left your gate open."

Brady grunted an indistinguishable explicative towards Haakon, then reached out to shake Sig's extended hand.

"Looks like you could use some help," Carlos said to Sig, cueing "the two new guys" to turn their attention back to the job.

He grabbed the wire bundle below Sig's grip to give him some relief. As he held on and Sig continued wrapping, he turned to Haakon and Brady.

"So we need to pull this wire down into the conduit—or as Sig calls it, the 'big plastic pipe'—and out the other end, over there by that pickup."

He gestured to his right by tipping his head. About a hundred feet away, a small pickup truck was parked next to another stub of conduit emerging from the ground.

Sig completed the wrapping, then turned to Haakon and Brady.

"Sorry, again, I chewed your ass out on the gate yesterday. Sometimes I can get kind of ornery."

"Sometimes?" Carlos questioned, rolling his eyes.

Sig gave Carlos a look of disapproval.

"That's because he's not getting any," Carlos said.

"Yeah, sadly that's true enough," Sig replied, sighing.

"Okay, now that you two have made up and we know all about Sig's love life or lack thereof, let me explain how this is gonna go down," Carlos stated. "I'm gonna slowly pull on the rope with the pickup over there. You two are going to carefully, and I mean carefully, make sure that the wires are feeding into the conduit. You may have to push the wires together, but make damn sure you keep your hands clear of the top of that conduit. That's the dangerous part."

"You guys have leather gloves?" Carlos asked.

Haakon and Brady each nodded yes.

"Okay, Sig will oversee and direct. If he notices a problem, he'll wave to me to stop."

It was a well thought-out plan that may have proceeded without a hitch had Carlos factored in Brady's propensity for bad luck. But who could have anticipated that Brady would have grabbed a pair of my uncle's leather work-gloves that had previously been used on a tar roof?

When the pickup truck began pulling and the wire started moving downward, Haakon and Brady took hold of the wire bundle and pushed them tight together. As the wire slowly descended into the conduit, Sig dutifully squirted ample amounts of the green lubricant out of the bottle and into the open hole.

Haakon and Brady had gripped the wire two feet above the conduit entrance, to not risk having their fingers pinched as the wires squeezed together. The problem occurred when they each attempted to reposition their grips. Haakon's gloved hands released. Brady's did not. Residual roof tar on his gloves, combined with his tight squeeze, locked his hands onto the wires. The gloves fit so tight, he could not quickly pull his hands out. Sig saw the impending crisis and screamed out at Carlos while frantically waving his arms.

"Stop! Stop the truck!"

Carlos hit the brakes of the truck, but there was a slight delay in his reaction. By the time the wires stopped moving, Brady had one hand stuck at the intersection of the wire and conduit. His face conveyed pain.

Sig screamed, "Back up the truck a little! Take off the tension!"

Carlos understood and quickly backed up a few feet so that the rope was slack. Then he jumped out of the cab and madly dug around the bed of the pickup truck. Carrying another rope in his hand, he ran towards Brady. When he caught sight of a forklift, he stopped and shoved two fingers into his mouth, then omitted the loudest human whistle sound that Haakon had ever heard, while simultaneously waving the coiled rope up in the air to get the operator's attention. He succeeded. By the time Carlos got over to Brady, the forklift was there to meet them.

Without a word, Carlos wrapped the rope several times around the wire bundle above Brady's hand. The forklift operator realized what Carlos was doing, so he moved his rig closer and lowered its two protruding forks just above their heads. Brady was still red-faced and expressing pain as Carlos threw the slack of the rope over one fork, looping it several times. Then he signaled for the operator to raise it. As soon as the upward tension was realized, Brady's hand came clear of the entrapment. Seeing this, the operator stopped lifting and Carlos pulled out his pocketknife.

"I'm gonna slit the top of your glove, then we can slide your hand out slowly," he said to Brady, who still looked in pain.

The razor-sharp knife easily cut through the leather.

"Okay pull, but slowly."

Brady seemed afraid to view what would come out of the glove, so he responded hesitantly. Grimacing, he gradually slid his hand out. It was a relief to see all of his fingers attached and, seemingly, in their proper positions—though two of them were bright red.

"Try to move your fingers," Carlos said as we each watched intently.

Brady obliged. Each of his fingers wiggled up and down. Carlos grabbed Brady's wrist and examined his fingers closely.

"I don't see any bends. Do they hurt?"

"They're a little sore, but I think they're all right," Brady answered.

His face looked reassured.

Carlos smiled then looked up at him, puzzled.

"What, have ya got glue on your gloves?"

"I don't know. Haakon's uncle is trying to fix me, I guess. Looks like he used them with tar or somethin."

Carlos reached over to pull the empty glove off of the wires. It did not give. He pulled again with more force, then it released unexpectedly, nearly throwing him off balance.

"That's a new one," he said.

Brady's pride was injured, but his hand, other than being sore, was fine. They finished pulling the wire with no more incidents. The task took the better part of two hours, but once completed, they all went about dismantling the wire spool stands, picking up the tools and supplies, then storing everything inside the van.

"Well, its close enough to quit'n time, guys," Carlos said. "Is your hand going to be okay, ya think?"

"It's fine," Brady answered curtly, still embarrassed at causing a scene.

"Tell ya what, if you guys are coming to Spaghetti Night at the Renfro Tav, I'll buy ya a beer," Carlos offered.

"That sounds good to me. We'll see you there," Haakon said, answering for both, knowing that their social calendar was wide-open.

"Not for me, guys. I've got some chores on the farm and a boy who is still young enough to miss me when I'm gone all day," Sig said. "I'll see ya tomorrow."

By the time Haakon and Brady arrived at the Renfro Tavern that evening, it was surrounded by pickup trucks of all colors and sizes. Many adults milled around the tavern doorway, talking to one another. Each time the door opened, music, laughter, and smoke poured out onto the street. Spaghetti Night had been a long-cherished tradition in Renfro. The gastronomic lure was a heaping plate of watery spaghetti, that might or might not have included a meatball, but *did* include a large piece of buttered toast, called "Texas toast"—presumably because it was a bit larger than a slice of bread that you might put in a toaster. If you added a draft beer, and nearly every patron did, you had what, some might consider, a balanced dinner for under five dollars. This was a good deal for the participants *and* the bar owner. The former got a cheap meal and a weekly social event. The latter generated revenue during an otherwise slow weeknight.

"Hawk, Brady!" a voice called out from the crowd as they entered.

The tavern was full of people, yet Haakon could recognize only Rachel and Swan who were scurrying behind the bar. Country music blared from the jukebox, pool balls clanged together, a the haze of cigarette smoke filled the air. It was so crowded, Haakon wondered how the pool players could find enough space to draw back their sticks.

There were a few tables dispersed throughout the large room—all occupied with people, beer, and plates of spaghetti. Each stool along the bar was also taken, as was the standing space between them.

"Hawk!" the voice yelled again.

This time Haakon recognized Landon leaning up against the bar with a beer in his hand and a cigarette dangling from his mouth.

"Come down here, I'll buy ya a beer."

Haakon and Brady worked their way through the crowd, trying not to knock anyone's glass of beer onto their clothes. Haakon suspected fights started on lesser offenses. As he walked, he also kept the corner of his eye on Rachel. At one point she noticed him and smiled. Haakon held up his hand as a wave and she nodded in acknowledgement, having no free hands to wave back with. Midway along the bar, sitting on a stool, Haakon also recognized Oscar. As Haakon passed, Oscar greeted him with his now familiar, "Damn hippy," with his head turned slightly towards Haakon to catch his reaction. Haakon smiled at him, then continued on down to Landon's side.

"Let me see that hand," Landon said to Brady.

"It's fine," Brady replied, keeping his hands tucked in their respective jeans pockets.

"I heard you really got it jammed," Landon continued, "and that your gloves had glue on them or something."

Brady did not appear amused.

"They had tar on them. I'll remember not to use roofing gloves next time I'm supposed to push giant wires into a small hole."

"He just smashed two of his fingers," Haakon said.

"Just two, that's all," Brady responded, seeming annoyed that Haakon minimized his injury.

"Oh, jeez! Ya got two other fingers and thumb, ya big baby!" Haakon said to him, seeing his exasperated expression.

"Yeah, I guess. But I wouldn't have gotten my hand stuck if I didn't have to do all the work," Brady replied. "Here's Haakon pushing the wire together."

He made a mocking gesture of Haakon gingerly pushing imaginary wire downward between his thumb and pinky finger.

"Yeah, well, at least I knew enough to not try to go down the hole *with* the wire."

"I'm glad you're not hurt," Landon said.

He turned to get Rachel's attention as she passed. When she stopped, Landon turned back to us.

"Get my Minnesota friends a couple'a Luckys?"

"Sounds good. Thanks." Haakon responded.

Then Haakon turned to her.

"Hi Rachel."

She smiled shyly, then hurried off to retrieve their beers.

"She likes ya, Hawk," Landon said.

"How do you know?"

"Because Swan asked her," he responded.

"Oh. That's good to know."

"Are ya gonna ask her out?"

"I think so… later, I think."

She returned and set the beers in front of them. Haakon and Rachel awkwardly stared at each other as though waiting for the other to speak. Then her eyes dropped as she took Landon's ten-dollar bill. As she walked away, Landon handed Haakon his beer.

"That would be a good idea. Sweet girl," Landon said. "You'll like her."

His eyes drifted beyond Haakon, towards the entrance door.

"Hey, there's Judd."

Both Haakon and Brady turned to see Judd walk in. He was clean-shaven and was wearing fresh clothes. He had even combed his hair. Two women greeted Judd almost immediately, causing Landon to shake his head.

"He's quite the lady's man. They fall all over'em. He must be pack'n sumpthin big because I can't figure out otherwise what it is about him… what they see."

"He's a lady's man?" Brady asked, parroting Landon's remark in question form.

"Yeah. I've never seen noth'n like it. Young, old, married. They all love'em," Landon said.

"Married? That can't work out too well," Haakon said.

"Ya wouldn't think. But he does it. No one messes with him," Landon replied, shaking his head. "I call him Big, Bad Leroy Brown, like the song."

Continuing to watch Judd in wonderment, Landon recited the song's lyrics.

"Baddest man in the whole damned town. Badder than old King Kong and meaner than a junkyard dog."

"Seriously? Judd?" Haakon asked, surprised.

"That guy's pretty strong," Brady said. "Did you see the guns on him? He's got biceps like Johnny Atlas."

"Big deal. So do I," Haakon said, smiling.

"Your arms are string beans compared to his," Brady replied. "One of his arms is three of yours."

"Now you're making me feel like a wimp," Haakon said.

"You *are* a wimp," Brady said, laughing.

Then they all laughed.

"Yeah, well, maybe working next to you makes me feel like a muscle man."

"In your dreams," Brady responded.

"He did some time, I heard," Landon added.

"In the 'Big House?'" Brady asked.

Landon chuckled.

"Yeah, I guess… in the state prison. I think he killed someone. Manslaughter."

"Really? Wow," Haakon replied. "Is that what the ladies like around here? Killers?"

"I don't know, but I wouldn't let him hear you say that," Landon said, still keeping his eyes on Judd. "Here he comes."

Judd came up behind Brady.

"I heard you smashed your hand," he said, addressing Brady.

"It's fine," Brady said.

Then he turned to address Haakon.

"So how was your first day? You guys gonna like it here?"

"Yeah, for sure," Haakon answered. "We like it a lot."

"Well, tomorrow's your lucky day. You're work'n with me. You two ever do any "conk" work?" Judd asked.

"Huh?"

"Concrete. You ever pour any concrete?"

"Oh, yeah. We have."

"Well, then you know it's hard work. We're do'n the floor in the new state garage north of town. It's four dump truck stalls wide. That's a lot of floor, that's a lot of "conk" to move, so ya best not stay out too late. You'll need a good night's sleep. I'm gonna work your tails off. Just ask Landon."

Landon had been taking a big gulp of beer, but when he heard his name he set it down.

"Yes, that's right. Judd's gonna work ya. No more easy street for *you* guys."

They all laughed. Then Judd moved on, down the bar towards a group of women.

Rachel returned.

"Are you guys gonna wanna order spaghetti? Mack's shutting the kitchen down pretty soon."

"I've already eaten, but you guys should," Landon said, looking at Haakon and Brady. "It's a good deal."

"Yes. Please. We're in. And can we get another round of beers too?" Haakon asked Rachel.

"Sure thing. I'll be right back with the beers. The spaghetti might take another ten minutes."

When she returned, Haakon was about to lean towards the bar to muster out the words to ask her out on a date. But as soon as she set down the glasses, someone in the crowd summoned her away. This deflated him. It had taken some time to build up courage. Haakon set his money on the bar, grabbed his beer, and hoped for another opportunity when she returned with the food.

The owner hurried out to the kitchen with four plates of spaghetti. Haakon marveled at how he balanced all of them at once.

Mack was a short, heavyset man who appeared behind the bar infrequently. Haakon did not get the impression he was a particularly affable person, and he wondered what compelled him to get into such a social-orientated business.

He wore a white t-shirt with a white apron that might have been clean at the beginning of the evening. But now the t-shirt was darkened with perspiration and the apron mottled with spaghetti sauce. Sweat dripped from his forehead as he carried the plates. Haakon cringed and wondered if his perspiration contributed to the wateriness of the noodles.

Someone yelled out, "Hey Mack, have you ever thought of straining the noodles?"

Mack tried to smile.

"Three bucks and you bellyache. Sure, I can strain them better, but then I'd have to double the price."

"I'm not bitch'n, I'm just wonder'n why you don't serve it in bowls."

"Cause if I served it in bowls, you'd bitch because I didn't give you a spoon. There would be no end to it. Once a bitcher, always a bitcher."

The complainer laughed.

"I learned long ago that you can't please everyone," Mack said. "So I say, screw'm all!… and the horses they rode in on!"

This comment made the harasser's entire table laugh hysterically. Haakon had the impression they all knew each other. He also had the impression if he had tried such banter with Mack, he would have found himself outside in a heap. Despite being short and fat, Mack looked as though he could effectively serve as his own "bar bouncer."

A finger tapped on Haakon's arm and he turned to see Swan.

"Rachel likes you. Ya gonna ask her out?"

Her question surprised Haakon at first. The dialogue reminded him of Junior High School.

"Yeah. I'd like to. She's been kind'a busy. I haven't been able to."

"Okay. I just didn't want you two to be ships passing in the dark, if you know what I mean. Seems like a good bet and you'd love Rachel."

"Well, I appreciate ya say'n that, Swan."

Rachel glanced over as she was making her way along the bar. As she passed behind, Swan reached back and stopped her.

"Let's get this over with," Swan said, while looking at Haakon.

She then turned to Rachel and spoke loud enough for Haakon to hear.

"Haakon was just going to ask you something."

A part of Haakon did not like being put on the spot. But the coward in him did. Haakon realized his capability to sink his own boat with shyness. He realized he could have easily missed the opportunity. With his hand forced, Haakon looked up into Rachel's expectant eyes. She appeared as nervous as he felt.

"Yes, yes… ah," Haakon muttered. "Would you… do you wanna do something Friday night?"

She smiled.

"I'd like that."

They both smiled and stared at each other again, but Swan quickly broke the trance.

"That's why they call me the broker. I should be in sales. I'd be rich."

Mack yelled from the kitchen door, "Spaghetti ready!"

His words put both women back into motion. Swan winked at Haakon as she walked off.

As Rachel retreated towards the kitchen, she turned her head and smiled.

"I'll be right back with your spaghetti."

5
THE FAMILY PORTRAIT

After her shift ended on Friday, Haakon met Rachel outside the tavern. She smiled when she saw him drive up and he took this as a good sign that she did not have pre-dating remorse. The ebbing sunlight shone half upon her, warming and softening her round facial features. It sparkled in one of her dark eyes. She was even lovelier than what he remembered from the last time he had seen her, and he thought it had to do with the low, natural lighting.

"Hi," Haakon said. "Are we still on for tonight?"

As he asked, he realized he had foolishly provided her with an easy exit from their date.

"Yes! I've been looking forward to it."

Haakon gulped in relief and then smiled again.

"You're gonna have to help me with ideas, as I really don't know what to do around here for fun."

She contemplated the question. Haakon could smell her perfume. It was having the effect on him that its manufacturer had doubtlessly intended.

"Ah… we could drive into Colterville and get something to eat, then go listen to the band at Moose's Saloon," Haakon suggested.

She did not answer right away. He assumed she was continuing to ponder the issue. Or, perhaps she realized the effect that her scent and presence was having on him and she wanted to prolong it. Either way, Haakon was in no hurry to break her spell.

"I don't really want to spend more time in a bar, as you might understand. It's such a beautiful evening. How about we grab a couple of burgers and some beer-to-go and find a nice place to just sit and talk?"

Burgers, beer, sit outside under the setting sun? Haakon wondered for a moment if he had met the girl of his dreams.

"I like how you think. That sounds perfect!"

"So, I'll go back in and make us two burgers?"

"I like it. I'll go pay for them and buy a six pack."

"Sounds like a plan," she said, smiling.

They both walked inside the tavern. She headed off towards the kitchen and Haakon approached Swan at the cash register.

"What are you two going to do tonight?" Swan asked.

"Nothing really. Just finding a nice spot outside to talk."

Haakon handed her a twenty-dollar bill.

"I need to pay for two burgers and a six pack of Lucky."

Swan grabbed the bill, then reached into the cooler for the beer.

"Tell Rachel to take you to Ormond's Overlook. That's where I'd go," she said, while setting the beer in front of Haakon.

Emerging from the kitchen, Rachel overheard Swan.

"Yeah, that's perfect. That's a good place to go, Haakon," she said, now beaming as though this "perfect place" had not occurred to her.

So, they left the tavern with beer and double-wrapped burgers in hand. As Haakon backed out of the parking spot, Rachel popped the caps off of two beers and handed him one.

"It still seems crazy to me you can legally drink a beer while you drive," Haakon said.

"Just as long as you're not drunk."

"Back in Minnesota, they'd haul you into jail for just having the cap off the bottle."

"That sounds harsh," she replied, as she tapped her bottle into his. "Cheers!"

Ormond's Overlook was a short distance from the tavern. Turning off the highway, they followed a rough narrow road for about a quarter mile. It dead-ended at a high overlook above the Cedar River, just four miles upstream from Camp One. When the Scout could travel no further, Haakon pulled up on the emergency brake and turned off the engine. From their seats, they could gaze across the river into a broad open meadow surrounded by a thick dark forest. There were many deer standing on the far shore. Long shadows made them more conspicuous. A few raised their heads and turned them in the Scout's direction. Apparently, concluding that it was far enough away and not presenting an imminent danger, they resumed their casual feeding.

"That's a lot of deer," Rachel said as she quietly opened her door and stepped out onto the tall grass.

Haakon followed suit, then the two of them walked closer to the river's overlook.

"I love it here. I don't know why I don't come here more often. It's too close, I guess," she said.

They had spoken very little on the drive, so Haakon was grateful she was attempting to break through his shyness.

"Yeah, sometimes I forget the places that are so close to get to. It's easy to take them for granted," Haakon replied, just trying to fill the uncomfortable silence.

"That's what it is. You're right."

They gazed at each other, as though realizing they had made a small connection. The nervousness prompted spontaneous laughter. Haakon wanted to lean over to kiss her, but he knew that it was too soon.

Instead, he broke off the moment and said, "I'll grab the burgers in the Scout."

He did, then the two of them looked around for a good place to sit. Rachel spotted a large fallen tree, so Haakon followed her there.

"Perfect!" he said. "What a great spot."

"It is," she answered, handing him a wrapped burger.

Haakon opened his partially, then turned to her and said, "Thanks for coming."

She smiled back at him, bashfully, as he tapped his burger against hers.

"Cheers!"

They giggled briefly, then took a bite of their dinner.

"I guess this makes me a cheap dater, but honestly I can't think of a better place to be right now," Haakon stated, sincerely.

Rachel swallowed quickly to answer.

"This is nice. You don't know how much I miss times like this. Having kids changes things."

Sadness seemed to come over her. Haakon was not sure if she regretted her comment or if she pined for times past.

"Don't get me wrong. I love my kids, but I miss this," she said, looking around her surroundings.

Haakon glanced at her without responding. He read truthfulness in her face.

"I mean, we do picnics and stuff *like* this... but its not like this... you know, the quiet. I miss *this*."

She looked into Haakon's face to see if he understood.

"Where are your kids tonight?" he asked.

"They're with the ex. He takes them every other weekend."

"Does he live nearby?"

"A whole block away."

"Wow. Does that work out okay?"

"Well, it's getting better. He's got a new wife. She's pretty much the reason we're not married anymore. That was hard, seeing her with him all the time. I felt like I had been robbed and there was nothing I could do about it."

"I'm sorry."

"Yeah, well life goes on. You can only live in the dumps for so long. I have kids to raise. I finally realized that I couldn't go moping around feeling sorry for myself forever. So you just learn to accept."

She took another bite of her burger, then seemed to contemplate while she chewed before continuing.

"Me and the ex get along fairly well these days. I even talk to his wife now and then. It's a hard pill to swallow, though. At times, I still have dreams of choking her to death."

"I can imagine."

But Haakon really could *not* imagine what her life was like.

"Tell me about you, Haakon. What's your story?"

There was more that he wanted to know about her, but he tried to give her a concise answer.

"Well, I'm going to college. I came out here with Brady to get a summer job. I couldn't find work at home… not a good-paying construction job anyway. No one is building anything back there," he explained. "But it's more than that. I was looking for a bit of an adventure too. I haven't been out West except to visit Glacier National Park and to go skiing in Colorado once. I love the mountains."

"The Go West Young Man thing?" she inquired.

"Yeah, I guess. I wanted to be a mountain man like Jeremiah Johnson."

"I loved that movie," she said.

Haakon smiled, then said, "It's probably my favorite."

They were silent for a minute, taking time to eat the rest of their hamburgers.

"So do you have a girlfriend back home?" she asked, surprising him.

"No, I'm pretty much a free agent."

"I'd think you'd be shaking off mobs of girls."

Though embarrassed, Haakon enjoyed hearing this and he grinned.

"Yeah, in my dreams I guess."

Simultaneously, they swigged from their respective bottles while watching each other. This made them giggle again.

"So what are your interests, Rachel? Do you like to fish? Are you a skier? Do you want to be the Governor of Montana?"

She appeared to be considering the question for several long seconds.

"When I was in high school, I thought I wanted to be a stewardess. I wanted to go places, see places."

She paused, appearing to go back into deep thought.

"But I got pregnant and that put the kibosh on *that* idea."

"Oh," was all Haakon could think to say.

"I was sixteen. I didn't even finish high school. But ya know, I was all right with that… at the time. I was in love."

She shook her head as though in disappointment with herself.

"So Jessie and I got married. Then we had two more kids."

"Is Jessie your age?"

"He's three years older. He had… has a job at the cedar mill—good job. I figured that we were all set. I was happy."

"Sixteen seems young."

"I guess it is, but it's not uncommon… not around here. I had a lot of friends who got pregnant and married in high school. It hasn't worked out for most of them. If I had to do it over, I'd definitely do it differently."

"You and Jessie didn't work out?"

"Oh, we worked out until he banged the neighbor. She was younger. I was only twenty then, but she was younger… cuter… no kids yet. So he traded me in for a newer model."

"That must've been tough."

"It wasn't great for my self-esteem… getting replaced. I don't recommend it to anyone," she said as she cracked a half smile.

"I shouldn't have asked."

"No, it's fine. Really. It is what it is."

Yet her facial expression cued Haakon to not pursue the topic any further. It seemed to have put her in a funk. But she quickly shook it off and purposely changed the topic, herself.

"What about you? You said you're going to college. What for? What do you wanna be?"

Haakon told her he planned to be an architect, but was uncertain. They talked about jobs and security—concepts that seemed so abstract to their young minds. They talked about everything, briefly: history, politics, weather, sports, music, and—when they began appearing in the darkening sky—stars and planets. It was as though each feared the discomfort of "dead air," so they kept their conversation alive.

A cool breeze descended into the valley. Rachel responded by wrapping her arms tightly around her chest. Haakon stood up and told her he was going back to the Scout for a minute. Then he returned with his jacket and without saying a word, draped it over her shoulders.

"Gee, thank you. I hadn't thought about it getting cold. What about you?"

"I'm fine," he answered, trying to surreptitiously overpower the chill.

"You say you enjoy music. What's your favorite? Who do you

like?" he asked.

"I like a lot of people, but my favorite today is probably Dan Fogelberg. I just bought his album," she said.

"Ah, I really like Fogelberg. *Souvenirs?*"

"No. *Home Free.*"

"That's his first album, I think. I've only heard a couple of songs from it."

She turned to Haakon and smiled.

"I have an idea. Why don't we go to my place and listen to it?"

He studied her face. Her offer seemed sincere.

"I'd love to hear it. Besides, it *is* getting kinda cold."

So they followed the Scout's headlight beams out the windy gravel road onto the highway again and drove the short distance back to Renfro. It was dark and quiet there except for the lights and sounds emitted from the tavern. Several cars and pickup trucks were parked outside and a few figures milled about them. As they passed, Haakon hoped not to draw anyone's attention for fear of being waved in. He wanted nothing to interrupt what might be an intimate evening with Rachel in her warm house.

She pointed up the hill and navigated Haakon through a neighborhood of old weathered houses—relics from Renfro's heydays. When they got near the top, she pointed to a dated mobile home, surrounded by a battered, once white, picket fence.

"Here's my palace," she said. "Sorry for the mess. I wasn't expecting any company."

Haakon assumed "the mess" that she referred to was the patchy yard covered with children's items—mostly outdoor items: colorful balls of all sizes, a bicycle, a tricycle, a Frisbee, a child's kitchen set, a hula-hoop, and what appeared to be a makeshift fort constructed from a large, empty appliance box.

She noticed him studying the grounds.

"I know. Looks like a storm passed through."

Haakon smiled and followed her to her doorway and waited at the bottom of the wooden steps as she fumbled with her keys in the dark. Once the door was unlocked, she swung it open and moved inside, then motioned for him.

"Come on in."

The steps were wobbly. Haakon wondered if they would support his weight. Yet, he thought it would be impolite to express this concern.

"I bet that you thought with that mess *outside*, there couldn't be anything left to mess up the *inside*," she said, appearing embarrassed. "Surprise!"

Haakon laughed as he looked around her toy-strewn living room.

"It looks like kids live here. Active kids."

"Active. You can say that again. You cannot stay ahead of them. It's not possible."

The mobile home's interior appeared even smaller than its exterior. It seemed modestly furnished, and what furniture there was, appeared old and worn.

"Sit down and make yourself comfortable, if you can find a place to sit," she said. "Just move the kids' toys. Would you like some wine? I have some white."

"Sure."

"Why don't you put on the album? It's there in the corner alongside the stereo," she said, pointing.

Haakon looked over and saw a long row of albums on the floor, all leaning against each other upright. Next to them on a deep shelf was a turntable sitting alongside a receiver. It was a much nicer stereo setup than he expected, measured against the other furnishings. Flipping through the album covers, he quickly came across her newest purchase. It surprised him, as he carefully removed the album from its cover, at how pristine the disk itself was. Whatever Rachel may have lacked in housekeeping skills did not transfer over to her care of record albums. Gently, as though he was handling a photograph, he placed the album on the turntable, pushed on the power button, then set the needle onto its outer edge. Within seconds the large speakers, that he had not until that moment noticed, began emitting the high piano keys and the familiar harmonious falsetto voice of Dan Fogelberg.

"I love this guy," Rachel said as she reentered the living room carrying two glasses of wine.

"Yeah, he's an incredible talent. Such beautiful music."

She sat alongside Haakon on the couch and they quietly listened to the music for a time, while sipping wine. As much as they enjoyed the album, listening to it intently conflicted with their desire to become more acquainted. So conversation soon overrode the music. The topics, like before, went everywhere. Somehow the discussion got on evolution, Genesis, and Adam and Eve. Rachel expressed her belief in the literal biblical explanation. And in reaction, Haakon committed the ultimate faux pas.

"You're joking, right?"

"No."

"I didn't think anyone believed that anymore," Haakon said, snickering.

Yet he realized by reading her face that his response was not being well received. So he desperately attempted to backpedal—though clumsily.

"I mean, you believe the Bible version is like a poetic take of how things really happened, not a literal one, right?"

"I believe it as the Bible says," she answered, unwavering.

Haakon sat dumbfounded, wondering how he could patch the hole that he just punched into his own boat. Surprising himself, Haakon had managed to both insult his host's religious beliefs and inadvertently question her intelligence. He felt like an arrogant college know-it-all jackass, because, he realized, he had just acted like one. He wished that he could take his words back. But he could not, so he lunged for an opportunity to change the subject. Dan Fogelberg's next song saved him.

"Oh, this is such a great song," Haakon said, instantly recognizing its first few notes.

It was a haunting melody that gripped the room's mood. Her stereo system superbly conveyed the sound's fullness. A smile returned to Rachel's face.

"It's my favorite," she said, without looking at Haakon.

It relieved him to see her cheerful demeanor return. They listened to the entire song in silence. And while listening, Haakon made a mental note to keep his mouth shut on topics of religion—and politics, for that matter. It was a prudent dating policy that he would from then on adhere to.

After the song, they returned to light conversation. In a short time, the discussion transformed into a lengthy stare, then an embrace, and then a long kiss. Gradually, they slid into horizontal positions on the couch and became less inhibited.

She whispered into Haakon's ear, "Let's go into the bedroom."

Without another word, they both rose to their feet. He followed her, leaving the music playing behind. Standing in the dark alongside her bed, they passionately embraced and kissed again. But when Haakon's eyes opened, he viewed a framed photograph hanging on the wall. There was just enough light from the hallway to illuminate a family portrait—Rachel, her three children, and her ex. He stared at it and the eyes of her three children stared back.

This startled Haakon and he pulled away from Rachel.

"What's wrong?" she asked, surprised.

He did not answer her, as he was trying to collect his thoughts.

"Did I do something?"

"No, no, um… I was just thinking…" he said, but then stopped.

She stared at Haakon with a puzzled expression.

"You know Rachel, you are a beautiful and sweet girl. But I don't think I'm doing the right thing here."

"What do you mean?"

"I feel like a jerk saying this, but seeing your young kids there…" he said, gesturing to the photograph, "I think I'm leading you on. I'm not really ready for the whole family thing, still being in school and all, and I'm afraid I'm wasting your time."

"Wasting my time?" she said, exasperated.

"I wasn't thinking this through. I really like you, but I'm not being fair to you," he continued.

"I'm not asking you to marry me!" she exclaimed.

"I know. But I'm afraid to start something. I know I'm not going to be what you want."

"How do you know what I want?"

"I'm thinking you need a guy that will be there for you and your family. I'm not that guy. I don't want to lead you on."

She looked down at the floor.

"I should have realized this from the 'get go,' knowing that you had kids… but I didn't want to know, as I am attracted to you. But seeing your kids there," Haakon said, gesturing to the photograph again, shaking his head, "I know I can't do this."

There was no graceful way to extricate himself from the situation he had created. They conversed more, but the discussion was circular. Eventually, he gave her a hug and said goodbye. Then Haakon walked out into the night and took a deep gulp of the cool, crisp air.

The nearly full moon illuminated thick swathes of fog that wove in and out of the trees on the far side of the valley. The mountaintops were not visible. The world around him felt cold, gray, and surreal.

Climbing into the Scout, he asked himself again what he had been thinking, since he knew ahead of time that Rachel had children. He concluded that he had not been thinking at all—that his decisions were hormone driven. This made Haakon feel like an ass all over again. He had not anticipated that the sudden immersion into a house of children would overwhelm him. Yet there it was—a slap to his face. Haakon knew in that moment he was not even close to wanting a serious relationship that instantly included three children. As inelegant as the act was, the sailor in him knew he had to "cut and run." And in the days ahead, he would have to work to rewind their relationship to where it started.

Though she thinly denied it, Rachel wanted a man in her life and she wanted to resume the family life she had lost. Who could blame her? Her wants and needs were so different from Haakon's. The family portrait had suddenly given him clarity. He understood his presence was interfering with the natural order of her world.

As Haakon rolled into Camp One, he said to himself out loud, "What a jerk."

6
LADY JANE'S LOG HOME

Jane Crenshaw retired as a Berkley sociology professor and moved to northwest Montana to escape the west coast rat race. She arrived in a shiny new Land Rover, as only a Californian would. Attired in drab green pants and a pressed khaki shirt, she looked like an eager "first day" park ranger. With her graying brown hair pulled close to her head and her makeup-less face hidden under large, dark rim glasses, her protective shell was nearly complete. But her piercing green eyes betrayed her. Jane had the eyes of a younger, yearning woman.

Kingsley found her to be difficult and cold, but Haakon instantly recognized her hard demeanor as a facade. It was forced and intentional—clearly intended to convey that she was no pushover. The way Haakon saw it, she knew keenly that construction was a man's world. As a single woman in a strange new place, she was not about to be taken advantage of. He admired her for this. And he should have said something in her defense when his working companions, who misread her haughtiness, nicknamed her Lady Jane.

There was a log home craze in 1976. The old was becoming the new—a full circle in home construction. This was partially driven by the romanticism of living a wilderness life and surrounding one's self with earthy things like raw timber. And it was partially driven by the energy crisis and the unfounded belief that logs had some magical insulation attributes. They were going up everywhere in the rural Northwest. To compliment her "safari car," ranger attire, and backwoods idealism, Jane ordered a pre-cut log home kit from a mill in Missoula, Montana.

But before the log kit arrived, Kingsley Construction had poured her concrete walkout basement foundation. Haakon aided with the form assembly and concrete pour, but he had not been on the crew that later capped it off with joists and a plywood subfloor. So, when he returned to the job-site ahead of the log kit, it astounded him how different it looked. Aside from now being an elevated flat brown plane, its tall, gray foundation walls had been tarred and backfilled. On the uphill side of the foundation, he could walk directly onto the subfloor without a ladder.

There is something extraordinary about the first subfloor stage of a building project. Suddenly the vision becomes tenable. No longer are you scratching abstract troughs in the ground. The dream ascends from the earth. Atop the newly created horizontal plane, you can conceptualize what will be, just as an artist can conceptualize a finished painting from a blank canvas. You can see the view from the living room's picture window or turn and look up at the tall rock fireplace. Perspective and dimensions make more sense.

Like a child obliged to stomp in a mud puddle, a builder is compelled to walk upon a newly created floor to see what there is now to see that could not be seen before. It is an unconscious act. And, though unsaid among construction workers, it is gratifying to experience what is fashioned from where only soil had previously existed. So, when Haakon returned to the job-site early, he walked onto the floor to get a glimpse of Jane's dream.

Breathing in the cool, moist morning air, with its potent scent of fresh lumber, he scanned her home's view and tried to imagine it completed. He could sense the log walls and the tall, rock fireplace and the massive, hewed overhead beams. It had been hard to imagine all of this from the ground precisely. But now, with its base established, it was all very clear. As Haakon stared out the window-to-be, a fog bank slowly floated down the river. A group of deer foraged unworried along its far bank. She had chosen well, he thought. Her setting was surely the antitheses of what she had left.

Brady sat semi-reclined in the Scout, logging a few more minutes of sleep before the start of work. Haakon and Brady had been assigned to assist the mill's expert log-layers as labors. It thrilled both of them to have the opportunity to work on a log home.

Haakon heard the door to a travel trailer open and close. He had noticed the trailer, along with the two pickup trucks parked alongside it, when he and Brady drove in. A short, thin, older man emerged, then wandered in the parked Scout's direction. He wore faded blue jeans and a plaid cowboy shirt. His dark tan face was leathery and not recently shaven. Short graying hair retreated from both his forehead and crown. Haakon figured him to be in his sixties, but at nineteen, he did not consider himself a good judge of age.

As Haakon stepped off of the subfloor and back onto the ground, he noticed Brady yawning. Brady must have heard the trailer door. He stepped out into the air and stretched as the three of them converged in front of the Scout's grill.

"You must be the men I've been waiting for," the man said. "Kingsley told me he was sending me his best."

Haakon wondered how many times he had used that line.

"Well, I don't know about the best, but we're here to work," Haakon answered for both of them. "I'm Haakon and this is Brady."

"Great! We'll have a truck of logs here within the hour. I've got an area I need you two to clear out for them," he said, wanting to get to it.

"I'm Jim and…"

He turned towards his trailer.

"That slowly awakening guy is Mike."

A younger, equally scruffy man stepped out of the trailer and approached in a slow saunter.

"Mike here is usually a little owly in the morning, but pay him no mind, he usually works out of it by quit'n time."

Mike looked to be in his mid-thirties. He was lean, muscular and slightly taller than Jim. His long, sun-bleached hair and mustache and tanned face, Haakon surmised, were no strangers to outdoor work. Even his eyes appeared sun-fatigued. But as he approached, he quickly pulled on his wraparound reflective sunglasses.

"I can hear you, old man. You're full of shit," Mike stated. "I'm always a ray of sunshine."

Then he turned to Haakon and Brady.

"Brady? Haa-kon? Nice to meet you. What kind of name is Haa-kon?"

"Norwegian, I'm told. Just call me Hawk."

"Good. I can't handle too many syllables this early in the morning," he retorted.

Then he turned back to Jim.

"You got any coffee made?"

"What am I, you're frick'n butler? The thermos is over there on the truck hood."

Jim gestured towards his pickup truck, then turned back.

"Do ya believe it? I let a guy bunk in my trailer and he thinks 5-star service comes along with it!"

Mike grumbled something under his breath as he ambled off towards the coffee.

"It's hard to find good help these days," Jim said.

When Mike was beyond earshot, Jim spoke quietly.

"Actually, he's a pretty good worker once he gets some caffeine in him. I just don't like to let him know I think he's a good worker. I figure job insecurity is a good work incentive," Jim said.

He looked back to make sure that Mike could not hear him before continuing.

"Not for you guys, of course. I just assume that you're good workers. But him… well, I gotta work with him nearly every day. It's good to keep him on edge a little."

Haakon and Brady chuckled. Then Jim, apparently determining that the greeting time had ended, abruptly changed his tenor.

"Well, I'd love to stand here and chat with you guys, but we have a log home to build. Let me show you what I need you to do first."

Haakon and Brady went about clearing a staging area for the incoming logs. Jim and Mike walked on to the capped-off foundation to assess the project. With blueprints in hand, Haakon could see them measuring and marking on the plywood floor. Before long, just as Jim had predicted, a semi-truck pulling a long open trailer loaded with blonde colored logs crept down the narrow, windy gravel drive, raising a tall cloud of dust.

"Holy smokes! Other than the light color, that looks like a giant Lincoln Log set," Haakon said to Brady, recalling his childhood canister of miniature building logs.

"Yeah. All that's missing are the green roof planks," he replied.

Then, minutes later, a second semi-truck appeared.

"Spoke too soon. There they are."

The second open trailer carried even more logs. And stacked behind them were long, green, metal roof panels.

"It *is* a giant Lincoln Log set!" Haakon said, astonished. "I've done this… hundreds of times. I think I already know how to build this house."

Unloading and organizing the logs and the other building materials took the better part of the morning. As buoyant and carefree as Jim appeared upon their first meeting, it soon became obvious he was neither. While Haakon and Brady lifted the logs off of the truck, Jim appeared very serious. He knew exactly how and where he wanted the logs laid out. Each was numbered, so there was a stacking order to follow. Haakon noticed that Jim and Mike spoke very little during this process. They moved about independently with resolve, seeming to know what to do and when, without having to confer with the other.

Jane lived in a medium-sized travel trailer about fifty yards from the construction site. It was her intention to oversee the entire building process and to make sure, Haakon presumed, the men did not take advantage of the lone woman. As Haakon carried his end of the long logs to their new location, he saw her watching from a distance. He got the impression she wanted to be right there with the workers, in the thick of the action, but was restraining herself.

"Shit! Those idiots should have made this up on the subfloor!" Jim yelled to Mike, shaking his head in disgust.

Haakon had learned, even before Montana, that as a building's construction proceeded skyward, the workmanship of the previous construction stage was always called into question. The roofers cursed the carpenters. The carpenters cursed the foundation workers. The foundation workers cursed the excavator. And the excavator cursed Mother Nature. Someone's previous work was always to blame for whatever problem was encountered.

"Who built this foundation? The Three Stooges?" Jim asked loudly, looking towards Haakon and Brady as they hoisted the first log on the subfloor.

By their expressions, Jim surely knew that neither was going to admit having anything to do with it. So Haakon and Brady each just shrugged their shoulders in response to his question. Jane suddenly appeared below Jim. She was looking up from where the foundation allowed for a walkout basement.

"Is there a problem?"

Jim, still looking at Haakon and Brady, grimaced theatrically when he heard her voice. Then he turned to see Jane behind and below him.

"No, not really," he answered in a much gentler tone. "The levels are a little off, but that's not uncommon. We can easily make up for it in the log courses."

"You had me concerned," she said.

"Oh, I tend to exaggerate sometimes," he said, meekly. "Don't worry. Everything looks fine. Outstanding, in fact! We'll get this done right for you."

As they continued to set the first course of logs up on the subfloor, Haakon noticed that Jim and Jane's conversation went on for a few more minutes. She would ask questions or voice concerns, he would answer with reassurance. When they finished talking, Jane turned to walk away. Jim, noticing Haakon and Brady watching him, mockingly held an imaginary noose to his neck and feigned pulling up. With one hand holding the imaginary rope up high, he cocked his head sideways and let his tongue hang out of his mouth as though he were dead. Both Haakon and Brady burst out laughing, then looked to see if Jane had witnessed his comedic acting. Thankfully she had not.

"Wow, that guy is gutsy," Haakon quietly said to Brady.

"You ain't a kiddin," he replied.

Mike moved over to Jim's side.

"I think she likes you," he exclaimed, now that Jane was out of sight.

Then he continued addressing Jim as he looked over at Haakon and Brady.

"I could definitely feel something going on."

"Of course, she likes me. All the ladies *love* me. They want me. Why does that surprise you?"

"Because you're an old man who hasn't shaved and bathed in God knows how long."

"I didn't know my personal hygiene was such a concern to you."

Haakon and Brady laughed, knowing the banter was largely for their entertainment.

"Well, it is a concern when I'm live'n in the same trailer with you."

"I have a thought," Jim said. "Why don't you move into your truck?"

"Maybe I will."

"Come to think of it, why don't you talk a little less and work a little more."

Mike chuckled, then went back to his business. Everyone did. But ten minutes later, there was cursing again. This time it was Mike.

"Oh shit! Jim, look at this."

Jim walked over to his side. Both Haakon and Brady watched with curiosity.

"Those dumb-asses put the tie-rods right through the doors and windows!"

"Nah," Jim responded in disbelief. "No one is *that* stupid."

"Look at the plans," Mike exclaimed, holding out the blueprints to Jim. "Look where the rods are."

"Oh. My mistake. There *are* people that stupid."

He turned to Haakon and Brady.

"Don't people know how to read around here?"

"What's wrong," Brady asked.

"Well, every four feet there is a threaded rod that goes from the foundation all the way up to the top log course. We drill holes in each course of logs and keep screwing on three foot threaded rod extensions as we go up. When we get to the top, we crank the logs down to the foundation, making the walls tight and strong."

"Yeah. Makes sense. I remember Landon putting the threaded boots in the concrete before it dried," Brady said.

"That's all fine. But obviously 'Landon the Genius' didn't realize that you don't put them where there're windows and doors!" Jim said, exasperated. "Didn't he look at the plans? Jeez!"

"I don't know. I was just a laborer like Hawk."

"What are we gonna do?" Mike asked Jim.

"Well, we're just not gonna have rods everywhere they ought to be."

"What's gonna support the walls," Brady asked.

"Glue. There's still a glue caulking that goes on every course. And they tie together and the roof weight presses them into place. They'll be strong enough," Jim answered, as though to convince himself.

Mike looked at Jim with astonishment.

"Don't tell Jane about this, she'll have a conniption," Jim said.

On the first day, Jim only trusted Haakon and Brady to pack the logs from the yard pile up onto the subfloor. In time, he realized that they were competent enough to measure and drill the rod holes as well. This made the log laying operation much smoother as both Jim and Mike could concentrate on laying and aligning each log. Yet Haakon suspected that his and Brady's proficiency threatened Mike.

"You guys got anything goin' the rest of the summer?" Jim asked as he set down a long log. "I could sure use you two."

Haakon knew that he said this partially as a cheerleading chant to encourage their work efforts. But it also seemed intended to poke at Mike's confidence. Compared to the inflated accolades that Jim laid upon Haakon and Brady, Mike never complimented them. Rather, he seemed purposely aloof. Haakon sensed he was jealous and oblivious to the fact he was being played by Jim.

"Yeah, we'll just be one big happy friggin family travel'n from job to job in a caravan," Mike inelegantly blurted out to Jim's question.

Jim did not respond to Mike's outburst but turned to Haakon and Brady with an exaggerated shocked look on his face. Mike noticed that he was being mocked.

"Eat fly larvae!" he said, addressing all of them.

"You've got to get more sleep, Mr. Crankypants," Jim said.

"I would if you didn't slam the trailer door when you have to get up and take a piss every five minutes at night, old man."

As the days progressed, everyone tried to be mindful of Jane's whereabouts. No one wanted to offend her with salty language, nor did they want to give her worries about the various construction challenges that were encountered. Usually, she came by for an inspection walkthrough in the mid-morning and the mid-afternoon. After each, she would confer with Jim, always looking very uneasy as she spoke. He, in turn, would look receptive to her trepidations. But, after she walked away, he would typically make some juvenile mocking gesture, usually vulgar. It shocked both Haakon and Brady that a job foreman would have such gall. Initially, his words and gestures towards Lady Jane gave them the impression that he despised her. In time, however, it became clear this was all for show.

"You never came home last night," Mike said to Jim, as they were unloading tools for the workday.

"What, are you my mother?" he replied.

"I just worry about you… you know, walking around these woods at night," Mike said, grinning at Haakon and Brady, knowing that he had Jim by the tail. "They got bears around here."

"Yeah, well I got a steel-toed boot that's gonna be up your ass in a minute if ya don't get to work," Jim said.

Then he looked to see Haakon and Brady smirking.

"What is this, an intervention? Get to work you guys! Jeez!"

"What is that wretched smell?" Mike then exclaimed. "Do I smell some cheap cologne? Who wears cologne to a building site?"

Mike mockingly scanned around him, then back to Jim.

"Ohhhh."

"You're beginning to irritate me," Jim chided.

"And I smell soap too," Mike continued.

Then he turned to Jim again.

"What the… you shaved!"

"You know, Brady and Hawk here are gonna have nightmares after they watch me kick your ass. You're pushin' it, buckaroo."

Haakon wondered if Mike was truly "pushing it" or if this was part of their usual jousting.

"Old man, you couldn't kick the ass of a chipmunk."

With that comment, Jim snapped into a boxer's pose with coiled fists in front of his face. But, just as Haakon and Brady were trying to assess if this was the start of a genuine fight, Jim dropped his arms to his side.

"You know, I'd like to stand here and have fun with you guys all day, but we've got a house to build. If it isn't too much trouble, would you guys mind get'n to work? I mean, I don't wanna put ya out or noth'n. Whenever you feel inspired. That works for me," Jim said, his words dripping in sarcasm.

In the second week, log assembly was becoming routine for Haakon and Brady. They did not even need instructions to start the day. The four of them worked together as a finely tuned log-home-assembling machine.

But, as they approached laying the last course of logs, Haakon and Brady knew that their work at Jane's job site would soon be over. Towards the end of that week, while working alone with Mike, Haakon took the opportunity to stroke his fragile ego.

"Jim says you and him go way back working together."

"Too long. I don't know why I put up with that old fool," Mike said. "I guess I feel sorry for him, being feeble and all."

"Well, he sure talks you up," Haakon said. "When you're not around anyway."

This seemed to surprise Mike as he paused for a moment in his actions, as though to reflect on Haakon's words.

"Well, he should. He'll never find anyone better. And he'll definitely never find anyone who will put up with all of his bullshit!"

Haakon chuckled.

"So, this works okay, you being away from your family for days on end."

Mike seemed to appreciate being acknowledged for his personal sacrifice. He lowered his shield.

"It's hard. All jokes aside, it's tough for my wife and kids. But it's seasonal. They get me full-time in the winter, probably more of me than they care for."

"What about Jim? Does he have any family?"

"No, he's a loner. He's got a gal from time to time back in Missoula, but he's found no one to replace his wife."

"She just up and left him, huh?"

"Yeah, but not in the way he jokes about. She died. Got cancer."

"Oh wow, I didn't pick up on that."

"He doesn't talk about it, cause it nearly took him out too. He had a rough patch after that. Fell into a bottle and didn't come out for a long time."

"Did you know him then?"

"I did, but he wasn't a good person to know back then."

"So how'd he get out of that?"

"I don't know. AA, I guess. Just figured it out. Never said just how, but he won't touch a drop anymore. Hasn't for many years."

"That's good to hear. Can you still drink around him?"

"Yeah, he's fine with that. I'm not much of a drinker, so it's not an issue—just a beer here and there."

"So is there something goin' on between him and Lady Jane?" Haakon asked, wanting to keep Mike "singing."

"You're sure a nosey guy!" Mike said, expressing again his familiar look of disdain.

"It helps the work day go by. I like to know all the dynamics going on around me."

"Whatever, but yeah, I think they have taken a liking to one another."

"Sure seems like an odd couple to me, though," Haakon said.

"That's because they're both odd people. But I don't know, Jim can clean up pretty good and Jane might be a fine looking older woman if she lets down her hair and loses that ranger outfit," Mike said. "I see possibilities here."

As the logs progressed skyward in the form of rafters, Haakon paid closer attention to Jane's behavior towards Jim. She continued to make her routine morning and afternoon inspection rounds. And she continued to confer with Jim at the conclusion of these rounds. As always, he would listen intently and would appear receptive to her concerns. Everything seemed normal until she left. But now, instead of rolling his eyes or mockingly grasping his neck with his two hands as though being choked or holding a hand to his head with an extended index finger suggesting a pistol, then recoiling it as though firing, or making some crude, repetitive sexual gesture, Jim did nothing.

"Where do you guys go next," Haakon asked during their last lunch together.

"I go home to Missoula," Mike said, "to see if my kids still recognize me and to find out if my wife has been out servicing the town."

"You should see this guy's wife," Jim said, with his eyes widening.

"Man, she's gorgeous. I don't know how he ever got her."

"I got her because of my good looks and winning personality. Everyone knows that."

"Like I said, I don't know how this guy ever got her," Jim repeated.

"Screw you old man."

"But all jokes aside, this guy's got a beautiful family. I wouldn't leave them alone so long, if it were me."

"How long are you away?" Brady asked Mike.

"I don't see them much until winter. Then I'm with them all the time. Eventually they tire of me, but then I'm back on the road in the spring."

"Can you imagine anyone tiring of him?" Jim asked, while rolling his eyes.

"What about you, Jim? You got a family?" Brady asked.

"Me? Naw. Not at home anyway," he answered. "Long ago, as I said, my wife got wise and left me."

Jim looked down in a shy manner.

"I've got two grown kids," he continued, "but they live far away. It's just me. So, it's easier for me to be on the road than Mike."

"Don't feel too sorry for the old sailor, he's got a lady in every port," Mike said.

"Oh, I wish," Jim replied.

"I'm getting the impression that you might stay on here after the logs are set," Mike said to Jim, making Haakon realize that they have not yet had this discussion.

"Well, Jane and I seem to have some things in common."

"Jane? What happened to Lady Jane?" Mike said.

"Act your age, would ya?" Jim snapped. "I'm trying to have a mature conversation here."

"This *is* me being mature."

"How does your wife put up with you? It must be like havin' a fourth kid for her."

"She puts up with me because I'm the best," Mike answered.

"You're delusional is what you are."

"I'm not so delusional to not know that you didn't come home last night."

"I was having a discussion with Jane and I fell asleep," Jim answered defensibly. "What, are we married or something? I'm beginning to think you're jealous."

"I just worry about you, old man. You might go senile on me and go wander'n off into the woods."

"You two sound like an old married couple," Brady said. "Have you ever thought of counseling?"

"That's kind of nasty, Brady. And here all along I had thought you were such a nice, quiet guy," Jim responded.

Brady's sudden comedic boldness truly surprised him. Everyone laughed.

Later that day, with the final log rafter set in place, all four log builders went about collecting tools and rolling up extension cords for the last time. Once everything had been loaded into their respective pickup trucks, they each stood facing one another as they did on the first morning.

"Well, it's been a lot of fun boys," Jim said, breaking the tongue-tied silence. "We must get together and do this again sometime."

The retiring crew laughed as they exchanged handshakes.

"I told Kingsley that whatever he's payin' you, it's not enough. He oughta give you guys a raise. You've been great! Of course, if you get a raise, I expect a cut."

"I hate to burst your bubbles, but he tells that to everyone," Mike said.

"You guys already know that Mike here is dealing with some mental issues. I've been trying to get him some help."

"I may be crazy, but at least I'm not senile."

"Like I said…" Jim replied.

Mike seemed giddy and eager to move on. He stood with his door open, halfway into his pickup truck cab.

"I hope that your wife is still there when you get home, Mike," Haakon said, trying to be funny.

Mike paused with his answer, making Haakon wonder if his comment had gone too far.

"Oh, I think she'll be there. Maybe it's actually good if she's making the rounds while I'm gone. She'll just realize all the more, how good I am."

"Have you ever asked her why your youngest son looks so much like me?" Jim asked.

"You're pushin' it, old man."

"That's exactly what she told me."

Mike cocked his right arm and formed a fist as though to strike Jim a blow.

"I'd smack you if I didn't feel so sorry for you."

Jim smiled and turned back to Haakon and Brady.

"Ya see. You guys get to move on with your lives. I've gotta put up with this guy on the next job. It just never ends. I'd retire, but he doesn't have the brains to run this operation himself. I'm kinda stuck."

"Who's the delusional one now?" Mike asked.

Then Mike climbed up onto his seat, closed the door, and stuck his head out of its window.

"I've got a woman back home who is longing for my manliness. It's been real, fellas. Adios!"

Mike saluted as he drove off.

"Are you headed back to Missoula too," Haakon asked Jim.

"No, I might stick around here for a few days, then go directly to our next job down in McCall."

He smiled.

"Jane's gonna show me a good fishing hole she found. The old gal ended up being all right. A little uptight at first, but I have a way of softening women."

Haakon and Brady did not return to Jane's job site again, but they heard from others that a pickup truck with Missoula County plates had been seen coming out of Jane's driveway from time to time. Haakon saw her in Renfro once, but she did not see him. He barely recognized her. She wore makeup, her hair was down, her glasses gone, and she was wearing tight jeans with a partially unsnapped cowboy shirt. Haakon thought it a good look for her.

Lady Jane was nowhere to be seen.

7
ICE CREAM & PERFUME

In late June, construction began on a large auto parts store in downtown Colterville. From the onset of setting the forms for its foundation, Kingsley assigned Haakon as Judd's assistant. Working at his side each day, Haakon got to know him better through his many anecdotes. Judd was a big talker and an unabashed braggart. But his stories were so amusing and enthusiastically delivered, Haakon forgave his vanity. Judd made the workday fun. And, the more Haakon listened to him, the more he became convinced the rumors about Judd were true. Judd was a walking, talking tale of intrigue.

No one would describe him as good-looking, but he was not an ugly person either. "Scrappy" is the word that came to mind when most mentioned his appearance. Haakon presumed that his alleged "many women" were drawn to his ruggedness—not unlike the cowboy models used to sell pickup trucks and Marlboro cigarettes on billboards. If Haakon visualized a cowboy hat on Judd's head, he could see him as the guy that ropes steers. A rutted face that included a prominent scar did nothing to dissuade from his "rugged guy" demeanor, nor did the fact that he was known to have been a talented prizefighter in his younger days and that he spent some years in Montana's Deer Lodge Prison. It was whispered that Judd had experienced more than a few hard knocks in life. He looked it. Though only in his early 40s, he had the complexion of a much older man. If it were not for his long, thick brown, wavy hair and his striking blue eyes, he could have easily passed for 60.

"I don't like to brag Haakon, but damn, I've got to manage my time with the ladies a little better. I've been spreading myself too thin," he stated, without being prompted. "It was hard get'n outta bed this morning. And she didn't wanna let me go."

Initially, Haakon had been skeptical of his countless "lady conquest" tales.

"It's tough all over," Haakon retorted, purposely looking unimpressed.

Haakon did not take the bait and ask him about the "she," though that did not stop Judd from elaborating.

"God, she was something!" he continued. "So little time, so many ladies!"

"It can't be easy being you, Judd."

"Ya got that right," he replied, beaming. "An average guy couldn't handle this kind of workload."

This made Haakon smile and Judd noticed.

"Ya got a girlfriend Haakon?"

"Not at the moment."

"Got any prospects?"

"Not at the moment."

"Jeez, when's the last time ya been laid?"

Haakon looked up from his crouched position with an annoyed expression on his face.

"Man, how do you even get up in the morning? What do ya have to look forward to?"

"Coffee, Judd. I get up in the morning so I can have coffee."

"You're pathetic."

"So I'm told."

"Ya got nothing goin' at all?"

"I've got my eye on the girl at the lumberyard, but I guess she's got a boyfriend," Haakon said.

Out of pride, Haakon was trying to make it sound like he had a shot at the lumberyard girl when he knew that he did not.

"So what!" Judd quipped. "A lotta my ladies have husbands and boyfriends. That means nothing."

He held out the "dumb end" of his tape measure.

"Hold this on the concrete, would ya?" Judd asked, gesturing towards the wall. "Ya just gotta schedule things right."

"I wouldn't know," Haakon said as he uncoiled the tape while walking.

"You talk'n about that redhead at the lumberyard, the owner's daughter? She's a beauty," he said. "She's interested in you?"

"Well, I'd like to think so, but… no."

"Hmm… that's tough."

Haakon had the impression Judd was beginning to feel sorry for him, for his lack of romantic prospects. Judd jotted down some measurements on a torn piece of cardboard, then dropped it into his tool belt and shoved the pencil behind his ear.

"Tell ya what. I'll have someone you can check out later this morning."

"You have girls coming here?"

"Yeah, well sorta. I've got Michelle from last night coming by with a lunch for me. She'll have her daughter Kim along. She's a cutie! I can set ya up."

"Well, let me get a look at her first."

Haakon was concerned Judd would embarrass him in front of the women.

"Yeah. Sure. Believe me, you'll like what ya see. She's hot. If I wasn't dating her mom, I'd be all over her."

"How old is she?"

"Ah, eighteen I think."

"Wouldn't that be a little young for you, even if you weren't dating her mom and all?"

"Eighteen? Naw. I've done eighteen," he answered, matter-of-factly. "But she's probably a better age match for you. How old are you, Haakon?"

"Nineteen."

"Perfect!"

Three hours later, as Judd had predicted, two good-looking women appeared outside on the sidewalk. One looked older than the other, but like an older sister, not like a mother. Haakon figured Michelle must have gotten pregnant as a teenager. How else could she look so young yet have a full-grown daughter?

Through the corner of his eye, Haakon watched Judd approach them. He hoped that Judd would not call him over to meet them. Haakon was shy in these matters and he preferred time to build up courage.

The daughter was a slightly taller and more refined version of Michelle. She, like her mother, had long, glossy, brown hair that hung down to her waist. Both wore short shorts, though the daughter's legs were toned like an athlete's. And the daughter had a soft glowing face that Judd had correctly described as "cute."

While Haakon was working close enough to recognize the women's beauty, he was too far to hear their conversation with Judd. At one point Judd gestured towards Haakon and the women's faces turned to look. Nervously, Haakon stared down at the 2x4s that he was stacking, fearful of making direct eye contact and being summoned. But Haakon's fear was unfounded. Judd kept his word.

After a few minutes, Haakon noticed Michelle handing Judd a paper sack. Judd glanced inside, then gave her a kiss. By the time Haakon mustered enough nerve to turn fully in their direction, they were gone, and Judd, surprisingly, was standing by his side. Haakon lurched in fright when he saw Judd nearly on top of him.

"Yikes! Did you fall from the sky?"

"I'm like a cat. I move around pretty quietly. I find this to be a helpful trait when dealing with married women," he said, chuckling. "Hey, you're all set up."

"Huh?"

"Yeah. You're all set up to meet Kim. She'd like to meet ya. I could tell that you were too damn shy to meet her now, so I set ya up for this afternoon."

"This afternoon?"

"Yeah. This afternoon. What, is your social calendar filled for the day?"

"No, no. I'm just trying to comprehend what you're saying."

"Well, it's not complicated, Einstein, so I don't think you'll even have to write this down," he said.

He stared at Haakon skeptically as a toothpick swiveled around his mouth.

"She's playing softball over there at the park this afternoon."

Judd pointed in the park's direction.

"She says if you want to meet her, come see her after her game. Ends about 4:30, she figures."

"Oh. Okay," Haakon said, apparently conveying some reluctance.

"What? I didn't make that easy enough for you? Do you want me to take you by the hand there to meet her?"

"No. I'm just surprised," Haakon said. "That was decent of you Judd... I think."

"I'm all about making people happy," he boasted. "I get up every morning and ask myself, 'Who can I make happy today?' I guess it's *your* lucky day, Haakon. Just be there. I have an image to uphold around here."

This prospect of a near "cold call" to an attractive young woman made Haakon nervous for the rest of the workday. He practiced introductions repeatedly in his head, but never got comfortable with any version. Yet, when work ended, Haakon sucked in his trepidation and, like a trooper, made his way on foot the short distance to the ball field. When he got close, his eyes acted as a radar beam and immediately picked her out from the crowd of uniforms. She was walking off of the diamond with two other girls that seemed very young. Kim was a full head taller than either of them.

Haakon knew she noticed his approach even though she did not look directly at him. Instead, she swung her long hair off of her face and attempted to arrange it with her hand. Then she turned towards Haakon, as did her friends, each smiling.

"Hi Kim. I'm Haakon."

His introduction seemed to cue her friends to depart. They told her goodbye, then walked off giggling.

"I hope I didn't scare them off," Haakon said, grasping for any words to break the ice.

"No, you didn't scare them," she said, smiling as she extended her hand. "Hi."

They shook and smiled at each other. Close up, her pale face was young, round, and soft—covered with more makeup and mascara than was necessary. She had stunning, clear brown eyes.

"Judd thought we should meet," Haakon said, still struggling for words.

"Yeah," she replied, seeming as shy as Haakon was.

"You like ice cream? Would you like to walk over and get a cone?" Haakon asked.

He thought of this proposal ahead of time. It was the best idea he could come up with.

"Yeah, sure."

As they walked to the ice cream shop on Main Street, Haakon asked Kim a series of questions, wanting to avoid any uneasy silence. At first, her responses were succinct "yes's and no's," but eventually she relaxed a bit and gave lengthier answers. She even asked some questions of her own. A few other young girls passed them on the sidewalk and they, like the ones before, giggled after they exchanged waves with Kim. Haakon thought it odd that she knew so many young girls. Even the teenage girl with braces, who made their cones, seemed to be Kim's friend.

With ice cream cones in hand, they ambled back towards the ballpark. By the time they got there, the cones were half eaten and their conversation had eased considerably. Their growing comfort enabled them to speak more freely.

Kim noticed another acquaintance walking in the distance with a young man. They caught each other's eyes and waved excitedly.

"That's my friend, Kathy. She just found out she's pregnant."

"Oh wow, that's tough. She looks so young," Haakon responded.

"No. She's happy. She loves kids."

"Yeah, but is she old enough to *have* kids?"

"She's fifteen. I've got a lot of friends that have gotten pregnant at fifteen."

"Really? Wow. That's young. That's gotta be hard."

"I guess, but they seem to manage. It makes me kind of envious sometimes."

"Envious to be pregnant so young?" Haakon asked, unable to withhold his surprise.

"I love kids!" Kim exclaimed.

"Well sure, but having kids so young. Doesn't that kind of screw up plans for college and careers and stuff?"

"Sometimes, I guess. But most of my friends have boyfriends who have good jobs in the mill. They don't plan to leave and go to college. They're happy here."

"But how do they know if they wouldn't be happier somewhere else if they don't leave for a while?"

"I don't know."

"Don't they have aspirations of saving the world or becoming scientists and doctors and pilots and lawyers?"

Kim's changed facial expression conveyed annoyance. Haakon feared he was coming across as a condescending "college prick" again.

"I don't know. They're happy. Isn't that enough?" Kim asked, indignantly.

Haakon sensed the conversation was headed for a dead-end.

"I don't want to wait too long to have a family. I don't want to be some old mother."

Haakon could not seem to help himself. He probed her thought process some more.

"But don't you want to explore a little bit before you get tied down for life? Travel? Go to college? Join the Peace Corps?"

"No. I don't want to do any of that. I love it here. I want three kids and a nice house… preferably with horses."

Her answer startled him and he looked to her face to see if she was being factious. Kim's sober expression informed Haakon she was not. Yet, he was concerned about being unduly judgmental.

"I'm sorry if I have offended you. I just don't understand why your friends wouldn't want to see what else is out there before they settle— why they wouldn't want to explore their own personal potential."

Haakon smiled when he asked this, trying to soften the inquiry.

"I don't know. They just don't," Kim said, defiantly.

"Well, at least you've waited for *your* kids and house and horse until after you've finished high school." he said, intending to be humorous.

Haakon quickly realized he sounded like a parent.

"Who knows, that's a ways off," she said.

"Didn't you just graduate?"

"Graduate? No. I'm only a freshman," Kim exclaimed.

"Freshman! How old *are* you?"

"Fifteen."

"Fifteen?" Haakon responded, shocked. "You're joking."

"How old did you think I was?"

"Eighteen! Judd said you were eighteen," Haakon answered, exasperated.

"Eighteen? *He* knows how old I am."

"Ah… well, I'm nineteen. I'm not exactly an old man yet, but four years seems like quite a gap for dating… at our age anyway."

"I've dated guys older than you," she said, as though bragging. "Besides, who says we're dating?"

"We're not. You're right," Haakon said, clarifying to Kim and, more importantly, to himself that he was not dating a fifteen-year-old.

They stood in silence for a moment, both of them staring at the ground. Kim seemed embarrassed. Haakon was still trying to process the disturbing information. Eventually, his thought process caught up and he broke the quiet with another question.

"Doesn't dating older guys bother your mother?"

"No. She's never said noth'n. But whatever!" Kim answered, now sounding hurt.

"Hey, I'm sorry, but fifteen is… well, fifteen."

"I'm nearly sixteen," she said, haughtily.

"Sixteen," Haakon muttered, still trying to comprehend the situation. "Kim, I'm sorry, but Judd told me you were eighteen. I thought we were close in age. You look eighteen."

The latter comment made her almost smile.

Haakon thought to himself, if they were each ten years older, this would not have mattered. But the dating line between high school and post high school was a precarious one. And the fact that she was not even close to graduation made the prospect untenable to him.

"Can we still be friends?" Haakon asked, holding out his hand. "I wish we were closer in age. I really do."

"Sure," Kim said, shaking his hand lightly and briefly.

She seemed disappointed. *He* was definitely disappointed—not just in her revealed age, but also in her lack of aspiration. Haakon felt like an arrogant ass thinking it, but he could not come to grips with a desire to marry and have children at such a young age. It made no sense to him. Yet he was learning it was not uncommon in Colterville.

Despite the pledge to be friends, their conversation dropped off quickly. Neither of them saw any point in investing any more time in the other. They cordially said goodbye, then walked off in opposite directions.

When Haakon arrived back at Camp One that evening, he found Brady sitting before a blazing campfire, roasting a hotdog on a stick.

"Grab some if you like. They're in the cooler," he said, motioning in its direction.

"Thanks. I will."

Haakon grabbed another stick that had already been dedicated to this purpose and pressed on two hotdogs. Then he sat across from Brady and focused on keeping them propped at just the right distance from the flame.

"Back from your date with the little schoolgirl early?" he asked nonchalantly.

Haakon realized then that the rumor mill at work had gotten ahead of him. Brady could be a brutal mocker. Give him red meat and he would rip into it like a famished *Velociraptor*.

"Shut up. Judd told me she was eighteen!"

"What was it that made you realize she wasn't? The schoolgirl uniform?"

"Laugh it up, jackass," Haakon said, conveying his annoyance.

"What I hear is that Judd tried to talk you *out* of dating her… say'n she was just a kid."

"You're enjoying yourself, I see."

Haakon's hotdogs burned due to his inattentiveness.

"There was no date. I met her. We had an ice cream cone."

"From where I come from, that's considered a date."

"Well, if that counts as a date from where you come from, Brady, then you had better step up your game."

He smirked and nodded his head. Haakon pulled his flaming hotdogs out of the fire and blew at them frantically.

"Maybe I should have loaned you my truck. Little girls like big trucks."

Brady had recently pooled his earnings with his savings to purchase a used tangerine-colored Ford pickup truck. It had a topper mounted over its bed, so this became Brady's new home. He abandoned the tent and moved his sleeping bag and personal effects inside. The truck also gave him independence from Haakon, which in turn gave Haakon much needed independence from him.

"Well, if that's true, the fact you even know *that* is more than a little troubling to me. You're creep'n me out, Brady."

The two sparred back and forth for the better part of the evening. Brady was enjoying the hammer he had acquired to hit Haakon with. Had it not been for the forthcoming "Spokane incident," he would have pounded Haakon mercilessly with "little girl" comments for weeks. But unbeknownst to Haakon, his romantic fate was about to change dramatically.

"Hey, Romeo, I heard it didn't go well," Judd shouted out to Haakon when he arrived at work the next morning.

Haakon turned to him, irritated.

"Oh, it went well until she told me she was fifteen! Jeez, Judd!"

"That bothers you, huh? I was afraid it might. That's why I didn't tell ya."

"Huh?"

"I figured once ya got to know her, you'd get beyond that."

"Beyond fifteen? You want me to go to jail? Fifteen?"

"Almost sixteen, I'm pretty sure."

"Seriously?"

"That's hot stuff for fifteen, huh?"

"Jeez, Judd, that's really young."

"Four years difference. Big friggin deal!"

"Not a big deal if I was thirty and she was twenty-six, but I'm *not* thirty and she's *not* twenty-six. I'm nineteen and she's a minor… by a mile!"

"Hell, you're in northwest Montana, Hawk. Families start at fifteen around here."

"That doesn't make it right… or a good idea."

This exchange concluded Judd's matchmaking attempts and perhaps, more importantly, his role as Haakon's romantic advisor.

Haakon dropped into a funk on the following days as he was both embarrassed by his fifteen-year-old encounter and depressed by the lack of romantic prospects. But then Kingsley, of all people, inadvertently threw Haakon a lifeline.

"Hey Hawk, I need you and Brady to drive the flatbed up to Spokane to help my daughter, Audrey, move into her new apartment."

"Yeah sure. When?"

"Now. Brady's already at the shop. You guys should be able to run up there, help her, and be back by dinnertime. Sound all right?"

"Whatever you want, Boss," he answered, smiling.

Haakon enjoyed driving to Spokane. From time to time, Kingsley would send him there in the shop's flatbed Ford truck to pick up various supplies. It was a pleasant, scenic drive and Haakon found the small city of Spokane easy to navigate—even in a large vehicle.

Driving with Brady would be an experience in itself. When not hampered by hitchhiker etiquette, Brady could be a colorful receptacle of stories and opinions—though they were always laced with negativity and sarcasm and delivered dryly between spits of tobacco. For a shy guy, Brady could be surprisingly talkative. And, for someone whose life was arguably a mess ninety percent of the time, he often offered logical and thoughtful solutions to a wide range of quandaries.

"Have you been trolling the schoolyards recently?" he asked, as Haakon steered out of the Kingsley Construction parking lot.

Haakon responded with a glare.

"You're so easy to get goin'," Brady said, chuckling. "Actually, Judd told me he would like to do her *and* the mom. Almost did."

"That's troubling."

"That guy's different, if you ask me."

"We can agree on *that*," Haakon said. "But I wouldn't mention that to his face."

"Right. He's probably killed guys for less," Brady said. "I've heard some stories."

"I've heard the same stories."

The two would talk cordially for a time, but Brady would always return to his "little girl" ribs. They were getting old to Haakon and they made for a long two-hour drive. But eventually, they entered the outskirts of Spokane and Brady, thankfully, became distracted by the new environment.

Kingsley's carefully drawn map led them directly to his daughter's apartment building. She was standing outside of the entrance waving as they turned in. Carlos had already tipped Haakon off that she was an attractive woman. And, at first glance, Haakon had to agree. Judging by Brady's silence and blank expression, Haakon suspected he found her to be the same.

"Hi, I recognized the truck," she said to his open window, as they rolled to a stop. "I'm Audrey."

She reached out her hand and Haakon met it by extending his out the window.

"I'm Haakon. This is Brady."

Haakon motioned towards him and Brady gave her a casual forehead salute.

Audrey was more than attractive. Carlos had sold her short. She was a doll—literally, a full-size version of a pixie-cut, blonde Barbie doll. She even came accessorized with full-size Barbie clothes—a waist-drawn shirt and Capri pants. They did not look like work clothes, but they served her figure well. Haakon was immediately drawn to her piercing hazel-colored eyes. They had been artistically embellished with mascara. It was hard to look away from her face. He found himself staring and smiling. Fortunately, she smiled back.

"You have some things to move?" Haakon asked, already knowing the answer.

Studying her, he wondered how it was possible she was Kingsley's offspring.

"I *do* have some things to move," she answered. "Mainly furniture. I've already moved a lot of the small things to the new apartment."

"Well, we'll get it all done for you."

With that declaration, Haakon and Brady went about transferring her belongings from apartment to apartment. Her furniture was not particularly heavy, nor did she really have much of it. She was going from a one-bedroom apartment to another one-bedroom apartment—albeit a much nicer one with a balcony that overlooked the Spokane Valley.

The two strong young men moved the big items on the first load, then returned to move the smaller items and boxes with Audrey's help. Each time Haakon passed her on the stairs or in the hallway, they gave each other prolonged glances and smiles. Haakon sensed she was interested in him and this, in turn, fueled his predisposition of being attracted to her. Since they had conversed little, he concluded it to be a mutual physical attraction. Regardless of what it was, it felt good and Haakon did not want it to end. He wished that she had more items to move.

"Well, that's it, I guess," Haakon said with disappointment as he loaded the dolly back on the truck. "Maybe I'll see you down in Colterville some time."

"Yeah, I would like that," she replied. "And if you ever get up here, drop me a line. I'll show you around Spokane."

She handed Haakon a card.

"Here's my number. I mean it."

Haakon grasped it between two fingers then waved it near his forehead, as though it would help formulate his thoughts.

"I was planning on being in town this coming Saturday," Haakon said, trying to think fast.

This was a lie, but he was willing to make it true.

"Any chance you want to get together then?"

"Sure," Audrey answered, visibly pleased. "Let's make it a date."

So they did—agreeing on a time to meet at her new apartment.

"Well, that's something," Brady said as the two of them drove off. "Going from a little girl to an old lady, all in the same week."

Haakon grinned.

"Yeah… what? What do ya mean, old lady?"

"She's twenty-eight."

"How would you know?"

"Oh, I know. I know things," he answered, smugly.

"You just happened to check her age before we drove up here?"

"Carlos told me all about her," he answered.

"So why have you been holding out?"

"I didn't know she would have any interest in you. Didn't seem relevant."

"I really don't know if she is interested in me."

"Give me a break. Her eyes were all over you during the move. I thought I would have to leave to give you two some privacy. It was getting embarrassing."

Haakon chuckled, then veered the truck onto the freeway and sped up.

"Well, I didn't catch all that, but I don't claim to be the keen observer that you are," Haakon said, purposely trying to flatter Brady to keep him talking. "So tell me what you know."

"She's twenty-eight. Recently divorced. No kids. Just got a job here at an insurance company or something."

"Twenty-eight? She looks younger."

"Yeah, like you're such a great judge of age," he quipped. "Oh, that's right. You like them young."

Brady turned away from Haakon, but his side profile still displayed a smirk.

"Yeah. Her husband was a high school teacher," he continued. "I guess he hooked up with one of his students."

"He had an affair with a student?"

"That's what broke 'em up."

"Carlos told you this?"

"That's what he said."

"Wow. That's tough."

"Yeah, I'd say."

Haakon shook his head, questioning the validity of Brady's words.

"We don't know this. Your talk'n secondhand rumor."

"Hey, I'm just tell'n ya what I hear."

They both fell silent for several minutes. Haakon focused on driving while Brady stared straight ahead.

"Just think, you've spanned thirteen years between dates. That's impressive for a nineteen-year-old."

Haakon chuckled again at the thought.

"It sort of is, Brady. Wow. It's funny how things work out."

"She's nine years older than you, Hawk. I've got a feel'n that she's gonna be schooling you on some things."

Haakon glanced at him, perplexed. Yet he spent the better part of the return trip pondering Brady's statement.

The remainder of the workweek passed painfully slow. Kingsley came by the job site and thanked Haakon for helping move his daughter, even though he had paid him to do so. It surprised Haakon that he was aware of their upcoming meeting on Saturday. Kingsley even asked Haakon to deliver a few small items to his daughter.

"Did he offer you a promotion?" Judd asked me after Kingsley had left the job site. "Are you going to be our new boss?"

Haakon laughed.

"No. But he didn't fire me, so I take that as a good sign."

When one o'clock Saturday arrived, Haakon was standing at Audrey's apartment entrance intercom as they had planned.

"You are very punctual," she said, as she opened the glass lobby door smiling.

"I try to be. Actually, I have been in town for an hour or so. It's hard to time such a long drive down to the minute."

"You should have called and come by earlier."

"No. I didn't want to surprise you. I figured you had enough to do, being in a new apartment and all."

"You are quite the gentleman. I'm impressed."

"That's the impression that I'm going for, for sure," Haakon said, smiling back at her.

Audrey wore a light summer dress that highlighted her long, smooth legs and a broad rim hat to, presumably, shield her fair complexion from the sun. Her short hair, extending below her hat, seemed softer than air—her eyes even brighter than Haakon remembered. And she smelled of flowers.

"Are you still up for a tour of Spokane?"

"I've been dreaming about Spokane all week," Haakon replied.

In truth, he had been dreaming about her.

"Well, you've come to the right place. How about I drive since I know where to go?"

"That sounds good to me, Audrey. But do you think my Scout will be okay here in your lot? I only park it in safe spots. You know, some people get jealous when they see my ride."

Audrey laughed. The fact that she picked up on his sarcasm, he thought, was encouraging.

"I'm jealous myself. All I have is a boring little Japanese car—nothing like your car."

"Oh, mine's no mere car. That's an all-terrain Scout. Big difference," Haakon said, trying to look serious.

"By the looks of it, and I mean this in the most respectful way, your Scout has some stories to tell."

"Yes, it's like an old warhorse. It's seen some things that a vehicle should never have to see. And it's a little out of its element here in the "big city" with all your fancy paved roads and all. You driving is probably a good thing."

So, with Audrey behind the wheel of her Honda sedan, they drove first to nearby Riverfront Park. Two years prior, this had been the site of the World's Fair.

"Can you believe that a few years ago this was an ugly, dingy, tangle of railroad tracks and rundown warehouses?" Audrey asked as they strolled along the Spokane River's edge.

"No, I can't. So they cleaned this all up for the Expo '74?"

"They did, after a lot of money, arguing, and hard work. But now this park is its legacy. I come here a lot."

"How long have you lived in Spokane?"

"Only a year. I used to live in Seattle," she answered. "I was married there."

"Oh," Haakon responded, as though he did not know. "You are not married here?"

"No. My husband was a high school teacher. He ran off with one of his students after she graduated. I guess I wasn't young enough for him."

"I'm sorry. He must be an idiot," Haakon said, thinking maybe he should not have.

"Yeah. *I* think so," she said, smiling shyly as she looked down.

"You're a beautiful woman, Audrey, and the more I talk to you, I realize that you are a beautiful person as well."

Haakon wondered if he had spoken too boldly as she seemed to hesitate with her response.

"Wow," she exclaimed, while looking down again.

He suspected she was on the verge of crying.

"Making you sad is the last thing I wanted to do."

"No, no. I'm not sad," Audrey replied, glimpsing in Haakon's direction. "That was such a nice thing to say."

"I'm just saying what I'm seeing. I'm sorry you had to experience that. It must have been hard."

"It was… and kind of crushing to the ego," Audrey replied, while turned towards Haakon. "I've gotten over it. Life goes on."

But Haakon sensed she had not gotten over it.

After the park, they drove to the top of Mount Spokane, a distinct peak that overlooked the city and the farmlands and seas of yellow-flowered meadows that surrounded it. From its 5,900-foot summit, they could even see into parts of nearby Idaho.

"This is beautiful up here, Audrey. Thanks for bringing me."

"I've enjoyed it. I like your company," she replied.

Haakon turned away from the mountain's view to face Audrey.

"Likewise," he said. "I've enjoyed talking with you, getting to know you."

They had talked nonstop since leaving Spokane, finding conversation easy. She told him her story and he told her his—the chain of events that led them to being together on an eastern Washington mountaintop.

"How long have you got here today," she asked.

"I have no schedule. I guess until you get sick of being my tour guide."

She laughed nervously.

"Well, if you're not in a hurry to get back, we could do something in town this evening—listen to music, go see a movie."

"I'm game for anything, Audrey."

"I've been wanting to see the remake of *A Star Is Born*. Any interest in that?"

"Sure. Is that some science fiction thing?"

Audrey laughed again.

"Are you serious? I guess you don't follow romance movies."

"No," Haakon said, smiling. "But I like science fiction. This is the movie where the giant star explodes, right?"

"No. There's no exploding star. This is a romance story with Barbara Streisand and Kris Kristofferson."

"I'm sure that's just as good."

"Men," Audrey said, shaking her head.

"I'm joking. I've heard of it. I'm not entirely a caveman. I *love* romance stories with Barbara Streisand and Kris Kristofferson."

"Now you're being a wise guy."

"I guess I am. But, no, seriously, I've heard its good. Let's go see it."

"Really?"

"Absolutely. I wouldn't miss it… even if it doesn't have an exploding star."

"Well, with that endorsement. How can we miss?"

"It looks like a beautiful evening coming. Do you have a favorite outdoor place where we can go to dinner before the movie?" Haakon asked.

"I do. I know just the place with a deck."

Haakon smiled at Audrey and she smiled back. Both stood staring at each other for a long moment.

They say there is a gravitational pull between any two objects. If you know the mass of each, you can determine the force. But in that moment, when the sun was making the smooth features of her face glow, Haakon did not need any equation to measure the attraction. He leaned towards her, hoping she would respond in kind. She did, and they kissed briefly. Then each retracted, slowly. Haakon was feeling embarrassed.

"I hope that was okay," he said.

She beamed.

"Yeah, it was okay."

Their afternoon tour evolved into a casual dinner at an outdoor cafe. It was perfect—the garden setting, the soft music, the mild weather, the low lighting, and, of course, the attractive company. They talked without a break, as though a reunion of longtime friends. Occasionally, they took each other's hand across the table. It seemed a subtle gesture of intimacy.

After the movie, they emerged into the cooling, dry air. It was dark now. Audrey shivered and Haakon put his arm around her as they walked towards the parking lot. She seemed receptive.

"I wish I had my jacket for you," he said. "Kris Kristofferson would have had a jacket for Barbara."

"This works," she said, looking up into Haakon's face smiling.

Haakon spent the following two weekends with Audrey in Spokane. Their romantic engine continued to roar along unfettered. By the third weekend, she announced she would come to Renfro for the 4th of July. It was the much-anticipated Bicentennial—the nation's 200th anniversary—and her parents were having a picnic at their home. They invited Haakon to attend.

"Don't worry about it, Hawk," Carlos said, trying to reassure him. "If Kingsley didn't like you, he wouldn't have invited you. In fact, he probably would have fired you by now. It's that simple."

"But that's gotta bug him, that someone as young as me, and an employee, is dating his daughter."

"What can he say? She's a grown woman. He knows this. Don't worry about it."

Carlos knew Kingsley well, and his words calmed Haakon.

But then he added, "If I were you, I'd be more concerned about Kingsley's son, Darrell. He'll give you a hard time. He likes to razz people."

"Oh great. I was just starting to get comfortable with this family picnic thing."

"Ah, don't worry about it. Just give'm shit back. He can take it. He's a good guy," Carlos said, trying to retract his words. "Besides, he and Kingsley are always fighting. This will give you cover."

His words shook Haakon's confidence again.

"I don't know what I've got myself into."

"Look at it this way. Play your cards right and this will be your construction company," Carlos said, laughing at his own joke.

Haakon gave him a bewildered look, and this prompted Carlos to stop.

"Hey, I just remembered," Carlos blurted excitedly. "I've got Holland Peak Lookout rented for the night of the 4th. I reserved it a year ago, but Lucy tells me that we've gotta go to her parents on account of her sister being in town."

"Holland Peak Lookout. Seems like I've heard of that," Haakon said.

"It's an old retired Forest Service fire-watch cabin they rent out for camping now. It's on the top of a mountain. It's very cool—incredible views! It would be a fantastic place to watch the fireworks. And a romantic place too. You and Audrey can have it for the night if you want it. It won't cost you a thing."

"That sounds great. That's a kind offer, Carlos. Let me check with

Audrey to see if she's interested."

Judd had been quietly working in the corner, listening to the conversation. When Carlos left the room, he beckoned Haakon over with a sideways head motion.

"So you're gonna take the boss's daughter up to a mountaintop and shag her," he stated, chuckling. "And you think *I* live dangerously pleasuring married women?"

"I wouldn't have worded it quite that way," Haakon replied.

"You wouldn't, but the boss will. I gotta hand it to ya, you've got balls, man."

"Do you think I'm making a big mistake here?"

"Nah! I'm just given ya shit. Truth is I'm jealous. She's a fox, but I doubt if she's my type."

"I thought all the women wanted you, Judd."

"You'd think, but no, there's a few out there that don't buy into my charm and good looks. I think she may be one. She's never given me the time of day."

"Well, I'm just lucky I guess."

"I'd say. And soon you'll probably be my boss, so I better watch what I say around you."

"Yeah, either that or I'll be in the unemployment line."

"She's a fine look'n lady. I had you figured wrong, Hawk. When you blew off Kim, I doubted you."

Judd grinned at Haakon while rotating the toothpick in his mouth.

"But you're quite the operator, as it happens. Ya work under the radar. I like that. I could probably learn some things from *you*."

Haakon laughed.

"I don't think so."

"Yeah. You don't just go for the girl. You go for the entire empire. Very Machiavellian."

"Maka what?"

"Don't they have schools in Minnesota?"

"Yeah, but I only went through the fifth grade. I didn't want to pass up my father."

They both laughed.

"Here I am, banging the common town girls while you're hold'n back, hold'n your cards, look'n at the big picture. You zero in on the princess. You're a regular frick'n strategist, Hawk—a real schemer. I had underestimated you."

"I assure you, there's no scheming here, just dumb luck… or maybe not. We'll see if I have a job at the end of all of this."

Judd would have nothing of Haakon's explanation. He and everyone else on the job were having too much fun at Haakon's expense. Dating the boss's daughter put a giant target on his back, so he had to endure a lot of incoming flack. This did not really bother Haakon, as he knew it was all in good fun. But he lived with fear that Kingsley would walk onto the construction site unexpectedly while something disparaging was being said about his daughter.

Audrey, to Haakon's surprise, was enthusiastic about the Holland Peak opportunity. He never envisioned her as a camping girl. And, as it turned out, she was not, but she wanted to try it. So, with her strong endorsement, they proceeded with a plan to drive up to the mountaintop after her parent's 4th of July picnic.

"Hi, I'm Haakon," he said, introducing himself to Audrey's mother as she opened the door.

Haakon had never met Kingsley's wife, nor had he been inside their house.

"Welcome. Happy 4th! Happy Bicentennial! I'm Lillian."

The Williams house was an oddity in Renfro and the subject of much ridicule. It was new and spacious—occupying two lots. And, though it was not garish, it appeared as such when surrounded by the considerably older, smaller, and weathered homes. Haakon had heard rumors that the locals resented the "fancy house" and "the Californians" for building it. They considered it showy—Kingsley's brick and wood declaration that he was better than they were. Admittedly, Haakon himself wondered what could have possessed Kingsley to build it where he did. There were many beautiful homes throughout the valley, but none of them, except his, was built in the middle of the rundown town.

Haakon was happy to see Audrey appear behind her mother.

"Hi!" she said, as she leaned past her mother to give him a kiss.

This surprised and embarrassed Haakon. Yet her mother seemed to think nothing of it. Still, he was relieved Kingsley was not a witness.

"Come on into the kitchen. Dad's in there," Audrey said, as she guided Haakon to the next room.

Kingsley was standing, watching a small, countertop black & white TV with a beer in his hand. He had a look of resignation.

"Hey Hawk. Happy 4th," he said, barely glancing up from the TV.

"Hi. Thank you for having me."

"Look at all this bullshit out east," Kingsley said, pointing at the TV screen with his bottle. "200th anniversary so they figure they can spend all the taxpayer money they want on their celebrations."

Though cordial, Kingsley was not wearing his jovial persona. Something seemed to be bothering Kingsley and Haakon hoped that the "something" was not him.

"Haakon and I are going camping on Holland Peak tonight," Audrey proudly announced.

What Haakon's paranoid ears heard, was, "Hey Dad, Haakon is going to bed me on a mountaintop tonight."

"Really?" Kingsley responded.

Haakon wished that Audrey had not brought this up right away. It risked an awkwardness overload. He was hoping Kingsley would have the opportunity to ease into this young-employee-dating-his-older-daughter situation.

Haakon fumbled for words, and when they came, he delivered them rapidly.

"Ah, I got the reservation from Carlos. He and Lucy had made the reservation months ago, but just found out that they couldn't go. So he handed them to me. I guess they're really hard to come by."

"That's what I hear," said Kingsley. "I've never been up there, but it's supposed to have a spectacular view. It's a small lookout. Only sleeps two."

Then his face seemed to register the words he had just said. Wanting to avoid an uncomfortable silence, Haakon continued explaining.

"Carlos says we'll be able to see fireworks in all directions from up there."

"I'll bet," Kingsley responded.

Then he took a long swig from his bottle.

"Do we need anything for up there?" Audrey asked.

"No, I've got all the camping stuff packed in the Scout already. A camp stove, utensils, food for dinner and breakfast, and two sleeping bags."

Haakon made sure that he emphasized the word "two," but Kingsley probably knew that two sleeping bags could be easily zipped together into one *big* sleeping bag.

As he monitored Kingsley's expressions, Haakon wondered if he should have asked her parents for permission to take her camping. This is how odd the conversation felt to him.

Thankfully, Audrey cut in.

"Hey, come outside and meet my brother and this family."

Welcoming the escape, Haakon dutifully followed her out the sliding glass door onto the patio. Kingsley's backyard was green and manicured as though it was in a suburban development. It had flowers and trimmed shrubs and lush, thick grass. Fortunately, a tall stockade fence surrounded it all, blocking out the shabby neighboring homes and their desolate, dry yards. Two small children were kicking a utility ball back and forth on the lawn while two adults sat under the shade of a large umbrella watching them.

"Haakon, this is my brother Darrell and his wife, Barbara," Audrey said as they came alongside where they sat.

Darrell was the spitting image of Kingsley, but larger and with a full head of hair. It surprised Haakon to see him wearing a long sleeve plaid shirt and long pants with suspenders, as though he had just walked out of the woods with a chainsaw. Everyone else was dressed in short sleeves and shorts.

"Hi," Haakon said, extending his hand to each of them.

"Hi. Haakon?" Darrell asked.

"Just call me Hawk," Haakon said, avoiding the explanation of his name.

"Was that you that pulled up in the puke-green bomb?"

"Darrell!" Audrey exclaimed.

Haakon laughed.

"That's okay. I've known it's a bomb for some time… though hearing it said out loud does kind of hurt," Haakon replied.

Darrell chuckled.

"I had you mistaken for one of those Forest Service Smokey Bear guys. I'd paint that another color if I were you. You're apt to get shot," Darrell said.

"As you are learning, Haakon, my brother is very shy," Audrey responded.

"I'm just mess'n with ya. I know you work for the old man," Darrell continued. "That's gotta be a treat."

"I do—for the summer, anyway. I enjoy it. I'll be going back to college this fall."

Haakon felt the need to clarify that being a construction laborer was not his life's aspiration.

"From Minnesota, I hear."

"Ya, you betcha," Haakon replied in stereotypical Minnesota-speak.

Non-Minnesotans often seemed amused at Scandinavian heritage self-mockery.

"There's lots of Minnesotans around here," he said. "They all seem to get a pass. But if you're from California like us, the grief you get is endless. If there's something wrong, it's *our* fault. Blame *us*."

"Yeah, I've picked up on that. Sorry," Haakon said, smiling.

"So, you're date'n my little sister. You seem young. How old are you?"

Haakon suspected the lineup of empty beer bottles in front of Darrell played a role in his lack of timidity.

"Nineteen," Haakon responded matter-of-factly.

Darrell raised his eyebrows, so Haakon felt a need to elaborate.

"Well, actually, nineteen and a half."

Darrell burst out laughing.

"You're alright, Hawk. But don't get a big head. Reed, her 'ex,' set the bar pretty low."

Haakon chuckled along with Darrell and Barbara politely, though Audrey appeared displeased. She handed Haakon a bottle of beer and he tipped it towards Darrell.

"Well, I'll take that as a compliment, anyway. Thanks," Haakon said.

Kingsley and Lillian came outside to join them with chips and dip in hand.

"Yeah, Reed was a real doozy," Kingsley added.

"Hey, Hawk and I are going up to camp at Holland Peak Lookout tonight. Have you ever been up there, Darrell?" Audrey asked, evidently wanting to change the subject.

"No. I have not. But I've heard great things about it," Darrell answered.

Then he turned to look up at Haakon.

"So you're going to sleep with my sister on the mountaintop tonight?"

"Darrell! Enough beer for you," his wife exclaimed, nervously laughing. "You're cut off."

"What? No!" Haakon responded, startled. "We are going camping."

Darrell caught Haakon flatfooted and he did not know how else to respond.

"Yeah, he said that they have two sleeping bags," Kingsley added, holding up a hand with two extended fingers.

Then Kingsley took another long swig of beer.

"Oh. Two huh," Darrell said, smiling. "I apologize for jumping to conclusions."

Darrell rolled his eyes in jest.

Audrey gave Haakon an "I am sorry" glance, then made another attempt at changing the course of the conversation.

"So what's the latest on the new bowling alley, Dad?"

"Well, we think that its gonna go. I'm waiting on approval from the county," Kingsley answered.

"You're building a bowling alley?" Haakon asked, surprised.

"Yep. We hope to start digging in September."

"Wow. That's exciting. That should be a big deal in Colterville," Haakon said.

"Well, we hope so. We'll be buying the current one, but it's too old and too small. This one will have twelve lanes. If it goes well, Lillian and I plan to run it and let you guys run Kingsley Construction."

Haakon was accustomed to Kingsley talking like this—including Haakon in the "you guys running the company." He frequently vocalized his vision of an employee-run contracting business, as though it would shore up worker morale. But no one gave it much credence. Even his son seemed skeptical.

"You're gonna have Carlos and Judd run'n your contracting business? Good luck with that," Darrell quipped.

"Well, it would have been yours to run if you had wanted it," Kingsley responded.

"I don't see that work'n, Kingsley."

Haakon was surprised Darrell referred to his father by his first name.

"It's a golden opportunity that you're foregoing. But it's a free country, I guess," Kingsley said, in a sarcastic tone. "That's what we're celebrating today after all."

"Hallelujah! I'll drink to that," Darrell said, raising his beer bottle in the air before taking a long swig.

Kingsley turned to Haakon.

"Darrell gave up a chance to run the business."

"We didn't exactly get along so well, working together," Darrell responded. "I'm just a realist."

It was easy to read the tension between them. And even though Haakon was an uncomfortable and unwilling spectator of it, he appreciated not being the focus of conversation anymore. Indeed, that pretty much summed up the entire afternoon—cordial but uncomfortable. Haakon was relieved when their predetermined departure time finally arrived.

"Have a good time up there," Darrell said as Audrey and Haakon began to leave. "I don't know if it occurred to you, but if you get cold, you can zip those two sleeping bags together. Just a thought."

Kingsley stared down at his beer bottle on the table. Darrell grinned broadly.

As they drove away from the house, Audrey leaned over and gave Haakon a kiss on the cheek.

"Was it that bad?" she asked.

"No. You have a great family. I enjoyed it," Haakon said, mostly lying.

Holland Peak was close to Renfro "as the crow flies." On a clear day, you could easily see the silhouette of its fire lookout. But the gravel road up to it was long and slow, traversing back and forth as it gradually climbed. Once they started up from the mountain's base, they lost sight of the lookout until the road's last stretch. Then it appeared straight above. At this point, the road became steep and the corners tight. Even with the stubby Scout, Haakon could not navigate the final switchbacks in one sweep. Instead, he had to first nose the Scout into the curve, then cut the wheel as he reversed precariously close to the road's cliff-side edge before proceeding forward again, but now at a reduced turning angle.

"This is scary," exclaimed Audrey. "I hope that your brakes are good."

"They are," Haakon replied, as he nervously maneuvered. "But ya gotta pump them a little."

When he glanced at Audrey, her face wore a horrified expression.

"I'm just kidding," Haakon said, relieved that he was back into first gear and slowly climbing away from the sharp turn.

To compound the steepness, the road also became rough with jagged rocks protruding from its surface.

"How are your tires?" Audrey asked, recognizing Haakon's concern as the Scout inched upward.

"Not great, to be honest," Haakon replied. "But I've got a spare."

"Good. I'd hate to have to walk home."

"But I don't have a jack," he added.

"You're joking, right?"

Haakon replied with another smile.

Luckily, the brakes and tires held. They arrived unscathed and parked next to the small lookout building.

"Wow," Audrey exclaimed as she stepped out of the Scout. "I feel like I'm on top of the world."

The sight amazed Haakon as well. Pivoting slowly around, he saw nothing but rugged mountainous terrain in all directions. Long shadows cast by the low sun made the ridges appear as giant waves in a vast, turbulent, green ocean. Standing on the highest peak, they had the view of lighthouse keepers.

"This is like that scene from *The Sound of Music*," Audrey said.

"It is, but fortunately without those pesky Nazis chasing us," Haakon responded. "I hate being chased by Nazis!"

"You're a silly guy, Haakon."

"Yeah, I get that a lot."

A wisp of cool air reminded them that daylight was waning,

so they went about unloading their supplies and setting things up inside the lookout. It was actually a small rustic cabin with a window-surrounded loft. You could access the loft by climbing a ladder, but since its windows were so old and dirty and nearly opaque, they saw no point in it. Instead, they focused their attentions on the cozy living quarters. This included a sink without running water, a small counter, a tiny table with two chairs, and two canvas cots.

"This will be fun. I haven't camped since I was a kid," she said, studying the sparse room.

Her skeptical face did not match her words.

"Well, staying in this cabin isn't really camping, but it's close enough," Haakon replied. "It's not exactly the Ritz, but I think we'll really appreciate its walls this evening. I've got a feeling that it can get pretty cold up here, even on the 4th of July."

They made a simple dinner on a camp stove, then sat on a large, flat boulder facing the setting sun while eating it, marveling at how good it tasted—eventually concluding that food, even simple food, just inexplicably tasted better when camping. Next, they cleaned up and prepared the cots and sleeping bags. Both wanted everything ready before nightfall and cold descended on them.

The fireworks did not begin until eleven o'clock. At northwest Montana's latitude, it took the summer sunlight that long to extinguish enough to provide an adequately dark backdrop. And, as advertised, the mountaintop *was* the ideal fireworks viewing perch. Not only could they watch the Colterville display, but they could view countless private firework shows distributed throughout the area.

Huddled in a blanket, Haakon and Audrey observed the show with the fascination of children—oddly looking down on the exploding colors as opposed to the more familiar pose of straining their necks upward. As though synchronized, a blast of cold wind coincided with the show's grand finale. They watched the flood of hues in awe while shivering and holding each other tightly. When the show abruptly ended, the two wasted no time in retreating inside the walls of the lookout.

That night on the mountaintop was, metaphorically, the height of their relationship. From the onset, Haakon was aware his time with Audrey would be short-lived. It was a subconscious feeling, bolstered by the distance between them, both in physical miles and in age. He believed she knew this too. They went into it willingly for their own respective needs. So Haakon was not surprised or saddened or regretful when it ended. Left unattended, their campfire faded. Once they were sufficiently warmed, they mutually allowed it to die out.

After the 4th of July, Audrey and Haakon's phone exchanges lessened and then finally stopped. A few weeks later, Haakon learned from Carlos that Audrey was back together with her ex-husband. Haakon hoped that this was a good thing.

8
ONCE UPON A ROOFTOP

By early August, northwest Montana was hot and dry. The surrounding woodlands were a tinderbox awaiting a devastating blast from a lightning bolt or a faint spark from a passing train. Either would have set the brittle world ablaze. The mornings started warm and by noon the sun seared exposed skin. Gravel roads were so parched that even slow drives lifted the fine glacial silt into high trailing tails of dust. And, fast drives created thick, bellowing clouds that resembled the exhaust gases of powerful rocket engines. The weatherman said the Dog Days had returned and that Sirius, the Dog Star, was back in the predawn sky.

Since his time with Audrey, Haakon had entered a dry spell himself. This was a tough plight for a young testosterone-charged male. The scarcity of female companionship combined with the heat made the days feel like weeks, and weeks like months. Haakon had finally given up on the lumberyard girl. She had "her guy" and despite Haakon's charm offensive, she exhibited no discernible interest. Continued efforts, he thought, were futile and likely bordering on pathetic. So, by the time Sirius arrived, the deprivation of love was taking hold of his psyche. And, as prophesied by the early Greeks, he could feel the Dog Days bringing on his own mental wilting and weakness.

Haakon's thoughts turned to summer's end and the return to school and, if extrapolated honestly, his return to female companionship opportunities. He had lost all hope for romance. There no longer seemed to be any available or interested women within his sphere. Renfro and Colterville were feeling small and confining. The allure of the Northwest that had rolled over him like a great tsunami in the spring, was now ebbing. Haakon was growing lonely and despondent.

To treat his melancholy, he made long, solitary, destination-less evening drives into the mountains. He would follow primitive Forest Service roads to see where they would take him. When he came upon a scenic overlook, he would usually stop to observe the world below and beyond. Breathing in the splendor, Haakon would yearn for more.

Ironically, August cued everyone in the building trades that summer was waning. Even though it was the hottest time of the year, builders and customers of builders looked nervously at their calendars. Since construction projects were invariably behind schedule, the customers began to panic. They feared the arrival of winter before the completion of their house or garage or family room addition or auto parts store. When they panicked, they would phone the contractor. These conversations would not be pleasant. Many would call Kingsley every name in the book. He, in turn, would keep his cool and make them promises he knew he could not fulfill. Then, after he hung up, the customers he spoke so highly of in the spring, he would now refer to as "jerks, sons of bitches, and assholes." It was a tense season to be a building contractor. And some of that tenseness rained down on his employees.

Reacting to pressure, Kingsley frantically sent his workers to whichever project needed them the most on a particular day. When needed everywhere, as they were by August, he would send his workers to the project that screamed the loudest, called him the worst names, or threatened him with an attorney—propagating the "squeaky wheel gets the grease" principle.

"Try to make a lot of people at least a little happy," was his adopted maxim.

So, throughout early August, Haakon and Brady bounced from

job site to job site, rarely for durations exceeding three days. Kingsley considered them moveable muscle. While they did not have the skill set of his experienced tradesmen—carpenters, plumbers, excavators, and electricians—they had the brawn to help the various tradesmen move along faster. Plus, their presence gave customers the reassurance that Kingsley was finally hearing them, at least for a day.

Since the beginning of the month, the two Minnesotans had packed, stacked, and assembled long, heavy logs for another pre-cut log home, insulated an oppressively hot pole building attic, set foundation forms for what would be a county vehicle repair shop, carried countless sheets of plywood up two flights of stairs and then nailed them down on top of joists to form a subfloor, and had hung what seemed like miles of ductwork from the high ceiling of a future auto parts store. The latter was a dream job because it took place in the shaded coolness of a concrete building set into a hill. Haakon was hoping to serve out his workweek in that relative comfort, but then Kingsley showed up with alternative plans for his labor chessboard.

"Hawk, you keep helping Sig finish up this duct work. Brady, I need to send you out to help wrap up a cedar shake roof. It's a few miles out of town," Kingsley instructed.

He handed Brady a sheet of paper with a crude map drawn on it and then abruptly left.

"You lucky bastard!" Brady said, while giving Haakon a dirty look.

"I just do what the boss says," Haakon replied. "If he wants me to stay cool and comfortable and for you to sizzle in the sun, what am I to do?"

Brady stomped off towards the exit door, carrying his tool belt. Just as he reached for the handle, it swung open and Kingsley's head popped back inside the store.

"Second thought, Hawk, why don't you go with Brady. I really need that roof knocked out today."

Kingsley's head disappeared as quickly as it had appeared. Brady stood next to the door, smiling at Haakon like the Cheshire Cat.

"Looks like we'll be sizzling together," he quipped, supporting the adage that "misery loves company."

Indignant, Haakon marched out the door into the heat.

Brady enjoyed pretending that his tall 4-wheel drive pickup truck

was a sports car. He charged down curvy, gravel roads with little regard
for its high center of balance. Haakon was accustomed to bracing
himself against the passenger door with his arm locked over the open
window. A high dust trail followed them as they ascended the hills
behind Colterville. Neither spoke. Haakon was still peeved that he
was going with Brady, so he just stared out at the passing scenery and
daydreamed about the much-anticipated end of summer.

Haakon and Brady had no experience installing cedar shake roofs.
Like many other tasks that summer, they would learn on the job. If it
were not for the oppressive heat, the task would have suited Haakon
just fine as he loved the smell of freshly split cedar. His enthusiasm,
however, was tempered when they turned into the driveway, bringing
the construction site into full view. The roof was an A-frame, high off
of the ground. It was so steep, Haakon could see that it required roof
jacks to hold the workers and materials from sliding off into the jagged
rocks and rubble below. Haakon did not care for heights in normal
conditions, but this appeared to be a particularly worrisome working
scenario. And, to make it more so, the rooftop was fully exposed to the
intense rays of the blazing August sun.

The house was being built for a recently retired Navy captain and
his wife. Like Lady Jane, the two of them lived in a large camping trailer
next to the building site so they could monitor its progress. When
work fell behind schedule, the captain voiced his concern to Kingsley.
Haakon and Brady's arrival on the job site directly resulted from that,
reportedly, "heated" conversation.

"I see that Kingsley has sent me his top guns," the captain said,
smiling as he met them in the parking area.

The captain had been waiting as they rolled in.

"Now I can get this job done."

Captain Hedquist was a tall, lean man with short gray hair and a
mustache. Other than in a movie or on television, Haakon had never
seen a navy captain before. But even without his uniform, he had "a
presence," an air of leadership—someone who, Haakon suspected, was
both unflappable and esteemed. He could picture the captain at a ship's
helm in a stormy sea.

"We'll give it our best, sir," Haakon said, feeling compelled to
address him as though in the Navy.

"I'm sure you boys will. I'm Robert Hedquist. Call me Bob. I'll introduce you to my wife, Rita, later and you'll probably run into Kari, my daughter, on the roof."

Haakon and Brady introduced themselves, then made their way inside the house to find Landon. He quickly gave them work instructions and within minutes both were hoisting bundles of aromatic red cedar shakes up to the top planks of scaffolding. Once they were all stacked, Haakon climbed onto the roof, bracing his boots against the springy 2x10 that spanned between the roof jacks. This standing position felt precarious to Haakon, as he knew each roof jack was secured in place by only three 16-penny nails that were, hopefully, squarely embedded into their respective underlying trusses.

Brady hoisted the shakes up to Haakon and he warily distributed them across the roof's surface above the current shake line. After Haakon placed the bundles, Brady handed up a large worm-drive circular saw. It was connected to what seemed to be a never-ending power extension cord, draping down to the ground far below.

"Could you have found a heavier Skilsaw?" Haakon said, quite surprised by its size and weight.

"Hey, it's what they had," Brady answered. "I just do what I'm told. Don't be a pussy."

Haakon shook his head, then pulled up the saw. Its long dangling cord made it heavier.

Tarpaper felt covered portions of the roof that was awaiting cedar shakes. Its blackness absorbed the sun's heat, making the roof even more uncomfortable. Haakon was sweating profusely as he climbed the steep grade, dragging along the circular saw, all the time thinking he should have stayed in Minnesota until he had found some cushy job in an air-conditioned department store. Or maybe he should have financed summer school so he could have sat in some climate-controlled classroom. Yet, even as his mind wandered, Haakon knew that his discontentment was more centered on his flailing love life than it was with his occupational discomfort.

Feeling sorry for himself, Haakon dragged the roofing materials upward towards the peak of the A-frame, wiping his sweating brow with nearly every other step. As he got closer, he could hear pounding on the other side. He surmised that this must have been the aforementioned "captain's daughter."

Haakon tried to envision a female who could do physically demanding work in such unpleasant conditions. His imagination did not flatter this person. He had expectations of bulging, "veiny," muscles, menacing tattoos, tobacco-stained teeth, and black leather—the kind of intemperate woman that might be seen leaning against a chopped Harley Davidson parked outside of a biker's bar. But, when his eyes finally breached the top edge of the roof, his expectations were abruptly flattened.

A few yards below him, down the steep pitch of the roof, was a goddess with an angelic face, auburn hair, long exposed legs, and freckled summer skin. Though looking up at Haakon, she was bent over her work just far enough for gravity to droop her elastic tank top, making her smooth tan breasts more visible than he would have dreamed possible.

Haakon froze in shock. A camera would likely have captured him as a cartoon character, with mouth aghast and detached eyes as large as saucers. It was as if an atom had split in front of him and his face was enduring its brilliant flash. Haakon's mind raced. Was this a mirage? Was the scorching sun inducing hallucinations? Was he like a lost soul crawling across the desert, so severely dehydrated that he was seeing illusions? Were deprived male hormones playing cruel tricks on his brain, maliciously mixing dreams with reality?

He became breathless as though his wind had been knocked out. Suddenly, feeling lightheaded and clumsy, Haakon staggered a bit and inadvertently released his grip on the circular saw. It dropped hard onto the plywood roof at his feet, then tumbled a few times before careening off of the A-frame's peak, down into the rocks below. Haakon heard it crash. Then he heard a screaming voice.

"What the hell! Are you trying to kill me?"

The distressed voice woke Haakon from his trance. He suddenly realized what he had done. But, hearing the voice reassured him he had not killed Brady.

Then the goddess spoke—she spoke to *him*, looking directly at Haakon with her bright blue eyes. Her words floated melodically through the air.

"Are you okay?"

"Yeah, I'm okay," Haakon answered, still staring at her. "I just dropped… something."

Haakon could hear Brady's yelling voice again.

"Nice work, Ace! You destroyed the saw!"

Haakon was not sure if the goddess could hear Brady or not, so he ignored him.

"Hi, I'm Haakon."

"Haakon. Like King Haakon?" she asked.

"Yeah," Haakon smiled, surprised. "Like King Haakon… but without the king."

He shook his head, perplexed.

"No one's ever gotten that."

"Norwegian grandfather," she said as an explanation, while looking resigned, "I've got all kinds of fun Norwegian facts drilled into my brain. But don't hold that against me."

She smiled and Haakon felt lightheaded again.

"I'm Kari."

Haakon decided in that moment that "Kari" was the most beautiful name he had ever known. They stared at each other until Kari broke the trance with more words.

"Do you think your friend is okay?"

"I don't know, I should check," Haakon answered, hesitant to turn away from her.

Straining to peer over the roof's edge, he saw Brady directly below, looking up. In Brady's two hands were several large pieces of what had previously been a perfectly operational circular saw. He held them up towards Haakon.

"Hey, Sir Edmund Hillary Haakon. Hello! Look what you did. Nice work! Kingsley will love this."

By now, Kari was curious about what was transpiring. She shuffled across her side of the roof so she could look down over its edge for herself. When Brady saw her face, he appeared as shocked as Haakon had felt.

"Hi," Brady said bashfully, staring up at her.

"Oh God, did you guys drop that?" she asked.

Brady, putting two and two together, quickly calculated what had just transpired.

"Us guys?" Brady retorted. "*Us* guys?" now said with more sarcasm. "No, *us* guys did not drop it. *That* guy," he said, pointing an accusatory finger up at Haakon. "*That* guy dropped it."

Haakon glanced over at Kari. She seemed puzzled by the conversation.

"I was just standing down here minding my own business, thinking I should have worn a hardhat today, when this heavy projectile with jagged edges came crashing down next to me," Brady said, with a sober face. "I should have known better with "Haakon the Gazelle" working above me."

Then he pointed his finger towards Haakon again.

"This guy is scary!"

Kari turned towards Haakon again and laughed.

"It's true. I *can* be scary," Haakon admitted.

"And graceful as a gazelle too," Brady added.

Haakon shrugged.

"Some days are better than others. What can I say?"

"You can say sorry, Brady, for almost killing me."

"I *am* sorry, Brady. All jokes aside."

"Oh, that's all right. I can see that you had more pressing matters to attend to than my personal safety."

"I really am sorry, Brady."

"Good thing that you weren't hurt," Kari interjected while listening to their discourse. "Hi Brady, I'm Kari."

"Hi," Brady responded. "Nice to meet you."

Brady paused in thought for a moment, then said, "Little tip for you, Kari. Don't work below Haakon."

"Yeah, I was thinking that he looks like trouble," she said.

"I *am* a dangerous man. I confess," Haakon said, playing along.

"I'll keep that in mind," Kari said, trying to look serious now.

Haakon sensed that she was emitting an interest in him, though perhaps not to his level of interest in *her*. Young men involuntarily emit "interest" when in the presence of attractive women, so his interaction would likely have seemed normal to Kari. But to have it reciprocated from a beautiful woman was an all too infrequent occurrence to Haakon. Nevertheless, this sense of reciprocated interest, real or not, gave him a jolt of euphoria—and with it, an equal dose of insecurity.

In that moment, Haakon felt intense pressure to "not drop the ball"—not lose the opportunity. He needed time for his brain to process his unexpected good fortune. He needed a plan quickly. Luckily, Landon provided Haakon with a crucial timeout.

"What the hell! Who busted this?"

Haakon realized Landon had just encountered the mangled saw.

"Oh, I don't know," Brady answered innocently, while staring up at Haakon. "I was just standing here and it landed next to my head."

Then Landon looked up to see a beautiful young woman standing near Haakon on the rooftop.

"Oh," is all Landon said, sizing up the situation.

Landon smiled, said something to Brady, shook his head and then walked away. Brady followed, but then abruptly stopped in his tracks and turned back up towards Haakon.

"Hey Gazelle, if you're through throwing down expensive tools, we need your help unloading a bathtub."

Haakon turned to Kari.

"I guess I gotta go."

"I guess you do," she responded.

They both stared at each other for several long seconds. Then Haakon turned and made his way off of the roof, smiling all the way down.

He did not see Kari for the rest of the workday. Yet, he could hear her talking and hammering, as she was working nearby on the other side of the A-frame's roof with Landon. Haakon figured Landon must have had the foresight, in the interest of productivity, to keep them separated. Or, more likely, Landon wanted to work next to a beauty himself. Either way, Haakon was not threatened by Landon. In fact, he was relieved it was Landon and not him working with her. Now that Haakon was in an insecure state of mind, he was not eager to exhibit to Kari how little he knew about cedar shake roofs. He did not want to make a fool out of himself a second time.

Though out of sight, Kari was all Haakon could think of that afternoon. As he hammered down the rows of shakes, he was trying to formulate a suave way to ask her out on a date. He needed to run into her again before the end of the day, because he had no idea if Kingsley would assign him to the captain's job site again. He feared he would not. So, Haakon decided he would "accidentally" cross paths with her as she was coming off of the roof at four o'clock. He did not have the nerve to just walk up and ask her out. Haakon needed to prompt a conversation so he could work up to "the big question."

It was a good plan, except she did not come off of the roof at four o'clock. As Haakon stood below her side of the roof, she was nowhere to be seen. She had already left.

With a sunken heart, Haakon considered walking over to the Hedquist trailer and knocking on its door. But that would have required nerve he did not possess. Yet he could see his window of opportunity closing. Everyone was walking to their vehicles to leave, even Brady.

"Let's head," Brady said.

Haakon was about to ask Brady to "hold up a minute" while he tried to muster up some courage. But, just as he was opening his mouth, the captain walked around the corner of the house with a beach towel draped around his neck.

"We're gonna drive down to the river and jump in and cool off. You guys can join us if you want," the captain offered.

Kari and her mother appeared behind him, also carrying towels. Both were wearing swimsuits underneath long t-shirts.

Haakon looked over at Brady, wondering what his response would be.

"I've got softball practice that I gotta get to," Brady responded.

"Damn," Haakon thought to himself.

His disappointment must have shown on his face.

"If you want to join us, I can give you a ride into town afterwards," Kari said. "I live in town."

"There truly is a God!" Haakon exclaimed to himself, hoping he had not lipped out the words.

"Really?" Haakon responded somewhat matter-of-factly while resisting the urge to attempt a somersault. "Yeah. That would be great. Thanks."

Haakon turned to Brady.

"I guess I've got a ride, so I'll see ya later at the ballpark."

Brady smiled and nodded his head, as though to say, "You lucky bastard."

Then he climbed into his cab and drove off.

"Okay," the captain said. "Kari, can you grab Haakon a towel?"

She nodded and made her way back to the trailer. Then the captain turned to his wife.

"Rita, have you met Haakon?"

"I have. We met from a distance when he was up on the roof."

She held out her hand to Haakon anyway.

"Nice to meet you again, Mrs. Hedquist."

Her grasp was weak. Haakon sensed something was amiss with her.

Kari suddenly pounced back, smiling with another towel in hand as though she were a retriever.

"Do you mind sitting in the bed with Jeb?" the captain asked Haakon. "There's no room in the cab for all of us. It's not very far."

Jeb was the captain's German shepherd.

"Of course not, as long as Jeb doesn't mind."

"I'll ride in the back *with* you," Kari piped in.

The captain half-smiled, then got in the cab with Rita. Kari and Haakon climbed into the back of the pickup where Jeb was already waiting. The two of them sat facing each other behind the cab with Jeb in between. They smiled at each other shyly as the pickup slowly made its way down the driveway.

"Have you lived here long?" Haakon asked, trying to strike up a conversation.

"No, just moved here," she answered. "I had been going to school in Seattle."

She turned to see if the pickup truck's rear vent window was open. It was not. She leaned towards Haakon.

"My mother is ill. I wanted to be here with her, so I moved back and took a job in town at the bank."

"Oh. I'm sorry to hear that... I mean about your mother. I didn't know."

Thinking he should say something positive, Haakon added, "She *looks* good."

Kari nodded.

"Yeah, she looks good."

But her expression conveyed otherwise.

"What about you? What's your story?"

"Oh, not much of a story," Haakon said.

He gave a synopsis of where he was from and why he was in northwest Montana. He concluded with, "That's why I'm here sitting in the back of a pickup truck with you and your dog."

She smiled at his sarcasm.

"So, you're here for just the summer?" she asked.

"Yeah, the plan is to go back to school next month."

This news seemed to make her smile fade a bit.

"Are *you* going to stay here?" Haakon asked.

"I don't know. My mother is sicker than she appears. I don't really know my future right now."

Haakon nodded in response and wondered if he had inquired too much. Their conversation fell off.

Fortunately, only minutes of silence passed until the captain steered his pickup into a small gravel parking area overlooking a Cedar River tributary. When he came to a stop, Haakon quickly disembarked, then offered his hand to assist Kari. She accepted it for balance and smiled as she stepped over the tailgate and onto the bumper, then onto the ground. Haakon lowered the tailgate for the anxious dog as the captain glanced at him, smirked, then threw him a towel. Without a word, the captain and his wife proceeded down a trail with Jeb in tow. They seemed to know Kari would not follow.

"I'll show you a great diving spot," Kari said.

"I'm not much of a diver."

"Well, I'll show you a great jumping spot then," she said. "You can jump can't you?"

"Yeah, I think I can do *that*."

Haakon followed her down a path that led in the opposite direction from where her parents had gone—all the way thinking to himself how perfect this all was. Only hours before, he was lonely and romantically frustrated. Now, inexplicably, he was following the long, tan legs of a goddess down a wooded trail to a swimming spot.

Yet a chill of paranoia swept over him. Could this be a sadistic trap set by the captain? His mind wandered to the many "Farmer's Daughter" tales, where the farmer would put a traveling salesman up for the night and, concurrently, place him in an impossible situation with his alluring daughter. The farmer would tell the salesman to "make himself at home." But he would qualify his offer with: "I do have one rule and only one rule. Keep your hands off of my daughter!" Of course, this would be the one rule that was impossible for the traveling salesman to abide by in the presence of his daughter's flirtation and irresistible beauty.

Haakon wondered if he could be analogous to a traveling salesman. It all seemed too good to be true.

Kari and Haakon arrived at a rock outcrop that dropped about ten feet, nearly straight down into the river. While the oppressive heat made jumping into the water appear inviting, the cliff's height was *not* so inviting. Yet, Kari, undeterred, pulled off her t-shirt and Haakon, for the second time, stood staring at her slack-jawed. Her bright blue, two-piece swimsuit was more revealing than he could have hoped for. It exposed nearly all of her smooth, tan skin. Her body was slim and taut. He feared he was staring too long, too intensely. Could "the farmer" be watching him? Was this a test of his will? If it was, he failed. Haakon could not look away. Kari was live art—a curvy, bronzed sculpture of divine splendor. He was mesmerized.

Though she did not turn directly towards Haakon, he knew she could see him staring. He got the impression she took pleasure in torturing him. But if his reaction to her exhibit provided reassurance to her ego, then Haakon was more than happy to oblige. Yet he worried his stare was dangerously approaching inappropriateness.

Thankfully, she broke his spell by walking to the cliff's edge and, without hesitation, diving gracefully into the water below— disappearing under a ring of bubbles. Seconds later, her head popped up above the water's surface a few feet beyond. She let out a shriek, then flung her auburn hair from side to side, throwing glimmering streams of water in all directions.

"Woo, that's cold!" she yelled, facing in Haakon's direction. "Are you coming in or what?"

Haakon pulled his shirt off, emptied the pockets of his blue jean cutoffs, removed his boots and socks, then made his way to the rock edge. It was painful walking over the sharp gravel with his bare feet. He tried to conceal his discomfort, but he could hear Kari giggling from below. Pausing at the edge, Haakon realized the cliff was higher than he had expected. But there was no turning back now. He had to jump. His honor was at stake.

Yet, despite being inherently uneasy with heights, Haakon could have been compelled to do anything at that moment: walk on hot coals, wrestle a grizzly bear, jump out of an airplane—anything she asked. So, in blind faith of smitten-ness, Haakon walked off the edge into empty air. It was not an artful maneuver. He merely dropped feet first into the river.

Forgetting to plug his nose, Haakon did not recall what caused more discomfort—suddenly being immersed in the frigid temperature or having water forced up into his nostrils. But pain was of a secondary concern to him. The impression he made with Kari was paramount. When Haakon came to the surface, he swiveled around to find her. And, when he did, he felt no pain, only gratitude that the cold splash did not wake him up. This was real. *She* was real.

"Oh, that feels good!" Haakon exclaimed.

"You're not a good liar."

"Well, I bet it will feel good… eventually."

She smiled. They each slowly waved their arms below the surface to keep their heads afloat. Haakon could see her upper body through the clear water. Her submerged skin appeared milky and supple.

"You're quite a diver," Haakon said.

"I used to do a lot of it. With my dad in the Navy, we were stationed all over the place—usually near water or at least a pool. Swimming was my thing. I was even a lifeguard for a while."

Haakon envisioned her in a bright red swimsuit, sitting up high on a tall lifeguard chair, and him purposely struggling in the water in front of her.

"I've never been much of a swimmer, I guess. I don't even really know how to dive properly."

"I thought Minnesota had a million lakes or something like that. How could you not be a swimmer?"

"The lakes there are filled with weeds and leeches," Haakon said, exaggerating. "By this time of summer they look like pea soup with all the algae. Not real inviting."

"Leeches?"

"Yeah, vile creatures," Haakon continued. "A cross between a tiny snake and an octopus. You can't pull them off without taking some of your skin with it. Ya need to pour salt on them. Then they fall off."

She looked appalled, so he went on.

"That's not the worst of it. The bottom of the lakes are basically decayed weeds and leeches and stuff. When you step into it, you sink like you're in quicksand, but it feels like you are stepping into cold oatmeal. It's not a good feeling."

"Yuck! How do people live there?"

"Beats me. Why do ya think I'm here?" Haakon asked, smiling. "Oh, it's got some good lakes too, especially up north. But it's not Montana. Not by a mile."

"Should I teach you how to dive?"

Haakon visualized them on the cliff's edge with her grasping his arms and legs, trying to shape his posture for a proper dive. He liked that idea.

"Sure," he answered.

They smiled and exchanged long glances until Haakon spoke again.

"Don't expect much from me though. I've been called a big lug more than once."

"You can do it. I'm a good teacher," she said, as she slowly made her way towards shore.

"Okay, then I'll be a good student."

Along the steep riverbank there was an opening that provided a natural rock staircase back to the top of the diving perch. As Kari pulled herself out, Haakon purposely delayed so he could watch. Her lean, sun-soaked body glistened with beads of water. He was enamored with how her backside curves so perfectly filled what little swimsuit fabric there was. Did her father know her swimsuit was so skimpy? Haakon took a deep breath and tried to relax. As she pulled at her hair, she turned her head towards him and smiled again, reminding Haakon of a shampoo commercial where the gorgeous model played to the camera with her captivating backward gaze. Surely, Kari had to know she was killing him.

"Come on out, you can't learn to dive from there."

"I'm just starting to get used to the cold, but okay coach."

Once they were both atop the diving perch, she tried to explain her technique. Unfortunately to Haakon's expectations, Kari's instructions were all verbal and she never laid a hand on him. As a result, he did not learn much, despite giving it several earnest tries. On his last attempt, he unintentionally did a belly flop.

"Oh God, are you all right?" Kari asked, looking down at Haakon, horrified.

The misguided plunge must have been loud, like a giant beaver's tail slapping the water's surface. The pain was intense and Haakon could not answer right away.

"That had to hurt," a voice called out from a distance.

Haakon looked up and saw it was the captain. He and his wife were standing atop the hill.

"Oh, great!" Haakon thought to himself, "The entire family saw my swift move."

"I'll be all right... in a day or two," Haakon feebly answered, successfully conjuring up a laugh from all.

Kari came back down the rock staircase to help him out. She grabbed his arm and then put her arm around his waist, as though to provide some lift. Haakon was fine by then, but he feigned lingering distress as it was being positively reinforced.

"Thanks," Haakon said, turning and looking into her face.

This was the closest he had been to her. The clarity of her eyes and the delicate texture of her skin nearly overwhelmed him with a longing pain. Their glances locked for an instance and he felt compelled to kiss her, but they were still in full view of her parents.

"You gonna be able to get back up here or are we gonna have to medevac you out, son?" the captain asked, sarcastically—surely realizing Haakon was employing some self-serving theatrics.

Both Kari and Haakon broke into broad smiles, and she pulled away.

"I'm fine," Haakon said to the captain. "Probably only a rib... or two... or maybe three ... but I've got others, so I'll be fine."

This got another laugh from everyone, making Haakon feel good. The captain and his wife turned to make their way back to the pickup. Kari and Haakon grabbed their towels and shirts and followed suit. As they walked, Haakon wondered if she was thinking about their near kiss. *He* was. The silent ride back to her parent's house confirmed to Haakon that she was as well. They both seemed overcome by shyness.

After Kari changed clothes and hugged her parents goodbye, she and Haakon climbed into her small Japanese car and drove out the driveway, waving as they left. Along the way to Colterville, Kari and Haakon discussed everything from sports to world history, never lacking words or interest in hearing the other's words. What had been such a long, boring ride earlier in the day, was now disappointingly short. Haakon was sorry to see the ballpark come into view. It was bustling with the activity of ball players and spectators.

"Are you sure Brady is here," she asked as they rolled to a stop.

Haakon scanned the parking lot and easily identified Brady's tall tangerine pickup truck.

"Yup, look's like I'm good," he said, hesitantly.

"I really had fun. Thanks," she said.

Kari looked at Haakon expectantly, as though cueing him to "return the ball." He looked back at her, hoping he was reading her expression correctly.

"Me too," Haakon shyly responded.

Then he continued with words that were so simple, yet so hard to muster.

"Hey, I'm working tomorrow, Saturday, but I'm pretty sure my boss is going to send me to another job, so I won't likely be back to your parent's house."

He swallowed hard, then continued.

"Is there any chance you would want to go out to do something tomorrow night?"

After saying the words, Haakon felt as though he was standing on the edge of a cliff again. He wondered if, in the next moment, his ego would fly high above the cliff or be a crushed heap at its bottom.

"Sure," Kari answered quickly, as though having expected the question.

Haakon gulped and tried to maintain his composure even though he wanted to erupt in joy.

"Great. We could have dinner, then go to Moose's. They have a decent band there," he suggested.

"Yeah, that sounds good. What time?"

"How about six? I'll pick ya up."

"Sure. Okay."

Haakon nodded and smiled meekly as he exited her car.

"Oh… I guess I don't know where you live."

They both laughed nervously.

"Yeah, that would help."

She pivoted in her seat and pointed up the hill behind them.

"I'm right there in that green house. Do you see it?"

His eyes followed hers.

"I do. I'll see you there tomorrow at six… at the green house."

As Kari drove off, Haakon swallowed hard.

9
FLOWERS & FISTS

At six o'clock sharp, Haakon turned the Scout into Kari's driveway. If he was anything, he was punctual. But since he was not driving a showcase car capable of impressing anyone but the most ardent backwoodsman, he thought it best to step up his "second impression" visuals, hoping to erase whatever "first impression" damage the Scout might have collared him with. So, as Haakon approached Kari's door, he had flowers in hand. Better to risk being taken as old-fashioned and corny than to be seen as an indigent, he surmised—even though he knew that it was socially acceptable to be an indigent college student. Yet Haakon was leaving nothing to chance. If she had peeked through the blinds and been taken aback by his vehicle's appearance, the array of floral colors would surely soften her.

He was right. Just as his knuckles were about to fall against Kari's front door, she swung it open in anticipation. Haakon found himself face to face with her radiance again. In their short time together, he had already seen her in enticing hot weather working apparel and in her sparse godsend to swimsuits. Now she stood before him "all dolled up" and smelling of lilacs. Her auburn hair shone and her soft cheeks had a trace of makeup. Mascara subtly accentuated her vivid blue eyes, and a faint pastel rose hue shimmered on her lips. She wore a light-colored western styled shirt—with several buttons open at the neck, exposing a silver necklace atop her tan, freckled chest—and faded, fitted blue jeans accented with cowboy boots. She was a cowgirl of dreams.

Haakon felt a sudden ache in his stomach. It was the sensation of a young man confronting overpowering splendor and deep-seated internal desire. The hurt was real, yet he did not want it to pass—not as long as his heart could handle the load anyway.

"My, you sure know how to impress a girl," she said mockingly but with a smile.

He stared up at her from the bottom of the steps.

"Yeah, sweet ride, isn't it?"

She laughed.

"I think I meant the flowers."

"*Oh!*" Haakon said, purposely exaggerating his surprise as he looked down at his hand. "You mean *these* old things?"

He held the flowers up to her and she raised them to her face to breathe in their scent. Haakon wished he had a camera at that moment, though no mortal photograph could have captured the intensity of her expression—her attractiveness, innocence, and youth, bounded by fragrance and vibrant natural colors.

"Thank you!" she exclaimed. "I *love* flowers!"

Then she turned to bring them inside.

"Come on in. I'll put them in some water."

Kari's home was simple and small with a scattering of mismatched furniture. It looked to be the same impromptu assembly of hand-me-downs and makeshift structures, like a brick and plank shelf, that was common amongst his peers.

"Welcome to my humble abode!" she shouted from the kitchen.

"It's nice."

"It's a start," she said, as she walked back into the living room, now carrying the flowers in a clear glass vase.

She placed them on the small table below the picture window and stood admiring them.

"Thank you," she said again, still looking at the flowers.

Kari turned her face towards Haakon's until their eyes met again and they held another long stare.

"Should we go?" Haakon asked. "If you're that pleased with the flowers, I can't wait until you get a ride in Scout. I even washed her in your honor."

"You've named your car *and* it's a her?" she asked.

"Yes, and yes."

"And you washed her for me?"

"Truth be told, I rinsed her. I was afraid that actually washing her might be too hard on her fragile old metal."

Kari chuckled.

"You're a funny guy, Haakon."

"I do what I can. I like to make people happy," Haakon said, borrowing from Judd. "I get up in the morning and the first thing that I ask myself is 'how can I make someone happy today?'"

"How admirable," Kari said, as they stepped outside. "You must be very proud of yourself."

"I don't like to brag," Haakon answered, shrugging his shoulders, "but sometimes it's hard not to."

They both broke out laughing in their mutual nervousness as they walked outside. Haakon opened the passenger door of the Scout and it creaked loudly.

"Pay no mind to that sound. It is not indicative of the overall driving experience of this fine vehicle."

Kari looked at Haakon with some doubt as he gestured for her to enter.

Downtown Colterville was just a few blocks from her house. During the brief ride, they traded jokes at the Scout's expense. Haakon enjoyed the banter, as it was an effective means to disguise his anxiety.

Hands down, the only restaurant he could consider taking his date to was The Riverside. It would be a stretch to call it a fancy restaurant, but it was the fanciest Colterville had. And, on this enchanting evening it offered an outdoor, riverside dining deck shaded by large cottonwood trees. While not a white linen place, it still set the perfect mood.

"I love this restaurant," she said as the maitre d' led them to their outdoor table.

"You've been here?"

"A couple of times with my parents. How about you?"

"Never. So far, the Renfro Tavern has been the pinnacle of my dining experiences. But if you haven't been there for 'spaghetti night,' you haven't truly lived yet."

Her smile encouraged Haakon.

"That may be, but I have a hunch that this place may also meet the high culinary standards set by the Renfro Tavern. But I wouldn't recommend the spaghetti."

They laughed. A gentle breeze from the river pushed Kari's bangs over her left eye. As she brushed it aside, their eyes met in another long stare.

"So tell me where you've been, what you've done. If you grew up in a military family, you must have lived everywhere," Haakon asked her, sincerely wanting to know.

"Yeah. Pretty much. Any place they could park a ship, I guess. Bahrain, Italy, Japan, Spain, and Hawaii."

"Wow. Where's your favorite place?"

"Oh, Hawaii. That's where I finished high school. Honolulu. I loved Hawaii. Have you been there?"

"No, I wish."

"I loved the landscape, the climate, the Polynesian culture. I learned to surf and dive there. It was a dream."

"Do you want to go back there to live some day?"

"I don't know. Part of me does, part of me doesn't. It was a time and place. I'm not sure I can go back... at least to what I enjoyed about it so much. Do you understand what I mean?"

"I think so."

"I don't really have many friends there. Being a 'Navy brat,' you move around all the time. So I didn't make a lot of friends. I was a bit of a loner and a bit of a bookworm. We weren't in Hawaii for that long really."

Haakon detected a hint of sadness in her face.

"I like it here now. This is beautiful country. I like the people. I like my job. It's a new experience. It's slow and simple... in a good way."

The waiter returned and they each ordered a glass of wine. Haakon followed Kari's lead, as he did not want to pretend he knew anything about wine. When it arrived, they each slowly sipped while delving more into their respective backgrounds—each of them trying to explain who they were and what made them tick. She was unexpectedly detailed about revealing who she was. It buoyed Haakon, giving him the impression she considered him a good investment of her time.

"I was such a loner that I did a lot of independent study. I even started taking college courses through my high school, starting at sixteen."

"Did you go to college after high school?"

"Yeah, I was going to 'U-Dub'… or the University of Washington in Seattle. With all the high school credits, I nearly finished this year. I just turned twenty-one, but I would have finished at twenty if I had stayed."

"Wow! That's fast," Haakon said, genuinely surprised. "I'm still a young'n myself, only nineteen. I've only got one year of college under my belt."

"Well, I don't know that I recommend what I've done. I think I missed out a lot on the non-academic part of college, the social part. I'm not sure why I rushed into being a working gal. It just sort of happened."

"So you don't mind being on a date with a younger man?"

She laughed.

"Now you are making me feel old."

They both laughed.

As the sun worked down towards the horizon, its increasingly ambient light illuminated the deck. The river was quiet—flowing wide, smooth, and slow. Occasionally, a recreational boat would slowly motor past. The cottonwood leaves rustled softly when an intermittent breeze found them. The sound seemed to complement the soft background music that played over the restaurant speakers, as though orchestrated. The air was sweet with a mix of pine and Kari's perfume. The heat of the day had fallen to a comfortable level. All factors were making the evening perfect—conducive for two souls to study each other.

"What about you? You said that you're going back to school. Where? Minnesota?"

"Yeah, the University."

"What are you taking?"

"Well, it may not be the most practical thing, but I want to go into art, watercolor painting." Haakon said, surprising himself that he said it.

He rarely told anyone about his genuine passion. Instead, he usually provided a safer, "more sensible" answer. Yet Haakon felt compelled to tell Kari the truth.

"Gosh, you want to be a painter?"

"I do, but I'm also thinking of architecture… probably a little more practical."

"Architecture would be fine, but why not follow your bliss? You only live once. If you want to be an artist, be an artist!"

Then she made a face as though cringing at her own words.

"I guess I'm being a little bold for hardly knowing you."

"No, you're not. You're right. Some days I think that. But, some days I think I should pick the safer route, the architecture route."

"Well, I guess you know *this* big mouth's point of view."

They both laughed.

Through dinner they never suffered an uncomfortable, silent pause. Her stories intrigued him and she seemed the same with his, or at least he hoped that he was reading her correctly. All the while the sun worked its way down through the cottonwoods and occasionally cast its light directly upon his eyes, causing him to hold his hand up as a shield so he would not lose sight of her face. When this occurred, the backlight illuminated Kari's soft auburn hair and enhanced a glow that his imagination had already encompassed her with.

They continued talking long after the food had gone and the waiter had turned his attentions to other tables. When it became painfully obvious they should free up the table, they hesitantly relented.

"It's still early," Haakon said. "Would you like to walk along the river path and talk some more?"

"Yeah, I'd like that."

The sunlight was ebbing, but the path had its own lights. They reflected on the river's mirror as they walked along.

"I don't mean to pry, but you mentioned that you moved back here because of your mother's health. Is she going to be okay?"

Kari paused as though in deep thought, then answered.

"She's not. There's really no treatment for her illness."

"Oh, I'm sorry."

"It's fine. I've already done all the crying, believe me… an ocean's worth. You come to know that it does no good and that it's best to just carry on and live what you have to live… and love who you have to love while you can."

Her eyes welled up.

"I'm really sorry."

He reached over to pull her to his side momentarily as they walked. Haakon honestly felt bad, and the brief side-hug was involuntary. When he released her, she glanced up at him for a moment as though to say, "it was okay." Then she looked back down at the path.

"It had always been my parent's plan to retire out here… build a house on their land. When my mom got sick and the treatment options ran out, they agreed to proceed anyway… actually ahead of their schedule. My mom loves horses and Dad thought this would be the best place to be."

Kari glanced at Haakon and smiled as though to concede this was true.

"I was finishing school in Seattle when I got the news. I decided I needed to come out here to be with her. I didn't really want to live with them. I wanted my independence, so I found my own place here in town and took the job at the bank."

"Do you have any brothers and sisters?" Haakon asked.

"No, it's just me—an only child," she answered, nearly smiling.

"This must be hard for you every single day," he said, questioning the wisdom of his own words, yet feeling compelled to acknowledge her pain.

"I'm trying to remain positive… philosophical, I guess. None of us has forever and not everyone knows when their time is up. I've just decided to enjoy spending time with my mother while I can—while she can still do things she loves… like ride horses."

"I can't imagine," he feebly replied.

"That's *my* story, Haakon. What about you?" she asked, signaling a desire to change the topic. "Are you liking it here?"

"I do like it… even more now that I've met you," he said, grinning.

After the words left his lips, he feared that they might have come across as overplayed and insincere.

"Likewise," she said coyly, smiling back.

Her reply restored his fragile confidence.

Their walk eventually led them within sight of Moose's Saloon, only a few blocks away from the restaurant. They could hear the loud country-rock music emanating through its walls, out into the street.

"Are you up for this?" Haakon asked.

"Absolutely. Sounds fun."

It was good they talked over dinner and during their walk, because the noise level in the saloon required any conversation to be shouted or lip-read. Live music blared from a band in the far corner. The joint was full of standing and sitting and dancing women and men of all ages. They conversed loudly, each trying to compensate for the background clamor, thus taking part in a perpetual cycle of audible chaos. Cigarette smoke haze filled the large room. Its smell, and that of spilled beer, was omnipresent. Yet a positive charge of electricity also filled the room. It was alive, when all was growing dark and quiet outside.

Kari and Haakon wove their way through the crowd along the long bar, while scanning for a place to sit. Haakon noticed Judd leaning against the bar and he nodded to Haakon just as Kari altered her course and headed for an opening table. Before Haakon could pursue her, Judd grabbed his arm and stopped him in his tracks.

"Hey Hawk, who's that?" he asked while his eyes followed Kari across the room.

"That's the captain's daughter. You know, the job up Deer Creek Road."

"Damn! My hat's off to you, my friend," he said, patting Haakon on the shoulder. "I guess I underestimated you. Like I said before, you work under the radar, man. Way to go."

Haakon smiled proudly, but Judd still had his eyes on Kari.

"Better go after her before someone else does," Judd advised.

Haakon was eager to do so for the very reason Judd stated. As soon as his arm was released, Haakon shuffled through the crowd to the table she had secured.

"Good work!" Haakon shouted.

But Kari cupped her hand on her ear, indicating she could not hear, so he gave her a "thumbs up" sign as they sat.

Beers were delivered to their table and each had only taken one sip when the band played the first few notes of a popular song—a song the entire saloon seemed to recognize. The surrounding tables cleared in a mass exodus to the dance floor. This made it all but impossible for Haakon to not ask Kari to dance. He was not keen on dancing, but he had, after all, invited her to a dancing bar. So Haakon signaled towards the floor and she nodded her instant approval.

Not being a good dancer, Haakon was out of his comfort zone. But watching Kari made his self-perceived dancing ineptness quickly slip from his thoughts. She clearly loved dancing. Her reaction was contagious. Gradually, Haakon lost his reservations and began to enjoy it too. Her delight was broadcast both on her face and in her movements as she freely swayed to the beat. If she recognized his dancing shortcomings, she did not let on. They danced through the fast-paced first, second, third, and fourth songs. Then finally, Haakon's dance floor courage was rewarded with a slow dance.

To a young man, this is what dancing is all about: having the opportunity to hold a girl close, really close, for the first time—to feel her warmth, her curves, her softness and to breathe her hair as it lies on your shoulder as you drift, side to side, to the gentle rhythm of a love song. If you are convinced that the attraction is love, genuine love, then this moment is even more monumental than the first time that you physically *make* love. The reason is not complicated. When you hold your love close for the first time, you ascend beyond yourself. You feel things unknown before—feelings that overwhelm all of your other senses. You feel the wonderment of nature.

They smiled shyly at each other when they realized the next dance would be slow. Then they clasped their hands on one side while holding the other's waist. Haakon held her timidly at first, but she pulled him closer, so he did the same. They swayed in a tight embrace with their heads nearly together. Then after their bodies made a full circle on the floor, Kari dropped her head onto his shoulder and gripped him tighter. The smell of her hair and perfume was enthralling. A jolt of elation flooded Haakon's body with an exhilarating sensation he had never known. It was as though he had been drugged and he instantly craved more of this drug. Haakon was not a praying person, but in that moment, he prayed for the song to never end.

When it did, they pulled apart and stared at each other as if to signify their mutual reverence. Then both giggled nervously. Haakon gently tried to usher her back to the table, but she indicated in sign-language that she needed to use the restroom. So, rather than go sit down himself, he escorted her, in a gentlemanly way, to the "ladies room" door, then stood nearby and waited.

The restrooms were near a pool table surrounded by a surly group of inebriated woodsmen, still in their work clothes. They were loud and foul and Haakon tried to ignore them, even looking down at the floor as he waited, not wanting to make eye contact and potentially attract the ire of a drunk. But, when Kari emerged from the restroom, one of them shouted out a crude remark and swatted her posterior as she rapidly walked by. He was not aware, or was too drunk to care, that she was with the man standing near the door.

Haakon was not a fighter by nature, as his size was nearly always a deterrent to such problems, but his response was involuntary and instantaneous. He took one step forward, then delivered his right fist into the drunk's smirking face. This sent the drunk staggering six feet or so before he finally lost his balance on the edge of the dance floor and fell onto his back.

He surprised himself, not realizing what adrenaline and a summer of packing heavy lumber could do for his swing. For a moment, Haakon relished the perfection of the knockdown. Then he turned to see Kari's stunned face. And just as he leaned to approach her, a fist met *his* face. Being an inexperienced fighter, it had not occurred to Haakon to watch the response of the drunk's friends. As it turned out, he had unwittingly set off a chain reaction. And, as big as Haakon was, he went flying several feet in the opposite direction.

The drunk's friend had apparently taken exception to Haakon's act. After he had knocked Haakon down, and Haakon was still on the floor, shaking his head, trying to get his wits about him, the drunk's friend cocked his leg back, intending to introduce Haakon's face to the tip of a cowboy boot. But, just as he recoiled for the impending blow, a calloused hand grabbed the drunk's friend on his shoulder.

"You don't wanna do that," a voice told him, matter-of-factly.

It was Judd. His voice disarmed everything. Even those who did not know Judd, knew *of* Judd. He was perceived as a one-man army and if he was on your side, you had the ultimate defense. If he were not on your side, you would do well to lie low. Judd's intervention assured that this fight had not only ended but would not resume, not even outside of the bar. And, behind Judd stood Brady and Landon. Each, presumably, was prepared to enter the fracas on Haakon's behalf, and this gave Haakon a reassuring feeling. The pool table group opted wisely not to further intervene.

"You gotta cause trouble everywhere you go?" Brady said, looking down at Haakon from the surrounding crowd, while offering his hand.

Haakon was speechless, still trying to assess the situation. Kari pushed through the crowd and crouched down to help him to his feet. Haakon remained stunned and numb to the pain of the blow.

"Your eye is going to swell," Kari said, as she and Brady pulled him up.

With his hand, he felt the point of impact. It stung and he grimaced at the discomfort. As he did this, the original drunk approached Haakon. His nose was bleeding. Haakon braced for a secondary attack, but as the drunk grew near he raised both of his open hands in a gesture of amity.

"I wanna apologize to the lady for being an ass," he said. Then he turned to Haakon, "I had it com'n, for sure."

He reached out his right hand and Haakon accepted it, begrudgingly. He could see Judd close by, watching the conversation. The drunk glanced over towards Judd, then grimaced and disappeared into his group of friends. Haakon suspected that the drunk and Judd had just concluded a discussion. Judd could be very persuasive.

Haakon gave Judd a wave and Judd nodded to acknowledge "the thank you." Then Haakon turned to Kari.

"This isn't what I had in mind tonight. How about we go outside for a minute to get some air?"

Kari did not answer him, but rather, commandingly, took Haakon by the hand and walked him down the bar towards the door.

Once open, they were surprised to find darkness. A few people stood outside near the saloon entrance with a cloud of pungent pot smoke lingering over their heads. Kari and Haakon walked past them and down the street along the many closed businesses. She still held his arm as though guiding an invalid. Haakon was not about to ask her to let go. He enjoyed it. They proceeded nearly to the end of the block when she abruptly stopped below a streetlamp and turned to look up into Haakon's eyes. She reached to adjust his head's angle so that its light would illuminate his face.

"Oh, that must hurt around your eye," Kari said, looking very concerned.

Haakon reveled at the attention and smiled down at her.

"Ah, for an ordinary guy maybe… but not for me."

Her expression conveyed that she knew he was lying. She grinned.

"So I guess this makes you my hero."

"Well, I don't know about that…"

Midway in Haakon's sentence, with her hands still on the sides of his face, Kari pulled his head down and hers up and planted her lips on his. Then Haakon pulled her body closer and engaged with her in a passionate kiss. He could not believe his good fortune. Sore eye or not, he would not let this moment slip by.

It was as though they were releasing their bottled up infatuation with one another. They kissed for several long seconds, neither wanting to stop. But then Haakon abruptly broke the kiss off and grasped the sides of Kari's face, wanting to look into *her* eyes. In them he thought he saw the same fervor and longing and desire and hope that he was feeling. They fell back into a long kiss. After a few minutes of this, they broke off from each other again, breathless. This time they did not nervously smile. Instead, they studied each other with a level of gravity—neither wanting to look away.

Finally, Kari spoke.

"We've got to get some ice on that. Let's go to my house."

Haakon would have gladly endured ten punches to his face to receive that invitation. Twenty minutes later, he was sitting on her couch and she was holding a sack of frozen peas on his battered eye. They talked. They shared a soda. They kissed more and eventually, while still in an impassioned embrace, they somehow shuffled their way into her bedroom.

As a young man, Haakon keenly knew the difference between sex and love, but he had never known the disparity to be so wide. What transpired that evening was a seismic event in his life. He would later learn that it was the same for her. Untapped passion was released in a physical unification of souls. Time stood still as their youthful bodies transcended through excitement, infatuation, trust, love, compassion, and then back to reverence. The two individuals that would emerge from the bedroom would be changed from the two that had excitedly stumbled into it. Together they had touched grace. And its beauty radiated outward as a ripple that raced across the universe.

10
SWEET SUNDAY

The morning light faintly illuminated the bedroom when Haakon awoke. It took a few seconds, but he slowly came to realize he had not been dreaming. Kari was sleeping next to him, covered in a sheet and blanket. He studied her peaceful face. The soft rays emanating through the window made her smooth skin glow. Her lips smiled slightly.

As Kari slowly awakened, she must have sensed Haakon's stare, because when her eyes opened, she smiled harder. Then she reached her hand up to his face.

"My hero who vanquished my tormentor," she whispered, mockingly yet sincerely.

"Well, I do what I can for the fair maidens of the world," Haakon said, stroking her hair.

She sat up rather abruptly, modestly holding the surrounding sheet over her naked body.

"You mean that you would do that for anyone… any fair maiden?"

"Oh no. Only for the fairest of the fair… m'lady."

This seemed to satisfy Kari, though her expression purposely retained a slight pout of doubt.

"Well, okay… I guess."

She reached out to Haakon's face again and tried to make out the swollen area around his eye.

"Still looks a little puffy. Does it hurt?"

"It's a little sore. For most guys—"

"I know," she said, purposely interrupting him, "For most guys it would hurt. They would probably cry, but not you. You're not most guys."

"No, I'm not most guys… and you're not just any fair maiden."

Kari smiled again, then leaned against the bed's headboard, still holding the sheet and blanket up to her shoulders to keep warm against the morning chill. Haakon sat upright, as well, at the foot of the bed with a pillow in his lap. They faced each other.

"I would really like to spend the day with you. Do you have anything going on?" she asked.

Haakon purposely hesitated and feigned giving the question serious contemplation.

"Let me check."

He reached down from the bed and rummaged through the scattered clothing on the floor until he found his shirt. In its pocket was a folded piece of paper. He opened it.

"Hmm… no, no… it looks like I've got some time today that I could spend with you, if I move some things around. You've picked me on a good day."

Kari leaned forward and grabbed the paper out of his hand.

"Milk, eggs, Wheaties? This isn't a schedule. This is a grocery list!"

Haakon shrugged his shoulders.

"A guy's gotta eat."

Then he thought the better of teasing her too much.

"I would like nothing more than to spend the day with you."

This made Kari smile again.

"Do you have something in mind?"

"I do," she said without hesitation. "How about horseback riding… and a picnic?"

He recalled that Kari's parents had horses on their property.

"I'm not much of a cowboy. I'm even less of a cowboy than I am a dancer. And I'm a little embarrassed to say so, but the last time I was on a horse, it rolled me off and then laid down on my leg, smashing my knee between it and a rock."

The light was rapidly improving, so he swung his leg out from under the pillow to show her a scar on his knee.

"They had to fix my cartilage. It was a fat horse."

"Wow. It must not have been a well-trained horse."

"Oh no, I think it was very well trained," Haakon answered. "It was trained enough to realize it had an idiot sitting on its back that didn't know how to pilot. I would have thrown me off too."

"Our horses would never do that to you."

"Well, you would have to give me some pointers on how to operate a horse correctly. I only showed you my knee to invoke sympathy and to lower your expectations of my horsemanship skills."

They both laughed. Kari glanced over at the time on her alarm clock.

"This is kind of awkward," she said, "but you have to leave before my neighbor wakes up. And he'll be waking up pretty quick now."

"Huh?" Haakon muttered, surprised.

"He's a friend of my dad's and—"

"Say no more. I understand."

Haakon grabbed for his clothes on the floor.

"Listen, how about I go now? I'll head back to Camp One, clean up and change."

"Camp One?"

"That's the name of my uncle's property in Renfro where I live. I'll have to give you the grand tour soon."

"I'd like that."

"How about if I come back at ten?"

"Ten is perfect!"

Haakon jumped up and started putting on his clothes. He could see her huddled against the backboard under the sheet and blanket, watching him.

"Would you mind throwing me my robe? It's hanging on the back of that door," she asked.

"I'd rather not. I'd rather that you had to get out from under the blanket and go across the room naked and get it yourself."

She looked at him cross.

"But I am a gentleman… dammit, anyway!"

He reached for her hanging robe, then tossed it to her. But Haakon was not gentleman enough to not watch her put it on. For a moment, the low light afforded him a glance of her gorgeous breasts that he had already known by touch. She noticed him watching her.

"I'm a gentleman. I never said I was an angel," he chuckled.

Then Haakon changed to a more serious tone.

"You are a beautiful woman, Kari."

She smiled shyly as he had both embarrassed and flattered her.

Once Haakon had his shoes on, he walked over to where she was still sitting on the bed.

"If I was leaving for more than a few hours, I would want to tell you how much I enjoyed last evening, last night… enjoyed being with you… every second of it."

He stared into her eyes to convey his earnestness.

"But since I'll soon be back, I will tell you this later… or again."

Their eyes remained locked and though both smiled, they were different smiles, no longer born of nervousness.

"Me too," Kari said.

They fell into a long embrace and another passionate kiss.

When Haakon finally stepped outside into the morning air, it surprised him how brisk it felt considering how warm the recent days had been. Kari's neighborhood was still and silent, making his quiet departure a challenge. The Scout's old door creaked loudly as he opened it and doing it slowly only extended the intrusive sound rather than diminish it. Even the clutch pedal emitted a loud scraping sound he had never noticed before. Luckily, the engine sprang to life with only a partial turn from the starter. This was rare and fortunate as few auto sounds are more grating than the endless churning of a motor seeking a spark. But, with the Scout alive, Haakon popped the transmission into gear and rolled swiftly and relatively quietly out of the sleepy neighborhood.

As he neared Camp One and dropped into Renfro Valley, it was as though he was seeing it for the first time. The low sun brightened half of the Montana wilderness and cast long shadows upon its leeward side.

Haakon thought to himself, "What a beautiful place this is." And he smiled.

Then he said aloud, "I think I'm in love."

Brady was splitting wood next to a campfire as Haakon drove in. He merely glanced up at Haakon's approach, then resumed his task.

"Are you cooking me breakfast?" Haakon asked through the Scout's open window.

"Yeah, I'm making crepes. I got a new French cookbook," Brady answered, sarcastically.

He glanced at Haakon again, but then did a double take.

"Have you seen your face today, Muhammad Ali?" he said, genuinely surprised.

"No."

Brady rolled his eyes, then said, "Ever heard of ducking?"

"Never saw it coming."

Brady shook his head.

"It's a good thing we were there. Those Paul Bunyan boys would've given you a whoop'n."

"Yeah, you're probably right. There were six of them, I think. Fighting five guys at once is my limit."

Brady smirked.

"Well, was she worth it?"

"Yeah. I really like this girl."

Brady nodded his head as though to acknowledge Haakon's sincerity. This was a rare reaction from a person prone to hurl out relentless verbal jabs.

"We're goin' horseback riding."

"Oh, that should be interesting. Did you tell her your horse story, Roy Rogers?"

"I did. She told me she would teach me and that her horses would never throw me."

"I wouldn't count on the not throw'n part," he quipped. "And I'm not sure if you're teachable."

"What, are you a horse expert now?"

"I know some things. I had a horse once."

"You had a donkey. They're different."

"It was a mule. But I had a horse too, when I was a kid."

"You mean the kind that has wheels? *I* had one of them."

"No, the real kind with hooves, you idiot."

"With all of your many talents, Brady, I didn't know that you were a cowboy too. How can I keep up?"

"You can't. It's futile," Brady said. "Just try your best. It won't be sufficient, but that's all you can do. What can I say?"

Brady did not smile, feigning seriousness.

"But if your girlfriend wants to ride with a *real* cowboy… well, you know who to call."

"I'll keep that in mind."

"And you may want to stay out of the saloons today. I won't be around to save you from your barroom brawls. I'm goin' fish'n."

"You can count on that. I like to keep my bar fights down to one per week."

"Good policy. Though I don't know if anyone would punch that face of yours now. They'd more than likely take pity on you."

Haakon reached up to his stinging cheek.

"I hope so. It's pretty sore. But it has gained me some very helpful sympathy from Kari. I'm kind of worried it will heal too soon."

"You're pathetic, Hawk."

"Maybe, but I'm pathetic in a pragmatic way."

By the time Haakon returned to Kari's house, she was packed and ready for their day's outing. He grinned at the implied eagerness. She returned a smile that exuded her excitement. They began conversing without words.

Kari's hair glowed. It appeared recently washed and hung neatly brushed just above her shoulders. She wore a lightweight plaid shirt that had tails tied above her waist, revealing her well-toned, tanned stomach. Partially visible underneath the shirt was what appeared to be her bikini top. She was expecting another hot day, he thought. Accentuating the entire getup were glorious short denim cutoffs that made her long, shapely legs a hallowed sight.

She greeted him with a passionate kiss. The feel of her skin and her smell brought him instantly back to the splendor of hours before. Then Kari pulled away and held Haakon at her arm's distance and studied his face.

"It looks like it still hurts."

"Only when I smile."

"I'll try not to make you smile today, then."

"Oh, please do. It's *so* worth the pain."

They drove the fourteen miles of windy gravel road back to Kari's parents, conversing nonstop—each craving more and more knowledge of the other. It was as though they had once been together and were now updating each other after having been apart for some years. There seemed to be so much to tell and so much to hear.

The captain heard their vehicle's approach and he and Rita were outside to greet them. When Haakon got out of the Scout and faced Kari's parents, they looked at him with a shocked expression.

"What the hell happened to you?" the captain asked.

"Oh, my face got in the way of someone's fist."

"Wow! Does the other guy look as bad as you?" the captain said, not expecting an answer.

Then he turned to his daughter and asked, in what Haakon hoped was a joking way, "Kari, are you dating some ruffian?"

"Dad, you would have been proud of Haakon," she gushed. "He valiantly defended your daughter's honor."

"I smacked a guy that was disrespectful to her. It was, sort of, involuntary."

"He did more than that, Dad. He sent the guy flying across the room. It was the creep's friend that got Haakon in the eye. Haakon's my hero today!"

"Heroes are a good thing. We can never have too many," the captain replied.

Then he played upon his daughter's enthusiasm.

"If you defended my little girl, then I want to thank you."

He reached out to shake Haakon's hand, then turned to look at Kari.

"This girl here, young woman, is one of the two most important things in my life," he said, nearly tearing up as he put his arm around both Kari and Rita.

Then the captain suddenly changed his demeanor, as though realizing that he was getting uncomfortably sentimental.

"I think you better practice ducking, Haakon."

"Yes sir. Good advice."

The captain turned to Kari.

"So, you're gonna ride horses today," he said, wanting to further divert away from his emotions.

"Yeah, I thought I would take Haakon up the Misty to Sky Pond. Thought we would do a picnic up there. Maybe swim."

"Oh, you'll definitely swim. It's gonna be a scorcher again today," the captain said. "I've got the horses ready for you, so you should be all set."

"And here's a dessert for you guys and the horses," Rita said, handing Kari a paper sack.

Kari peeked inside the bag.

"Thanks Mom!"

She gave both her mother and father a kiss on the cheek.

"And thanks, Dad!"

It seemed that the captain purposely tried not to hover over Kari and her new "friend," though Haakon was certain he would have preferred to. The captain walked with Rita somewhat hesitantly back up the path that led to their trailer, like a father who was still struggling with the fact that his baby girl had grown into a woman.

As Haakon watched her parents walk away, Kari motioned for him to follow her down the hill to the horse barn.

Forest surrounded the newly constructed house on three sides, but its face overlooked a large open pasture of tall grass. The captain had fenced it so their two horses could freely roam its acres. Within view of the house, he built a barn that afforded the horses a comfortable shelter. This was a place Kari and her mother spent much of their time together, tending to Omar and Burt.

As the captain had promised, both horses were saddled and ready to go.

"You'll want to pet Omar on the nose here, so he gets to know you."

Kari motioned Haakon towards her. He reached out for the horse's nose and it snorted and recoiled.

"You do recall my horse story from earlier, don't you? I don't have a great history with these things."

"Omar will treat you well. And he's not a 'thing.' He's a gentleman like you. You'll get along fine."

As though on cue, the horse turned its head toward Haakon and snorted again.

"He's kind of looking at me funny. I think he knows I'm not a horse guy."

"No, he just knows you're a guy. He's a little jealous, that's all."

"Jealous? You want me to ride a jealous horse into the mountains?" Kari chuckled.

"Trust me, he's mellow. All ya gotta do is get up on him. He'll follow me and Burt. You won't even have to steer."

"What if I lose you? I won't even know how to turn him. Plus, he's jealous. It would be in his interest to buck me off over a cliff or something."

"Don't be a sissy. Man up, Haakon! Didn't you ever want to be a cowboy when you were little?"

"Sure I did… until I actually rode a horse. Then I switched over to wanting to be an astronaut."

She laughed again.

"Ever seen the inside of a space capsule? They squeeze those guys in there like sardines. At least cowboys have lots of room."

"Yeah, okay. I'll be a cowboy for you. But I wouldn't do it for just anyone."

"I'm honored. Should I give you a cowboy name? Something like Hopalong Haakon?"

"I like that. It's got a nice ring to it," Haakon said, grinning. "What about you? Calamity Kari?"

She smiled, then said, "That's pretty good… okay. It's settled. Hopalong and Calamity."

After two fumbled mounting attempts, Kari managed to get Haakon up into the driver's seat of Omar. Once his feet were in the stirrups and his hands on the reins and horn, still holding the bridle, Kari walked up to face the horse.

"Now you behave, Omar, and be patient with Haakon."

The horse snorted in response.

"I don't claim to speak horse, but did he just say 'no way'?"

Kari giggled.

"I think he said that he kind of likes you."

"You're not a good liar, Calamity. Whatever he said was not nice, that much I know. I've got a bad feeling that by the end of the day, I'm gonna have another horse lying on top of me."

"Even if he's a little jealous, he wouldn't do that."

Kari turned to Omar and put her face to his.

"Will you?"

He snorted again. Then Kari turned to look back up at Haakon.

"It'll be fine."

"Yeah, that's what Custer and the captain of the Titanic said. It'll be fine."

"Where's that brave man that vanquished my honor last night?"

"Well, that drunk pool player only went for a couple hundred pounds. This guy looks to be the better part of a ton—and a jealous ton at that!"

Kari smiled at Haakon and as he looked down on her adorable face, he thought to himself that he would ride a wild horse bareback across the Sahara desert for her.

She mounted Burt effortlessly, then the two of them sauntered over to Haakon's side.

"Once I start off, just give Omar a little shake of the reins and he will follow me."

"Hopefully with me still on top," Haakon answered, apprehensively. "Does he have a throttle? How fast will he want to go?"

She smiled.

"Don't worry. We'll go slow. He's gentle. He'll just follow me. You and he will be best friends."

"Well, I would like that. I really should get new friends and I've always wanted a horse friend."

Kari looked at Haakon cross.

"These are my babies. Be nice. If you're nice to them, they'll be nice to you."

"Oh, I can promise that. I'm not gonna start something with *this* big fella."

"Good," she said, looking at Haakon with some skepticism. "Let's go."

She was right. Omar behaved for the most part. He followed Kari and Burt obediently across the pasture towards a shortcut path

that would link up with the Misty Trail, even though Haakon knew
Omar would have preferred carrying Kari. And he could understand
that. Haakon would have been happy to carry her up the trail too, if he
could.

It did not take long for Haakon to realize this horseback ride was a
very pleasant outing. First, it did not require much effort from him. The
horse seemed to operate on autopilot as long as Kari was ahead for him
to follow. Second, from Haakon's catbird seat, he could stare endlessly
at Kari without feeling gawky. He enjoyed watching her in her element,
doing what she loved doing. From time to time, Kari would turn her
head back to check on Haakon. And, each time that she did this, a little
more of Haakon's heart would melt. But, it was the moments when Kari
was not focused on his welfare, that he could sense her absorbing her
world—not just her surroundings, but the whole of the experience. Kari
was riding high in the wild on a creature she adored, seeming to be in a
state of euphoria. Haakon liked to think his accompaniment was part of
her bliss, but he was not sure.

"The Misty" was the name that locals applied to the steep valley
formed by Misty Creek. It fell from a high park in the mountains
and was fed by a tiny alpine lake appropriately named Sky Pond. A
trail followed the creek closely, except where the grade forced it into
switchbacks. Then it would leave and return, in wide zigzag patterns,
ascending the steepness gradually. The route was rocky and smelled of
hearty pines and fir. The views along the way began as picturesque, but
evolved to "flat-out" stunning as they climbed. When the trail finally
reached the turn into the high park, the panorama afforded was nothing
short of breathtaking.

Kari stopped her horse at this point and motioned Haakon over
to her side. Haakon clicked his tongue and slightly shook the reins,
prompting Omar to approach her. Kari watched Haakon's face and
awaited his response.

"Wow! This is amazing!" he said, though he thought his words
inadequate.

Far below them was a long, narrow valley scattered with a handful
of houses, meandering roads, and rolling grass meadows. A wall of
wooded mountains defined the valley's far side. Some of the mountains
exceeded the tree line, still harboring traces of snow in the high crevices

hidden from the sun. The vivid greens of spring had faded by this late dry summer date, but the muted greens of the vast forest were all-pervading.

"I love it here," Kari said as she looked out. "I've been here a hundred times and I never tire of the view."

Haakon nodded, not being sure if she even noticed his response. She was in a trance, as was he. But Haakon's trance was watching Kari scanning her environment. As much as he enjoyed what they were doing and where they were, his growing infatuation distracted him. He could not really control his focus. He felt as though he was in an emotional freefall. The more time Haakon spent with Kari, the more arresting she became. It was all that he could think about.

Eventually, Kari turned to look back at Haakon. She did not seem surprised to see him observing her. They stared at each other again, neither of them smiling—studying each other as though one knew what the other was feeling. It appeared they were moving beyond nervousness and insecurity and that their mindsets were bonding. It was a beautiful sensation to experience in such grand surroundings.

"You know I want to kiss you right now, Haakon," she said, breaking the silence. "I'm kind of getting to like you."

"Oh, I know little lady," Haakon responded, trying to imitate his idea of a cowboy drawl. "I've kinda take'n a like'n to you too."

Kari seemed amused.

"And, if I wasn't on this damn horse, I would accept that kiss with pleasure, ma'am. I surely would."

Looking intent, Kari skillfully maneuvered her horse alongside his. Then she leaned over towards Haakon as if to give him a kiss, but stopped short—her face mere inches from his.

"Two rules, cowboy. Don't call me ma'am and don't ever 'damn' my horse. If you can agree to that Hopalong Haakon, I shall grant you that sought kiss."

"Well, bust my saddle, Missy. You surely drive a hard bargain. But if those be your terms, I shall accept. And you, therefore, have my most sincere apology for addressing you unsuitably and disparaging this fine horse that I sit upon."

They both giggled until their heads slowly fell together and their lips met. Omar stirred and moved slightly away, enough to part their faces—making them laugh again.

"Oh yes, a fine horse, I say—the absolute finest. But please don't be getting this horse mad at me, Kari. I've only got one good knee left."

"I do think Omar's a little jealous," she said. "It took him awhile to get used to Burt too."

"Oh great. And you waited until we were up the mountain, just inches away from a cliff, to tell me this?"

They laughed again, this time making Haakon's swollen eye sting, but he did not care.

"There's a little lake just a short distance through that gap," she said, pointing behind Haakon, towards a cut in a rock wall. "Let's go there and see if we can stand the cold water."

"Nothing can be colder than my camp baths."

"I'm pretty sure you are wrong about that," Kari replied, beaming. "Let's go see."

The trail turned away from the overlook and proceeded into a narrow passage through a tall rock outcrop. On the other side, the path leveled out and entered a thick forest of subalpine firs. Omar and Haakon followed behind at a slow, steady pace. Kari said nothing, seemingly transfixed by the imposing setting.

Haakon sensed a sudden drop in temperature. When a tall mountain peak came into view, still harboring patches of snow, he suspected it was the source.

Eventually, the trail sloped downwards and, when it did, a brilliant turquoise lake came into view. Its surface shimmered as though sprinkled with floating diamonds. Behind the lake was an abrupt wall of rock that defined the bottom reaches of Misty Peak. High on the wall, narrow ribbon falls careened out of snowbanks, cascading along abrupt ledges on their way down. The closer they got to the lake, the more apparent it was that they were entering a deep glacial cirque—a gigantic rock amphitheater. Dwarfed by its scale and awed by its splendor of vivid colors, it was easily the most dramatic lake background Haakon had ever laid eyes on.

"Wow!" he said, again feeling the verbal expression lacking.

Without looking back at Haakon, mesmerized by the scenery herself, Kari exclaimed the same.

They continued towards the end of the trail, each gazing upward to scan the rocky heights that appeared before them. Kari stopped short of the lake's edge, alongside a narrow horizontal rail constructed by the Forest Service.

"Let's tie off here," she said.

Quickly, Kari jumped off of her horse and then reached out for his.

"I'll tie them on the rail, but I'll hold Omar while you get off."

Kari correctly surmised that Haakon's dismount would not likely be graceful. Indeed, his foot got stuck in a stirrup and he nearly fell backwards. Yet, he caught himself just in time and then tried, unsuccessfully, to pretend his ungainly maneuver did not happen. Kari was trying to conceal her laughter.

"All right, we've established that I'm no cowboy," Haakon said, slightly embarrassed. "But I've got other skills."

She laughed openly now.

"I just can't think of those other skills at the moment, but they'll come to me."

"Swimming perhaps?" she asked, smiling.

"Perhaps," he answered, returning the smile, but with a sinister variation.

Kari secured both horses. When she turned back, it surprised her to discover Haakon standing close behind. They embraced again. Then their lips met for another long, passionate kiss.

When they stopped for air, he said, "I've been waiting to do this."

"Why?"

"Why have I been *waiting*?"

"Yes, why?"

Their heads fell back into a kiss. This went on for several minutes until Omar seemed to get annoyed with them carrying on. He let out a loud snort which startled Haakon and made both of them break out laughing.

"Let's jump in," Kari suggested.

Now, the high sun was delivering its full midday strength. Even though the air was colder here in the cirque, it did not overcome the overall heat. The chill of mountain water still sounded inviting.

"I'll race you there," Haakon said.

Then he quickly pulled off his shirt and kicked off his tennis shoes. Kari followed his lead, revealing the bikini he knew and loved from the other day. Pausing briefly to watch her, Haakon lost valuable time, allowing her to start off down the short path ahead of him. He may have had a chance of catching up, but he immediately realized the mistake of casting off his shoes. Small, sharp rocks covered the trail. He grimaced as he tiptoed around them as best he could. Yet each misstep punished the tender soles of his feet with pain.

Kari did not remove her shoes until she was at the lake's edge. And, after they were off, she wasted no time in running into the water. Once knee deep, she dove in. When her head reemerged, she let out an agonizing scream. The piercing sound echoed off of the surrounding cliffs.

"This is freeeeeezing!"

Haakon would have laughed out loud had he not been struggling down the final yards of the path.

"I can't believe it! Nothing can be this cold!"

She quickly swam back to where most of her body could stand out of the water, allowing the blazing sun's rays to heat her skin. She appeared as a sculpted sea nymph, standing in the turquoise plane of the majestic rock and ice setting—her arms embracing her own exposed flesh to generate warmth. Haakon would have relished watching her if he was not having such difficulty.

"You think you're in pain. Try walking down this path barefoot. It's torture!"

"I would never do that," she said, chuckling.

He returned a mocking glance of scorn. After Haakon finally picked his way to the lake's edge, he continued walking into the water. The frigid temperature stunned him, but he was relieved to discover that the lake's submerged gravel consisted of small rounded stones. This made them relatively comfortable to step on, so compared to the "trail of pain," the lake's water temperature was only a secondary discomfort.

When he arrived at Kari's side, he was standing nearly knee deep in the lake. Haakon reached his arms out to her, to pull her close. She was quivering and seemed to appreciate the warmth of his body pressed against hers.

"You should have told me about the shoes. You're the local expert, ya know."

"In a race," Kari said with some difficulty, her jaw still clattering from the cold, "it's every man and woman for themselves. I take every advantage I can."

"Hmm... I'm truly sorry to hear that."

He quickly lifted her up and swung her back, preparing to throw her into the deeper water.

"Don't you dare!" she shrieked.

Ignoring her warning, Haakon tossed her several feet into the lake. But questioning the wisdom of this act, he immediately dove in next to her to grab her thrashing, screaming body. He pulled her back to the shallow water where they could stand again. The excitement of retrieving her counteracted the temperature shock to his body. Kari had been right. It was excruciatingly cold water—much colder than the river bath at Camp One. They stood knee deep again, laughing uncontrollably. He hugged her and she hugged back, pulling him even closer with her arms. Then Kari lifted her legs up out of the water and wrapped them around Haakon's waist. Her head was above his. Her breasts pressed against his cheeks.

"I'm not going back in there. Don't even think of throwing me again. I mean it!"

She looked down at Haakon with a stern expression.

"Well, if you mean it and all, I guess I better not."

Yet he shifted his body and repositioned her as though preparing to throw her again.

"I mean it Haakon! I'm not kidding!"

Kari was now cradled in his arms and he looked down into her face.

"You look mad. I've never seen you mad," Haakon said, genuinely surprised.

"Oh, this isn't mad. This is my serious look. You'll know if and when I'm mad. And, if you throw me back in, you'll see that side of me... and you'll wish that you had not, Haakon."

"That sounds like a threat. You're a pretty big talker for someone in such a precarious position."

"Maybe I'll change my approach then."

She reached up and wrapped her arms around Haakon's neck, pulling her face close to his.

"Please, oh please don't throw me back in, big, bad cowboy," Kari said with an exaggerated pouty expression.

"I don't know," Haakon said, joking with her. "You just threatened me and all. Is that all you got?"

She pulled Haakon's face to hers and kissed him.

"Oh, maybe I *shouldn't* toss you again."

But then he abruptly shifted his stance, feigning another throw.

"But maybe I *should!*"

Kari screamed again and then they both giggled.

"Let me try harder to convince you," she said.

This time Kari wrapped her legs around Haakon's waist again and grasped the sides of his head with her hands, pulling her lips tightly to his. Her legs tightened around him, so he pulled her closer with his arms. The warmth of their wet tan skin glistened in the bright sunlight. To an observer, they may have appeared as a single sculpture surrounded by sparkling turquoise and sheer rock walls and a vivid cerulean ceiling. It was all quite surreal.

Clumsily, Haakon walked Kari back to the shore, still holding her above the water as they continued kissing. He struggled with each step, trying to find stable footing on the shifting underwater stones. Once on dry ground, he gently released Kari next to where she had placed her shoes and she quickly pulled them back on.

"I'm gonna run up to the horses to grab our stuff… and I'll get your shoes. I'll be right back," she said.

When Kari returned, she was wrapped in a towel for warmth. She handed Haakon his shoes and he quickly pulled them on.

"I've got a blanket in the pack. Let's go over there for our picnic," Kari said, pointing to a flat open space a short distance down the shoreline, well off of the trail.

Haakon grabbed the pack and followed her. And, once there, without a word, the two of them hastily spread the blanket out across the patch of grass. Then they stood facing each other on its opposite ends.

"Are you hungry?" Kari asked.

"Depends what you mean by hungry."

Haakon walked around the blanket's edge to Kari's side. As they stood close, they studied each other's faces. He reached up to feel Kari's cheeks and she recoiled, as his hands were still cold. Then he slowly dropped them down to her shoulders and pulled off her towel. She quivered for a moment until Haakon wrapped his arms around her and pulled her close. Then, in unison, they slowly dropped to the blanket. Haakon reclined on his back, gentling drawing Kari on top of him. With eyes remaining locked on to one another, they grappled to remove the small amount of clothing they wore. Each of them shivered until their movements coalesced. Their passion quickly generated its own warmth.

Unlike the night before, Haakon could now visibly see the fervor in Kari's eyes. At times, her head would block the high sun, making her auburn hair take on a glorious backlight. As it danced in the air, it glowed like the fiery edge of an eclipse. Haakon ran his hands up her sides and visually absorbed the delicate splendor that he had known by caress. It was overwhelming. And when he reached higher and lightly grasped Kari's hair, Haakon was convinced he was touching Heaven.

Their two young adoring souls merged into nature's majesty—forest, rock, water, and them. The intense sun cast its warm rays upon their coupling. The very star that formed the earth, fashioned the oceans and lakes and forests, and tectonically pressed the Rocky Mountains high into the sky, was the same star that now fueled the fire of Kari and Haakon's infatuation.

While they made love, they did not differ from their surroundings. They *were* the earth. They were one. They were the stuff of stars.

11
ENDLESS SUMMER

In the weeks that followed their horseback ride up to Sky Pond—a day that Haakon came to remember as "Sweet Sunday"—he and Kari were inseparable. They spent practically every non-working hour together. Haakon could not get enough of Kari and the allure was mutual. To an outside observer, their display of adoration and incessant fawning may have appeared juvenile and, at times, insufferable. But to them it was reflexive, involuntary. It was as though their youth and vigor spawned its own torrent of gravitation—its pull beyond their control. They became corresponding laser beams, parallel and acute. What occurred beyond their narrow sights seemed of secondary importance.

Haakon became somewhat adept at playing cowboy as they spent more time on horseback. Occasionally, they even rode them at a gallop's pace—something he could never have imagined doing after his first, pre-Kari, horse encounter. The two of them embarked on more day-trips into the forest. And, though billed as "picnics," these outings often evolved into love making under the warm sun, surrounded by the solitude and majesty of Montana wilderness.

"I think we've redefined the meaning of 'picnic,'" Kari said to Haakon, as they lay in the open.

He turned to her and smiled. She smiled back. Her bright blue eyes dominated his view, but his peripheral vision could still make out her body's curves and her skin's alternating hues of summer tan. Part of him wanted to scoot back to a distance where he could fully study her in the light, like an artist assessing the details of a nude poser. But he loved being so close to her eyes. They were magnetic.

Kari reached her hand to the top of Haakon's head and lightly stroked his hair.

"I don't know how to say it. This may sound corny, but you fulfill me. You fill a void in me."

Their eyes remained locked.

"That's exactly what I was thinking," Haakon said. "That, and on this giant planet, somehow we found each other… and on a rooftop out in the middle of the woods in northwest Montana, of all places. Do you realize the astronomical odds of that?"

"There's something else at play here, Haakon."

He slowly nodded in agreement. A sudden breeze pushed up against a nearby stand of pines as though to concur, shaking the needles and making them sing like a million tiny wind chimes. The coolness fell upon their exposed bodies and they reacted by pulling closer.

Sometimes they hiked. Sometimes they camped. Each had a reverence of the wild and enjoyed being in it, particularly with someone who shared its wonder. Sometimes they stayed awake late to lie out on their blanket so they could stare up into the stars and discuss the profound topics inspired by observing something so incomprehensible. These conversations would make them feel small but never insignificant. They were young and confident, and they believed their love to be too strong to be an inconsequential force in the cosmos.

Among the many things they did that summer, Kari taught Haakon to be a fly-fisherman—or at least how to cast in a way that would not provoke outright laughter from spectators. She had mastered the craft from her father while stationed on Puget Sound's Whidbey Island. She learned well. Kari had both the patience and instinct to be adept at landing just the right fly at just the right spot on a stream. Haakon enjoyed watching her fish more than he enjoyed fishing. She was an artist, graceful and succinct. And, from his perspective, the artist had the added benefit of being gorgeous.

"The thing is, you need to have your lure *in* the water in order to catch a fish. They're not apt to come on the shore looking for it," Kari said more than once, noticing Haakon watching her.

Although she teased, he knew his attention flattered her.

Besides not being much of a fisherman, Haakon was not much of a dancer either. But he tried to be for Kari. And, she was not much of a drinker, though she sought saloons that had live bands. More often than not, it would be a country western band. And that was fine by her. She just wanted to be out on the floor moving to the rhythm. In time, as with fly-fishing and horseback riding, Haakon lost his self-consciousness and learned to enjoy dancing. Naturally, he always preferred the slow dances where he could hold Kari close. She would rest her head against his shoulder as they swayed, telegraphing her ease and contentment through his body. The closeness, combined with the melancholy nature of the slow song, would sometimes nearly make Haakon cry. But fearing a display of weakness, he would instead channel the overwhelming sentiment through the strength in his arms and he would pull Kari even closer and tighter.

Colterville was no entertainment mecca. Yet, aside from the three saloons that sporadically hosted dancing bands, it had a drive-in theater and a bowling alley. The Scout was their preferred outdoor movie vehicle since it had a bench seat, as opposed to her car's less intimate bucket seats. Though it was not particularly comfortable, it enabled them to snuggle side by side as they watched. Haakon never mentioned to her the sore back it gave him. He considered it a small price to pay for cinema coziness.

When Kari wanted a livelier evening and there was no dancing band to be found, they would sometimes try their luck at knocking over bowling pins. Haakon never developed the aptitude for this sport either, but Kari had grown up with it on the various Navy bases. Haakon suspected she purposely "threw" some matches so as not to make him feel too inadequate. He did not have the heart to tell Kari he really did not care if he was a good bowler or not.

Yet Haakon never reciprocated Kari's bowling alley grace when playing croquet on her parent's yard. This had been his childhood game and few contemporaries were in his league of play—certainly not in northwest Montana and certainly not Kari. But she, as it turned out, did not like losing in *any* game. Haakon came to realize Kari was a very competitive person.

"Croquet is no game for the squeamish. If you can't handle the heat, you should not be in the kitchen," Haakon said, purposely goading her.

"Do you think my couch is long enough for you to sleep on?" she replied, knowing that her parents could not hear.

Kari's mannerism gave Haakon the impression she was serious, so he toned down the teasing. He may have even "thrown" a few croquet matches for his own self-interest.

On perhaps the hottest day of that summer, they worked together collecting bales of hay for Sig's uncle and aunt. The farmers found themselves shorthanded and desperately in need of moving their hay bales before the forecast rain. So Kari, sharing the cab with Little Sig, slowly navigated the farm pickup truck around the rolling field, while Haakon and Sig "bucked" the heavy bales up onto the truck's tailgate. Carlos, standing in the truck bed, would then pick them up and swing them onto a stack he was building behind the cab.

"This isn't so bad," Haakon remembered saying to Sig after planting a dozen or so bales on the tailgate.

Sig's only response was to grin at Haakon. He knew what Haakon would come to know after the bales numbered in the hundreds. Yet, as tired and uncomfortable as Haakon later became, he stayed with it. He could see Kari's face peering back at him in the pickup's side mirror and he did not want her to think of him as some wimpy "city boy." Girls, he recalled thinking, with some exasperation—particularly good-looking ones—have an intrinsic ability to muster that extra bit of energy out of young males.

But Haakon had a limit. After enjoying a sizeable, multi-course dinner at the farmhouse that evening and then returning to Kari's house to shower, he lay on her bed. His next recollection was waking in the morning by her side. She told him that despite her best attempts to rouse him that night, he was unresponsive. Haakon doubted that was possible, but when he turned his body towards her, sore muscles convinced him otherwise.

Haakon made up for it the following evening. After dinner at Kari's house, she wanted to teach him how to salsa dance. And, though he was still sore from bucking hay bales, he could not refuse her. She had already cleared a space in her living room to serve as their dance floor and Tito Puente was cued up on the stereo's turntable.

"Just watch how I move my feet," she instructed. "It's just like walking."

It was *nothing* like walking, he thought. Kari led Haakon backwards through the basic steps, resolved to drill them into his brain. As he stumbled about, he smiled at the determination written on her face as she whispered the count, "one, two, three, pause, five, six, seven, pause." But Kari was too focused on his moves to smile back. He realized he would do well to take the dance seriously.

Eventually, Haakon got it and was able to complete a few movements without dropping the count. Kari beamed proudly.

"And you said that you couldn't dance. Look at you!"

"Yes. The more that I do this, the more I am convinced that I was born to dance," Haakon said.

"Don't get ahead of yourself, but I *do* see promise."

Haakon had to admit, he was pleased with his sudden dancing flair. And there was something very erotic about moving in unison to the beat while holding each other—man-to-woman, face-to-face, eyes-to-eyes. It was fervid and it led to even better things for Haakon as the evening wore on. It *did* occur to him that his accelerated learning was akin to the Pavlov's Dog technique. Like his canine counterpart, positive reinforcement undeniably motivated Haakon.

Although they never made it official, Kari and Haakon came to live together. During the working weekdays, he stayed at her house. He always left for work a little early to assure that her neighbor would not see him leave, though it was unlikely that they were fooling anyone, particularly her father. The captain had to know Haakon was staying with his daughter. Yet he never said a word about it to either of them. Haakon liked to think that Kari's father remained silent because he approved of him. But, Haakon knew it was more probable that, as a pragmatic military man, the captain wanted to avoid a battle on two fronts. His hands were full dealing with his wife's failing health. He did not need a conflict with his daughter. That summer, the captain was a fragile man.

Initially, on the weekends, Kari would stay with Haakon at Camp One. Like a trooper, she would willingly endure the inconvenience of the outhouse and the frigid makeshift river-bathtub for the novelty of "roughing it" and breathing in the ever-present aroma of pine and fir. Kari loved campfires, so they made one nearly every night. And she was a good sport about the tiny living quarters of the trailer.

"I have always wondered what it would be like to be an astronaut and to live in a small space," she said. "Now I wonder no more."

On these camp weekends, Brady no doubt felt like the odd man out—particularly when Kari and Haakon huddled near the fire. The couple never conveyed that he was unwelcome, in fact they enjoyed his company and dry wit. Brady's overly sarcastic storytelling made for some colorful campfire entertainment. But sitting across from the lovers must have made Brady feel lonely. And, this loneliness, and the likely longing for his high school heydays, prompted Brady to return to Minnesota. In early September, he threw his few belongings into the back of his pickup truck. Then, in his classic Brady style, he bid Haakon an unemotional goodbye.

"Well, it's been real… see ya around."

Yet, as hard as he tried to conceal it, Haakon knew Brady was sad to go.

He never asked if Haakon was returning with him as had been originally planned. Brady just came to realize he was not. As a keen observer, he would have recognized what had developed between Kari and Haakon. So it did not surprise Haakon that Brady chose not to waste the words.

Though, at times, an insufferable "pain in the ass," Brady had a heart that was too big for even his intractable personality to hide. Haakon was sorry to see him go and he stood for a long time watching the bold white "F-O-R-D" letters, painted across his tailgate, recede down the gravel drive.

"Did he leave because of me?" Kari asked.

"Yes and no," Haakon answered. "He marches to his own drummer, whether it's on a path to glory or over a cliff. It's both his best and worst quality… and it's not alterable."

"I'll miss him. He was funny… even charming sometimes."

Haakon turned to Kari and rolled his eyes.

"Charming?" he questioned. "I've heard him called a lot of things, but charming? I'll have to think on that one."

Haakon chuckled to himself as he watched Brady's pickup truck turn north onto the highway, because, in truth, he knew Brady *could* be charming.

In the weeks that followed Brady's departure, as if orchestrated to bolster Haakon's relationship with Kari, autumn was postponed. The heat subsided, but the cold was held at bay as well. The bridge to winter became a never-ending Indian Summer. The favorable weather enabled them to enjoy the camp weekends late into the year. And this was true of all outdoor activities.

As the daylight hours grew shorter, Kari and Haakon made it a custom to go on long evening strolls. Sometimes they hiked along the creek. Often they walked down the gravel drive and around the property. Occasionally, they walked on the railroad tracks. When they did, each competed to see who could balance themselves, walking along a single rail the furthest. Kari had been a high school gymnast, so Haakon was out of his league from the "get go." Consequently, to retain his dignity, he was reduced to cheating.

"BOO!" he screamed after charging Kari from behind, trying to scare her off of her equilibrium.

"Knock it off, cheater! Can't you just compete fair and square?"

"I wasn't raised on a parallel bar like some of us."

"Well, life isn't fair. Deal with it, buttercup!"

Haakon grabbed Kari and lifted her off of the rail with her legs kicking in protest. But within a minute they were standing face-to-face in an embrace.

"Why do I put up with you, Haakon?"

"My good looks?"

"No, it's not that."

"My swanky truck?"

"Seriously? No, it's not that. And it's not really a truck."

"Well, that only leaves my charismatic personality."

"No. It's because I feel sorry for you… that you are such a poor rail-walker you feel compelled to cheat. How pathetic!"

"You love me because I'm pathetic?"

"Yes. Because you're pathetic and you need my help."

"That's good enough for me," Haakon responded. "I'll take your affection anyway I can get it."

He leaned down to kiss her.

Often in the evenings, before Haakon started a campfire, they would go down to the hillside that overlooked the creek and sit on its smooth granite outcropping. The natural porch was always warm, its thermal mass retaining the day's rays of sunshine long into the twilight, so it made for a comfortable perch from which to watch the sun set behind the distant mountains. Usually, they sat tightly next to one another—she leaning into him, neither of them saying much of anything. While taking comfort in each other's warmth, they would observe the sky slowly exploding with pastel hues.

And they would sometimes talk about serious things.

"I've decided to not go back for fall quarter."

Kari's face turned towards Haakon, surprised.

"What?"

"I don't want to go back. I can't… now."

"But you've got to finish college."

"I don't know. Maybe not. I've been talking to Kingsley. He wants me to become an electrician's apprentice. Says he'll put it all together for me."

"You want to be an electrician?"

"I enjoy the trade. It's a good job," Haakon said, selling the idea to not only her but to himself. "I love it here… and I can't imagine leaving here… leaving you. I've never been happier… never been so content."

"You're going from being an artist to an electrician?"

"Yeah, does that seem weird?"

"Kind of."

Kari's arm slipped behind Haakon and she pulled closer, resting her head on his shoulder.

"You know that you could go to the university down in Missoula," she said, thinking through the possibilities. "At least you could come back on weekends."

"I thought of that. I still wouldn't want to be away from you so much though."

"I wouldn't want you to be away so much either, but I don't want you to forego your dreams for me. We can do both," she reasoned.

"The U of Montana doesn't really have the program I want, either. And even if it did, I'd have to pay out-of-state tuition, which I can't afford."

"You know, I would go back to Minnesota with you if it weren't for my mom."

"I know you would. And I know you can't. But I don't think I can go either. And I think I might really enjoy being an electrician."

They sat silent for several long seconds.

"My schooling future doesn't have to be all decided now. I'm just going to take fall quarter off and go from there. It doesn't mean that I'm necessarily foregoing college."

"Hmm…" she responded.

Then Kari squeezed Haakon tightly again.

"Well, I would love nothing more, of course. I've been dreading the day that you go back to school. To be honest, I've cried about it… a lot."

He turned to Kari and she looked up into his eyes. The amber twilight made her soft cheeks glow while glistening like tiny flames in her pupils. Haakon reached out for her chin and lightly pulled her lips to his. They said nothing more on the topic that night.

The splendid mild weather continued into early October. It seemed summer would never end. Wanting to take advantage of it, Landon proposed "a couples weekend canoe trip" on the south fork of the upper Cedar River. The expedition would be comprised of Landon, Swan, Kari, and Haakon. They would drive two cars up the Renfro Valley and drop one at the final destination. The other vehicle, carrying the four paddlers, their camping gear, and their two canoes, would continue on up to the launch point. This would enable them to paddle one-way downstream to a waiting vehicle.

Kari loved the idea of a canoe camping trip, so on Saturday morning the four precariously climbed aboard two unsteady aluminum canoes loaded with their gear. Swan and Landon were in one canoe and Kari and Haakon shared the other. In each, the lighter women sat up in the bow seats to better distribute the weight.

Haakon was the only paddler with real canoeing experience, so he tried to coach the others in proper canoe navigation. After a half-hour of errant steering, followed by laughter and screams, the two teams finally "got their groove." They learned how to coordinate their strokes, and the canoes, thereafter, traveled in the general direction intended.

The Cedar River's south fork cut deep into the rocks of the surrounding mountains. Though it must have lived a tumultuous past, somehow the ever-falling water, fed by the winter snows of nearby peaks, evolved over the eons into a gentle ribbon that flowed quietly at the feet of giants. Tall, daunting rock cliffs walled some of the route. These sections were so grand to behold that the paddlers could not help but stare up into the heights and wonder how water and time could have been such a masterful artist. With necks strained upward in awe, they found it difficult to form words. During this rare speech void, Haakon detected a subtle echo of moving water.

When the valley opened, the glossy river surface reflected the forest and stunning rock outcroppings that made up its shores. The current was discernible, but not worrisome. It carried the boats at a comfortable pace, so they did not have to work hard to make progress. Instead, they talked and laughed while casually paddling. It was a perfect day and they glided along with ease. Landon was lavishly praised for encouraging the outing.

"This must feel like home to you, Hawk," Landon said.

Haakon's expressions showed that he was reveling in this. He had previously reminisced to Landon about his many canoe adventures into the Boundary Waters Canoe Area Wilderness of northern Minnesota.

"Well, take away the mountains and it sort of is familiar," Haakon answered. "This is amazing!"

"It's unbelievable," Kari added.

"My dad used to bring me and my brothers up here," Landon said. "I haven't been back in a long time. It's so close, I'm now asking myself why."

Several times, Haakon noticed Swan sitting silently in the bow of her canoe, gazing forward with a paddle rested across her lap. It was almost as though she was meditating. He wondered if being Native American gave her a leg up on connecting with the wild surroundings. Could she read it better? Could she hear things he could not hear? Haakon knew next to nothing about Native Americans—only their stereotypical depictions from movies and television. But he believed, or wanted to believe, that they had a primal extrasensory bond with the land. This perceived "earthy mysticism" intrigued him.

He had been told that Swan was a descendant of Chief Joseph—the fabled Nez Perce chief of one-hundred years prior, who, legend claimed, skillfully evaded and outmaneuvered the U.S. Cavalry for over three months. The Chief accomplished this impossible feat with relatively few warriors, while traveling nearly 1,200 miles through rugged terrain. And, he did it with hundreds of women, children, and elders in tow. Haakon wondered if Swan had inherited any of his indomitable spirit. For a person of small stature, she had a formidable enigmatic aura about her.

Their plan was to paddle fifteen miles to Cottonwood Falls, the only whitewater aberration along the route. Here they would disembark from the canoes ahead of the falls, then portage the short distance to its other side. Once underway again, they would paddle only another half mile to a campsite. Since they encountered no other people, they thought it likely to be vacant.

When the canoes landed on the shore of the portage point, each rose out of their canoes to stretch their legs and to view the waterfall. From a rocky perch just below the falls, they could fully assess its full splendor and might.

"Oh my God, this is beautiful!" Kari exclaimed, over the roar of falling water.

"Wow. Pretty impressive," Haakon agreed.

The waterfall was slightly wider than two canoe lengths. It dropped at about a thirty-degree angle, actually bending more than free-falling. With a relatively smooth and transparent surface, you could see its underlying rock base. The water did not get white and frothy until it slammed into the lower step of the river, four feet below. Then the water churned briefly before being released into a broad, gentle pool. On its far end, the pool narrowed into the continuance of the river. Eventually, it would meet the larger Cedar River, then the Saleesh River. The converged waters meandered to Lake Pend Oreille and finally the Columbia River, the Northwest's freshwater highway to the Pacific Ocean.

Despite its name, Cottonwood Falls looked as though an

experienced paddler could successfully navigate it. Even if one miscalculated and tipped, there were no jagged rocks to slam into. The river poured gracefully into the pool below, like water out of a slightly tipped bucket. Yet Haakon assessed it as deceivingly difficult.

"Come on. We can paddle over this," Kari said, looking for his response.

"Oh, I don't think so," Haakon answered.

"It would be fun, let's do it," Swan said.

"What's the worst that can happen?" Kari continued. "We just fall into the pool. It would be fun either way."

"No. Bad idea," Haakon said.

He knew that neither Kari nor Swan had any prior canoeing experience.

"Note that this is not named Cottonwood Rapids, it's Cottonwood Falls."

"Why don't you and I do it?" Swan asked Kari.

"All right, I'm game," Kari answered.

"Hawk's right. This is not a good idea," Landon finally interjected.

"Oh, you guys are soft. Us girls can do this. Let's show them how," Swan taunted.

A momentum of dare had built between the two girls. Against Haakon's better judgment, he contemplated the possibility.

"Well, if you do it, do it with an empty canoe," Haakon said. "After you tip over, you'll at least still have dry clothes and dry sleeping bags."

"Fine, let's carry the stuff across. Then you and Landon can watch from down here as we show you up," Swan said.

By now the women had something to prove. Haakon should have known that could be a dangerous motivator. Yet, he and Landon did what the women proposed. They carried one canoe and all of their camping provisions to the lower side of the waterfall. Then Haakon stood below to observe as Landon went above the falls with the women to help launch them. Everyone was out of Haakon's view until Landon appeared on the rock ledge above.

"Here they come," Landon shouted down at Haakon, trying to have his words carry over the crashing water.

The bow of the canoe, seating Kari, appeared at the waterfall's upper edge first. Right away, things went awry. The canoe struck an unseen boulder that was just inches below the water surface. The jolt surprised Kari and she dropped her paddle overboard, eliminating her ability to help steer. The current pulled the canoe sideways into the falls. Then gravity rolled it over, turning it inwards, towards the waterfall. Both women tipped into the turbulence.

The current pushed Swan out into the pool and away from the falls. But Kari remained out of view for a few seconds. The water's force carried her into the waterfall's undercurrent, where physics seemed defied. Counter-intuitively, the current pulled her upstream and held her under the weight of the falling water. By the time Haakon thought to react, her bobbing head suddenly appeared in the pool, a short distance from Swan. Haakon sighed with relief. Then Landon, who was still watching from above, broke out laughing at the mishap. As if taking his cue, Haakon nervously laughed too.

"Excellent!" Landon shouted down to the two women.

Assuming them both out of danger, Haakon began scanning the river for the two wood paddles they had dropped. On a previous Boundary Waters canoe trip, Haakon's party snapped nearly all the paddles fighting against strong head winds. They literally broke in two and the paddlers faced the prospect of traveling thirty miles in canoes without paddles. So, since that incident, Haakon had "paddle conservation" embedded in his brain.

He spotted both paddles floating in the center of the pool, slowly drifting downstream. Instinctively, he jumped into the empty canoe beside him and pushed off alone to retrieve them. Just as Haakon was about to reach into the water to grab the first paddle he came upon, a voice softly called out from behind him. It was an eerily weak voice. Haakon sensed danger. So, leaving the paddle floating, he pulled hard to the left and pivoted his canoe into the opposite direction. Then he heard the faint voice again and this time he could understand it. Almost indecipherably, the voice said, "Help."

Yet Haakon still could not detect the source. His heart pounded as he frantically searched the surrounding water. Suddenly, Kari's head appeared, barely breaking the glassy surface of the pool. She was only a canoe length away, so one strong paddle stroke put him beside her. He reached over to grab her shirt and pulled her alongside the canoe, while shifting his legs in the opposite direction to counterbalance. Haakon could not pull her into the boat without flipping it, so he held her shirt tightly with one hand as he paddled with the other, back towards the shore. Out of the corner of Haakon's eye, he could see Swan crawling onto the bank with Landon's help. Landon pulled their half submerged canoe onto the shore with her.

Once in shallow water, Haakon jumped out of the canoe and pulled Kari upright. Her face was ashen.

"Can you talk?" Haakon nearly shouted, holding Kari's face up so he could see her expression.

"Yes," she whispered, but her body was nearly limp and her skin bluish.

"Oh God," he blurted.

Haakon drew her close, both for warmth and for reassurance that she was whole. Kari shivered violently.

"We've got to get them warm, fast!" Haakon shouted to Landon.

From a distance, Swan appeared fine. She was standing on her own, talking to Landon.

Haakon turned back to Kari's face.

"I'm so sorry. I'm such an idiot!" he muttered with his speech broken with sobs.

Kari responded softly, "I'm okay."

But she was not.

Landon and Swan appeared by Kari and Haakon's side. Swan was visibly shivering as well.

"We've got to get them warm," Haakon repeated.

Landon nodded in agreement.

"Can you start a fire?"

Being a born woodsman, Landon had a campfire started in minutes. Haakon had already peeled Kari's wet clothes off and had her bundled into a dry sleeping bag. Quickly, Haakon stripped to his underwear and climbed in with her to transfer his body's heat—something he had learned from a winter survival class.

Swan had much more strength. She had already changed to dry clothing on her own and had moved towards the heat of the fire. Once it was blazing, Haakon climbed out of the sleeping bag, then carried Kari, still in the bag, to the fire's edge. She responded almost

immediately to its warmth. Haakon could literally see color return
to her skin. He lowered himself to the ground, next to the fire, with
Kari still in his arms. Holding her in his lap, Haakon watched her face
intently. She stared back but said nothing, still looking distraught—no
doubt contemplating, as Haakon was, what had nearly happened.

While recreating the event in his mind, it occurred to Haakon
that Swan had been wearing a water-skier's lifebelt. It was not much
of a floatation device, but it was better than nothing—which was
what Kari was wearing. Both women were strong swimmers, but both
women were fully clothed. When weighted with water, their clothing
counteracted their swimming abilities.

Haakon felt like an idiot for not having thought this out before
the failed canoe stunt. The gentleness of the river appeased him and he
had assumed swimming from the tipped canoe would be effortless. But
without a lifejacket and after being held underwater by the current, Kari
had been handicapped and thus imperiled.

He would later learn Kari had quietly dropped below the water's
surface several times. Each time she rallied and fought her way back up,
but it was unlikely she had another surge in her. On one resurface, she
grabbed onto Swan. But realizing that the minimal lifebelt could not
support them both and that she was pulling them both under, Kari let
go.

She had been on the cusp of drowning and Haakon had not even
been aware. By sheer dumb luck, he had given chase to a canoe paddle.
And this unlikely act had put him in the pool in a position to save her.

"You're my knight again," Kari whispered to Haakon as she
regained some strength.

His eyes welled up.

"I'm not a knight, I'm an idiot! God, I'm so sorry, Kari."

He sobbed and gripped her tight.

As the sunlight dimmed, the group decided to make camp where
they were. Fully recovered, Swan, with Landon's help, pitched both of
the tents and made dinner. Haakon stayed by Kari's side. Landon even
managed to retrieve the two wayward paddles.

When darkness fell, all four sat around the fire in near silence.
Even though Kari continued to improve, the gravity of what had
transpired seemed to hang over them like a dark cloud. They tried to

converse, but could never quite break out of the solemn funk.

The only comic relief of the evening came later when both couples were in their respective tents. As Kari and Haakon lay together in silence, they could hear the crackling fire and the roar of the waterfall. But they soon could also discern "oohing and aahing" sounds coming from the other tent. This made Kari and Haakon both burst out into laughter. Kari had recovered.

"When I paddled out into the pool today," Haakon whispered to Kari, "I was not going after you. I just assumed you were okay. I was going after the paddles. That's the truth of it."

Haakon tried to continue explaining why he was chasing the paddles, but Kari interrupted.

"I was stupid. I didn't even think to put on a lifejacket. I'm a great swimmer, I thought."

"Don't you understand? If I had not gone after those paddles, I would not have been out to you soon enough. It was just dumb luck."

He shook his head, still trying to comprehend the incident.

"But you *were* there," she said matter-of-factly.

"If I had not been on a trip where we broke seven paddles, you would have drowned."

"But you *were* on the trip and you *did* save me."

This bizarre connection of unrelated events would haunt Haakon forever. Over time, he would sometimes apply religious explanations to make sense of it. But on this night, he felt both foolish and grateful. Haakon would have easily given his life for the same outcome and he found this realization to be exceedingly sobering.

"I'll never leave you, Kari. I love you. I can't be without you."

Haakon wanted to say more, but words failed him as he sobbed again. It was as though Kari's recovery gave him the freedom to chastise himself for not foreseeing the danger. But she would have none of it.

"I love you too, so much," Kari said, pulling Haakon closer. "But I never know how to tell you how much. I can't think of the right words to say."

The faint campfire light, filtering through the thin tent fabric, illuminated her eyes. They were sincere.

"It's like the song. 'Wherever I am, I'm always walking with you. Whoever I'm with, I'm always talking to you…' I've never felt this way about anyone, before."

"Nor have I, Kari."

They stared into each other's faces until she fell asleep. Then Haakon watched alone, absorbing Kari's presence. Eventually, *he* fell asleep and she merged into his dream.

12
THE HUNT

Despite the unseasonable long run of warm weather, the aspen trees remained on their primordial schedule. By mid-October, wide swathes of the mountains transformed into an array of brilliant golds, blending harmonically with the predominant evergreens. By early November, these varied hues were contrasted with intricate shapes of snow, forming majestic crowns on the high peaks. As the days progressed, the reach of white gradually descended towards the valley floor. This transition of color, along with the ebbing hours of daylight, was the stark visual cue of winter's approach.

Mornings grew crisp, then utterly cold. Windshields displayed the frost born of the predawn freeze. In partial darkness, Haakon tried in vain to scrape the ice off of the Scout's glass without making noise. It probably did not matter, as it was no longer a secret that he was living with Kari. Dropping temperatures forced him to abandon Camp One. The trailer's small furnace and thin walls could not fend off the wind and chill. And the river-bathing practice became painfully impractical.

Yet he tried to minimize the scraping noise by creating a visual hole in the windshield just large enough for him to find his way down to the highway. It was not ideal or particularly safe, though he rarely encountered other passing vehicles at this hour. Haakon hoped the engine heat would eventually finish the de-icing job as he drove along. But usually, by the time he arrived at the job site, the defroster had only begun to gnaw away at the hole's edges.

Each dawn seemed a little colder than the previous. And each working day was harder to start. It was an unwelcome transition that Haakon had never known—to abruptly move from a warm bed to a frigid construction site. He underestimated the impact of working in cold. Despite being from Minnesota and being no stranger to winters, Haakon never knew it at such an early hour. He had passed briefly through the morning chill, from house to car and from car to school. And he had played in it plenty as a child and had snow skied in it as a teen. But voluntarily recreating in cold was not the same as mandatorily working in it. Climbing icy scaffolding, unraveling stiff extension cords, setting up frosty equipment, and hammering nails while wearing gloves was a sobering experience to him. It was a difficult adjustment.

On some days it would take him an hour or two to warm up. It would be even quicker when the sun came out. But fall sunshine was not commonplace in the Inland Northwest.

"You'll get used to it," Carlos would say, looking somewhat ridiculous wearing his blaze orange fake-fur-lined bomber hat with its earflaps down. "If I can move here after growing up in El Paso, you can certainly survive the transition from Siberia… or Minnesota, or whatever icebox you are from."

But Haakon was unconvinced.

With the footings just poured for the new Colterville bowling alley, the crew was building skyward against time and weather. Getting the exterior walls up would make way for the trusses. Once placed, they could nail down the sheets of plywood and then sheath and enclose the walls and roof. It was all hands on deck for this task, whether a tradesman or a laborer. Because once the building was sealed, it could be insulated, then heated—at least enough to take the chill out of its inside air. And this promise of comfort was a huge motivator. Yet, even moving hard and fast, they were still looking at two weeks of cold outside work.

The construction site was only four blocks from Kari's workplace, so Haakon met her for lunch in a nearby cafe on what turned out to be the coldest fall day.

"You look like Hatchet Jack from the movie *Jeremiah Johnson*," she exclaimed upon seeing him approach up the sidewalk.

"I *feel* a bit like a frozen Hatchet Jack. It's been a pretty cool, breezy morning."

She looked cold as well, so they quickly ducked into the cafe and found an empty table.

"Do you recall the rifle that Hatchet Jack had frozen in his hands?" Haakon asked.

"Why, I do, Mr. Haakon. It was a .50 caliber Hawken," she said, her face displaying pride in knowing the answer.

They laughed.

"Seriously, you look totally frozen. Your cheeks are bright red."

"Well, that's better than the pale white of frostbite, I am told."

Kari grimaced at his words.

"Yeah, it's pretty cold working out there today. But hey, I can start to feel my fingers again."

Haakon moved them up and down in front of her as though he was playing piano keys.

"You know, you're a young guy now, but you might not like doing this stuff so much when you're older."

"Well, I don't like this cold stuff so much *now*, but are you trying to talk me out of this?"

Kari's face turned serious.

"No. I mean yeah… maybe. I want you to make the right decision for your life. I don't want you to do this job for me."

"I have thought about it. I mean, I'm tough enough to take a little cold outside work. Heck, I'm from Minnesota. That's like being a Laplander. But I've thought about it more lately. Not the being with you part, the career part. Some days I have mixed feelings on the career part, but never on the being with you part."

The waitress came and quickly jotted down their orders. As she turned to walk away, Kari and Haakon picked up the conversation where they had left off.

"The appeal of being an electrician is not quite the same this time of year as it was during the summer, I'll admit."

"I get it, of course," she said.

"I don't know. I guess it's not a good day to be assessing it. Tomorrow, if it's warm and sunny, I could be singing a different tune."

"You know my dad thinks you should go back to school."

"He must want me gone."

"That's not true. He likes you. But he's a big believer in college."

Kari stared at Haakon for a long moment.

"You know if you want to go back, I'll wait for you."

"You must want me gone too."

"You know that's not true. It would kill me!" she exclaimed.

He detected annoyance in Kari's face.

"Don't screw up your education because of me. I can tell you are not really liking your work as much as you did. I've been seeing this in you even *before* it got cold."

"You can tell?"

"I think I know you pretty well, Haakon. I can see it and hear it in what you say—and don't say."

"Well, it's true. It's a big decision."

"That's okay. Now's the time to figure these things out," she responded.

They both sat quietly for a few minutes, reflecting.

"What if we both went back to Minnesota?"

"I can't do that. You know that. My mom. I can't leave her."

"I know. I'm sorry. I don't even know why I said it."

"Well, that would be the answer in a perfect world."

"Listen, let's not have this discussion now. I need to be in a more neutral state of mind, not when my brain is half-frozen."

They dropped the topic for the rest of their lunch visit, but Haakon could tell Kari was cognizant of the impending fracture in his plans.

Weather that was not ideal for outdoor construction *was* ideal for deer and elk tracking. Early November was prime hunting season in northwest Montana and practically every able-bodied Montana male was a hunter. It was a "big deal," akin to a "Holy month." To many, it was the pinnacle of the entire year. To them, the months before and after hunting season were merely for talking about and preparing for the next hunting season. Some local businesses closed during these weeks and those that did not, like the mills, endured a significant uptick in worker sick days.

Given that nearly everyone hunted, Haakon received many offers to join in. He was not interested in the kill aspect, but he *was* interested in its camaraderie-while-slogging-through-the-woods aspect. The killing was not a moral issue with Haakon as he was an unapologetic carnivore—a lover of burgers, steaks, and practically all things meat. He just preferred to acquire his meat pre-packaged in a grocery store. Haakon had no inherent desire to "meet the meat that he eats" as some did. Yet the fatalist in him surmised it was probably a good idea to know how to hunt just in case it ever became necessary. One never knew when there might be some disaster, like a nuclear war, that could set mankind back to the pre-grocery-store Stone Age.

Hunting was not entirely new to Haakon. His uncle had taken him along on a deer hunt once in northern Minnesota and had first insisted that Haakon complete a gun safety course. This brief experience hardly qualified him as a gun expert, but it introduced Haakon to the basics of how to clean a gun, how to dress out a deer, and how to handle a rifle safely. He had forgotten much of the deer processing part, but gun safety had been thoroughly drilled into his skull.

"Let's go get your license. I can vouch that you're a resident," Carlos offered. "I've got a rifle you can use."

"I wouldn't want to slow you guys up. I've only gone once before."

"It's not a race. It's more of a waiting game," he said. "Besides, I need a big guy to help drag my elk out when I get one—and I always get one. Normal guys don't always get one, but as you know, I'm not a normal guy."

So Haakon relented and signed on with Carlos's hunting group for opening day.

Since Kari's father was sitting out the hunting season, he lent Haakon his blaze orange insulated jumpsuit and hat. Wearing it, while holding a lunch bucket and thermos, made Haakon an irresistible target of Kari's mockery.

"Will you be providing for me, great white hunter?"

"Me bring you home meat to fill stomach and elk hide to warm you on cold nights," Haakon responded in jest, while pounding a fist on his chest.

Kari mimicked a sexy growl.

"That kind of cave-talk turns me on."

He smiled.

"Well, I've got an entire repertoire of caveman talk that I'll save for later on."

Kari smiled back for a moment, but then turned serious.

"Be careful."

"I will. I'm in no competition with these guys. If I get something, I get something."

This answer seemed to satisfy Kari, so he kissed her goodbye and walked out into the cold Saturday pre-dawn and then into Carlos's waiting, warm, idling Jeep Wagoneer. Haakon squeezed into the rear seat between Landon and Sig. Without turning, Judd from the front passenger seat immediately addressed him.

"Hawk, you're a damn fool to get out of a cozy bed with that captain's daughter to go with us."

"I must provide," Haakon replied.

Everyone laughed.

"I'll bet you must," Judd said, garnering another laugh. "Let me know if it ever gets to be too much of a workload for you. I've got a lot of experience and I'm always available to help out."

"That's good to know. I'll keep that in mind."

"Hey, what are friends for?"

Haakon took more ribbings about the "captain's daughter" as they made their way out of town. It did not bother him, as he understood he was the rookie on the team and therefore the designated target. Taunting went with the turf. Besides, Haakon was certain that any of them, with the exception perhaps of Carlos, would have traded places with him in a heartbeat. So Haakon was impervious to their barbs.

The Wagoneer traveled up a gravel Forest Service road, somewhere above and north of Colterville. When they got high in the mountains, Carlos pulled off onto a spot widened for passing logging trucks. They all climbed out into the cold and stretched and yawned and groaned about the temperature. Then each shuffled to the back hatch to retrieve their respective rifles.

The not-yet-visible sun began to silhouette the distant peaks to the east. There was just enough illumination for Haakon to make out a fog bank in the valley below. Its buoyancy gently weaved through the treetops that protruded up and out of its embrace, like a lost and fallen cloud trying to find its way home. The air was sweet with pine and all was quiet save the cry of an unseen raven. Haakon realized, in that moment, he was standing in his idyllic vision of the Northwest— mountains, tall trees, and fog. It was a surreal world of blue that felt enclosed and consoling.

Carlos's plan was to split the group into two. He and Judd would drop into a large clearing below where they stood, then make their way east. Haakon was to walk another quarter-mile up the road with Sig and Landon to the next clearing. Then they would also drop from the road and make their way west towards Carlos and Judd. The idea was to scare any deer or elk into the sights of the other party. This was a workable plan as long as the other party was sure of its target and certain that they were not firing on the other hunters.

Since they were each dressed in blaze orange outfits, being mistaken for a game animal seemed impossible. Yet Haakon knew it sometimes happened. There is no vision or intelligence test given when you apply for a hunting license. It is assumed you can differentiate between a large brown elk and a blaze-orange human being. And Haakon assumed that each member of his group was a competent hunter who knew how to handle firearms safely. But it did not take long to become disavowed of that belief.

As Sig, Landon, and Haakon walked off of the road, down into the clearing, Haakon was immediately troubled with how Landon was carrying his rifle. Frequently, he allowed the trajectory of his rifle barrel to pass across both Sig and Haakon. This was taboo in gun safety. The assumption was always that the gun was loaded, the safety off, and it was ready to fire, even if you were "certain" it was not loaded and not ready to fire. Following this reasoning, the barrel direction should never pass across a human being, or anything other than the sky, the ground, or the intended target.

"Landon, you're making me nervous with that barrel aiming at me," Haakon finally said.

"What a pussy! I've got the safety on," he replied, defensively.

"Yeah, maybe so, but I'd feel a whole lot better if you kept it pointed up or down," Haakon said. "I guess I'm a pussy, but I just don't like look'n down the barrel of a gun."

"What do you know about hunting? You're a city boy," he protested. "Plus, it's not a gun, it's a rifle."

Haakon took offense at both the "rifle" and "city" comment.

"I don't know much about hunting. And I don't know much about rifles either. But I know which end of the barrel the bullets come out of."

Sig spoke up.

"I'd kind of appreciate it too, Landon. I patched up too many guys in Nam. Not look'n to do it again here today."

"Fine!" Landon said, indignantly.

"And, by the way, I'm from a small town *near* a city. I'm not a city boy," Haakon stated, feeling it necessary to set the record straight.

For a time, Landon was careful. But, eventually the barrel was swinging where it should not have, once again. It was as though he was incapable of staying focused. So, rather than lambaste him, Haakon walked behind and suggested Sig do the same.

The area they were hunting was a mix of fields and forest. Sawyers had harvested much of the timber years before, affording the openness and the ability for grasses and sporadic low brush to grow. The clear-cut, with all of its protruding stumps, made the area look a bit like a grown over war zone. But it was very conducive to elk hunting.

All the terrain was hilly and the ground surface uneven, making it difficult to walk. The group hoped that they would spot an elk wandering out of the protective trees and into the clearing. Keeping the hunt near the road made the recovery of any potential kill significantly easier. It was not difficult to imagine that packing quartered sections of a large elk, through miles of hilly and obstacle riddled terrain, would be arduous. The closer the kill was to the road, the less work expended.

Surrounded by calm morning wilderness and walking well behind Landon, Haakon's thoughts became introspective. Again he tried to resolve his impending dilemma with Kari. As much as he found comfort in the land and the people of northwest Montana, and as much as he loved Kari, Haakon was increasingly questioning the decision to forego college. He knew he could enjoy many aspects of the construction trades, but he wondered if he would value it the same when he grew older, as she had warned. In Haakon's heart, he knew the correct answer. Just the fact he was asking himself this question made him realize he *needed* to go back. But, how he would broach this to Kari, he did not know. It was one thing for her to say that she would be supportive, but he feared it would be another thing altogether to have it actually happen.

As they trekked across the clearing, Haakon's brain was so lost in thought that he allowed himself to get ahead of Landon. And this would prove to be a fateful moment of bad timing. For some inexplicable reason, Landon's supposed safety-latched rifle fired. Its piercing blast reverberated across the otherwise near silent setting, echoing in the valley below. Instinctively, all three hunters froze in their tracks.

"What the hell, Landon!" Sig shouted, glaring at him.

"That was so close I could feel the air move next to my foot," Haakon said.

Sig glanced at Haakon's feet.

"You're hit!" he exclaimed.

Haakon looked down at his boot and bright red blood was oozing out.

"Shit!" he said, now alarmed even though he could not feel pain.

"Oh, man! I'm sorry! I'm sorry!" Landon screamed, looking at Haakon's foot in shock.

"All right, all right, settle down," Sig said. "Let me get a look at that."

Sig set down his rifle, then lowered a pack from his back and set it on the ground next to Haakon.

"Let's sit ya down, Hawk, and get that boot off."

He took Haakon's rifle, opened the magazine to remove the cartridge, then set it next to his. He and Landon helped lower Haakon to the ground, while keeping the injured foot extended outward.

"Is it hurt'n?" Sig asked, now on his knees unlacing Haakon's boot.

"Yeah, it's not feel'n too good," Haakon said, now detecting the onset of pain.

"Ah, Hawk, I'm such an idiot," Landon blurted, still looking panicked.

Haakon did not respond, being preoccupied with Sig sliding off his boot. He was afraid of what its removal would reveal. As it slowly came off, Sig looked up at Haakon's face to watch for an expression of discomfort.

"We okay?" he asked as he gingerly pulled the boot off.

"Yeah," Haakon responded nervously, realizing that the blood-soaked sock was next.

"Tell ya what. I'll cut this off," Sig said.

He pulled a small scissors out of a red first aid kit, that was now visible inside of his open backpack, and began cutting the fabric away from the wound.

"So, you were a medic in Vietnam?" Haakon asked, still watching Sig's actions closely.

"I was," he answered, looking up at Haakon's face again. "I know how to patch these kinds of holes—I've done it a lot."

"So, if I guy's gonna get shot in the woods, it's probably best to do it next to an Army medic, huh?" Haakon said, trying to inject a little diversionary humor.

"Yeah, I think that's right," Sig said, smirking as he slowly peeled the sock away. "Today's your lucky, unlucky day."

Sig got quiet for a moment as he carefully examined Haakon's foot.

"It's not too bad, Hawk. It may have nicked the bone, but it went clear through. I'm gonna clean it up and bandage it to stop the bleeding and we'll get you down to the hospital. You'll be fine."

While Sig tended to the foot, Haakon tried to be brave and not express the pain that was setting in. Landon paced nervously in circles around them, muttering unintelligible words. Minutes later, Carlos and Judd appeared. They heard the shot and assumed there was a game kill. But when they got close, it occurred to them there had been an accident.

"What the Hell?" Carlos exclaimed as he approached.

"I shot'im," Landon exclaimed. "I'm such an idiot. I shot'im!"

"Jeez! Is it bad?" Carlos asked, now crouched down next to Sig.

"No, he'll be fine. Bullet passed through his foot. Might have grazed the bone though," Sig answered, as he began wrapping the wound. "Can you guys get the Jeep up here? We need to get him down to the hospital."

"Yeah, I'm on it," Judd said, standing behind Carlos. "Hand me the keys."

Carlos frantically fumbled through his pockets, then exclaimed, "Oh shit! I left them in the ignition."

"Well, I'll head down there," Judd said. "Hopefully, you didn't lock them in."

Then Judd turned to Haakon.

"You ain't gonna die while I'm gone, are you?"

"I'll try not, but can we chat later? This is kinda begin'n to hurt," Haakon answered.

"Aw right, ya big baby. I'll be right back. Just hang on," he said.

Haakon realized that Judd was trying to make light of the incident for his benefit.

"Hey, if they're locked in, find a rock and break the window," Carlos said.

Judd nodded in acknowledgement.

"But if ya gotta break one, break the passenger window, would ya? It's already screwed up."

"Aye, aye," Judd said, as he turned to jog down the gravel road.

"I'm sorry guys," Landon said, now slightly more composed.

"Holy smokes, Landon!" Carlos said, shaking his head. "Sorry this happened, Hawk. That can't feel too good."

"Ah... it would probably hurt a normal guy, Carlos," Haakon responded, using Carlos's own manner of speech. "But, of course, I'm not a normal guy. And, as it turns out, I'm not bulletproof either."

"I guess not," Carlos said smiling. "This will be a good story for ya. I don't think Kari will like hearing it though."

"I'm sorry, Hawk. I'm sorry," Landon blurted out again, as he continued pacing.

"Shut up, Landon!" Carlos shouted. "You're making us all nervous."

"I'll be fine, Landon. Settle down," Haakon said, now feeling reassured that he was being properly cared for.

Within ten minutes, Judd arrived in the Wagoneer with all the windows intact. And within forty minutes they were at the Colterville Hospital emergency room.

"I called Kari at her parents', like you asked," Carlos told Haakon after they redressed his foot.

"Was she pretty upset?"

"She didn't sound too pleased, but I reassured her you were okay and that there was no reason to race back here," Carlos said. "I told her we don't need her to get into a car accident on top of it."

"Good message. Thanks."

After being released from the emergency room, Carlos and Sig helped Haakon into Kari's house. By the time she arrived, they had left, and Haakon sat reclined on her sofa with his foot propped up on her coffee table, watching television.

"Haakon, are you trying to give me a heart attack?"

Kari looked as though she had been crying.

"Sorry. I hadn't anticipated being shot at."

"Does it hurt?"

"Yeah, it aches a little, but they gave me some stuff."

"Any long-term damage?"

"No, they don't think so, but I've got to keep my weight off it for a while. I'm on crutches for maybe a month."

Kari leaned down to hug Haakon. He could hear her sobbing quietly. Once composed, she pulled her head away from his and stared into his eyes closely. Kari's eyes were red. Mascara had run down her cheeks.

"Getting a phone call from Carlos at my parent's house… I feared the worst," she said, sobbing.

"Sorry to give you the scare."

"I'm just so grateful it wasn't worse."

"Yeah, he came close to shattering my foot. I'm pretty lucky."

She nodded her head in agreement, then tried to regain her composure by wiping her cheeks dry.

"This kind of messes up your work," Kari said, trying to sound collected.

"Yeah."

"You know I was thinking as I drove back, this will probably make your going back to school an easy decision."

"That thought had occurred to me."

Haakon observed Kari's face for emotion.

"Maybe that idiot Landon did you a favor, assuming this heals back to normal. You were teetering on the decision before."

"Yeah," he said, looking down now. "I was getting soft on the electrician thing as a career."

Haakon looked up into Kari's face again. They stared at each other with solemn expressions for several seconds.

"Well, that's it then," she responded. "You really only have one course here, Haakon."

He dropped his head into his hands and rubbed his forehead.

"I know."

13
WINTER BLUE

On Thanksgiving morning, the snowline descended from the mountains and swallowed up the entire valley. Kari and Haakon awoke to several inches of powder on the ground. Viewing it through the picture window gave Haakon the same nostalgic feeling that first snowfall always did, conjuring up tender childhood memories—a mental Norman Rockwell painting where children excitedly pulled sleds and threw snowballs as their sidewalk shoveling parents laughed in admiration. It was never *really* like that, but there was something to be said of a sudden white-flocked world and its air of enchantment. It was nature's renewed palette—fresh and full of possibilities.

Haakon looked forward to spending the day with Kari's parents. He had grown to enjoy their company and he had the impression that they liked him as well—perhaps even as an acceptable mate for their daughter. They were aware of his injury and understood why Kari was chauffeuring him around. Haakon had recently discarded the crutches, but a removable cast still prevented him from flexing and bending his injured right foot. With fresh snow on the ground, his inability to drive was a good thing. Kari's car, at her father's insistence, had new tires.

Haakon's old Scout's had tires that were cracked and worn, with only faint traces of tread. Despite being 4-wheel-drive, it was useless on slick, snowy surfaces.

With its veneer of white, the familiar route to her parents' seemed alien.

"Wow. This is quite spectacular," Haakon said, truly impressed by nature's makeover.

"It is almost unrecognizable," she said, not taking her eyes off of the road.

Kari was an attentive driver. The snow had been light and dry and did not present any significant challenge, but she would take no chances.

"You know, this is kind of nice being in the passenger seat."

"You like this, do you?"

He did. He enjoyed the freedom of being able to watch her and not the road. Sometimes, when Haakon awoke early, if the light afforded it, he would just stare at her. She was so content sleeping and her radiance made him ache inside, but in a good way—a longing of sorts. Observing her driving was quiet different. Though Kari would rarely look over at Haakon, he was convinced she knew he was looking at her. Kari's lips curved slightly upward, revealing an unconscious pleasure.

"Daytime Kari" had carefully-brushed hair, slight eye shadow, rouge cheeks, and a subtle glaze of glossy color on her soft lips—all of which enhanced her innate beauty. Haakon studied her facial features and wondered what aggregate of minute details was responsible for such perfection. She was every bit the goddess revealed on that hot summer rooftop. And this realization only worsened his dilemma. He could not stand to be away from her. Haakon felt fortunate to be with Kari and even more fortunate to be the recipient of her love. Yet, the practical, unemotional side of him knew what he had to do. It whispered inside of his head, "Don't lose this college opportunity or you may forever regret it."

They had talked little on this drive. There was something in the air and both knew what it was. As she turned into her parent's driveway, Kari spoke up.

"Something is bothering you. I can feel it."

"Why do you say that?"

"I think I know what it is," she said as she let the car roll to a stop far short of the house.

"What is it?" he asked, almost indignantly.

"You're not happy… not happy like you were in the summer anyway."

"I'm not happy. I don't know how I can go back. I wish that I could just go to school down in Missoula," Haakon said shaking his head. "Then I could at least come back on weekends."

"That'd be nice, but what's the point if they don't have the program you want and if you can't afford the out-of-state tuition?"

"No point," he said sadly.

"I don't want you to go, but I don't want you to regret not finishing school, then blaming me later."

"How could I blame you?"

"You've gotta be happy with your decision, Haakon. When all is said and done, if you're not happy, I can't be happy."

He reluctantly nodded in agreement.

"I'm fearful things wouldn't work out in the long run. You would grow to resent me. That's just the truth."

Kari's eyes grew glossy with near tears.

"I could never resent you," Haakon said, looking down at the floor mats. "It's not possible."

"It *is* possible," she retorted.

Haakon sat silent for a moment, not wanting to respond.

Then he said, "I know that there's something to what you say."

He turned to see a tear fall from her eye.

"Let's shake this off. Your parents are gonna think we're fighting."

Kari tried to smile as she dried her cheek with a tissue, glancing up at her face in the visor mirror.

"I love you, you know that," he said.

She turned to Haakon. Her face brightened a bit.

"Yeah, I know. And I love you. If we didn't love each other, this wouldn't be a problem," she responded in a nervous chuckle.

Looking into her eyes he nodded again.

Kari put the car back into gear and slowly proceeded up to the house. As they approached, her parents came outside to greet them.

They must have noticed the car parked on the driveway, but they never let on that they did. Haakon had not seen Kari's mother for several weeks and already he noted a decline in both her appearance and demeanor. She was waning. He glanced over to Kari and saw that she was fighting tears. The captain noticed Kari too, and as she walked past him following her mother into the house, he grabbed Kari and pulled her close.

"Be strong for her," he whispered in Kari's ear, though loud enough for Haakon to hear.

Then he turned to Haakon and said, "This is hard on my girls."

Yet his face wore the same emotion as Kari's.

There was a reprieve from the sadness as they all conversed with drinks prior to the dinner. But, the cloud came back when the family sat and bowed their heads for the captain's Thanksgiving prayer. All eyes were closed but Haakon's and he observed three people fighting to maintain their composure. This display of pain nearly made Haakon break out sobbing himself. And, if he had, he was convinced it would have set off a contagious cascade of tears across the table. So Haakon swallowed hard and somehow maintained his poise. When Kari opened her eyes and looked over towards Haakon, she noticed his struggle. Yet she said nothing and the conversation quickly transformed into the words that helped coordinate the movement of platters and bowls of food around the table.

After the feast and after the joint group cleanup effort, Kari and Haakon donned there coats, hats, and gloves and stepped outside for a stroll in the twilight. Holding hands, the couple made their way down the hill towards the horse barn. The overcast sky filtered what light remained, so the world was cast in a bluish-white hue. These same clouds produced large, yet sparse, flakes of snow that drifted casually downward. Even though they appeared weightless in the muffled silence of their snowy surroundings, Haakon could hear them softly impacting the ground.

Midway down the hill, Kari abruptly stopped and turned towards Haakon, grabbing his other hand as she looked up into his face as though to garner his full attention.

"I love you, Haakon."

The dim blue light stressed the blueness of Kari's eyes.

"I love you too," he responded, somewhat surprised.

He realized a further explanation was coming from her.

"I have never felt so strongly about anyone before."

Haakon said nothing but continued to stare into her eyes.

"I feel you make me whole—I truly do. I feel you and I are one... and of like mind, but so much more than that."

She reached up and grasped Haakon's face with her two hands.

"The last thing in the world that I want is for you to leave. You know that. But you can't give away your education. And you can't have regrets. Now's the time."

Her watery eyes shined up at him.

"Being an electrician would have been great if that had been your dream. But I don't think it ever was. I know you're troubled, you're doubting. I think you're trying to find a way to stay."

Haakon did not know how to respond. She was right and he knew that Kari was far more introspective than he.

She pulled her forehead up to his and their eyes locked closely. Both stood like this, frozen and silent, for what seemed an hour. Giant snowflakes floated dreamlike around them in the blue light.

The same delicate snow fell two weeks later on the evening she drove Haakon to the bus stop. They arrived ahead of the bus and sat wordlessly in the car for several minutes, neither wanting to start the long-dreaded farewell. It had been an intense journey since their meeting on the hot summer rooftop. Now their ride jarred to a sudden stop.

Winter solstice was near, so darkness came early. It was cold outside, yet warm in the car with the engine running and the heater fan blowing. The snowflakes melted as they landed on the warm windshield, then ran down the glass in little ribbons of water. At first Kari sat motionless behind the steering wheel, staring forward as though she was still driving. Haakon watched her but could not speak. Then suddenly, without turning, she leaned into him and wept.

"God, I didn't want this day to come," she whispered.

He stroked the hair that fell out of her stocking cap.

"I know," he said, wishing that he had more words.

"Summer is six months away. I can do that," Kari said, as though to convince herself. "I know we'll write and talk on the phone and time will go by. I know I can do that."

But she was withholding words and Haakon knew what these words were.

"I'm afraid that you won't come back. I'm afraid that you'll find someone else… fall in love with someone else."

She turned to look up into Haakon's face for reassurance.

"I'll be back. Of course, I'll be back. God, I love you. This is killing me," he replied, hoping that the words would ease her angst.

Reading Kari's face, he could not tell whether he was seeing comfort or doubt.

They sat embraced together for many more minutes until the headlights of the bus appeared. He looked at her with a frown, then got out of the car and grabbed his pack from the backseat. Kari followed him outside. The two of them fell into a final embrace. As the bus pulled over to the curb, Haakon kissed her—first on the lips, then on her stocking cap covered forehead.

"I've gotta go. Are you going to be all right driving home?"

"Yeah, I'm fine," she said unconvincingly with tears in her eyes. "Really, I'm fine driving. I'll sit here for a bit before I go home."

Haakon mustered half of a smile. Kari did as well.

"I'll let you know when I get there," he said.

Then Haakon turned and walked to the bus, feeling as though he had taken a blow to the stomach.

As he stood in line with the other two boarding passengers, Haakon looked over to see her watching. Neither of them smiled. They just stared at each other as though telepathically relaying their sentiments. When his turn came to board, he reluctantly stepped up, still wondering if this was the right thing to do. Part of him wanted to turn and jump back onto the sidewalk, while the door was still open behind him.

He did not.

Instead, Haakon shuffled his way down the aisle and found an open seat. He could see her through the window, but she could not see him. He waved, but she stood unresponsive alongside her car. When the bus rolled forward, Haakon blew her a kiss then stamped it on the glass, still hoping for her response.

There was none.

Illuminated by the street lamp, Haakon could see large snowflakes gently falling all around her. Kari stood motionless, looking deflated. He thought of yelling out to the bus driver to stop. He envisioned running back to her—appearing suddenly before her from out of the darkness.

But he did not.

Within minutes, the bus turned off of Main and she was gone.

14
TWO DOES DRANK

An unseasonable cold surge dropped from Canada, engulfing the entire Inland Northwest. It met a wave of moisture that swept east across the lush, blooming Wenatchee apple orchards, then over the broad Columbia River basin. Gradually, the moist air climbed towards the western foothills of the Rocky Mountains. Where the weather systems merged, an offspring of leisurely descending snowflakes was born. They were colossal, and their resulting white veneer atop the green earth temporarily concealed the progress of spring.

Two deer emerged from the snow-clad trees on the river's far side. Misty watched them with silent curiosity. They ambled to the water's edge. The falling snow eased up, and a narrow ray of sunlight found its way through the clouds and fell upon them for nearly a minute, illuminating their sleek reddish spring coats. As one drank, the other cautiously gazed up. She sensed the man and dog's presence, yet was not compelled to flee. Then they both drank.

Misty and Haakon watched them for several minutes until the faint crunching sound of rubber on snow-covered gravel distracted them. Misty growled as she assessed the level of danger—ready to bark out an alarm. Haakon turned and saw a large black pickup truck slowly approach. It pulled up near, behind Haakon's car and trailer. Misty barked and danced about nervously. The pickup stopped and its single occupant climbed out—a tall man wearing a weathered Carhartt jacket and a cowboy hat. Haakon did not recognize him.

"It's okay, Misty," Haakon said to the unconvinced dog.

"Ya gotta keep that gate closed," the man said to Haakon as he walked nearer. "Don't ya know we got cattle that can get loose?"

Misty emitted a single persuasive bark to notify the stranger to stop approaching.

"It's okay, Misty," Haakon said again, without really knowing.

Initially, the audacity of the stranger surprised Haakon. But, in a moment, his tired brain caught up.

"Jeez! Little Sig?"

"Hi Haakon. Good to see ya back."

"Wow! It's one thing to talk to ya on the phone. It's another thing to actually see you. You're all grown up."

Sig smiled.

"Yeah, I've been all grown up for awhile now. You're sound'n like an old man."

"I *am* an old man!"

"Well, you're admittedly a little grayer… your hair's shorter than what I remember, but you're look'n pretty good."

"Well, there's no get'n around that," Haakon responded, chuckling. "But damn! If your father could see you now."

Haakon shook his head in disbelief again.

"I wasn't feeling like an old man until I saw you. Guess I can't call you Little Sig anymore."

"Ah, call me whatever. I'm not particular."

Sig smiled again and reached out his hand. Misty stared at him warily. Haakon took Sig's hand and with his other arm, gave Sig a brief hug. Stepping back, Haakon studied him again.

"Damn! You look like your father… but older," Haakon said. "How's that possible? I feel as though I just stepped through a time tunnel."

Sig was still smiling as he crouched down and offered his hand to Misty for her scent analysis. She seemed reassured, so Sig reached up to pat the top of her head.

"Nice looking dog. German Shepard?"

"She's a Shepard Lab mix—the look of a killer with the temperament of a lover."

"I saw you pull in. Can I give you a hand unloading?" Sig asked, glancing at the trailer.

"Oh, I've been driving for over twenty hours. I'm zonked out. I'll probably get to it tomorrow."

"Well, if you need a hand, call me."

"I should be able to get it. There's nothing really heavy. But thanks."

"Well, you know where I'm at. Don't hesitate to ask. Anything you need to get setup here."

"I appreciate that, Sig."

"After living in that little camper, you probably won't know what to do with all of this room."

Haakon turned to look at the house.

"Yeah, it looks a bit roomier. I hear it even has indoor plumbing."

Sig laughed.

"Your uncle built a nice shack here. I wouldn't mind trade'n it for the farmhouse. I'd say you and I had pretty nice uncles… or in my case, great-uncle."

"We're lucky guys, you and I, Sig. And not *just* because we're so good-looking and have great personalities."

They both laughed.

"But all jokes aside, you are right. Here we are, barons of our own estates, because of the hard work of our uncles. We are indeed lucky guys, Sig."

"Have you gone inside yet?" Sig asked, gesturing to the house.

"No. I only know this house from photographs."

"It's a beautiful log home. I got to help your uncle with a lot of it."

"It looks like something out of a fairytale. He couldn't have built it in a more stunning place."

Both men stared at the handsome log structure in silence for several seconds.

"God, it's good to be back!" Haakon exclaimed.

"How many years has it been?"

"Forty-six," Haakon answered. "I haven't stood here for forty-six years. I still can't believe it. It just seems like a few years ago."

"Did you end up marrying that cute girl from Colterville?"

"You remember her?"

"Of course. I may have been young, but I was still a boy with eyes."

Haakon's smile drooped into a frown.

"No, I ended up marrying someone else. Turned out not to be my best decision in life, but I got two beautiful daughters out of the deal and four grandkids."

"Oh. You two seemed pretty serious. I just thought—"

"No," Haakon interrupted, while looking down at the ground. "It's not how it turned out."

"Life's funny," Sig said.

"Yeah, it can be."

Haakon looked back up at him.

"Hey, my uncle told me that you have a beautiful family."

"You'll meet my wife, Rose Mary. We've got two boys and a girl. They're all grown up too and on their own with their own families."

"Are any working on the farm with you?"

"No. They all moved away with their careers. It's hard to keep kids in small towns these days. It's just me and Rose Mary."

"Damn. I still can't believe my eyes."

Sig smiled again.

"Little Sig," Haakon muttered while continuing to stare at him.

"Well, I've gotta run to town. We'll have plenty of time to catch up. Again, don't hesitate to ask for help."

"Thanks Sig. I won't," he said as he watched Sig climb back into his pickup truck.

When he shifted into reverse and began backing up, Haakon yelled out to him.

"Hey!"

Sig rolled down his window in response and looked back.

Haakon walked towards him and said, "Make sure you close the gate when ya leave, would ya? I don't want to be chase'n cows."

Sig smiled, then gave him a lazy wave before turning his eyes back to the driveway. Misty and Haakon watched his pickup truck go up the hill until it was out of view. Then they turned to look for the two does.

15
IMPLAUSIBLE HAPPENSTANCE

It was Haakon's intention in retirement to become the painter that he always wanted to be—a dream long delayed. Now, suddenly, he had some financial security and all the free time in the world to pursue it. No more busy schedules, no more deadlines, and no more incessant ringing phones. He even had the perfect inspirational setting for an art studio. What artist could ask for a better place to paint than a secluded log cabin overlooking a serene river in the woods? Haakon thought to himself more than once that, by good fortune, he now lived in "artistic nirvana."

It was no trouble for him to shift gears and pursue his new venture. The way Haakon saw it, he had over four decades of pent-up artistic drive wanting exploitation. So once he setup a workspace in the cabin's den—a room that conveniently had both a view of the river and natural lighting from the north—he dove into painting with vigor.

Haakon was not particularly good at it at first, but he was indisputably prolific. Failure was his friend, he told himself. So, early on, Haakon had a lot of "friends" in the form of unfinished paintings. The more mistakes he made, the more lessons he absorbed. Haakon convinced himself that if he kept at it, he would persevere.

"I know you're skeptical of all this, Misty, but I'm determined to power through."

Sitting beside him, the dog stared up into Haakon's face, then tilted her head sideways.

"Yeah, it looks hopeless to me also. But I'm too stubborn to quit."

Misty whimpered in what Haakon interpreted as despair, then rolled into a lying position near his feet.

The downside to this "all in" method was that it consumed large quantities of painting supplies. But fortunately for Haakon—and "more fortunately" for the proprietor—there was an excellent art supply store in Colterville. Apparently northwest Montana's beauty attracted others with artistic aspirations. As necessity would dictate, Haakon became a frequent visitor there—so much so that the owner knew him by name.

"I just got my paint shelves stocked and now you're gonna clear me out again?"

"I'm a painting fool, Ben. I'm afraid I may go through a truckload or two of paint before I'm any good at it."

"Well, the upside is that my kids have never eaten so well. We love beginners. You purchase as many truckloads of paint as you like."

"I'm always happy to help out."

"We're get'n kind of dependent on you, so don't get too good too fast. I still have my youngest to put through college."

Haakon smiled.

"You know us artists are kind of sensitive people. How do you know that you're not hurting my feelings?"

"It's just a hunch *I've* got. Us art supply store owners have feelings too, and a sixth sense. I've seen a lot of "wannebe" artists come and go over the years, but I think you're tougher than most. You can take a little jousting."

"God help the artist that can't," Haakon replied. "This hobby can be hard on a guy's ego. But don't count on me wasting paint forever. I might just get good at this some day."

"I don't like to hear that, but I'm a realist. I keep tell'n my kids its time to think about moving on… you know, leave the nest."

Ben was being facetious. His adult kids had long ago moved out of "the nest."

"Well, tell your kids there's no reason to worry for a long while."

Ben smiled and nodded without looking up from his task.

"Haakon, I would like you if you were a good painter too. You know that, right?"

"Sure."

"But just not as much."

"Why do I come here to get abused?"

"I'm just trying to prepare you for the real art world out there, Haakon. Ya gotta have thick skin to make it."

"Yeah, I'm thankful to you on so many levels."

"Well, we just like to help out artists."

"Is that why you got into the business?"

"Heck no. I got into it to make big money. I was told to either open up a chainsaw shop or an art supply store. That's where the big bucks are, they said."

"Well, I'd like ya even if you sold chainsaws… just not as much."

"Touché, my friend!"

Haakon noticed a woman studying a shelf towards the back of the store.

"I'd love to stand here and chat with you, but I've only got so many years to become a famous painter, so I'm gonna go get some more paint."

"Yes, yes. Go re-supply. If ya need a shopping cart or a dolly, let me know."

Even though Haakon always purchased the same eleven colors, he enjoyed viewing Ben's entire selection of paints. There was something about seeing all the colors laid out in one place in full-untapped tubes that spoke to the artist in him. Perhaps he saw infinite possibilities and this, in itself, inspired him. Haakon wondered, as he stood there, if this was a big part of his frequent visits—to get a dose of motivation.

"Maybe so," Haakon told himself out loud as he studied the shelf. "Whatever it takes."

"Excuse me?" a woman's voice said.

Haakon looked up to see the voice's source. She was looking at him from across the top shelf, from the next aisle.

"Oh, I'm sorry. I'm talking to myself again," Haakon replied, embarrassed. "I guess I've been out in the woods alone too long."

She smiled. An alarm went off in the deep recesses of Haakon's head.

"I thought you were talking to me," she said.

She was beautiful. And, she was disconcertingly familiar to Haakon, though not visually—not in appearance. His mind whirled as it rummaged through its memory files, trying to identify what was setting off his internal alert.

The voice—there was something in her voice that made Haakon nearly freeze in place. It was a similar awakening sensation to hearing the first three notes of a once beloved song, where the brain, using an astonishingly minimal cue, instantly fills in the remaining musical notes.

"Haakon?"

Hearing her voice a third time supported the unbelievable conclusion that his brain had just provided. He studied her face for visual confirmation. Slowly, he could see her. His perplexity had to have been apparent in his expression. Haakon inelegantly paused, but then mustered the courage to respond.

"Kari?"

The woman before him was not the young woman whose image had long been embedded in Haakon's mind—an image he had viewed nearly every day. Haakon's eyes struggled to see Kari in this woman's face. She was attractive to be sure, but it took time for the firing neurons in his brain to mesh the two Karis together. Yet, gradually they merged her physical features with his dated mental photograph. It was like a veil being slowly lifted. He began to recognize her eyes, her facial lines, and, most surprisingly, her distinct aura. And while this realization brought on an incredible surge of warmth to Haakon's heart, it simultaneously produced a wrenching pain in his stomach.

"Yes," she said, and her surprised expression slowly transformed into a smile.

It was definitely Kari's smile.

A few times in Haakon's life, and only a few times, an event had unraveled so perfectly that it seemed implausible to be explained away as mere happenstance. Its beauty appeared designed—more akin to the artistic intent of a masterful hand. Mere probability seemed an unsatisfactory explanation for such perfection, especially considering that it was born of a vast, chaotic universe.

Despite the improbability, like their chance first meeting on a remote Montana rooftop, Kari stood before Haakon a second time.

Their stares became self-conscious. Both fumbled to find words, forming their lips, gasping for air as though to omit some sounds. For a long moment, nothing came from either. So, instead of uttering words, they each broke out laughing, nervously. They laughed so hard their eyes teared up, though Haakon thought he was actually crying.

"I'm… speechless," Haakon finally got out of his mouth, stating the obvious.

Kari held her hand to her chest as though to suppress laughter.

"Me too," she said.

Then after a pause she regained her composure and continued.

"It's good to see you, Haakon. You're all grown up."

He chuckled at that.

"It's good to see you too, Kari. I can't believe my eyes."

"I can't believe that I'm looking at you either."

"God, you look great!" he said, wondering if she believed him.

Kari said nothing in reply.

"I froze when I heard your voice," Haakon said, still nervously chuckling. "Did you see? I couldn't move!"

They were still on opposite sides of the shelf.

"Can I come around and hug you?" Haakon blurted out.

He feared that he had asked something inappropriate. Kari did not answer, but instead stood motionless, continuing to stare at him. Then her eyes glossed over and each slowly made their way to the end of the aisle. Rounding the corner, facing each other, they each extended their arms and fell into an embrace. It was brief, as Haakon did not want to make her uncomfortable. Yet, for that moment, her touch and smell triggered a plethora of memories. It was excruciatingly painful for him to release her.

They broke away and looked at each other again, now at arm's length. Neither of them was smiling. Each had watery eyes. Haakon was barely staying composed, but then Kari averted the discomfort by resuming the conversation.

"What are you doing here?"

He took her cue and shook off the deep emotions that had flooded him. Haakon felt more comfortable—at least he felt less pain.

"I live here now. I moved back."

"You live *here*?" she asked, surprised.

"My uncle passed away a few years back. He left me Camp One."

"So you moved back into the trailer?"

He chuckled.

"I think I *would* have. I have so many great memories from it. But no," Haakon said, "He built a cabin. It's actually a beautiful log home. He put it right where the trailer used to be."

There was another awkward pause while they both stared at one another.

"I am retired now. I thought it was time to learn how to paint… finally… after all these years."

He smiled at her. She smiled back.

"I remember. You wanted to be a watercolor artist."

"Well, I didn't quite have the nerve to jump into it, so I became an architect. At least I could do watercolor renditions of buildings, I figured."

Kari grinned and nodded.

"That's why I'm here now… to buy more paint. I waste a lot of paint. I keep Ben over there in business."

Haakon gestured over to where they both could see Ben going through a box on the checkout counter. They both nervously laughed again.

"I'm glad to hear that you are painting."

"What are *you* doing here?" Haakon inquired. "I had asked about you and your family at the post office and they told me you moved away long ago."

"Yes, I moved to Portland after my mother died."

Haakon wanted to say that he was sorry for her loss and that he really enjoyed knowing her mother, but he feared it would lead to the larger topic that could abruptly end their conversation. He looked back at her with a remorseful expression instead.

"My father passed away just recently. I'm actually here to take care of some legal matters with his house."

"That I heard too," Haakon said. "I'm sorry, Kari. I really thought a lot of your parents."

She stared at Haakon blankly, but he knew that Kari's mind was racing behind her face.

"God, it's good to see you!" Haakon said, almost involuntarily.

He hoped that she would not notice his eyes welling up again.

Kari nodded her head slowly while clenching her lips tight. She seemed to hold back a torrent of emotion.

In Haakon's shock, he was at a loss of words, yet it compelled him to say something, anything, to fill the void.

"Are you here to get art supplies? Did you become an artist?"

"No. No, not quite. In fact, I'm a terrible painter. I can't even paint a wall in a house without making a mess," she said, chuckling nervously again. "I needed stationery."

Another long pause transpired and Haakon feared that an opportunity was about to slip from his grip.

"Do you have time to go get some coffee? I would love to hear about you… your life." he asked sheepishly, mentally hedging the possibility of being turned down.

Kari did not answer immediately. She was clearly giving the question considerable thought. He sensed reluctance, but then she surprised him.

"Yeah, sure. I've got some time."

Haakon suggested that they walk to the nearby cafe and she agreed.

As they passed Ben on their way to the door, Haakon said to him, "I'll be back. You know I'll be back."

"I and my family are count'n on it," Ben answered.

Kari gave Haakon a puzzled glance.

"We've got this symbiotic relationship going, Ben and I."

"Sounds like something I don't want to know about," Kari responded, and each laughed as they stepped out onto the sidewalk.

Haakon regarded her sense of humor as an encouraging sign.

It was late morning and the old-timer coffee drinkers had moved on. Kari and Haakon found an empty table against the large front window. It looked out into the heart of downtown Colterville. There was not much activity outside, but enough to make the view interesting. They smiled at each other again as they sat down on opposite sides, facing each other. Haakon was still nervous. His brain was continuing to process the improbability of their encounter.

"I've gotta ask Kari, married? Kids?"

She half-smiled.

"I *was* married."

"Oh," is all Haakon could think to respond with.

"And I had a son, Kyle… but I lost him… in the Gulf War."

"Oh, my God! I'm so sorry, Kari. I'm so sorry," Haakon said sincerely, slowly shaking his head. "I can't imagine—"

"Yeah. Neither can I to be truthful. It's been twenty-five years and I still can't come to grips with it."

"Was he in the Army?"

"No. Navy like his grandfather."

"Of course, your father was a Navy captain. Of course, he would be Navy," Haakon said, embarrassed.

"My father took it hard. They were very close… and he felt responsible for guiding Kyle's Navy career," she explained impassively. "Kyle worshipped my father."

"I suppose he wanted to *be* like your father," Haakon said, hoping she received the words as a compliment to her father.

"He did. He wanted to make him proud. And he did that. He became a Seal and he was doing what Seals are trained to do."

She began to tear up.

Haakon shook his head and frowned.

"Oh Kari, I'm so sorry," he said again, wishing he could come up with better words.

But then Haakon thought to ask, "Do you have a photo of your son?"

This made Kari smile.

"Yes, of course."

She reached into her purse and removed a wallet. Opening it revealed an image of a young man with a stern expression dressed in his Navy's finest.

"What a handsome guy," Haakon said. "I see you in him."

"Yeah," she responded, staring down at the photo. "He was a handsome guy and an all-around wonderful human being. I miss him dearly."

Haakon reached across the table and took hold of her free hand with both of his. He could not think of what to say, but he hoped that the gesture would speak to his sorrow for her pain. They looked into each other's sad eyes. Haakon feared that she would recoil and withdraw her hand in offense, but she did not.

The waitress arrived to take their coffee order and Haakon took his hands back.

"After my son's death, Sean, my husband and I... well, we sort of went adrift. Neither of us could ever quite come to grips with it all. Nothing was ever the same after that."

Haakon studied her pained face as she spoke.

"He ended up marrying again. And he had a couple more kids. We talk now and then, but it's all quite distant, the two of us."

Kari's eyes grew watery again.

"How about you, Haakon?"

"I was married," he answered, half-smiling. "About the time our daughters—I have two girls—went off to college, she decided that she wanted to be with my business partner... and friend, or so I thought."

"Oh, I'm sorry Haakon."

"Yeah, well things happen," he said nonchalantly while shrugging his shoulders, feigning he was not pained. "Now she's living in L.A. with my best old ex-friend, Ray."

"What?"

"I kid you not. Just like the song," Haakon said, now shaking his head. "His name is Ray and they live in Los Angeles. You can't make this stuff up."

Sensing that *he* was about to tear up, Kari reached for *his* hand that sat near his coffee cup.

"I'm not on the verge of crying because of her," Haakon said, nearly sobbing. "I'm on the verge of crying because I can't believe that you are here, sitting in front of me, right now."

He grasped her extended hand with his other hand.

"This is all very surreal, Kari."

"It is," she replied, half-smiling again.

Haakon regained his composure and their hands slid apart.

"I have two daughters, two beautiful girls. They're all grown up now. Both are married. Both have a couple of kids."

"So you are a grandfather?" she smiled, seeming surprised.

"Yeah, I'm a grandfather," he said, hesitantly acknowledging that he was old enough to be. "It's a tough title to get used to at first, but it's a fun role."

"What did your girls and grandkids think of you moving out here?"

"Actually, they moved first—one family to the east coast and the other family to the west coast. They wanted me to stay in our old house in Minnesota, but yet they were rarely there anymore."

"I think that's common."

"Yeah, I guess. But I needed a change. And they knew that. They just didn't *want* to know that," Haakon said. "But they're getting over it."

They both smiled at each other again.

"So you retired from being an architect. Were you doing skyscrapers, houses, what?"

"Primarily commercial stuff… buildings. No skyscrapers."

"Did you enjoy it?"

"Yeah. Yeah, it was good. But it was never my passion. I guess I just didn't have the guts to go out and be an artist. I chose the safe route."

"Well, there's nothing wrong with that," Kari said.

Haakon was unconvinced she meant it.

"What about you?" he asked.

"Oh. Well, I'm an interior decorator."

"Really. Homes? Commercial work?"

"I've done it all. I used to work for a large firm in Portland. But in later years I ventured off on my own."

"I can see it. You're smart and creative. It makes sense."

Kari blushed.

"I'm not working as much as I used to, by choice. I'm pretty much just doing work for my favorite clients."

"It sounds like a nice position to be in."

"I enjoy it."

For a moment, Haakon fell into a trance observing her. There was another pause in their conversation. He nervously chuckled, then glanced out the large window, noticing a familiar building.

"Do you remember "fight-night" at Moose's Saloon?" Haakon asked, turning back to her, smiling.

Kari smiled back.

"Yes, of course I do. How many bar fights do you think I've attended?"

Haakon laughed. Then he gestured to the building over her shoulder and she turned to look. As she did, the sun caught the side of her face and its bright contrast removed the years. Before Haakon, sat the young Kari—the Kari from his mind's photograph. His heart pounded.

Kari turned back and smiled shallowly, as if she knew what he had seen.

"It doesn't feel like that long ago," she said.

Haakon displayed a smile of regret.

"No, it doesn't."

They continued talking for nearly an hour on topics pertaining to the previous forty-six years. But never in the conversation did they touch upon Haakon's broken promise. Yet, it was there during the entire visit—a giant pink elephant, sitting in the cafe's corner glaring at him.

"Well, I've got a meeting with an attorney, so I had better get going," Kari grimaced, seeming to not want to end their talk.

"Oh, yeah," Haakon said surprised. "I shouldn't have kept you so long. I just go blathering on and on."

"No, it was good. It was really good. I've enjoyed this, Haakon."

They both stood up, nervously facing each other. He wondered if he could move towards her to embrace again. He wanted to, but he still feared she would rebuff him. She had every reason to do so. Haakon could see the elephant, still in the corner, staring. True, she had allowed him to hug her in the art supply store, but she was arguably in shock then. Now, after such a long conversation, her mind had surely replayed Haakon's abandonment of her. It was very possible that, despite their cordial discussion, she had rage ready to erupt.

Haakon had to risk it. He moved towards Kari and gestured with his open arms. Thankfully, she was receptive and they hugged. Again, feeling Kari against him, smelling her so close, caused him almost unbearable pain. Their hold was brief—still a bit discomfited.

As they pulled apart, Kari nervously said, "It's really been great to see you."

Facing her, his mind flashed back to junior high school when he first mustered up enough courage to ask a girl out on a date. Like then, he swallowed hard, then walked out onto a plank—fully exposing himself to the possibility of falling directly into the snapping jaws below of his mind's sharks. So what followed their brief embrace was a torrent of words delivered in rapid succession in hopes of somehow not allowing an opportunity for rejection.

"Listen, I don't know what your schedule is and how much time you have, but ah… but are you available to come over for dinner this evening? See the cabin? I can show you my paintings. I would love to hear more about what's going on in your life. I feel there is just so much more to talk about."

Haakon broke off his salvo of words and stood awaiting her response.

Kari hesitated as she had with the coffee shop invite. Was she not even going to honor his question with an answer? He feared she would turn away and walk out the door, giving him a small taste of his own medicine. He knew he had it coming. Even the elephant in the corner was smirking, knowing he had it coming too. The long pause made the snapping shark jaws grow louder. Haakon braced for the worst.

"I…"

Her lips seemed to search for an excuse. Then she stopped trying to form words. Kari just stared at Haakon with no expression. He expected her to decline. But then her head moved, slowly, subtly, up and down.

"Sure. Okay."

16
GLACIER LILIES

If not for Misty's excited barking, Haakon may have missed her knock. It was a faint tap. He wondered if its meekness suggested her hesitation. He could understand if it did. But before Kari could reconsider, Haakon quickly made his way to the front door.

Since the encounter in town, there had not been time for Haakon to process what had occurred. The return from Colterville launched a race to transform his evolving "mancave" into a presentable human domicile. This, and his ambitious cooking endeavor, occupied most of his thoughts. So, when he opened the door and saw her again, the wave of reality crashed into Haakon nearly as hard as it had hours earlier. A stab of anxiety not known since his youth, when he was first attracted to girls, struck him hard again. If he did not know better, he could have mistaken his pain as a sign of coronary failure.

Despite not initially recognizing her in the art store, Kari still struck Haakon as gorgeous. And somehow, in the few hours since, she became even more beautiful. Her hair was shinier and her mascara and blush were more pronounced. Under an open jacket she wore a blue-flowered dress that emphasized the slim, fit figure he remembered so well. Her perfume radiated like a waft of sweet springtime air.

Misty did not seem threatened, yet Haakon held her collar to prevent the dog from excitedly jumping up on Kari.

Haakon wanted to say aloud, "God, you're stunning and to see your face again is killing me inside." But he did not have the nerve. A deluge of intense emotions, questions, doubts, and regrets were bombarding his brain.

So he disappointed himself and instead said, "Hi! I hope you weren't standing there too long. I didn't hear your knock until Misty barked."

"Misty?" she asked, surprised, as she leaned down to pet the dog's head. "Your dog is named Misty?"

"Yeah, I named her after Misty Peak and the trail."

Kari stared at Haakon for a moment, seeming to be taken aback.

"She's a good girl," Haakon said as he leaned down to rub Misty's neck. "I got her a year ago as a pup."

"She's a pretty dog."

"Yeah, and she knows it, don't ya Misty?" Haakon said, pulling the dog's face close to his.

Kari smiled and said, "No, I was just standing out there twenty minutes or so."

"You're joking, right?"

"I *am* joking, but I didn't want to do the Gestapo knock and give you a heart attack. You need a doorbell."

"I guess I do. I didn't know that until I had my first guest... which is you."

"Well, that is quite an honor... I think."

They both laughed nervously as they had upon their earlier encounter.

"Come in. I'm so happy you came."

Kari walked inside and presented Haakon with a bottle of wine.

He studied it for a moment then said, "Oh great! Thank you. Let's open this."

She smiled as though she was purposely constraining her emotions.

Then she looked beyond Haakon and said, "What a stunning house!"

Haakon's hours of toil had nearly restored it to the charming log home that he had inherited. His uncle had taken great pains to adorn it with unique knickknacks and western artwork. Haakon considered his uncle's discerning interior decorating an impressive feat for "a guy." It was warm and cozy—very informal, but in an elegant, rustic way. Having a roaring fire in its tall stone fireplace only added to its inviting ambiance.

"When did your uncle build this?" Kari asked, now in the middle of the living room, slowly revolving while scanning her surroundings.

"About seventeen years ago. He retired here. Let me take your jacket."

She slipped it off and handed it to him, then walked to the far end of the room and began viewing Haakon's many paintings. Haakon stood watching her awestruck, as though his favorite movie actress had come to visit. She did not face Haakon, but he suspected she was aware his eyes were following her.

"These are yours? These are great, Haakon! Wow!"

"Well, none of them are finished."

"Really? They *look* finished."

"I think I don't finish them so I always have that excuse for any of their shortcomings. It's sort of a mind game I play with myself, I guess."

"Well, you shouldn't make any excuses. These are beautiful. I'm impressed! And I've seen a lot of art in my career. I know of what I speak."

Kari turned towards Haakon.

"And I'm glad to see you pursuing your dream."

"Thanks. I'm enjoying it."

Kari walked across the room to the large picture window and Haakon followed.

"God, I remember this view, this incredible view!"

As though responding to her words, a faraway cloud parted, allowing the setting sun's afterglow to illuminate the distant mountains. Their reticulate patterns of snow took on a majestic pink hue, magnifying the splendor.

"Yeah, it's something you never forget. Sort of got etched into my brain too."

She nodded in agreement, still transfixed by the scene and possibly by the memories it stirred.

The snow had melted and spring was in full rebound. The greens were vivid as they drew from the moisture to replenish their vigor and growth. Accommodating the recent melt, the river ran strong and fast— working into a froth of white water where the rocks below resisted. Sediment gnawed from sandy banks turned the water's clarity to an opaque tan.

"The river is really running hard," she observed. "I bet its freezing cold."

"Yeah, I'm sure glad my uncle put plumbing in this house. I don't know if I could still do the river baths."

"That was freezing even in the summer," she responded.

Then, after saying that, she looked at Haakon shyly. He wondered if she suddenly recalled what *he* had suddenly recalled: the times they bathed in the shallow river together—laughing, screaming, and embracing in the frigid water. He glanced back at her with the same timidity.

"Should I open that bottle?" he asked, wanting to end the uncomfortable silence.

"Please. Yes."

This broke her trance and she followed Haakon into the kitchen.

"It's so inspirational here. It's got to be a good place to be an artist, I would think."

Haakon struggled with the bottle's cork.

"Yeah, that's the hope. If I can't be artistically motivated here, I don't think I could be motivated anywhere."

"I can't get over this place!" she exclaimed, with her eyes still wandering. "What a charming house."

"I'm very lucky. I believe that I had the world's best uncle."

Haakon slowly poured the wine into the glasses. Handing her one, he proposed a toast.

"To our meeting again, Kari."

She smiled, almost sadly, then tapped his glass.

"Yes," she whispered.

Standing close, they watched each other take a sip. Then, as though choreographed, each set their glasses down and continued staring at each other—not smiling, not frowning—just staring. It was as though one was waiting for the other to blink. But then, simultaneously, they moved towards each other as though drawn by gravity. They fell into each other's arms. Unlike the embrace of earlier in the day, this was a tight embrace, an ardent embrace. Haakon could not see her face, but he sensed she was crying. He was too. They held each other for a long minute, tightly, as though loosening the hug would allow them to fall apart again.

Haakon felt elated, grateful to have her in his arms. His mind raced, trying to contemplate the odds of them being together again, while at the same time trying to reconcile why he never returned to her. It was a torrent of thoughts that his brain was incapable of processing as he held her. He tried to relax and be content Kari was in his arms, for whatever reason and whatever improbability.

Then their embrace brusquely ended. Kari pushed away. She was still close and Haakon reached up to grasp the sides of her face with his hands. They stared into each other's watery eyes. Hers were still the vivid blue of youth. Mascara ran from them now, down upon her blushed cheeks. For an instant, Haakon was looking at the young Kari from the "Endless Summer" of all of those years back. Despite the contortion of emotion, redness, tears, and black streaks, her radiating beauty engulfed him.

Their faces pulled together into a passionate kiss, and with his eyes closed, Haakon was transported back in time. Immediately, her soft lips were familiar. Silently, he prayed for the kiss to not end. There was nothing he would have rather been doing or no place that he would have rather been than having Kari right there in his arms. Decades of pent-up adoration poured out as an overwhelming energy—a force that he had not known for a very long time.

But then Kari abruptly pushed off of Haakon again, this time more forcefully. She pounded her fist hard on his chest.

"You bastard!"

Her girlish face of fright and vulnerability contorted with rage.

"You bastard!" Kari shouted again, this time nearly choking in tears. "We were supposed to be together! We were supposed to have a family together! We were supposed to grow old together! Why did you never come back? How could you never come back? You promised me! You promised—"

Uncontrolled sobbing cut off her speech. Kari bent over slightly, holding her stomach as though someone had punched her. Haakon reached out and tried to hold her again, but she pushed him away.

"You never came back," she said quietly, looking up at Haakon as though wanting an answer to a question she did not ask. "You left me… and you never came back like you promised… and you never said why."

Kari walked in visible pain the short distance into the living room, then fell upon the couch in a near-fetal pose with her legs pulled up off of the floor, still sobbing.

The elephant from the cafe had come out into the open finally. Haakon knew that dealing with it would not be pleasant, if he could deal with it at all. Yet it was necessary to try. Haakon wanted to make amends, if he could somehow. And he wanted to apologize.

He followed her into the living room.

"I don't know how to redo the past, Kari." Haakon said, standing next to her, looking down. "I don't always understand how things happen as they do. I really don't. I wish I did."

Kari seemed to listen but did not look up at him.

"When I got back to Minnesota, I got swept up," he stated, trying to explain while knowing that his explanation would fall short. "Everything went so fast. It was a whirlwind—new friends, the goings on of college…"

Pausing for a moment, Haakon tried to carefully gather his next words.

"In time, I met Hannah… I met her and we fell in love. I didn't stop loving you, Kari, but I fell in love again. I don't know how it's possible, but it is. It was."

Still Kari would not look up.

"And then things happened fast," Haakon said. "I feel like a jerk saying it like this, but it's the truth. When I look back now, it was like being swept up in a riptide. Hannah was there, you were not, and things evolved."

He paused for a moment, looking for any reaction or movement from Kari. There was none.

"I can look at it sort of objectively now, but I couldn't then. It was all emotions and everything was fast. That part of my life was such a blur."

A burning log tumbled in the fireplace—its thud making Haakon glance up for a moment. Kari did not.

"I was nineteen. I just remember everything going so fast."

Kari's face remained hidden in her folded arms, but she stopped sobbing. She still seemed to be listening to his words.

"This will sound cold, but I've thought about it a lot. I think much of what happens in our lives has to do with when and where we are and who we are with. In the end, life just happens. It takes a course of its own and things fall into place as they do."

Haakon glanced up at the fire and tried to arrange his thoughts coherently.

"I'm not sure I believe it is fate. Sometimes it seems like fate. If you had been there, things may have turned out different. That's my fault and it seems like an insensitive thing to say, but we can't know these things."

He wiped his eyes and then reached down and placed a hand on Kari's shoulder, hoping she would not shake it off. She did not.

"I guess I'm making it sound like I was some kind of victim. I wasn't. I don't know that I can explain myself well, but I'm just trying to set the stage of the time and place of what was influencing my decisions. But they were *my* decisions. I own them. I was a big boy. I knew what I was doing. With you, I was a coward. I'm not proud of this."

Kari's head remained tucked into her arms, but she still seemed to be listening.

"Abandoning you without a word is easily the worst thing I have ever done in my life. And I've always felt guilty about it. And to tell you now that I'm sorry just doesn't seem adequate. I know that."

He paused again, trying to conjure up words that would better convey his sincerity. But he came up short. The words may not have existed.

"But I am... I am so truly sorry. And until I can think of better words, that's all I can say. It was a cruel decision that I made... and I have to own up to the decision... as spineless as it was."

His hand still rested on her shoulder and Kari, continuing to look down, reached across her chest to place her hand on top of it. Haakon felt undeserving, yet so very grateful for the gesture. Then she squeezed his hand tightly and sobbed again.

"I'm trying to be honest with you, Kari. I can't tell you I regret my life and my family. But there are parts I regret. Parts I am remorseful for, more than you know. Parts that I want back."

Haakon's own words made him sob harder. He struggled to regain enough composure to continue talking.

"I regret hurting you. I so regret hurting you. There is nothing I regret more. Nothing. I regret not having you in my life these past decades. It literally burns me inside. But I can't regret my family. I don't. And I know deep inside you have to know this."

Still looking down, she sat motionless. But her hand still clasped his.

"Even if we could redo our pasts, we wouldn't be able to redo just parts of our past. It's a package deal, I think. Redoing parts would be redoing everything, and I wouldn't want to redo all of it."

Keeping his hand on her shoulder, Haakon crouched down on his knees beside her.

"You wouldn't want a past that didn't include Kyle and I wouldn't want a past that didn't include my girls and their families. They're all part of what we became and the paths we chose, for right or wrong. In the end, they are right and they are as much a part of us now as our arms and legs."

She squeezed Haakon's hand more firmly.

He was struggling to put into words something that he never understood himself. Yet he feared his words would worsen her regard of him. Still, Haakon wanted to be truthful. He owed her that.

"I loved my family. I loved what I had. I loved my wife, then. I still love what she and I once had. And I love my girls."

Haakon was looking directly at Kari's concealed face and he suspected that she could see him from the corner of her eye.

"If you take nothing else from my inadequate words, please know that I never stopped loving you. Seeing you again, being here with you again, reminds me of how much."

Kari's subtle sobbing resumed.

"I owe you a better explanation, but I don't have one. I truly don't have a grasp of it all… and I guess that sounds like a cop-out, but it's the truth."

"The older I get, the less I understand. I think because as I get older, I realize that there is so much more to understand than my finite brain is capable of comprehending. I often think of James Taylor singing the words, 'Einstein said he could never understand it all. Planets spinning through space, the smile upon your face.'"

Haakon paused for a moment before continuing.

"The intricacies of our very existence are so mind boggling when I think about it," he said, feigning a chuckle. "So, I rarely think about it, because it hurts my head too much."

Haakon glanced toward what he could see of her face and she seemed to smirk.

"I don't deserve your visit here now. I know that. But I am grateful that you came. I am truly sorry for the pain that I have caused you. And selfishly, I'm sorry for the time lost between us."

Then Haakon sat back on the floor, releasing his hand from her shoulder.

"God, this is so surreal, this moment right now. You being here... after all of these years. I feel like I am in some parallel universe."

Without a word from her, Kari looked over at Haakon and reached over to pull his head to hers. They remained silent and motionless for several minutes. It was an uncomfortable posture for Haakon, but he endured it, as he was grateful for her reaction. He hoped that the gesture indicated the beginning of her forgiveness.

As much as Haakon wanted to remain locked against her, he felt they needed to get up and shake off the air's heaviness. Slowly, he pulled his head away and turned towards Kari's face. She turned towards his. Her eyes were sad and swollen from crying. Mascara ran down her cheeks.

"Let's go for a walk before dinner," Haakon suggested. "I have some things I would like to show you."

She nodded and smiled slightly. Haakon's heart sank. He loved this face, this person, and this soul. He had forgotten how much. Looking at her so defeated, Haakon felt an immense wave of guilt and remorse, as though he had beaten a puppy.

Kari moved into the bathroom to freshen up and Haakon looked in on his dinner project, putting everything on hold and hoping for the best. They each donned a jacket and stepped out into the spring evening with Misty in tow. The evergreen-scented mountain air was crisp and cooling rapidly. But Haakon needed to move his legs, and he suspected she did too. He put his arm around her as they walked and she seemed receptive, her body falling into his. At first, they said nothing, no doubt both still digesting what had just transpired. But the mood changed when they reached the property gate, bringing the full valley into view.

"I miss this place," Kari said, looking off toward the distant mountains.

The low light partially illuminated her face, reminding Haakon of their first date.

"It stays with you wherever you go."

Haakon nodded his head in agreement as she turned slightly and looked off to a small meadow on a distant hillside.

"Do you remember that place?"

Haakon smiled.

"Maybe every day."

"Me too."

They both giggled shyly.

"And how about the rock outcropping?"

She looked back now towards the smooth slab of granite that overlooked the river.

"Probably every day of my life."

The reminiscing went on for several minutes. It lightened the air. All those years ago they had expressed their love to one another, both verbally and physically, in many valley locations. Haakon had not forgotten a single spot or occurrence and it flattered him that she had not forgotten either.

"Since we are reminiscing, there is something I would like to show you," he said.

Haakon gestured for her to follow and he led her to a pole building up the hill, behind the house. When he got to its garage door, he stopped and turned to her.

"Are you ready?" Haakon asked, as he leaned down to grip the door's lift handle.

"I'm not sure," she responded.

Like unveiling an art sculpture, Haakon pulled the garage door up and open, suddenly revealing its contents.

"Oh my God!" Kari exclaimed.

"That's what *I* said when I first saw it. I had no idea that my uncle still had it."

Sitting inside the garage stall was the old International Scout, looking as rusty and weathered as it had forty-six years before. Misty briefly walked around it while inspecting with her nose.

"It looks exactly the same," she said.

"Yeah, ageless utilitarian beauty. It sure doesn't look any better, but it's amazing that it hasn't disintegrated. I think it has a little more rust, but it's pretty much how I remember it."

"Does it run?"

"I'm not sure. I haven't even put the battery in yet."

"Wow. This *is* like a time warp," she said as she walked around it, peering inside. "Looks like your uncle put in new upholstery."

"Yeah. He must have used it. He just never mentioned anything about it, and I never asked. So this was a big surprise. I spent a lot of time in this rig."

"Well, when you get a break from your paintings, there's a project for you."

Haakon chuckled.

"I'm going to give it a try one of these days. I thought it would be fun to run around in it again, though I should probably donate it to the Smithsonian."

Kari laughed. Haakon pulled the garage door closed and they resumed their walk.

Eventually, they arrived at the flat granite outcrop that overlooked the river. They had spent countless sunset hours on this rock.

"Can we sit for a while," Kari asked.

"Sure, of course. Why don't I get you a blanket?"

"No. I'll be fine. Let's sit together," she replied. "Will the dinner be okay?"

"Well, I'm not sure if the dinner was ever really going to be okay, so sure… it should be fine," Haakon joked.

They sat on the rock side by side, just as they had decades before. It still retained the heat from the afternoon sun. Their timing was ideal. The sun had just dropped behind a mountain and the sky was filling with amber. They said little, both absorbing the natural spectacle and, for Haakon's part, their chance mutual presence. It stirred his memories of that distant summer. He suspected that hers were too. For several minutes they seemed to speak without uttering a word.

"I should have reached out to you, Haakon. When you didn't write, I should have reached out."

Kari turned to stare into Haakon's eyes. He was taken by her earnest expression.

"I have to take some responsibility. I felt rejected and I let my pride get the best of me."

"No. I own this, Kari. Us not being together is my doing. I let the fire die and I'm so sorry. Even selfishly, I'm so sorry for myself."

"We were young," she responded, as though the few words best explained their fate.

"Yes, we were young," Haakon said, looking into her eyes, nodding in agreement.

When the light faded, a chill dropped in from the upper valley, prompting them to move back inside the house. They each had another glass of wine and cordially conversed while Haakon did his best to salvage the dinner. Nothing turned out well, but Kari was polite and did not let on. They continued talking nonstop through dinner, though the conversation grew heavier—about their marriages, about his girls, and about her son.

"After Kyle's death, my father went into a deep depression," she said. "As I told you this afternoon, I think he felt responsible for ushering him into being a Seal, with all of his Navy stories and all. I honestly believe my father's depression helped keep me afloat, because I was the only one that could keep *him* afloat. It was a rough time. It still is. It always *will* be."

"I'm sorry that I brought it up again."

"Oh God, don't be. That's my greatest fear, that Kyle will be forgotten. I'll talk about him anytime, anywhere. I might cry, but believe me, I *want* to talk about him."

Kari's face wore the conviction of her words.

"I couldn't talk to Sean about him. He was incapable. He couldn't deal with it. He wanted me to move on, but that was impossible. When my dad was alive, we talked about Kyle all the time. I miss that."

"Your dad was a good guy. If your son was anything like him… well, it speaks for itself."

"He was *a lot* like him and, yes, they were *good* guys."

"I guess 'good guys' sounds like an understatement, but I regard it as the simplest, most flattering way to be remembered. I hope you realize that is how it was intended."

"Absolutely. You are right. At the 'end of the day,' they were 'good guys' who made the world a little better. It is a fitting tribute."

Kari raised her wineglass and Haakon, following suit, raised his and tapped it into hers. Then they each took another sip while watching each other.

When dinner was over, Kari helped Haakon clean up and put the food away. Then they moved into the living room to sit in front of the fire. She took a seat on the couch while Haakon stoked the flame. He returned with a blanket and laid it across her lap. Kari patted the spot next to her, gesturing for him to sit alongside. As he did, she pulled the blanket across Haakon's lap, then moved closer to his side and dropped her head on his shoulder. They said nothing for a time, spellbound by the warmth, the dancing flames, and their memories. Haakon's brain continued to struggle with the fact that she was actually there. And, even when his brain accepted this reality, he still assumed that she would rise to leave.

But instead, something miraculous happened—something wonderful and quite unexpected. Perhaps it was stirred by the ambience of near darkness, save the fire's glow. Perhaps it was the culmination of decades of pent up longing and loneliness.

After they had huddled closely together for the better part of an hour, Kari turned to him and said, "Haakon, I want to make love."

It would be difficult to equate the passion they exhibited that night with the past, yet their lovemaking was a sweet journey back through time. The decades fell away. While joined as one, Haakon was nineteen again and what he experienced then, he experienced again. He wanted to stay there—back in that time before deaths and divorces and betrayals and bills and responsibilities and the realization of one's mortality. He wanted to stay in the innocent age of youth. Kari's eyes told him she wanted the same. So they continued until they could no longer—their age finally ringing their bell. Then they rolled into each other's arms and into a deep, comforting sleep.

During the night, Haakon awoke to see Kari standing by the

window, peering out at the nearly full moon. Wearing only his shirt, she had a tranquil elegance. Her long exposed legs, still shapely as he remembered, and her hair, now tussled, gave her a wild look. The diffused moonlight was drawn to half her face. She appeared angelic and he almost said something, but caught himself. Kari seemed to be in deep contemplation. Their reunion was a lot to process, so he thought it best to leave her be. Haakon was still coming to grips with it himself.

When morning came, Haakon awoke early. The sun was breaking over the mountains and by now was casting a long, sharp light on Kari's sleeping face. It reminded him of the first time he had seen her skin glow in the early light. He stood and stared at her. She was still angelic. Haakon's heart melted. He praised the fate that brought them together again—if only for this one night. Fearing the light would wake her, he pulled the drapes closed and quietly left the room.

With an extra dose of exuberance, Haakon embarked on another ambitious cooking foray. Aside from preparing a grand breakfast for his guest, he even picked some glacier lilies from the yard and placed them in a vase at the center of the table. Eventually, Kari appeared at the dining room entrance, momentarily startling Misty. She wore the shirt she had on in the moonlight. Though still partially in slumber, Kari's subtle sexuality nearly knocked Haakon over.

"Good morning," she said, smiling as she stretched.

"Good morning. Were you comfortable last night?"

"I was."

"I noticed that you got up."

"I did. I was looking at the moon. It was so beautiful."

"And I was looking at the moonlight shining on your face as you stood there."

She smiled, then sat down.

"Would you like some coffee?"

"I would love some. Thanks."

She noticed the flowers.

"They're beautiful. Do you pick them every morning?"

"I don't believe I have ever picked flowers before."

"Gosh, I feel honored."

"That's what I was aiming for."

They smiled at each other, then Haakon turned back to his culinary task, glancing back to her when he could. She sipped at the coffee and gazed out the window.

"I hope that you are hungry. I made enough omelet for an army."

They ate and talked. And after eating, they sat at the kitchen table and continued talking—covering more highlights of the many lost years. She told him more about her son and her career and her marriage and her parents. He told her about his life with Hannah and about his daughters and about his career. Again, they laughed and cried—their outer reactions to their inner remorse of vanished time and missed opportunities.

When the discussion turned to the present and the future, Kari took on an unexpected somber expression. She reached out across the table for both of Haakon's hands. Her change of demeanor alarmed him.

"There is something more," Kari said, staring into Haakon's face intently. "Something else that I need to tell you."

He looked back at her with trepidation and braced himself mentally as best he could.

"The condition that my mother had," she explained, "it looks as though I have it too."

This was a piercing arrow. Haakon knew immediately what this meant.

"Are you certain?" he asked, shocked and grasping for the right way to respond.

"No. I am not certain, but it seems very likely." she answered. "I had symptoms. I went in just before this trip… had some tests. I'll know more when I get back to Portland. But after cajoling my doctor, he admitted that the odds are pretty good that it is the same."

"If that's the case, there must be things they can do today? Your mother was so long ago."

"Not really. The verdict is still the same."

"But you don't know for sure," Haakon stated.

"No, I don't know for sure," Kari answered, though he suspected she was cueing into the fact that he wanted some hope. "I'll know when I get back."

"Jeez! This must scare you," he said, regretting his words as they came out.

"Yeah, for sure. When I first suspected something was wrong, a couple of weeks ago, I was pretty messed up. I guess that I'm still messed up, but I have lived with it for enough days that I've gotten kind of numb."

She paused for a moment, while continuing to look into Haakon's eyes.

"I was beginning to accept the inevitability of it, I suppose. But now, seeing you, I'm feeling a bit messed up all over again."

Kari looked down and sobbed quietly, then muttered, "I promised myself that I wouldn't do this."

Haakon squeezed Kari's hands tightly for a moment, then their grips relaxed while they stared into each other's faces—again, communicating without words.

After several seconds, he said, "Listen, Kari, what can I do to help you with this? I want to help you."

Her composure returned and she stopped sobbing.

Haakon reached over for a box of tissues and handed it to her. She took one and dabbed at her eyes.

"Oh Haakon, this has been wonderful being with you again… last night. It took me back… and it took my mind off of this… took me far away. God, I loved that. But we have our own lives now. I'm fine dealing with this."

"I want to go back to Portland with you. Maybe I can be of help."

"No, Haakon. I'm fine. Really."

They still held hands.

"I understand if you would rather me not be there. I have no right to push myself into your life," Haakon said while staring hard into her eyes. "But if you would like me to be there, I would rather be at no other place."

Kari shook her head.

"No. Let this go. We're fine… you and I. The past is the past. Things are as they are. You don't need this," she said with surprising composure. "I'm really glad that we've had this time again… this talk… it means a lot to me. It's closure, sort of. I mean this in a positive way. But we've had our own lives now. Let's let this go. I didn't tell you this to draw sympathy."

"I know that," Haakon said, feeling offended.

He got up from his chair and turned to look out the window. Several deer were carefully making their way across the shallow, fast running river.

"What has this been, all this crying and hugging and reminiscing?" Haakon asked, while still facing the window.

He turned back to her.

"I love you, Kari. I have always loved you. I am grateful for this reunion. I can't tell you how grateful I am. I don't know how it happened. I don't deserve it. But I don't want it to end… unless you do… unless you really do."

"But it is going to end, Haakon. Either way."

"You don't know that!"

"Yes, I do know. I'm not a fatalist, Haakon. But I *am* a realist. I know what's going on inside of me. They're running these tests as a long shot, but I know the outcome. I was with my mother nearly every day. I know how this goes."

Kari sat with her head looking down in silence for a moment.

Then she said, "I love you too, Haakon. But it's late for us. I can't ask you to be with me when it's the end. It's not a good ending."

He walked over to her side and knelt next to her, taking her hands into his again.

"I don't want you to leave me. And I don't want to leave you a second time."

Kari leaned her head into his and sobbed.

Haakon again tried to fight off crying himself. But when he gained enough composure, he continued talking.

"Let me go to Portland with you. Let me help you. Unless you swear that you don't want me, I'm coming. I will not let you face this alone."

"We've had a beautiful moment in our lives, here—this chance meeting. Let's leave it at that. I don't want you to see me decline. I want you to remember me now… as I am now… forever. I don't want regrets."

"If you go back to Portland without me, I will regret *that*. Of that I am certain."

This time Kari paused before she replied.

"I don't think you really know what you're getting into, Haakon. Come with if you want. I would love nothing more than to have your company... truly."

She grabbed the sides of Haakon's face with both of her hands. Her eyes pierced into his.

"But, if you get cold feet—get them sooner than later. Promise me *that*. I won't blame you. If you opt out, opt out early... while I'm strong. Do you know what I mean?"

"I do. But I'm not leaving you again."

Haakon said this to give Kari reassurance, but her eyes had doubt—and he understood this.

17
SKY POND

"Come back to Camp One with me."

"No. I will not put you through that."

This was the essence of the conversation they had three days after the Portland doctors gave Kari the news she had expected—two days after the crying and the hugging and the futile words of consoling.

Kari had allowed Haakon to sit in and listen as they told her, with solemn faces, that she could expect several months of relatively good health—but then, by autumn she would likely begin to fail. One doctor thought it possible that she could last well into winter, but the other two, after being pressed for candor, believed that she would not see the year's end.

Following their verdict, Haakon went through a brief phase of denial. But Kari, being stronger and more mentally prepared, walked him through it. She was well aware of what she was up against and had chosen to wear a brave face. For a time, *she* became the healer and *he* the patient.

"I'm through feeling sorry for myself and I don't want others' pity either. It is what it is. We all have to play the cards we're dealt."

The doctors offered her no remedial treatment, as none was available for her condition. In a way, this was liberating. She had no hard choice to make—brutal treatment and a miserable, slightly extended lifespan versus comfort treatment and reasonably good-quality remaining days, albeit fewer days. Kari's clock would run out naturally. She had no vote.

"I'm retired. I have the time to care for you. I *want* to take care of you."

Kari smiled.

"I would rather that you remember me as I am now, Haakon… and as we were all those years ago. We have glorious memories and with our chance reunion we've created a beautiful new memory. Let's leave it at that."

"I can't… not again."

Haakon was in a chair, leaning into her bed. She was sitting upright, stroking his hair as she spoke.

"As you said to me last week, sometimes life just goes its own way. I'm not sure we have as many choices as we think we do."

"Sometimes we *do* have choices, though," Haakon replied. "When we *can* steer our destiny, we should."

Kari said nothing in reply, but continued to stroke his hair.

"God knows I don't deserve it, but if you won't do it for you, please do it for me. Come back with me. Do it for me."

By the end of the week, Haakon had worn Kari down and she relented to his request. Unbeknownst to her, several visiting friends pulled Haakon away from Kari for interrogation. They did not know him, so they were skeptical of his commitment to her well-being. Haakon took no offense to this. They confronted him out of love for her. He would have done the same, if he were in their shoes.

He did his best to convince them he would make it his life's mission to give her what comfort and happiness he could muster. Of course, they had doubt in their eyes. A few knew that Haakon had hurt Kari badly in the past, so his arguments did not start from a persuasive foundation. One of her girlfriends even threatened Haakon with, "You hurt her again and by God I will find a way to hurt you, buddy." And he had the impression she meant it.

Haakon told each friend that they were always welcome to

come visit Kari in Montana, and this seemed to help console them. Before Kari and Haakon left, one of her friends held a farewell party. And, though the gathering was a peculiar mix of celebration and sorrow, Haakon believed her friends became more at ease with him. They did not want Kari to be alone in the end either. Yet, as Kari and Haakon prepared to leave for Montana, the friend who had previously threatened Haakon glared into his face and held a stern finger an inch from his nose. Without uttering a word, she conveyed her message again. Haakon, with a submissive face, nodded in consent.

The following morning, in a car stuffed with her belongings, the two of them left Portland.

"I heard that Robyn threatened to kick your ass," Kari said to Haakon as they wound along the Columbia River.

He turned to her and smiled.

"Your friends care about you—that was the message *I* heard."

A slight smile came to Kari's face and she nodded in acknowledgement.

"But you do promise that if you have second thoughts, you have them soon, while I'm still strong?" she continued.

"Not gonna happen. But, yes, I promise."

Early summer in northwest Montana is a time of lush foliage and ever-present falling water. Warmer temperatures combine with moist air to reinvigorate the winter-dormant world. The rugged landscape that had appeared barren with ice and snow, exuded life and infused the atmosphere with its sweetness. High country snow packs melted into ribbons of water that skirted down sheer granite faces. Where the rocks folded, the ribbons converged into streamlets and, after long descents, into creeks. Then creeks poured into rivers and the rivers eventually merged into *the* river of the Northwest—the sea-bound Columbia. The mountain snowmelt from Camp One's view, spurred on by gravity, would eventually find its way into the Pacific Ocean.

The forest and grasslands, savoring the rain and snowmelt, turned into an array of vivid greens, harkening back life. And the renewed life permeated the air with a sweet fragrance of pine and fir. The abundance of released moisture filled the cool mornings with banks of fog. When the early rays of pink light shone through them, it set the stage of mysticism. It created a natural theater that could easily harbor elves and unicorns, if they were to exist. In a world locked in ice and snow just a few weeks prior, life and renewal abounded. Everything seemed possible. It was easy to be optimistic.

Haakon was not sure if Kari had always been an early riser, but after the move to Camp One, she was usually up within an hour of him and he was a *very* early riser. On their third morning back, she came up behind Haakon as he was painting.

"Oh, I like that," Kari said, looking over his shoulder.

Once his brush hand moved away from the painting, she leaned down to hug Haakon's neck and kiss him on the top of his head. He smiled but kept his eyes on the painting, focusing on where to direct the brush next. Kari's head sat on his shoulder and they both studied the colors.

"I thought that we should go for a horseback ride today," Haakon said. "I've found someone who will deliver two horses at the Misty trailhead for us. You interested?"

"I'd love that! I haven't been on a horse for years," Kari answered, excited.

Setting his brush down, Haakon swiveled the chair around so he could grasp Kari's body and pull her onto his lap.

"Then I will make it so."

That afternoon, they were back on saddles, with Misty following, ascending the same Misty Trail as they had on "Sweet Sunday," all of those decades before.

Little had changed along the trail. Kari commanded the route as though she had never left. It was good to see her on horseback again. It seemed to reinvigorate her psyche and Haakon detected a boost in her physically. It was subtle, but it was there. Her motions were quicker and more deliberate. Her eyes appeared brighter and wider. And her smiles were more forthcoming. This was Kari's realm and she fed upon it like a flame in a breeze.

When they reached the first overlook along the steep switchbacks, Kari stared out onto the valley as she had on their first visit. Haakon knew that her mind was refueling and he chose not to interrupt her thoughts with his inane words. Kari turned to find him staring, and this made her blush.

"Bring back memories?" Haakon asked.

"Yes," she answered, turning back to the view.

"You must have a hundred memories from this place. I have only one, and it is one of my favorites."

Kari turned back to face Haakon.

"I have hundreds of memories from here, but none that come close to *our* day."

Then she gave her horse a light tap of the heel, followed by a slight shake of the reigns and continued up the trail. Misty followed while Haakon stayed put for a moment, as he enjoyed watching her ride. But his horse soon twitched nervously, seeming displeased to be left behind the other horse. So Haakon relented and shook the rein to follow behind.

When Sky Pond's diamond studded turquoise-blue water came into view, they halted their horses. It was even more impressive than what Haakon recalled. This time, the steep rock walls were enhanced with more snow. The intricate stark white shapes created fascinating patterns against the blue, gray, and reddish hues of the granite—dictated by geological shifting eons ago. The bright, nearly blinding whiteness of the snow contrasted with the surrounding colors of rock and tree, making their hues appear even more vivid.

There was no need to waste words. Their expressions conveyed mutual awe of the setting. Instead, each lowered themselves from the horses and then led them to the nearby hitching rail. This time, rather than run down to the lake in swimsuits, they each grabbed a jacket out of their packs, then proceeded slowly to the lake's edge, hand in hand. Misty followed behind.

A light breeze skirted upon the lake from its far side. It met their faces with sharp coolness and the sweet scent of pine. The tall cirque walls were largely hidden from the sun, assuring that much of the snow would remain well into the summer. Where the clumps of snow melted, white threads of water emerged, free-falling until they hit a step of rock. Then, more often than not, they disappeared for a distance before reappearing from a different point. The wall contained more ribbon falls than Haakon could count. His eyes wandered from one to the other, in wonder of the spectacle.

After a long silence of reverence, Haakon spoke.

"We *are* swimming again, right?"

"What?"

"Have you grown soft?" he teased.

"Yes. Yes, I have grown soft. And smarter too," Kari answered, appearing concerned that Haakon was serious.

"That's nothing to brag about. I think we should do it."

"I think we should do *it* too. But not the swimming part," she counter-offered.

This made Haakon smile. He knew what Kari was referring to. Without another word, she squeezed his hand, rose, then led him, with Misty trailing, to the place on the shore where they had laid forty-six years prior. Kari leaned down into her pack and pulled out a blanket.

"Is that the same blanket? I remember the colors and the plaid patterns," Haakon said, surprised.

"I'm impressed that you remember. Males are not known for recalling such details. I've stored a lot of things away, Haakon... mostly in my heart."

Making love in the daylight in your mid-60s is not the same as when you are young. This becomes clear upon the first shed article of clothing. But, what might have been missed in youthful wonderment was regained in age-honed introspection. Many have argued that "youth is wasted on the young" and Haakon was convinced it was true. The lovemaking was as passionate—perhaps more so as it compiled the past with knowledge of what would be. Physically though, it was hampered by lessened muscle range and a reduced tolerance for the hard ground. When those moments of discomfort occurred, they stopped briefly and laughed at themselves. But they did not stop for long.

Misty, sitting upright alongside the blanket, seemed curious and amused by their activity.

Afterwards, they laid face up, side-by-side, soaking in the intense rays of the sun—still benefiting from the heat that their motions had created.

"I'm going to be sore tomorrow morning, but God, that was beautiful... truly beautiful," Kari said, staring up into the sky.

She rolled over towards Haakon and looked into his face. He smiled in reply.

"This is surreal. Being here again with you. I feel like I'm in a dream and I'm afraid to wake up," Kari continued.

"I'm with you on that. Don't wake up. Please don't wake up," Haakon said jokingly. "I'm afraid if you do, my dream will go away with yours."

"My dream won't leave," Kari said, looking at Haakon earnestly, rubbing her hand along his cheek.

"And mine won't go either."

Kari rolled the edge of the blanket over her body for added warmth and they remained in each other's arms facing the sky.

"It makes you wonder about time… about reality… how it is that we are even here," Kari said.

"Sounds heavy for a daytime topic when there are no stars to stare up at," Haakon said, continuing to look skyward. "I don't know. I guess you get to a point when you realize that existence is beyond our comprehension. We think we know so much when we are young. But then, one day, you realize that you don't know shit. No one does."

Haakon turned to face Kari.

"We go every day thinking we go on forever. Then you begin to understand that the ride ends… for everyone… at least as we know it," he said. "I think about that. Now with you, I think about it a whole lot more."

"I'm afraid, Haakon."

He reached for Kari's cheek.

"Don't be afraid. We'll travel this together. Maybe what's on the other side is even better, though at this very moment I can't imagine that possible."

Haakon stroked Kari's hair and she smiled back at him. They stared at each other in silence for several minutes. A cool breeze fell down the walls of the mountain and crossed the lake, forming tiny ripples before it met them.

"Wow. Is that ever cold!" Haakon said, when it arrived.

"Yeah, let's get dressed," Kari said, equally startled by the sudden chill.

They each emitted various moans as they rose, now aware of the taxed muscles.

"Gosh, it sounds like we both need to be put in 'a home,'" Kari said.

Both laughed as they rapidly pulled their clothes back on.

"My mind is still young, but my body apparently isn't," she said.

But looking at Kari in that moment, as she tugged and positioned her shirt, Haakon thought she appeared young. Kari turned and caught him watching.

"Like I told you long ago," Haakon said, smiling. "I'm a gentleman, but I never claimed to be an angel."

Much of that spring and summer was a replay of their original time together—what they came to know as their fabled "Endless Summer of Youth." This even included retracing the near disastrous river canoe trip, though this time with just the two of them in a single canoe. Even Misty was left behind with Sig, as they considered a large dog to be a potential balancing wildcard in a tippy boat. And this second time they portaged around the deceivingly dangerous Cottonwood Falls. For long stretches along the route they would not talk, preferring to breathe in the route's natural splendor. They could hear the faint sounds of the slow-moving river and that of their paddles, dipping into and pushing against it. In the quietness, they could make out subtle sounds—sounds that they really had to focus on hearing. There were many emanating from the surrounding woods that could not be identified, adding to the journey's enchantment. Although they enjoyed the company of Landon and Swan on the first trip, their company inadvertently caused them to miss out on much of the wilderness experience.

Camping, again, below Cottonwood Falls brought back powerful feelings, particularly when they snuggled around the campfire. Both knew it would, but they wanted to "face their fears" per se. It was a closure thing. But, sleeping on the hard ground—even though they had thin inflatable mattresses—distracted from their reminiscing. The ground was harder than what either could remember.

"That was an incredible evening," Kari said as they packed the tent the following morning. "But let's not do it again… this tent thing."

Standing while stretching the kinks in his back, Haakon nodded in full agreement.

Their "Endless Summer" redux included many riverside dinners at the same location of their first date. The restaurant had been renamed, but the evening atmosphere was much the same. The outdoor setting was still conducive to romance and, on weekend evenings, the restaurant hosted a country-western band on its outdoor patio. So, early in the season, they would stay on after their dinner to dance.

"You know, I really haven't done much of this dancing since *our* summer," Haakon said to her, as they slow-danced on a warm evening under a canopy of stars.

"Your wife wasn't much of a dancer?"

"Not so much. It was kind of limited to weddings."

"So, this is something that is, sort of, ours?"

"Yes, that's true," he replied. "But it needs refreshing. I wanted to warn you before I stepped all over your feet."

But Haakon did not step on her feet. Like riding a bicycle, dancing, for the most part, came back to him. And, what he had forgotten, she patiently re-taught him.

Haakon awoke one morning to noise emanating from the back closet. He feared a raccoon had snuck into the house, so he went to investigate with a long handled fishing net in hand. It surprised him to find Kari rummaging through his uncle's fly-fishing gear with Misty alongside her, watching in anticipation. Haakon's sudden appearance both startled and embarrassed Kari.

"I guess I should have asked before I dug through this stuff," she said to him sheepishly.

"No. Have at it. I forgot it was there and worse, I forgot that you had such a strong interest in fly-fishing."

"It takes me back to my dad."

"I understand. Let's get licenses and go today," Haakon suggested.

Three hours later, they were standing knee-deep in a nearby trout stream. Haakon never took to fly-fishing, but he still remembered the basics Kari had taught him. So he could fumble along and sometimes get his lure near its intended destination. Haakon knew his form was not pretty, but fortunately there was no one there to see it other than Kari. And, if his fly-fishing style had mattered to her, he figured she would have dumped him that very first summer.

His enjoyment was in watching the master—watching Kari work the rod and the waters. She was a cross between an artist and a magician who somehow defied gravity and kept the swirling line suspended above her head for an inordinately long period. And when she let loose—holding the rod out like an extended magician's wand, sending the fly off to its intended target—he knew from her expression it was another bull's-eye.

When Kari reeled in a trout, she would always hold it up for Haakon to see. He, in turn, would always beg her to keep it.

"What's the point of all of this if we can't eat the fish?"

"The art is the point," she would answer. "You as an artist should know that."

"All I know as an artist is that trout looks pretty on a barbeque. It tastes even better."

However, his argument would be to no avail. As a fly-fishing purist, Kari would ignore his pleas and carefully release the fish back into the stream. Sometimes, they would debate this "catch and release" practice on their drive home. But it would always be a brief discussion. Within ten minutes, she would be fast asleep. Haakon would glance over to see her serene face far off in another trout stream, or in another dance, or on another horseback ride. Kari put her *all* into everything she did.

Haakon surprised Kari one evening after dinner, by pulling up to the house in the recommissioned Scout. She was busy in the kitchen and to get her attention, he honked its horn. Kari's face appeared above him through the dining-room window. She looked puzzled at first, but then burst out laughing. Within seconds, she was outside on the deck.

"The Scout!" Kari exclaimed, while looking down on Haakon.

"Sweet ride, huh?" he responded, while sitting high on the backrest of the front seat, extending his arms out to draw attention to the vehicle as though he was a model at a car show.

"Yeah, but where's the roof?"

"I took it off. It is not exactly a convertible sports car, but the entire topper, which includes the cab top, comes right off with just a few screws," he replied.

"I don't remember you doing this to it before."

"I didn't realize that it came off that easily."

"Well, it doesn't make it any prettier," Kari said.

"Nah, but it makes it perfect for an evening convertible drive in the mountains. Come on. Hop in."

Fifteen minutes later they were traveling up a gravel Forest Service road into the mountains. The higher they climbed, the windier the route got. Haakon was retracing much of what he had traveled on those lonely "Dog Day" evenings.

"Up here is where I would come before I met you," Haakon said loudly as they slowly rolled along. "I would just drive and drive, not really knowing where I was going."

"Do you know where you are going now?" Kari asked.

"No, but I have a full tank of gas and I brought the chainsaw," he said, turning to smile at her. "We can go pretty much anywhere."

Kari smiled back at him.

They spoke very little, each seeming to soak up the endless oncoming panoramas of Montana wilderness. The higher they traveled, the more grand the view became. Eventually, they arrived on a road that was cut along a mountaintop ridge. Since it was narrow with steep grades on both sides, traveling on it was unnerving. But it afforded spectacular views in all directions. And, as the sun dropped in the sky, shadows accentuated the views by contrasting the trees and the contours of the landscape.

When they arrived at the road's apex, they stopped and climbed out of the Scout. From the overlook, both peered down into a deep valley that hosted a raging white river. Even from the mountaintop perch, they could hear the water roar as it violently cascaded downward to the will of gravity.

"This is a spectacular place," Kari said, visibly enjoying the sight.

"I remember this. I would sit here and feel both lonely and in awe," Haakon said, as he turned to her. "I had no idea back then, I was about to meet a goddess on a rooftop."

She smiled. The low light made Kari's face glow. A breeze pushed her hair in front of her face and Haakon fell back in time. He pulled Kari to his side and they stood silently for several minutes, absorbing the setting and their love.

When they climbed back into the Scout, the magic of the evening was nearly overridden. Haakon reached down to turn the Scout's key and nothing happened. The engine merely omitted a loud clicking sound. Kari looked at him with a worried expression.

"That didn't sound good."

"No, it didn't. I'm thinking I should have bought a new battery."

"Are you telling me we are walking home?" Kari asked, concerned.

Haakon contemplated her question for a moment.

"Well, if I was a normal guy, probably. But as you know—"

"Yes, I know, you're not a normal guy."

"That's right, because a normal guy would have parked in a low spot, but not me."

"Right, you parked in a high spot. So what does that do for our predicament?" she asked.

"It does *this*," he answered as he pressed his foot down on the clutch.

The Scout began to slowly roll forward.

"We're gonna coast home?"

"I hope not," he said as he switched the ignition key on.

Once the Scout was rolling at a fast walking speed, he lifted his foot off of the clutch. This engaged the first gear, forcing the engine to turn over. Immediately, it fired to life.

"I'm impressed… and relieved," Kari said smiling.

"It's what I do," Haakon responded smugly while shrugging his shoulders.

They backtracked down the windy gravel roads with the sun setting behind them. Kari slid over to his side as the open air took on a chill.

"Sitting here reminds me of the drive-in theater. I miss that," she said.

"Yeah, I wish they still had one."

Kari nodded in agreement.

The next evening, after the sun set, Haakon surprised Kari again.

"Put your jacket on please, I've got something to show you."

She did and he led her outside to the parked Scout. Aimed towards the river, it had a large flat screen TV resting on its hood.

"May I introduce you to the new Camp One Drive-In Theater?"

Kari burst out laughing.

"Are you serious?" she asked.

"If you want a drive-in theater, I give you a drive-in theater."

She smiled, then hugged him.

"Oh, it gets better," Haakon said, looking down at her face as they embraced. "Tonight's feature film is *Jeremiah Johnson*."

She laughed.

"I'm not sure that would be my first choice, but how can I complain?"

"You'll love it! It's the extended editor's edition with an additional full hour of Jeremiah crawling around the mountains doing what mountain men do."

"Hmm… well, at least I know I'll enjoy sitting next to *my* mountain man."

"There's more. I've even got popcorn."

"How can a girl say no to that?"

They never made it to the end of the movie, but for nearly an hour they returned to the drive-in of their memories. Like then, Haakon's poor sitting posture resulted in a sore back. But, like then, he still considered it a small price to pay for sitting tightly by Kari's side while sharing a bowl of popcorn in front of their version of the "silver screen."

Several days later, Kari surprised *him* by announcing she wanted to learn how to paint with watercolors.

"Do you know anyone that could teach me?" she asked, jokingly.

"I know people. Let me see what I can find out. I'll get back to you."

"What if I make it worth *your* while?"

Haakon looked at her coyly and smiled.

"Let's talk," he said.

So with a promise of "repayment," Haakon set her up with a workspace near his and went about teaching her the fundamentals of the painting medium.

"This is really hard," Kari said, "much harder than it looks. The paint just goes wherever it wants."

"True. Sometimes it seems as though it has a mind of its own," he said. "Ya just have to go with it. You don't always get to the place you had intended. Sometimes you get results that are better, that you didn't expect. Sometimes not so much."

"Well, I'm getting the 'not so much,' right now," Kari said, frustrated.

"Stay with it," Haakon said. "It's kind of like fly-fishing. You develop a feel for the interaction of paper and paint. But unlike fly-fishing, you get to keep the nice paintings."

Kari glanced up from her artwork for a moment and glared at Haakon.

"You better play your cards right, buddy," she said.

"Hey, a deal's a deal. Are you threatening to renege?"

"There're different degrees of compensation, teacher. There're apples, but there can be a lot more… if you know what I mean."

Haakon smiled.

"I'm afraid I do. I retract my callous fish analogy."

"Smart move," she said, without looking up from her painting struggles.

If Kari decided that she was going to learn something, she followed through. Haakon could not think of an exception to this.

Of course, Ben at the art supply store was delighted he had another novice painter as a customer.

"I think I'll call the family and tell'em that it's steak and lobster tonight!" he said, upon hearing of Kari's new art venture.

"Maybe tonight," Haakon replied. "But it probably won't be a very long gravy train with her. She's a fast learner."

"Well, that's disappointing. You know I don't like fast learners, Haakon. Please don't teach her so well."

Haakon smiled. He was half-joking, but he ended up being right. Kari zeroed in on her style and soon had few failures. She tended to paint landscapes and, those that she painted, tended to be abstract—not much for detail, but big on boldness. They were expressive pieces of art that, Haakon suspected, reflected her interior, her inner turmoil. Yet, this struggle with mortality manifested itself not in dark, morose depictions, but in vivid, audacious colors. Kari seemed incapable of viewing her world in dark tones.

Her painting attention span impressed Haakon as well. She could stay on task far longer than he could—an ingrained aspect of her resolute personality. Kari sat down to pursue her vision and rarely looked up until she finished it. It was as though she had a lifetime of inspiration needing expression or perhaps it was a ninth inning run for immortality.

"If you weren't so beautiful, I would say that I have created a monster," Haakon said to her as she busily worked her brush.

"Monsters are not always bad," Kari responded without lifting her eyes off of the paper. "Sometimes they scare you into doing something more, something better. I'm getting to like my painting monster."

That evening Kari suggested that we go sit on "their rock" to watch the show of flowing water under an emerging crimson canopy. Haakon turned on some music first, then pointed the deck-mounted speakers outward toward the river. It was a random selection of songs, so he had no idea that by the time he walked over to her, it would be playing the familiar clave of a Cuban song. Feeling invigorated, Haakon approached her in a dance cadence. This seemed to surprise both Kari and Misty.

"You remember how to salsa?" she exclaimed.

"Oh yeah. I've considered changing my middle name to Salsa," Haakon replied, now getting more dramatic in his movements. "I'm all about salsa. Care to join me?"

"I thought you hadn't danced much?"

"Not in public. But when I hear good Cuban music, I get happy feet—wherever I am."

This was not true and the more Haakon danced, the more apparent this became to her. Yet Kari smiled and rose to meet him. Their hands clasped and they moved with a unison tempo, as though they had been practicing for weeks—all the time their eyes were locked onto one another's. Haakon did not speak for fear of losing his concentration and lessening the passion. Misty stood nearby, watching their every movement with great interest.

Once Haakon became confident, he motioned for a spin and like two Olympian figure skaters executing side-by-side triple lutzes, they pulled it off effortlessly—at least in his mind they did. Then she fell towards his body backwards and he held her waist as they continued swaying. It was an ideal moment of dance and outdoor sunset ambiance. They both realized this, so when the song ended and a new one began, there was no attempt to repeat the perfection.

The dimming light grew more enchanting, and it cued the night's coolness to slide down into the valley. It descended along the river where it eventually found the couple still standing on the granite slab, embracing from their dance. The abrupt chill drove them into the warmth of the cabin.

Once inside, the phone rang and Haakon answered it to some disappointing news. Neither of his daughters nor their families would visit that summer. The two families had planned a joint trip. But now it was canceled because of the varied summer schedules of the grandkids—summer sports and camp activities and such.

"I don't understand how it was 'all go' before and now, suddenly, it's not," Haakon said in frustration after he hung up with his eldest daughter.

"Maybe it's me," Kari said, as she sat scratching Misty's ears.

"How could it be you?"

"Well, you've always said that your daughters were never acceptant of your divorce. The little girls inside of them may still desire you back together. I represent an obstacle to that dream."

"We would never get back together!" Haakon exclaimed.

"*You* know that, but, as you once said, *they* may not want to know that."

"Doesn't make any sense."

"It might if you were a woman."

Haakon looked at Kari puzzled.

"I don't take it personally," she said. "It's who I represent, not who I am."

Haakon thought about this, realizing she might have had a point. He remembered a recent phone conversation with his youngest daughter.

"So, you're telling me that if you had stayed with Kari all those years ago, you would not have met my mother… and I wouldn't exist?"

"That's true," Haakon answered. "A lot of things in our lives hang by thin threads."

"Since you and Mom didn't work out, do you regret coming back to Minnesota back then?"

"No. Never. I regret hurting Kari, but I will never regret what we had as a family. It was good and I'm sorry that your mom and I ended."

"Well, as a daughter, it's admittedly hard to hear about another woman in my mother's place. But as an adult, I know that you deserve to move on in your life, like Mom did."

Haakon did not respond.

"It sounds like it will be a tough road for you ahead, with Kari's health. I hope that you know what you're in for."

"I'm sure I don't. I force myself to not think about it. But I don't consider it optional."

Haakon knew that his daughters were compassionate people, so they would genuinely sympathize with Kari's plight. Yet he knew that these two adult girls never came to grips with the breakup between their parents. So Kari's theory might have had merit. Regardless, they never came out that summer and they never met Kari, and this deeply saddened Haakon.

"They may reconsider later in the summer," Kari said, seeing Haakon was upset.

"Yeah, maybe," he replied, but he doubted it.

By late August, she was still strong and Haakon grew hopeful, questioning the initial dire predictions of the doctors. She even suggested that they try helping the neighbors buck bales of hay as they did during the "Endless Summer." Haakon explained to her that Little Sig no longer made the small rectangular hay bales. His modern equipment created massive round bales that required a forklift to move them. So, disappointed, she proposed that the two of them go walk the field one evening instead.

To get there, they took the route along the railroad tracks. And, without prompting, Kari instinctively stepped up onto a single rail and began walking foot in front of foot, with her arms extended off to her sides to regulate her balance. Taking her cue, Haakon hopped up onto the parallel rail and tried to keep up with her pace, just as he had done so many times in their youth. Giggling, they strode along—each glancing at the other as they concentrated on their equilibriums. Misty followed between the rails, looking from side to side, seeming to want to take part in the game. As in the past, Kari maintained her balance unfettered, like a seasoned circus tightrope performer. Haakon, on the other hand, stumbled along, spending half of his time off of the rail— more akin to a circus clown.

"You've obviously been practicing," he said to her, observing the flawless performance.

"Oh yeah, I walk railroad tracks all the time. It's how I commuted to work in Portland."

Haakon smiled, then said, "I remember how to even this up."

"After all of these years, you would still resort to cheating?" Kari said, while continuing her seemingly effortless motion. "Can't you try to out railroad walk me, honorably?"

"Nope. I've tried that," he answered. "But, as one beautiful unnamed competitive person once told me, you gotta take every advantage you can!"

Haakon suddenly lunged towards her, like a linebacker seeking a tackle. Misty began barking excitedly. Startled, Kari lost her balance. But before she stepped off of the rail, Haakon grabbed and lifted her, cradling her in his arms.

"You're still pathetic," she said, giggling, looking up into his face.

Misty relaxed, but stared at the two adult-children anxiously.

"Yeah, after all of these years, I still need your help in making me a less pathetic person."

"That's a pretty tall order, Haakon."

"I guess so, but the joy is in the journey, they say."

"Yes, I think it is," Kari said, as she pulled her face up to his and kissed him.

They could detect the sweet scent of freshly cut hay, well before arriving at the field. It filled much of the valley with its pleasing aroma—its coumarin boldly stating, aromatically, it was summer. Long shadows extended from the base of the hay bales, like drag marks, as though the giant shapes had slid towards the sun. The light was low and the air golden.

"Did you realize that hay is one of mankind's most important inventions?" Kari asked, as they strolled hand in hand among the giant round bales.

"I did not. It just seems like dry grass to me," Haakon replied.

"It enabled civilization to spread north into the temperate zones, because it provided a means of storing animal feed during the non-growing seasons. *Before* hay, the great civilizations were all in the lower, warm latitudes."

"You're a pretty smart girl."

"I paid attention in class. I didn't have you to distract me."

He smiled at her, then said, "I never thought of that, but it makes sense. So it must have been handy for our ancestors."

"I imagine."

"What you're basically telling me is that if hay had not been invented for our northern European ancestors, you and I would probably not exist."

"Yeah, I guess so," she replied, pondering the point. "I hadn't thought of it *that* way."

"Hey, speaking of hay, what's such a smart girl like you doing hanging out with such a dunce like me? I'm not filled with all these interesting facts like the creation of hay."

She smiled at Haakon and said, "I told you, you're pathetic and I feel sorry for you."

Haakon stopped and took Kari's other hand.

"Then I may be the only person on the earth thankful for being pathetic... that is, after being thankful for the invention of hay."

Looking up at Haakon, her face beamed.

"Do you ever feel the passage of time is accelerating?" she asked as they resumed walking, still hand in hand.

"Every day."

Kari grasped his arm and for a moment leaned her head on his shoulder as they continued walking. Haakon felt a surge of sadness realizing they had been so long gone from each other.

"It just blows me away that it has been decades since we last walked this field. It feels like it was yesterday," Kari said.

"It *was* yesterday. It's right now too... if you believe physicists," Haakon replied. "They say that time is a human invention and what was, *is*. Somewhere in space-time, yesterday and tomorrow are occurring now... whatever "now" is. Oddly enough, this hard-to-grasp theory actually comforts me."

"And you say you are a dunce. I can't even understand that," she said.

"Oh, I know a few things, but it *is* hard to understand. Yet I don't know if it is any harder to understand than how we even exist at all. Still, here you and I are, walking through a field on a beautiful summer evening, on a giant sphere that is spinning around a star while it, and everything, are hurtling across the universe."

Haakon stopped to look into Kari's eyes.

"It's all true, but how can we get our heads around *that*?" he asked.

She did not seem to notice, but Haakon could see the shadow of their joined silhouettes broadcast on the side of a hay bale.

"Sometimes I stand and watch the sunrise and I think… I feel rather, that I understand things," Haakon said. "Everything seems so whole, so right. It's like a wave of enlightenment that overcomes me."

Kari's face glowed amber in the low light.

"But then the sun rises higher and the color and the intensity fade and the world brightens… and then I fall out of the dream-state—not in a sad way though. It's more like a realization that your mind can't burn that brightly for very long."

Kari stared up into Haakon's face, seeming to listen intently.

"And then I try to remember that overwhelming sensation that I had just experienced. But I can't. I can only remember that I had it. Sometimes it feels close enough to grab onto. And sometimes it feels like a dream… like it's far away. But I know that it *had* been close and real… as real as real can be, I guess."

Kari reached up and grasped both sides of Haakon's face.

"Our love is real, Haakon."

"Our love is absolute," he replied.

18
WHERE ALL THINGS MERGE

As the summer progressed, Kari would awaken earlier than Haakon. Occasionally, he would hear the front door open and close. On these mornings, looking through the dining-room window, he would see her standing outside on the granite slab, in a robe, with a shawl across her shoulders, staring out into the mist above the river. She was a beautiful soul, and few memories better embodied this than the sight of her nobly facing the dawn light. Kari had an elegance about her—an air, a grace. Her posture and expression conveyed deep introspection and dignity. Though tempted to go be by her side and comfort her, Haakon knew she wanted to be alone.

They did a lot of talking while walking that summer. They discussed everything. In time, it felt like they had covered all the lost years, but that was not possible. Yet neither had secrets. Both talked about their marriages. Haakon talked about Hannah and while Kari seemed to have some understanding, he did not believe she really liked hearing about her. They talked about Sean and Kari's marriage before their great loss. Haakon talked about his daughters and their independent lives with their families. And, of course, Kari talked about her son. Nearly every day Haakon would ask something about him. By summer's end, Haakon thought he knew Kyle—at least he could recognize the parts of Kari embedded into Kyle's personality.

When the evening walks became difficult for her, they would watch the sunsets, sitting out on the granite overlooking the river. Haakon would usually drape a blanket over her back before moving close enough to provide some of his body's heat. At times, they would sit silently, breathing in the majestic world around them. But more often they would embark into a deep discussion. Towards the end, Haakon returned to the topic of his broken promise and he apologized to her again, wanting to rid his conscience of something "un-riddable." But Kari would have none of it, growing more reflective as her health failed.

"Haakon, who knows what our story would have been if you had returned? Maybe we wouldn't have stayed together. Who knows these things?" she asked.

"It's hard to imagine us not staying together."

"It is today, but that was a different time, a different stage of our lives," she replied.

Haakon nodded in agreement.

"Now and then, I believe in fate. Maybe if you had come back, you would not be here with me today."

Kari turned to face Haakon with a solemn expression.

"And today is when I really *need* you."

Turning back towards the sunset, she was silent for a moment as though collecting her thoughts. He glanced at Kari and noted the warm hue of the ebbing light on her skin and the reflective glassiness in the corner of her eye.

"Our lives came together by chance all those years ago," she said, without turning back towards him. "And our lives parted for whatever reasons. We lived separate lives with separate families... and decades later we met again."

Kari paused for a few seconds, then turned back to Haakon.

"By chance? Is it all by chance? Us meeting on a rooftop in the woods of northwest Montana? Us re-meeting in an art store? I don't know."

She shook her head.

"All I know is that it's a beautiful thing… poetic… it's an artistry of life."

Haakon stared into Kari's eyes as she said this. The words seemed to make her strong. After a moment, she looked up into the sky where the receding light was making way for the brightest stars.

"Of all the possible outcomes of the comings and goings of the universe up there…"

Kari stopped speaking, then turned from the sky to Haakon.

"Well, here we are… you and me. How can that be?"

Subtly, Haakon nodded in acknowledgement of Kari's words while continuing to look into her eyes. Her face wore something between a smile and a frown.

She turned towards the remnant light of the sun that by now had dropped below the mountain. In silence for several minutes, Kari seemed in deep thought again.

"I don't understand it all, Haakon. I don't understand the concept of time. I don't understand living. I certainly don't understand dying. I don't understand how it is that we even exist in this vast universe… or even why. Maybe I'll know once I'm gone. Maybe the answer is out there. I would like to know these things."

Kari glanced skyward, then turned towards Haakon again and clutched his arm tightly. For a moment he saw the face of the girl from that bicentennial summer—that "Endless Summer." His heart swelled and he longed for all that was past.

"But I understand love," Kari continued. "I understand what is between us, Haakon. And of all the things there are to know, that's all that I really need to know."

She paused while looking directly into Haakon's eyes, then resumed in a calm voice.

"I take comfort that you have your daughters and your grandkids after I am gone… and Misty."

Haakon began to tear up.

"I want you to realize how much I cherish that I have you *now*… that I have your love *now*," Kari said, sobbing quietly as her head dropped onto his shoulder.

He stroked her hair.

"My greatest fear in life was to leave alone, unloved."

Haakon pulled Kari closer and held her tight. It took all of his might to emotionally hang on.

"I will always love you," he whispered into her ear. "I *have* always loved you."

By late September, Kari was showing clear signs of lost stamina, but she still insisted on revisiting Sky Pond. So Haakon planned with the outfitter to drop the same two horses at the trailhead. When he awoke that morning, the air was calm and the sun was shining. It looked to be the perfect fall day for a horseback ride in the mountains, though it troubled Haakon to see a fresh coat of white on the upper peaks. At the high elevations, this could equate to "feet" of snow. He feared that the window for a Sky Pond visit had closed for the season and he told this to Kari when she woke.

"It's a beautiful day. Let's just ride up as high as we can and take it from there," she answered, unconcerned.

So they met the outfitter as planned and he sent Kari and Haakon off on the trail with his well wish of a nice day. The air was brisk, but the rising sun provided ample heat as their horses ambled on at their slow, steady pace. The two did not talk much as they ascended the mountain. Kari was taking it all in, enjoying every second, every step of the ride.

They met a thin coat of snow on the ground once they reached the valley overlook. It was just enough to change the tenor of their surrounding environment. But as the horses strode up the remaining leg of the path, the snow became deeper. It clung to the boughs of the trees, as this portion of the trail was in the mountain's shadow. Yet, Kari and Haakon could see sunshine reflecting ahead, so they rode on. Now surrounded by snow, it was as though they entered a white tunnel and were enticed forward by the distant illumination. The horses trudged along with small puffs of fog erupting from their laboring nostrils— their hoof sounds muffled by the six inches of powder.

Haakon had expected to be awed by Sky Pond. His two previous visits had instilled reverence of its unique geology and its seemingly artful design. But as they approached its edge, his senses were overwhelmed. The snow and ice had transformed the dramatic cirque into a dreamlike winter wonderland—a grand palace of shimmering icy walls that reached boldly into the distant sky. The mountain lake itself, frozen smooth and undistorted, was a near perfect mirror of it all.

"My God, this is unbelievable!" Haakon said.

Kari stared out onto the lake as though in a trance, unable to utter any sound or reaction. Her eyes were tearing up.

"Are you okay?"

"This is so beautiful," Kari said in a near whisper, still staring ahead. "I'm almost breathless."

Haakon turned to look out again. They both seemed to absorb the majesty of the moment. He climbed off his horse and helped Kari off hers. Then he hitched both to the branch of a fallen tree. After brushing the snow off, they both sat on the same tree trunk and resumed their reverie with the surroundings. In time, they conversed again.

"Haakon, I nearly fell from my horse when I saw this. It was like I could faint. This is intense. I thought I had felt nothing like this before… but I had."

He turned towards Kari and her eyes were wide and bright.

"When I first fell in love with you, I felt this too," she continued. "It's like I told you all of those years back, that I couldn't think of how to tell you how much I loved you. It was, it is, so intense. Like this— overpowering!"

Kari looked at Haakon with an expression of astonishment. Her eyes were glassy.

"This is what it must be like in the end… this intensity… this moving power of beauty… and love."

Haakon slid closer to Kari's side and reached around her waist.

"Love is Heaven. Heaven is love. It's one and the same. I know it. I feel it," Kari said, as though experiencing a revelation.

Haakon continued to hold her tight and she eventually relaxed a bit and rested her head on his shoulder. They both sat there in the sun for well over an hour, gazing out into the grandeur, savoring the energy that it provided. Then, after a long period of silence, Kari spoke to Haakon softly. He could feel the subtle waves of her words fall onto his chest.

"Haakon, it's time for me to go."

There would be no Indian Summer that year. Autumn did its

usual best to temper the earth's heat to usher in the cold season. Kari did not make it to the first day of winter, but she stayed long enough to see the riverbank's first coating of snow. She marveled at how the whiteness could so quickly transform a complex world into such simple quiet and beauty. She would sit transfixed at the window, as if drawing in the splendor as a remedy or perhaps a soother. When Kari could no longer rise from bed, Haakon painted the window's view, then mounted it high on the wall within her sight. He tried to convey with watercolors the warmth she recognized within fresh sunlit snow. She told him the painting was her favorite and it seemed to bring her comfort.

Towards the end, when Kari's voice was weak and barely audible, she said, "Haakon, I hope the walls in Heaven are painted with watercolors."

The day that Kari left Haakon was not unlike the day he left her. The sunlight had vanished and whiteness wove together with strands of gray fog. Trees and mountains ascended in and out of view, with no discernable beginning or ending. The all-encompassing mist was the foreteller of a long, hard, cold winter. And in the ensuing weeks, Haakon would find the season of low light to be almost unbearable.

He fell back into a dark quagmire. He had known it before when his marriage ended, but this was darker. Once again, the ruin of the world lay atop him and he pitied himself. His daughters tried to buoy him and together they came to visit. Both urged their father to leave Montana for the winter, but he would not. Even Misty, in her own way, tried to cheer Haakon by frequently dropping her toys at his feet, then looking up into his eyes expectantly, as if to say, "Come on, man, snap out of this."

Part of Haakon considered his anguish to be penance for not fulfilling the promise of returning to Kari all of those decades ago. And this paradoxically was self-preserving, because he felt that if he ceased to live he would cease to feel his earned pain.

But life did eventually resume. Like an overturned sailboat, the physics of gravity and an off-balance mass ultimately righted Haakon's psyche. Gradually, the sun moved higher in the sky and the days grew longer. Spring recaptured, then rejuvenated the world around him. Music followed and then came splendor. Haakon crawled out of his hole and saw and heard and felt again.

Kari had requested that he spread her ashes upon the Montana landscape that she so loved. But rather than do so in the winter, Haakon waited until early summer when the mountains were lush and covered with glacier lilies. He was loath to give her up. As morbid as it may seem, her ashes had kept him company through the dark season. On the longest and hardest days, when he looked up to the mantle, she would be there.

And Haakon was not eager to travel solo on horseback up into the mountains, even though she never asked him to do so. But he knew what was right for her. So, with the outfitter's reassurance, Haakon secured Kari's urn onto the saddle of the trailing horse, and together, with Misty trotting alongside, they made their way back up to Sky Pond.

When they came to the lake's edge, Haakon sat quietly atop his horse for a time, breathing in the reflective lake's opulence. Both horses and Misty were patient with Haakon that day, perhaps realizing the heaviness of his heart and perhaps sensing Kari's presence.

"I know you are here, Kari. I can feel your hand on the reins," Haakon said aloud.

Then he dismounted, tied the horses off, and carried her urn, with Misty following, to the clearing where they had twice lain. Standing there, Haakon cast her into the still morning air. A breeze lifted from where there had been none. It carried the lightest of Kari upward and Haakon tilted his head to watch as she danced and spun above him for a moment. Then, inexplicably, she raced sideways, this way and then that, before gently descending to the earth.

Haakon smiled because Kari knew he would be coming back to her.

A fog bank slowly eased its way over Sky Pond's surface. The horses began to snort and shimmy in place—their restlessness beckoning Haakon to go. Even Misty seemed anxious. So, with watery eyes, Haakon blew a kiss into the clear mountain air and walked back to the horses.

Approaching the top of the shallow basin, the horses stopped and Haakon turned back on his mount. The fog was weaving in and out of the pines on the distant shore. In minutes, it thickened and blanketed all that was below. Still, the sun was visible above. It shone on his face and drew long tree shadows atop the fog. In that moment, Haakon could feel coolness and warmth as he was on the edge of both.

With Misty leading, they proceeded higher into the warmth. When Haakon felt Kari let go of the reins, he turned back one last time to look for her. Haakon could see only mountains, tall trees, and fog. It was difficult to distinguish where the mountaintops ended and the sky began.

Yet, he knew where they merged, she was there.

THANK YOU

for reading my novel, *Sometimes It Feels Like Far*.

If you enjoyed it, please consider leaving a review on the book's Amazon page. **<u>Reviews are very helpful to the sale of my book</u>**. AND, please consider sharing the book's Amazon page on your favorite social media platform(s)—Facebook, Instagram, Twitter, Pinterest, etc.

Here is the book's Amazon page link:
https://www.amazon.com/dp/B08QRMJQYK

Also, I hope you check out my other book—my purported "humorous childhood memoir." I am told it puts the fun in dysFUNctional!

Searching for Alpha Centauri in a '64 Chevy
www.spetz.com/searching

If you would like notification of my next book
(a sailing comedy/adventure), or of any special promotions,
please sign on to my email list:
www.spetz.com/far

About the Author

Gary Spetz is also the author of the humorous, childhood memoir, *Searching for Alpha Centauri in a '64 Chevy*.

And, as a "signature member" artist of the National Watercolor Society, he has hosted, scripted, filmed, and co-produced—with his wife, Marlene—three painting/travel series (111 episodes) for Public Television (distributed via American Public Television): *Painting Wild Places*, *Watercolor Quest*, and *Color World*.

His artwork has also been depicted in various art publications, including *Watercolor, Artists, Watercolor Magic, Searching For The Artist Within*, and *Art From The Parks*. And his paintings have been included in the "Top 100" of the National Park Academy of the Arts.

Gary and his wife reside in Northwest Montana, where—when not trying to outsmart a trout—he continues to paint and write.

For more information about Gary
and his writings, artwork, and Public Television series,
please visit:

www.spetz.com

Acknowledgments

Even after 40 years of marriage, my wife, Marlene, still surprised me—this time with her keen storyline editing skills. During the proofing phase, she challenged various directions of the manuscript while offering quite creative alternative paths. Her female perspective drove part of this. But most of it, I think, was driven by her exceptional insight—a quality of hers I had long recognized in non-writing scenarios. As in our marriage, I often came to agree with her line of reasoning. And this, alas, resulted in an improved novel.

So, aside from being my "wind" (as cited in the book's dedication) and my definition of love, Marlene has proven to be my very-adept-in-house storyline editor as well.

I'm a lucky guy.

I would also like to acknowledge and thank Jan Kerley, Meredith Fuller, Susan Handy, and Deborah Newell for their early constructive input. As a male author working on a not-meant-to-be-a-love-story manuscript that eventually evolved into a love story, I often felt "out on a limb." They helped me crawl on and off of the limb with less apprehension.

And I would like to acknowledge and thank the many members of my Advanced Reader Team (ART, ironically). They kindly shared their time and impressions—ultimately providing me with the confidence to see this project through. Much to my embarrassment, they also caught me on more than a few typos.

A special thanks to the sharp eyes of Eileen George, Jane Michael, and "Motorcycle Guy Jim." Admittedly, I play "fast and loose," at times, with the English language. This had to have caused pain to those ART members taught (born, I think) to be meticulous wordsmiths. However, their pain ended up being the book's gain.